FAIRY TALES FROM
HANS CHRISTIAN
ANDERSEN

FAIRY TALES FROM
Hans Christian
ANDERSEN

REBO
PRODUCTIONS

Contents

© 1995 Rebo Productions, Lisse
© 1997 Rebo Productions Ltd.

adaptation text: Rindert K. de Groot
illustrations: Maan Jansen
cover design: Ton Wienbelt, Den Haag
production: TextCase, Groningen
typesetting: Michele Thurnim, TextCase
translation: First Edition Translators Ltd, Great Britain

ISBN 1 901 094 685

The little match girl

It was New Year's Eve and bitterly cold outside. It had been snowing for some time, and a harsh wind blew. The kind of biting wind that blows right through you in winter.

But in spite of the weather the street was crowded, because everyone was doing their last-minute shopping. Nearly everyone had something which they had to rush out and fetch from the shops. And because it was so cold, and they wanted to get back as quickly as possible to their warm fires at home, everyone was in a hurry.

In the middle of all those hurrying people walked a little girl. She walked barefoot, her eyes were red, and her hair fluttered round her face in the wind.

That girl was not celebrating because it was the last day of the year. She was cold, very cold, and she still had to sell all her matches. She carried those matches in a big tray, a heavy tray that hung on a strap round her neck.

Yet to make herself look a little bit pretty, the girl had put a ribbon in her hair. She had found the ribbon on the street. It was lying where it had been blown off someone's present by the strong wind.

The girl didn't have much luck, because no one wanted to buy her matches. After a while she felt very lonely and she walked through the streets completely numb with cold.

It gradually became quieter in the streets, as the shops began to shut. Everyone was going back home, where it was nice and warm and comfortable.

Most of the children had Christmas trees, decorated with lights, and gold and silver balls.

The little girl had a home, but no Christmas tree. And she couldn't go home till she'd sold all her matches.

Here in the cold she got sadder and sadder. Everything round her was chill and grey; there was a little leafless shrub, a wall battered by the wind, and

the cold snow covered everything with a layer of white. It went on snowing, and everything was covered, flake by flake, with a white blanket. She walked on, shivering in the icy cold.

It got later and colder, but she had to go on. She had to sell her matches so that she could take some money home. Her father would be terribly angry if she went home with all her matches and no money. Perhaps he would even beat her.

He always got angry very quickly, because he was so poor. He almost never went out, but always stayed within the four cold, damp walls of their house. There were four straw mattresses inside those four walls. When you lay on them, you could see the holes in the roof.

The little girl walked on, and thought about her family. She hadn't a grandmother any more, because a little while ago her grandmother had become very sick and had died. Now her mother was very sick, too, and because of the cold her cough kept getting worse.

Oh, she must sell her matches! If she could take some money home, everyone in the house would cheer up for a while. They would be able to

dream of nice things, and forget how hungry they were. They might not have cakes and roast goose on their table, but at least it would be a good start to the New Year.

The little match girl walked on. She had now reached a part of the town where the rich people lived. They had big houses with gardens in front. The girl began to be a bit more hopeful. All the windows were lit up, and she could see in easily. If she wanted to, she could dream about all the people inside, who could hardly wait before starting to eat all that lovely food.

But here, too, everyone was in a hurry, everyone wanted to start the party. So no one took any notice of the poor little match girl. She didn't really want to stay there any longer. Everything else was so nice here, but the people weren't nice. The poor little match girl knew that no one would look at her and buy something from her. Even if she had walked so far and was so cold.

She pulled her shawl round her a bit closer, and went on walking. She walked into a wide street. The houses in this street were a bit smaller, and behind one of the windows she saw a little boy who had a lovely Christmas tree. She could see that he was very happy. He looked out into the garden, at a lovely snowman with a thick scarf. The scarf was much thicker and better than the little match girl's shawl.

The little match girl could easily have taken that soft white woollen scarf, because the snowman wouldn't miss it. She needed that scarf so much, because she was so cold, and the snowman couldn't feel the raw wind at all. But she didn't take it, because she was always very honest.

Two little birds were playing happily in the snow. One pecked at some crumbs, and the other played about on the snowman's broom.

It was still snowing. The snow piled up against the walls. The little girl could hardly walk any further. She tried to walk in other people's footprints, but that was very difficult. Their footprints were frozen hard, and that made it very painful for her little feet, which were all purple with cold. She could hardly feel them any more, they were so cold... They seemed to be quite frozen.

What a pity about her slippers! This morning she could hardly get them on because they fitted so badly. Her mother had repaired them so often, they hardly looked like slippers any more. Yet the little girl had to make do with them, because her father and mother had no money for proper warm shoes. This morning, when the little girl had to run to cross the road, they had come off. When she went back to look for them, one had been run over by a cart; it was squashed quite flat. The cart had driven on. The

other had been picked up by a boy, who gave her a nasty look. The little girl had asked him to give her slipper back. The boy wouldn't; he only laughed at her, ran away fast, and threw her slipper into the river.

She went on walking through the long streets, and got colder and unhappier. She kept thinking of all the horrid things that had happened to her today: the snow that kept on snowing, the matches she couldn't sell, the slippers she had lost... it all came back to her.

Quite worn out she went to sit against a wall. She huddled down to protect herself from the cold wind. She was cold through and through, and wasn't quite sure where she was.

How far had she walked? Was she already a long way from the place where the little boy, the two little birds, and the snowman were? She didn't know any more.

She felt miserable, and her whole body hurt, it was so cold. And that was not all, because her tummy hurt, too, because she was so hungry.

The little girl almost couldn't stand it any more; what should she do? She didn't really dare go home, with all those unsold matches. Suddenly she knew what to do, she would think about her grandmother. Her grandmother had always been so nice to her. She used to tell her lots of stories about elves and fairies.

The little girl cowered down a little further, and suddenly saw her tray of matches.

She had completely forgotten the tray when she had taken it off, trembling with unhappiness, cold, and pain. Now she discovered it again. There was no food in it, but there were matches! So far the matches hadn't brought her much luck. But if she now took just one and lit it, surely her father wouldn't notice?

In any case, she would feel a bit warmer, how lovely that would be. She only had to strike the match against the wall to light it. A flash, and it was light all round her. At first she was startled by the noise it made as she struck it, but she quickly held her hand round the flame to stop it going out.

Oh how lovely, how nice and warm! She could move her cold, stiff little fingers again a little. She felt her whole body warm up, she even felt as if her curls were on fire.

The little girl looked at the flame burning in her hands. The flame made her warm and dizzy, and suddenly something strange happened. She saw herself sitting in front of a lovely big cast-iron stove with a brass cover. The fire in it was alight. Oh, how lovely and warm it was by that stove. The little girl dreamed that it was her stove. She had bought it from rich people, who were very kind; she'd had to pay very little for the stove. She was very pleased, you didn't often come across a stove so cheaply. The stove looked a bit dull, but she would give it to her parents when she had cleaned it up. She had been polishing that stove for three weeks now with the cloths and scouring powder that nice lady had given her. How nice it looked! The little girl felt more and more pleased every time a pretty curl or decoration showed up under her polishing. The stove had curly feet and a fluted chimney, the two doors were slightly open, so that you could look at the flames inside it.

When the stove was sparkling clean, the little girl wanted to see if it worked properly before she gave it to her parents. How nice and warm their house was going to be! She had carefully lit a fire in it. The flames danced in the stove, and the little girl quickly stretched her cold little feet towards the stove to warm them.

But suddenly the stove disappeared. The little girl was sitting outside again, holding a half burnt-out wooden matchstick.

She was very sad to have lost her stove. Quickly she struck another match; perhaps she would see it again!

But no, the stove didn't come back. The light of the match shone on the wall, and made the wall transparent. She could see exactly what was happening in the room behind the wall.

There was a big table, covered with a fine white tablecloth and a beautiful china dinner service. In the middle of the table was a lovely roast goose on a silver dish, garnished with plums and slices of apple. It smelt marvellous, and the smell wafted towards the little girl. She went to the table to share in the feast. She saw all sorts of other delicious things: dishes of lovely roast potatoes and vegetables, a gorgeous chocolate cake, and large goblets full of ice cream...

At last she would be able to fill her empty tummy. She shuffled carefully past all the people standing in the room. She was invisible, she felt as if she was floating. She could eat as much as she liked, nobody could see her, and nobody was going to chase her away because she hadn't been invited.

But now what was happening? At the very moment she was about to seize one of the juicy pieces of roast meat, the goose began to move.

The bird rolled off the dish onto the floor, and the little girl saw it turning to attack her. She was frightened, and imagined all the awful things the goose might want to do.

Then the match went out. She was back sitting against the cold, wet wall. There was nothing to eat any more, and no angry goose.

The match girl was disappointed. She had felt the warmth of the strange cast-iron stove with the brass cover, she had seen a fine roast goose with a garnish of apples and plums.

But now she was back here again, quite alone, cold, and hungry. She couldn't go on. She shut her eyes, and tried to think of nice things. That was all she could do now, her legs were so cold and weak that she couldn't walk any more.

To get a little warmer inside, she tried to think of the two best days of her life. The first day was when she saw the king's children. Then she had heard the nicest thing said to her ever. She stood there watching in her tattered old clothes, but a policeman had whispered to her that she looked just like the youngest princess!

The second day two nice things had happened. First she was on the lake, which had frozen over. People were skating there. That was such a splendid and happy sight, that the little girl couldn't get enough of it. And after that she had gone to the circus, where they had animals doing all kinds of fantastic things.

That day the little girl did not have to sell any matches, she was allowed to go skating on the lake. She couldn't get enough of sliding and twisting on

the ice. With her tiny body she looked like a ballerina from a musical box. Lots of people watched her, they thought that the girl with her pale face and red cheeks was very pretty.

A boy and his sister had come up to her, and given her a bag of roast chestnuts and a ticket for the circus. In the circus she had laughed her head off, and she had been able to give its bottle to a monkey dressed like a baby. That day was like a fairy tale.

It was no fairy tale now: everything round her was just as cold as the frozen lake where she had gone skating, but now it wasn't at all happy and cheerful.

The little girl began to run a high fever, she began to glow all over. Yet by the light of the third match, which she had just lit, she still looked pretty. She had chosen that match from the smallest box. She had chosen one with the smallest head. Perhaps it wouldn't even work. Psst, rrsst, the match made the same sound as the other two, though perhaps a little softer. But this match, too, produced the same bright, blinding light.

Again something happened: the little girl was sitting in front of a lovely Christmas tree. The tree was bigger than the one she'd seen at the little

boy's house, and even more beautiful than the tree she'd seen last year at a rich shopkeeper's. There were a thousand coloured candles burning in its branches, which were hung with coloured balls, sparkling in the light. Besides, the branches were decorated with artificial snow, and tasty sweets were hidden among them. There were all kinds of little surprises hidden in the tree.

The little match girl stretched out her hand to take the very smallest present off the tree. She was so pleased there was something for her, which she could keep for ever.

What would there be in the parcel? She hoped it was a doll. She wanted one so much. Then she could tell the doll all her secrets. She would take her with her whenever she had to sell matches, and she could sleep in her bed at night. She would hold the doll in her arms. It wouldn't be worried by the cold draught that came through the holes in the roof. The doll would comfort her and love her; no one else did. The little girl smiled, and went to get the doll. Then the match went out. It looked as if the tree disappeared into the sky, and as if all the candles became stars.

Suddenly one of those little lights fell to the ground. A long trail of light hung in the air.

Someone is dying, thought the little girl, when she saw the falling star, because that's what her grandmother had taught her. Her grandmother, the only one who had always loved her, had often told her earlier: "When a star falls, someone goes to heaven."

Unfortunately grandmother wasn't here now.

The little girl struck another match, and was immediately surrounded by a great light. In the light her grandmother appeared, and smiled at her.

"Grandmother, dear grandmother," cried the little girl. "Take me away with you while the flame is still alight. I don't want you to disappear, like the warm stove, the delicious goose, and the lovely Christmas tree! I don't want to be left behind here, with just a burnt-out match."

She lit another match, and another, and then she lit the whole boxful. She wanted to keep grandmother as long as possible. All those matches at once made a lovely fire, making hissing and spurting noises with each new flame.

Grandmother looked much prettier than when she had died. She didn't look so old, and looked happy. Then she took the little girl by the hand. She went up into the sky, and took the little girl with her in her arms. She took the little girl to heaven, where there was no cold, no hunger, and nobody was sad.

The next morning the little match girl was found by passers-by. They found her holding a bundle of burnt-out matches, leaning against a cold

wall. During the night she had died of cold. That was the night when many people had parties to celebrate the start of the new year.

Some people wondered how the little girl had got such red cheeks, and why she held a fan of burnt-out matches in her hand. And no one could explain why she was smiling…

The Chinese nightingale

Hundreds of years ago, and very far away, in China in the old days, there lived an emperor in a porcelain palace. The palace had very many rooms, and every room was different. It looked magnificent; you don't see such a beautiful palace in such lovely colours anywhere today. Wonderful flowers, in all the colours of the rainbow, grew in the palace gardens. The flowers swayed gently in the breeze. Tall stems of bamboo rustled, and everywhere you could hear the quiet chatter of birds.

The emperor's estate was so large that it couldn't all be kept as beautifully as it was near the palace, where the gardener made sure that everything was tidy. He couldn't do everything. He didn't get to the far end of the garden so often, so that there were bigger trees there than nearer the palace. In one of those trees – a very old one – lived a little bird. The bird was very difficult to see, and not particularly beautiful, but he could sing. His song was so lovely that everyone who heard it was completely enchanted. That bird was a nightingale.

Behind the wood was a small lake, where fishermen went every day. They heard the nightingale, and told everyone who wanted to listen how beautifully the nightingale sang in the emperor's wood.

One day the emperor heard from one of his servants that somewhere in his woods there was a bird that sang so beautifully that tears came to the eyes of everyone who heard him.

The emperor sent for his first minister.

"Fetch me that nightingale immediately," said the emperor.

"If you fail, I'll dismiss you."

You will realize, of course, that the first minister wanted to keep his job. He had a nice house, and could buy anything he liked, because as first minister he earned a lot of money. So he had to find that nightingale somehow. He ran frantically through the palace until he saw a servant. He asked: "Where is the nightingale? Take me to the nightingale!" But the servant couldn't help him. He had never heard the bird. The first minister ran on, but everyone he asked where the nightingale was shook their heads. Some of them had heard of him, but they had never heard the bird sing themselves.

It began to get dark. The first minister was afraid that the emperor would fire him any minute. He looked round him. He'd asked everyone, hadn't he? He saw a door leading to the kitchen. Perhaps the kitchenmaid might know, he thought. He went in, and asked the girl: "Do you know where I can find the nightingale?" The girl answered: "I think so. One night when I went to visit my sick mother I sat down in the wood to rest on my way. Then I heard a bird singing beautifully. It sounded wonderful; tears came to my eyes, it was so lovely."

"Take me there, take me there!" cried the first minister. "I will cover you in gold."

"I'll take you there," said the girl at once. She hoped she would get enough money to pay for a doctor for her sick mother. Besides, she thought she had washed up enough of the emperor's dishes; she'd been doing it all her life.

If she could really get a lot of money, perhaps she wouldn't have to work in the kitchen any more. Then she could take care of her mother.

Together the first minister and the girl went into the wood. They had to walk quite a long way before they reached the first really tall trees. The first minister, who was very fat, could only with difficulty keep up with the girl. Besides, the gardener hadn't been working this far out, so that there were hardly any paths; they were all overgrown.

After walking for some minutes they heard a mooing noise. "Is that the voice of the nightingale?" asked the first minister. "No," said the girl, "that's a cow."

A little later they heard: "Caw, caw," and the first minister asked: "Is that the nightingale singing?" "No," said the kitchenmaid, "that's a crow. You mustn't be so impatient, we are still a long way off, you know."

They walked further still, and suddenly they heard a lovely sound. It was the nightingale. He was singing his heart out.

"How marvellous," cried the first minister. He was quite silenced. They walked to the tree where the bird sat. The nightingale stopped singing. With his head to one side, he looked from his branch at the first minister, who stood huffing and puffing by the tree.

The first minister looked at the nightingale, and said: "Dear nightingale, I invite you to come to the palace. The emperor of China would like to hear you sing. Everyone will fall silent in admiration of you, and you can be introduced to the whole court."

The nightingale had to think about it. He would really rather stay in the wood, because he loved the trees and the flowers all round him. But it was the emperor of China who was asking, so he decided to go along.

"All right, that's agreed," said the nightingale, "I'll go with you." The first minister bowed to the nightingale, and the minister, the kitchenmaid, and the nightingale went off to the palace.

In the palace the emperor was waiting in his throne room. There were low porcelain tables, with porcelain decoration. The emperor sat on a porcelain throne, and his whole court sat round him, all wearing their finest clothes. The clothes were not made of porcelain, because that's impossible, but everything else you could see in the room was. The emperor thought nothing was quite as beautiful as porcelain.

The bird perched on a golden perch in the porcelain cage the emperor had had made for him. The first minister said: "Here is the emperor's nightingale!"

The nightingale began to sing. It was magnificent. He sang the loveliest melodies anyone had ever heard. And he sang so clearly. It was brilliant.

After an hour it was over. The whole court was silenced by it, and the emperor most of all. He cried softly, he had thought it so lovely.

"Nightingale, would you like to live in the palace?" he asked the bird on its golden perch. He didn't even wait for the little bird's answer, but told his servants to lock the bird's cage, so that the nightingale couldn't get out any more. The cage was put on a porcelain table in front of the window, so that the nightingale could still look at the trees.

The nightingale wasn't as happy as he had been in the woods, but he still sang for the emperor every day. He was let out twice a day. Then he had twelve silk ribbons tied to him, six to each foot, which were held by twelve servants. He was allowed to flutter up in the air for a few moments, but not for long, and after a few minutes he had to go back to his cage.

He had to sing in the morning, and he had to sing in the evening, and he had to sing whenever the emperor felt like it all through the day. And that was nearly always.

One day an envoy came from the emperor of another country, Japan. He brought a present from his master for the emperor of China. The emperor received him in his throne room.

"What have you brought me?" he asked with curiosity.

"A bird which sings more sweetly than you've ever heard," said the envoy. The emperor got angry.

"That's impossible," he cried. "The bird that can sing most sweetly is my nightingale."

"Just listen to this one," said the Japanese emperor's envoy, and he brought out the bird. It was an imitation bird. It was much prettier than the emperor of China's nightingale, which was a grey colour. The bird the emperor of Japan had sent as a present shimmered all over from the diamonds on its back. And what wasn't covered with diamonds was of pure gold with porcelain decoration.

The envoy wound the bird up by a spring at the back. When he let the spring go, the bird began to sing. It sounded so lovely, that the emperor could hardly believe his ears.

"Do it again," he cried when the bird had finished. The envoy wound the bird up again, and let it play again. It sounded exactly the same as before.

"My nightingale must hear this," said the emperor. "And after that the two birds must sing a duet."

26

He gave orders for the nightingale to be brought out of his cage and put on his golden perch, which still hung beside him. The nightingale always had to perch on it when he sang for the emperor.

"Just listen, nightingale," said the emperor to his own bird, once he was on his perch.

The envoy rewound the imitation bird, and let it play again. Everyone was very impressed, and again it sounded just like the last time.

"And the best of it is," said the emperor of Japan's envoy, "the clockwork mechanism means that the bird can always be played again. Have a look how it works."

Everyone looked at the back of the bird. It was indeed a very clever idea, a spring you could wind the bird up with.

The Chinese nightingale didn't look. He was very unhappy. Why was everyone listening to a fake bird? Surely it was no good? He thought that he could sing much better. At least he sounded real, and not mechanical. And besides, he sounded different each time, while the clockwork bird always sang exactly the same tune.

Everyone was still very impressed by the imitation bird, and was examining how it worked. The window was open, because it was midsummer and very hot.

"I'll just fly away," thought the nightingale. "Nobody likes my songs any more."

He jumped off his perch, and flew through the open window. Nobody saw him fly away, because everyone was interested only in the imitation bird.

Now the emperor of China wanted the two birds to sing a duet together. He asked: "Nightingale, what did you think..." but he never finished the sentence, because he saw that the nightingale had disappeared.

"The nightingale has gone," shouted the emperor. "Quick, find the nightingale!" But the first minister said: "Let him fly away, we still have the best one here."

And the emperor agreed with him.

For the year that followed everyone worshipped the imitation bird. Every day it sang in the palace throne room, and everyone who came to see the emperor, and that was a whole lot of people, thought the bird's song was wonderful.

At night the bird stood on a silken cushion beside the emperor's bed. When he went to bed the emperor wound the bird up, let it play, and before the bird had finished he was asleep. Then he dreamed about the nicest things, and particularly about birds.

One night the emperor lay in bed listening to the bird singing. It sounded just as beautiful as ever.

But what was that? Suddenly the bird sang a wrong note. The emperor was shocked, and jumped out of bed. He bent over the bird. At that moment the emperor heard an enormous bang inside the toy bird. It trembled for a moment, and then stopped.

Although it was late at night, the emperor immediately sent for the best and most expensive doctor he could find.

"Doctor, what is wrong with my bird? Make it better," said the emperor to him.

The doctor worked for hours, but couldn't do anything for the bird. "Fetch the clockmaker," cried the emperor, and that was done.

The clockmaker tried to repair the bird as best he could. At last he said: "The clockwork mechanism is worn out, majesty. I advise you not to make the bird sing more than once a year."

That was terrible for the emperor. He cried, he was so unhappy that he could only make the bird sing once a year.

For the next twenty-five years the imitation bird only sang once every year. It did that on the emperor's birthday. Then the bird was very carefully wound up, and everyone could listen to its song.

Of course, it was still the same song, but no one thought that mattered. It sounded lovely, and besides, no one could learn it by heart. It was a very difficult little melody, and if you could only hear it once a year, it was not easy to learn it by heart.

"With a real nightingale you have to wait to find out what you are going to hear," said the emperor. "At least with this nightingale we know what it's going to sing. If we open it up we can see exactly how it works, and how it is put together, because it's a machine."

But that, of course, didn't alter the fact that the nightingale could only be played once a year.

And then the emperor got ill. At first he was just a little off-colour, but then he got really sick, and looked very pale.

The people of China were very worried at the emperor being so ill, because he was a very good emperor. Much better than the one before in any case.

All the doctors in the whole country came to look at him, and even dozens of doctors from other countries, but none of them could help him. The emperor got worse and worse.

One night he lay in bed and felt he was going to die. He could hardly breathe any more, and had difficulty keeping his eyes open. He called all his friends to him and said goodbye to them. Everyone in the palace was sad and sorrowful. They knew for certain that the emperor would die that night. All the arrangements for his funeral were made.

The emperor had sent everyone away from his bedroom, and now lay alone in the dark. He wouldn't last much longer, he thought.

Suddenly he heard a lovely song. Wonderful notes combined to make a brilliant melody. It was the nightingale! The real nightingale from the emperor's garden!

The emperor's blood began to run faster. A little colour came back to his cheeks. The bird went on singing. He sang so beautifully that the emperor

felt a little better. He mumbled: "Thank you," to the bird, and fell asleep. The emperor slept well that night. He wasn't dying, he felt it, and as a result of that sleep, which the nightingale's singing had given him, he felt much better again.

The next morning a queue of people waited outside the emperor's bedroom door. Everyone was sure that by now the emperor would have died, and they wanted to have a last look at him.
Cautiously they opened the door, and they thought that they would find a dead emperor in the bed. But what did they see when they opened the curtains? The emperor, yes, but he wasn't dead.
He was sitting straight up in bed, there was colour in his cheeks, and he said: "Good morning!"
That taught the emperor and everyone else at his court the difference between a real nightingale and an imitation one. And the emperor didn't make the same mistake again. For the rest of his life he loved his own live Chinese nightingale best.

The gardener and his masters

A very long time ago there was a king in every country, and there were lots of counts and barons, too. These distinguished gentlemen lived in large castles, ate the nicest food you can think of, and gave splendid parties on every possible occasion. The one who had most money and gave most parties was the most important man in that country.

In one country, a long way from here, there were a count and a countess, who also lived in a beautiful castle. The castle had forty rooms and twelve

turrets, and it was furnished with the most beautiful chairs, sofas, and beds that could be bought. They hoped to make an impression on the other barons and dukes. In every room hung the most splendid paintings, with labels saying who had painted them, and how much they were worth. The count and countess thought everyone should know how much money they had paid for their paintings, because they were inordinately proud of them.

Not only was the castle beautiful on the inside, but also outside. There was a large piece of land round it. This was the castle garden, but it was so large that you couldn't really call it a garden any more. Round the garden there were stately old trees, and dense shrubs. There were not only a lot of flowers, there were also big greenhouses, in which vegetables and fruit could be grown all through the year.

Nobody knew how long the family of the count and countess had owned this castle, but it had to be a long time, because the trees, which stood neatly in a row along the drive, were at least a hundred years old.

The count who lived in the castle had a gardener, whose name was Larsen. Larsen was a very good gardener. He knew the names of all the plants by heart, and he was very good at laying out gardens. He had laid out this garden, too; he had given each shrub, each flower, and each tree its own place. And that was not his only duty. He also had to mow the lawn, look after the flowers and plants, and rake the drive. And in addition he had been taken on to cultivate the vegetables and fruit in the greenhouses.

The count and the countess were very pleased with Larsen's work. The garden always looked very tidy, and the flowers were magnificent.

Unfortunately Larsen himself was not satisfied at all: the centuries-old trees along the drive were not to his taste. They were bare, and they were responsible for a lot of noise; all the rooks were building their nests in them. What a lot of cawing! It was enough to deafen anybody.

"Can I cut down those trees some time? Their branches spoil the view, and there is such a noise from them!" he complained to the count.

The count did not agree with him. He said: "Those trees belong to the birds. They build their nests in them, and live in them all day long. Where would they go, if you cut down the trees? They can't go to the trees round the outside of the garden. There are never any birds there, you know that. Besides, you've got enough to do."

There was certainly enough to do for a gardener. The count and countess were pleased with the results of his work. The flowers in the garden smelt lovely. And there were so many of them! Carnations, roses, tulips, all

sorts of flowers could be found in the count's garden, and everyone enjoyed the fruit and vegetables, too.

One day the count sent for his gardener. He told him that he'd had lunch with one of the barons the day before.

"The food was delicious," he said, "but the dessert was the best I ever tasted. There were fresh cherries, melons, pomegranates, and peaches, larger and juicier than I've ever seen before."

When he told him that, the count felt hungry again, he had enjoyed the baron's food so much. He said: "I think that the fruit came from a far country. It was delivered by the best greengrocer in town. Go and have a look, Larsen, and tell me where it comes from. Then I will get them to send some young trees out to me. And then we'll have that delicious fruit ourselves, soon." The gardener did as he was told, and went to the greengrocer. The greengrocer knew Larsen quite well, because every year he bought any left-over crops from him.

"Where did all that delicious fruit come from?" Larsen asked the greengrocer.

"That was your own fruit, which I sold to the baron," said the greengrocer. "It didn't come from a far country at all."

"Excellent," thought Larsen, "I wonder what the count will have to say about that?"

He went back to the castle to tell the count and countess.

"My lord," he said to the count, "the fruit comes from our own kitchen garden!" Larsen looked very proud when he told him that.

"That's odd!" the nobleman said. He didn't really believe it. "Go back to the greengrocer and ask him to sign a statement that the fruit is indeed from our own kitchen garden. Only then can I be sure."

The gardener went back to town and went into the greengrocer's shop. "You have to put your signature to a letter, in which you declare that the fruit really comes from the count's kitchen garden," he said. The greengrocer did so.

When Larsen got back to the castle again, he told the count: "Look, here is the greengrocer's statement. I grew the fruit myself!" and he gave the letter to his master.

"That's tremendous!" cried the count. He called in all his servants and said: "Put fruit dishes all over the castle, filled with the best fruit in the garden! Send a large basket full of apples, pears, pineapples, melons, cherries, strawberries, and plums to all the barons and counts in the country! Decorate the whole castle with the best fruit you can find! In a week's time I will give a large fruit party!"

There was a hustle and bustle in the castle. Everyone was busy decorating the whole castle with fruit, from top to bottom. A week later the fruit party was held. Hundreds of barons and counts came and, of course, the king himself, too.

The count was smiling from ear to ear when he saw how much everyone enjoyed the party.

The next day he called the gardener in.

"What is it, sir?" asked Larsen. The count answered: "That was a very successful party yesterday, but you know that the crops have been good everywhere, don't you? It is so hot that apples and pears all over the country have done very well!" That was not a nice thing to say. The count was simply jealous that Larsen had managed to grow such wonderful fruit. All he could do was simply play at being a count. He didn't even know how to mow the lawn.

Several months passed, until one day a letter arrived from the king. The count was very pleased when he read it: he and his wife were invited to an enormous party the king was giving.

It was a splendid feast. The royal palace was beautifully decorated, and the food was delicious. Especially… the melons. The king had put melons everywhere, which were so sweet and juicy that you almost ate your fingers as well.

The next day, when the party was over and the count was back in his own castle, he said to Larsen: "See to it that you grow the same kind of

melons, Larsen. Go to the king's gardener, and buy some of the seeds. And don't worry about the cost."

"Well," said Larsen, "that's going to be difficult, because the seeds come from our own garden. The king's gardener ordered them from me himself, and I myself collected them and sent them to him."

"Then the king's gardener must have planted them in different soil, and in another garden," said the count.

"No, the king's crop failed, so he asked me to supply the melons. So the melons you liked so much at the king's party were our own," answered the gardener.

"Then you will have to sign a statement," said the count, "otherwise I won't believe you." And Larsen did so.

Now the count and countess told everyone who wanted to know how good their fruit was. Their fruit and vegetables became known in all corners of the world, and seeds were sent out to people everywhere.

"As long as Larsen doesn't get too big for his boots," said the count to his wife. It wasn't very kind of them to be so nasty to their gardener. Because instead of having a rest after all his hard labours in the garden and in the

greenhouses, Larsen worked harder than ever before. Every year he tried to grow new varieties in his garden. And nearly always he succeeded.

Several times a week Larsen did the flowers in the castle. He tried to arrange them as attractively as possible, and put them in the prettiest vases. One day the countess said to him: "Dear Larsen, those arrangements are quite pretty, but it is a pity that you don't do more for them. You just throw some flowers together and then you think you have a flower arrangement."

That wasn't true, because the gardener really did his best.

One day Larsen brought in a blue flower. It was a simple flower, but very pretty just the same.

"Oh," said the countess. "I am sure that must be a Hindustani lotus!" She had read that name in a book once, and this flower was so beautiful that it just had to come from somewhere a long way away.

The count and countess spent the whole day admiring the flower. They kept moving it to a different place, so that it was in the sun all the time. All the counts and barons in the neighbourhood came to look at this wonderful sight. They all said they had never seen anything so beautiful,

and that it must be very rare. In the end even the princess came to admire this exotic flower.

"What a magnificent flower!" said the princess.

The count gave it to her. "Because you are so beautiful yourself," he said to her courteously. He didn't think she was at all beautiful, but he wanted the king to like him. And he thought it was worth giving away his precious flower for that. And moreover, even if the princess was not beautiful, she was certainly nice.

When the princess had left, the count wanted to know what kind of flower it really was. He went into the greenhouses, and looked for the flower everywhere, but he couldn't find it.

He went to look for Larsen. "What kind of flower was that?" he asked him. "That was just a perfectly ordinary flower," said the gardener, "the flower of an artichoke."

"What?" shouted the countess. That gave her quite a shock, because an artichoke is the kind of vegetable you can find anywhere. "Why didn't you tell us before? We have given the blue flower to the king's daughter, and told her that it came from a far-away country. She knows everything about flowers! She will think that we were trying to make her look foolish. Now we will never be asked to the king's parties again!"

They went straight to the king's palace to offer their apologies to the princess. They blamed the gardener. "He always plays tricks on us," they said, and told her that they had punished him.

When the princess heard that, she said: "That is unfair! Why should you blame someone who discovers that a simple flower can also be beautiful? As long as the artichokes are in bloom, you must bring me a fresh flower every day."

And that is what happened. The artichokes flowered for another two months, and for two months the count took a flower to the princess every day.

The summer was over, and the leaves fell from the trees. It rained nearly every day, and the wind blew. It got colder and colder. Everyone spent as little time as possible outside, and hurried back to their firesides.

One evening the wind blew harder than ever. Large, black clouds scudded across the sky. There was such a storm, that the trees swayed backwards and forwards. It blew so hard, that one of the trees along the drive blew over. It made a tremendous noise. But that was not the whole of it; all the tall trees with the rookeries blew over, one by one. You could hear the shrieking of the rooks until morning came. They were so frightened, they flew up against the windows of the castle.

What a night! No one had had much sleep, but fortunately the weather improved a little the next morning; the storm had died down.

"Now you've got what you want, Larsen," said the count to the gardener, when they were having breakfast. "Now there is enough room for new plants. A pity there is nothing left to remind us of the past."

Larsen didn't care much about that. Now he could grow what he liked in the open spaces. He had never understood why the count didn't want those ugly old trees cut down.

The gardener walked to the drive where the trees had once stood. Now there were bits of tree strewn about on the ground. Lots of old beeches and birches had blown over. Larsen thought about all the things he could plant on that sunny, open ground.

For days he walked through the woods and across fields in the neighbourhood. He had a good look at all the flowers, shrubs, and trees that grew there. Only then would he decide what he was going to plant. First he couldn't think what to choose, but suddenly he had an idea.

He cleared away all the branches, and raked the piece of ground. Then he made a drawing of hedges and wildflowers on a piece of paper. That was

his plan for a beautiful garden. It took a little while, but at last he was ready. He began by planting a whole lot of shrubs. He planted a green holly-tree, and found space for large ferns, which looked like palm trees. Here and there he put some wildflowers close together. It was a lovely sight. It looked just like a picture, it was so beautiful.

A few days before Christmas the gardener raised a flagpole on the spot where the old trees once stood. That was the thing to do in that country. Next to the flag he put a few sticks in the ground, and hung barley on them. He was sure the birds would like that, and then they could have a bit of Christmas, too.

"You can see that Larsen is getting old," said the count and his wife to each other. That was really not very fair, because the gardener was full of good intentions.

A little later there was a piece in the paper with a photo of the castle. The garden was very beautiful, it said, and it was a good thing that the old custom of putting barley out for the birds had been revived.

The count and the countess were very jealous again. They said to the gardener: "You have all the luck, Larsen, because people always think that anything you do is marvellous. And you don't even do anything for it!"

The count and the countess may have been jealous of Larsen, but couldn't help being pleased with him, too. They could have dismissed him any day, but they didn't. Because they thought that they should be good masters.

That is the story of the gardener and his masters. It all really happened in a far-away country, long ago.

The boy who couldn't shudder

Once upon a time there was a man with two sons. The eldest was a bright, clever boy. He could cope with the most difficult tasks, but deep in his heart he was really a scaredy-cat. He was scared of everything, and often said: "Father, please don't send me out in the dark, because then I get so frightened that I shudder the whole time. I get so afraid that I go into a cold sweat. I keep hearing sinister noises everywhere, and in the end I'm just rigid with fright."

Whenever the younger son heard that, he muttered in amazement: "Shuddering, what's that? Here's something else I don't know, I have an awful lot to learn. Father, let me go, because I would like to learn to shudder. It seems a very good idea for me to learn what it is!"

One day the sexton came to visit. He came for a nice cup of coffee and a chat. And while the sexton was enjoying his company, the father of the two young men suddenly had a wonderful idea.

"Sexton," he said, "I need your help. My youngest son is not afraid of anything. Whatever happens, he has absolutely no fear. And my eldest son is always afraid. Now my younger son wants to know what it's like to be afraid, too. May he become a bellringer in your church? Churches are always a bit spooky at night. And I think that in such a large building, full of all sorts of strange noises, my younger son might get frightened. And then perhaps you can pretend to be a ghost. If he's not afraid of that, then I don't know what we can try. Then I'll give up."

The sexton protested a little. What an odd idea, a young man who was never frightened! And a sexton surely shouldn't start playing at being a ghost. What would people think... Suppose someone saw him! Then everyone would think that the sexton had gone mad.

But the man gave the sexton two gold pieces for his poor box and... Oh well, all right then, just this once the sexton would do as he asked.

A few days later the boy was high up in the church tower, under the roof beams.

Of course, he wasn't frightened. He thought it was grand to be up at the top of the tower. He could look out over the whole village, and in the distance he could see the house where he lived. He could even see his father walking in the meadow. Look, his father was taking some oats to the horse.

The youngest son found it exactly to his liking, up there in the top of the tower.

He didn't mind if there was a bit of wind. He liked fresh air! And the feeling as if the tower was swaying from side to side in the wind was fun. You didn't feel that every day.

But just at the moment when he wanted to ring the bells at midnight, a floating white shape suddenly appeared.

"Shiver and shake, miserable human," cried the ghost in a strange, hollow voice.

"Get away, or tell me what you want here, if you've got any guts!" shouted the boy.

He was certainly surprised, but not afraid. Who was that, that madman in a white sheet saying silly things to him? He would have to teach him a lesson. Just imagine if the sexton were to hear that funny people in white sheets were climbing up to his tower! The sexton had just told him to look after the tower properly. He wasn't allowed to let anyone go up.

The ghost kept waving his arms and saying funny things in that strange voice. The boy had had enough, and gave the ghost a sharp push, so that he rolled down the stairs. Then he went peacefully to sleep. That silly ghost had certainly learned his lesson by now!

The next day the sexton's wife found her husband. He lay groaning on the floor at the bottom of the tower stairs. He had a broken leg, and a strange white sheet lay next to him.

Whimpering, the sexton told her what had happened, and the sexton's wife went to complain to the boy's father.

His father was so angry when he heard what had happened to the sexton that he drove his son out of the house. He gave him fifty gold coins to take with him and said he would have to manage for himself from now on. He, his father, had given up. Who ever had a son who was never afraid? He just couldn't stand it any more.

In good spirits the young man took to the road. Perhaps now, at last, he would learn to shudder. He had travelled quite a long way along the dusty road when he was overtaken by a horse and cart. Cheerfully the driver called out to him: "Hey there, friend, where are you going? It looks as if you're not sure of your way. But whatever you do, don't take the road that curves off to the right and disappears among the trees. That leads to the haunted castle. Even the bravest of the king's soldiers don't go there, it's so spooky."

The young man immediately decided to go to the haunted castle. There he should at last learn to shudder.

He went to pay his respects to the king whose castle it was. He bowed deeply and said: "Please, majesty, give me a workbench, a knife, and the means to make a good fire. I would like to pass three nights in your castle."

"Very good," said the king. "If you are successful, you may marry my daughter, because it will mean you must be very brave. No one has ever dared spend three nights in my haunted castle."

When night fell, the young man went to sit by his crackling fire. As usual, he quite enjoyed himself. The fire kept him nice and warm, and there was no one near to spoil things by complaining.

Towards midnight he blew on the glowing coals, and suddenly two enormous jet-black tomcats jumped out of the fire. They stretched out

their huge claws, and spat at him. And they looked at the young man with blazing eyes, as if they just wanted to tear him to pieces.

"Your nails are much too long," said the young man, and he took the cats by the scruffs of their necks, and clamped their feet in the vice on the workbench. Only then did he realize that he had to deal with two very dangerous sorcerers. They had turned themselves into black tomcats to plague people and harm them. But that didn't work with this young man. He seized the tomcats and threw them in the moat.

A little later he noticed a bed in one corner of the room. He dropped down on the feather mattress to have a good sleep.

But he was no sooner lying down, than the bed set off on a walkabout. It travelled through the whole castle, from one room to the next. It went faster and faster, and ended by running down the corridors till it stormed into the great hall. The young man thought it was wonderful. This was really good, a travelling bed!

Suddenly the bed threw its passenger off, quilt and all. The young man fell on the floor, drew the bedclothes over him, and fell asleep.

The next day he went to the king, and said: "Majesty, I still can't shudder,

but perhaps I'll learn tonight. I find your castle very entertaining. All kinds of interesting things keep happening."

That evening he sat by the fire again.

It was exactly midnight when he heard a loud roaring noise in the chimney. He jumped up and grabbed a stool. The bottom half of a man was coming down out of the soot.

Two large feet appeared in velvet stockings, then two sturdy calves with silk garters round them, and finally a very smart pair of short breeches decorated with ribbons. And that was all!

There the man stopped. He had no upper half, no arms, and no head, or eyes, or nose. There was nothing of all that.

When he saw it, the young man burst out laughing. He bent forward, stuck his head in the chimney of the fireplace, and shouted: "Half a man to keep me company, what use is that? A whole one would be much better! Then at least we could have a chat together."

The young man heard a lot of violent cursing, and then the other half of the man arrived. The top half jumped onto the bottom half, and there was the whole man.

The young man just laughed fit to burst. Where did you ever see such a thing, a man in two halves, which got together occasionally?

Meanwhile the two halves of the man went on cursing and swearing. He was certainly in a very bad mood today.

And that was not all, no, far from it. All kinds of odd people and animals kept coming down the chimney, and out of the fireplace. Each one seemed even odder than the last, but they were all in a foul temper. They all stood there cursing and swearing.

And the young man? He just fell about laughing. He had never seen such a collection of freaks together before.

When at last nobody else came down the chimney, the freaks began a little game. They had seven bones and a skull, with which they began to play skittles. The young man would have liked to take part in the game, but when he looked more closely at the skull, he said: "I would very much like to have a go, but first I must plane down this ball a bit; it's not round enough."

He cheerfully went to sit at his workbench, and whistled as he made the skull nice and smooth. He lost the first game of skittles, and won the

second. When the clock struck one, all the freaks vanished, and the young man was alone again in the haunted castle. He went soundly to sleep, because with one thing and another it had got quite late.

The third night in the haunted castle nothing happened at all, and the young man slept well.

Early in the morning the king arrived to ask him how things had gone. "Well, young man, have you learned to shudder at last?"

"Absolutely not, your majesty, but I think I have chased away all the ghosts from this castle. People won't be able to call it a haunted castle any more."

"Well done," cried the king. "You may marry my daughter, as I promised."

The whole kingdom celebrated in honour of their new prince. He was very happy, but occasionally he sighed and said: "If only I could be afraid, I would so much like to shudder! I still don't know what it means."

One night the princess's chambermaid put a big bucket of cold water down near the head of the bed where the prince and princess slept. Tiny fishes sparkled in the water. The prince didn't notice, because he'd been fast asleep for some time.

The chambermaid gave the little fishes one by one to the princess, and the princess slipped a handful of them inside the prince's nightshirt.

And what the sexton hadn't been able to do, and what the ghosts, the sorcerers, and the strange freaks had none of them been able to do, the princess did with her icy-cold slippery fishes: at last the prince shook. He had at last learned to shudder. Now he knew just as much as his elder brother. Now he was completely happy, because now and then he shuddered delightfully, together with the princess.

The little mermaid

Long ago, at the bottom of the deep blue sea, far below the waves, lived some girls who were half human, half fish. The top of their body looked just like that of a human girl, but the bottom half looked like that of a fish. They were called mermaids.

Only people who had almost drowned at sea, when they had fallen off their ships, had ever seen a mermaid.

The mermaids often went to the surface of the sea to rescue shipwrecked sailors. They took them to a safe beach. That wasn't difficult for them,

because they could swim very well with their fishtails. But otherwise no one saw them, because they never showed themselves on land.

No one believed the sailors when they said they had fallen into the sea and been rescued by mermaids, who had no legs, but a scaly fishtail. And yet their stories were true.

The mermaids lived in a beautiful palace made of gold, silver, green, blue, yellow, and red sea shells that sparkled when the sun shone on the water. They looked just like pearls and diamonds.

Round the castle was a large garden, overgrown with brown and green seaweed. The seaweed swayed backwards and forwards in the flow of the sea.

In the palace lived the sea-king. His wife had died some years ago, so he had no one to share his responsibilities with. He had to see to it that life under water went smoothly. The mermaids had to rescue wrecked sailors, there had to be enough fish around, and the seawater had to be kept clean and should not flood over the human peoples' dikes and dunes. Of course, the king didn't have time to bring up his six beautiful daughters himself, so he had asked his mother, the girls' grandmother, if she would

teach her grandchildren all they needed to know. She was happy to do that.

She knew that the children of a king had to be brought up with nice manners, otherwise they would not be good princesses. So she taught them manners, and all kinds of things that would make them well-educated mermaids.

The six mermaid princesses were all beautiful, but the youngest was the prettiest of all. She had long fair hair that glistened, a perfect pink skin, and blue eyes. She was so incredibly beautiful that it made her father swell with pride! No wonder, with such a daughter!

And yet, things weren't going quite right for this youngest daughter. Although everyone loved her and all the seafolk thought she was the most beautiful mermaid they'd ever seen, she was often unhappy. Then her face was sad.

Her sisters, the king, and her grandmother all wondered what was wrong with her. Was the most beautiful princess ill? Or was something else wrong?

More and more often the princess went to her own room in the palace to be by herself, or looked for a quiet spot in the large garden. She liked to sit there and dream, far from the laughter and play of her sisters.

"Will you come and join us? We are playing a game together!" her sisters would call. "I don't feel like it today," said the little mermaid, "you go and play a game between the five of you."

Her sisters thought it was a pity that the youngest princess didn't want to join in. That happened more and more often, these days. What could be the matter?

When they were having dinner that night, the oldest princess asked her youngest sister: "What is the matter with you these days? Why are you always so sad?"

"Well," the mermaid began. She saw that everyone was looking at her. Why should they be so interested? "I have found a marble bust of a young man. It probably fell overboard when his ship was in trouble in that storm a few weeks ago."

So that was the problem. The little mermaid was in love, in love with a marble bust!

As often as she could, the little mermaid talked to her grandmother, who could tell her all kinds of things about life on land. The princess listened with bated breath.

"On land men and women live in large towns and villages. The sun shines

much more fiercely than here, because the rays don't have to penetrate all that water first."

Grandmother knew so much about the world, the girl thought. She became more and more curious. After all, if the marble bust of the young man had made her heart beat faster, then there must be an awful lot more to life on land, she thought.

"When you are fifteen," said grandmother, "you may rise to the surface for a day, just like all other mermaids, and look at the world of humans."

First her eldest sister was fifteen. After endless warnings from her grandmother to be careful, she swam to the surface. She had to be back again that evening.

How envious the youngest princess was. She so much wanted to go up, too, to look at the people who lived on land. She had a few more years to wait, but at least she could ask her sister lots of questions. And she did.

"What was it like up there?" she asked her sister, as soon as she was back down below. "Fantastic!" said her eldest sister, and never stopped talking about everything she had seen. The youngest princess became more and more impatient; she wanted to go, too! The next year it was the king's second daughter's turn. She, too, went to the surface, but she swam in another direction. She learned about other landscapes and other people, and she told her youngest sister all about them. A year later the third princess went yet another way, and so it went on until at long last the youngest princess had her fifteenth birthday. How pleased she was! This was the best day of her life; today she would be allowed to go to the surface and look at the world of people!

Her grandmother was even more worried than before.

"Will you be very careful when you see people?" she warned. "Oh yes," said the princess. "I will simply swim away if it gets too dangerous; they won't follow me."

"And beware of scary beasts!" said grandmother.

"Oh, but we've got some here, haven't we? They are just a little bit different," answered the little mermaid. "Make sure you're home on time," added her grandmother, "because tomorrow we are having your birthday party. All the fishes, seals, and seahorses have been invited, so you must not be late back."

"Don't worry, grandmother," said the princess.

When her grandmother could not think of anything else to worry about,

she said goodbye, and gave her a kiss. The mermaid swam away fast.
She used all her strength to swim as fast as she could towards the sky she
could see above her head. When she reached the surface, she stuck her
head out of the water to look at the sun as it went down, and coloured the
sky red. How beautiful! You didn't see that down below. There it just got
dark when the sun went down. While she was floating on the water, the
mermaid suddenly saw a magnificent ship. There was a party on board,
and hundreds of little lights hung on the rigging. A handsome prince was
standing on the decorated bows of the ship. The princess swam a little
closer to the ship to have a better look. What a wonderful sight!
As she got closer, the wind suddenly began to blow, and it started to rain.
The weather got worse and worse, and suddenly she saw lightning and
heard thunder.
The bad weather had struck so suddenly, that the crew on board had not
been able to haul the sails down in time. Everyone had been so busy
having a party, that no one had seen the angry clouds gathering. And now
it was too late...

The ship was lifted right up into the sky, and when it came down again it
landed so hard on the waves that it broke in two. The two halves sank,
and all the people on board were thrown into the water.
For a moment the princess hoped that the young man would come with
her to the sea-kingdom, but just in time she remembered that people die
if they have no air to breathe. Her grandmother had told her that.
Then the little princess saw the handsome young man swimming. Quickly
she swam towards him, and pulled him along with her, while she held his

head above water. When she was almost exhausted they reached the beach. Quickly she pulled the prince onto dry land. He was unconscious. The princess decided to have a little sleep, because she had to rest before she could swim back to the castle. She crawled towards the prince, and lay down beside him. She shut her eyes, and soon fell asleep.

The night passed, and morning dawned. The storm had passed, and the sea was as smooth as a mirror. For a moment the princess thought she had dreamed everything. But the prince lay next to her. His face looked very much like the face of the marble bust she had found, and which was now in her garden. The mermaid kissed the prince on his forehead. Still the young man did not stir. Surely he wasn't dead? The mermaid decided that she had to take him to his people, because she couldn't do anything for him here. Because she couldn't move across country with her fishtail, she pulled him back into the water, and took him to a bay not far away. There were people living there, who would surely find the prince. The mermaid put him down again on the beach, and hid behind a rock, so that she should not be seen.

Soon a young woman found the prince, and called for help. Quickly two men came running along, and pulled the young man upright, so that he began to recover. The first thing he saw was the face of the young woman who had found him on the beach.

The little mermaid, who had fallen in love with the young man, was pleased that she had been able to do something for him. She dived into the sea, and returned to her kingdom. At home she wouldn't say anything at all about her trip. The king, her grandmother, and her sisters thought that rather odd.

From now on the princess spent days on end in her little garden, in front of the bust of the prince.

Sometimes she went to the beach where she left him. She hoped she would find him there again, but that didn't happen.

Years went by. Every day the girl grew sadder. Her grandmother was sorry for her. She thought of something which might help her granddaughter. She called her, and asked: "Would you rather live on land instead of at the bottom of the sea?"

The girl would like that; then she could look for her prince. But why did her grandmother ask? Surely mermaids couldn't live on land?

"Far away there is a witch who lives at the bottom of the sea. She can give you legs, but..."
The girl did not stop to listen to what else her grandmother had to say about the witch, because she had swum away fast, she was so eager to become human and look for her prince.

What a long way it was to the witch's place. Sometimes she was so tired, she bumped into the hard coral, and made her tail bleed, but that did not worry the princess. She so much wanted to see the prince of her dreams again.
"Ha, there you are," cackled the witch, who was as ugly as sin. "I was expecting you." There was a horrible stench from the kettle beside her.
"I know what you want," said the ugly creature. "I must say you have a nerve! I will grant you your wish, but the price will be high! You will get a pair of legs in exchange for your voice, so you will never be able to say another word... You will never be a mermaid again. And if you can't conquer the heart of the man you love, you will die...
Apart from that," she added maliciously, "each step you take will hurt you. Your feet will bleed, but you will have to go on smiling, and no one must see that it hurts. Do you still want legs?"
"I am quite determined," said the brave little mermaid. "I want to become human, whatever price I have to pay."
Bravely she drank from the smelly potion the witch had prepared. For a moment she couldn't see anything, but suddenly she found herself back

on the beach. How it hurt! Her fishtail had disappeared, and instead she had two lovely legs. The princess cried, because they hurt her so much. She tried to walk, but her new legs were rather awkward. She fainted.

When she opened her eyes again, she saw someone standing in front of her. It was the prince! The prince, too, had gone to the beach. He kept going back there hoping to meet the young woman who had saved his life.

The prince took the girl with him. But he did not know that she was the one who had saved his life. He still thought that he had been rescued by the girl he'd first seen when he woke up. And the girl who had been a mermaid couldn't tell him anything; she had exchanged her voice for a pair of legs.

The prince introduced her to his parents. Everyone liked the girl, and at parties she danced the night through. Her feet hurt her terribly, just as the old witch had told her, but she went on smiling brilliantly. As soon as she was alone, she would go to the beach and bathe her feet in the sea.

How unhappy she was! The prince liked her very much, but not in the way she wanted. He loved her like a sister, or a good friend...

Sometimes he told her what was bothering him. He told the little mermaid that he had seen such a lovely girl, who had saved him. And now that girl had gone, and he didn't know where she lived. And she was the girl he would like to marry. But how could he find her?

The prince didn't mind telling the little mermaid his story, because he knew she would keep his secret. After all, she couldn't talk! If only he'd known what she was thinking!

The prince no longer dared hope that he would ever meet the girl on the beach again. But one day he was invited to visit a neighbouring king. And who turned out to be the king's daughter? He recognized her at once: the girl who had saved him!

The young princess had also fallen in love with the unknown young man on the beach, that same night. She was overjoyed when they met again. They decided to get married at once, and a few days later that is what happened.

The wedding was celebrated on a brilliantly decorated and lighted ship. The little mermaid kept on smiling. That was very difficult, because she was very unhappy. Her legs would hardly carry her, but she danced all night.

She knew that this would be her last night. The prince had married another girl, and the mermaid had to return to the sea. She would drown, because she had become a human girl. But she didn't care. She couldn't live without her prince! Sadly she stood by the rails and looked at the sea. It wouldn't be long before the sun would rise.

When she was ready to throw herself into the waves, she suddenly saw her sisters. But what was that? They were completely bald!

"Come," they shouted to her, "we've sold our hair to the witch in exchange for your life. But there was one condition: before the sun rises the prince's blood must flow onto your legs. Then you will get your fishtail back again. Please, take this knife and kill the prince. Do it quickly, otherwise you'll die..."

The little mermaid started to cry. She didn't want to kill the prince at all. She loved him so much! She threw the knife into the sea.

The first rays of sunshine could be seen. The princess jumped into the sea, because now she had to die. And that is what happened, because now that she was human, she could not do without air. No longer could she live like her sisters and the fishes.

She went to the land of the spirits, where she would be for many years to come. From on high she looked out on the world, and saw the prince and his wife, who were happy together. She cried softly, but she was still

pleased that the prince was happy with his princess. And even if she was sad herself, she wished the prince and his princess every happiness, for as long as they lived.

The drummer's son

On a Sunday morning, long ago, a woman walked into the village church. She saw at once the angels carved out of wood. They were hung on the walls and were magnificently decorated. They were painted with gold and their hair was made from golden thread. How beautiful they were.

The woman, who was expecting a baby, thought to herself: I do so hope that my little one will have golden hair too. Then it will look just like the sun when it rises: when golden rays of sunlight shine over the earth so that the day can begin again. The idea of a son with golden hair made her break into a smile, and at that moment, she knew that she would have such a son.

After a while she bore a child. "He has truly golden hair", she cried out, when she first held her child in her arms. How happy she was! She had a son with golden locks, more beautiful than anyone's she had ever seen.

Her husband, the father of the boy with the golden hair, was a drummer. When a fire broke out in the village, he had to keep on drumming until all the fire fighters had heard him. They would then quickly get buckets of water and start to put out the fire. In those days there were still no fire engines nor yet any fire sirens.

The drummer took a good look at his son and said: "I'm terribly sorry, but our son doesn't have golden hair at all. It's as red as the setting sun."

"That isn't true", said his wife. "His hair is golden." And that is what she stuck to. The village folk agreed with the father. The little boy's hair was indeed red.

The father and mother named their son Peter. Everyone in the village knew who 'Peter with the red hair' was. But his mother persisted in her belief that his hair's colour was gold. She always said to him "My golden darling" which made it seem as if it were his real name.

The drummer's son had a beautiful singing voice. He knew many songs by heart and he made up lovely tunes. Since the birds could sing so sweetly, he decided that he wanted to sing just as well, which he did his very best to do.

"I hope that he'll get into the church choir", said his mother. "Then he'll be singing below the golden angels." She saw the whole scene in her mind's eye, her golden darling underneath the golden angels.

"Fire-head!" is what the village children called him. "Don't go sleeping in the attic or else the thatched roof will catch alight!" they said to Peter. Peter did not mind all that much. He had red hair and nobody else that he knew had that. He was proud of it.

Peter was very musical. The town musician came by one day and when he heard how beautifully Peter could sing, he said to him: "What a lovely melody! Did you make it up all by yourself? In that case you are sure to be able to play the violin splendidly too." His parents bought Peter a violin from their savings and every week he was given a lesson from the town musician.

Peter was very pleased that he could play so beautifully but nonetheless it still bothered him a little, since if things continued in this fashion he would become the town musician and that was not what he wanted.

"I want to be a soldier", he told his parents. The idea of marching with a sabre in his hand to the beat of a drum seemed wonderful.

His father said: "I wouldn't think it so bad if you were to become a soldier.

But in that case you would have to rise to the rank of general, since generals are the only really important soldiers. But you can only become a general if a war breaks out."

Peter's mother turned pale when she heard what her husband had to say. "I don't want anything to happen to my golden darling", she said. "He'll only come back without an arm and then he won't be able to play the violin anymore."

War did break out one day because the king of Peter's country had got into an argument with another king. All the young men from the village, including Peter, the drummer's son, had to go and fight the enemy.

His father hoped that he would return with a big medal for bravery pinned to his chest. His mother feared that he would be wounded almost at once.

She was deeply sad when it was time for him to go. "Will you be careful?" said his mother to him one more time.

Peter was a good soldier. He was the drummer boy who had to beat the

drum. He was always cheerful even when he was given the hardest chores to do. Above all, he was healthy and strong.

Peter did not have to fight at first, but the day came when the enemy was within sight. The drum rolls could now be heard in the distance. They were given the order to advance. The enemy, too, came ever closer until the fighting began. Because the battle was so intense and it all happened so quickly one could no longer see anything through the gunpowder smoke. How hard the soldiers fought! Bullets flew in all directions and the sabres glittered in the sun.

Peter kept on beating his drum. He continued giving the signal to go forward. "Onwards, onwards!" he shouted as he made the loudest drum roll that he could.

Naturally, things can also go too far and this is what now began to happen somewhat. They were losing more and more men, so it did not take long before someone gave the order to cease fighting. Peter did not want to listen and kept his drum roll going. "Onwards! Onwards!"

Peter was not wounded. Neither did anything happen to the soldiers' dog which always followed on behind him. Together they walked on still further. Peter kept beating his drum until he could go on no more.

The battle had cost the lives of a great many soldiers. Even so, the enemy was defeated. Peter was very proud, since if he had let the soldiers stop

fighting, as he should have done in fact, they would have then given up and his army would have certainly lost. He might even have been taken prisoner.

The drummer and his wife sat at the kitchen table. It was the middle of the night and neither of them could sleep.

"I so much want Peter to come home", said his mother.

"So do I, so do I", said her husband. They had talked the whole evening and night about their son who was fighting the enemy.

"Perhaps he will come back without any arms or legs", said his mother.

"I reckon that his jacket coat will be studded with medals", said the drummer. He was going to be so proud when that happened.

The drummer and his wife went on talking for a while until they became so tired that their eyes closed by themselves. "I feel so exhausted", said the mother. "But I still don't know whether or not I'll be able to sleep. I keep on thinking about Peter."

It took a time, but after a while Peter's mother fell asleep. She dreamed that she entered the church and there stood the wooden angels. One of them began to move. It was Peter.

Peter's father dreamed as well. He dreamed how his son returned with his chest covered in ribbons and gold and silver medals.

Peter awoke and looked about him. What he saw was horrible. The soldiers had fallen asleep soon after the battle had ended. Now he could see just how terrible it had been. Many soldiers had died. Peter beat on his drum. "Get up, everyone get up!" The other soldiers woke up. They were pleased that they had won but now they wanted to return home quickly, and Peter more than any of them because he wanted to see his father, the drummer, and his mother.

They started the return journey, which would take seven weeks, for that is how far they were from home. Peter beat on his drum to let everyone know that they were leaving. "Onwards, back home!"

After a very long journey Peter arrived home. He looked hale and hearty and was brown from the sun. His eyes shone on entering his parents' cottage.

"Peter!" cried his mother in surprise, running towards him. "You're back, you're back!" she wept. Her tears were not ones of sorrow, but of happiness that her son still had all his arms and legs.

"Hmmm", said his father, "you don't have any medals."

Yet he was so happy to see his son again, even so, that he beat out the loudest drum roll on his drum that he possibly could.

"My golden darling", said his mother. She was overjoyed.

Everyone was talking about Peter in the village. His eyes were shining still and it seemed as if his hair shone too. In any case, that is what his mother kept on saying and she still kept calling her son 'golden darling'.

"Peter should dye his hair", said the woman next door when visiting the drummer's wife. "That's what the baker's daughter did and within three weeks she had a fiancé."

"Yes", said the drummer's wife, "but the only thing is that she has to keep dyeing it every week. If she forgets one week it turns green."

She gave her neighbour a very angry look and meant it too. She was extremely proud of her son with his beautiful hair.

The next day the mayor's wife came to visit with her daughter Lotte.

"Play us something on your violin", said Peter's mother to her son. Peter did not need to be asked twice. He took his violin from its case, placed it against his chin and began to play. He did not play a tune which everyone would already know. No, he played a tune which he had made up himself. It sounded exquisite. Peter was truly very talented.

Tears sprang up in the eyes of the mayor's wife when she heard Peter playing.

"How beautiful", she stammered. Her daughter thought it charming too.

"Mother, may I have a violin as well?" she asked. Naturally, the mayor's wife could not very well say no with the drummer's wife sitting next to her. It would look like the drummer did have money enough for a violin while she, the mayor's wife, did not. That was unimaginable, of course.

"You may", she replied at length, "but in that case you will have to take lessons from Peter." Everyone agreed on that point and they arranged that Lotte would come for her first lesson the next day.

Lotte rapidly learned to play the violin. She did not have nearly as much talent as Peter but she came a long way. She soon learned a few tunes by heart.

Peter loved teaching Lotte to play the violin. She was kind and friendly. Furthermore, she was always jolly. And she was so pretty ... When Lotte was playing, Peter found himself looking more and more often at her face. He completely forgot to make sure that she was playing the violin well.

One day, something unexpected happened. Peter suddenly gave Lotte a kiss on the cheek. Lotte blushed all over. "Lotte ...", Peter began to say, but he was unable to finish his sentence. At that moment the mayor entered in order to introduce the town clerk's son to his daughter. He was

called Gerard and had an ugly face. His nose was crooked which made him look as if he were always cross. Perhaps he was too.

In the lessons Peter gave to Lotte that followed, he stayed ever longer. Lotte behaved very pleasantly to him. Peter fell ever more in love with Lotte. He lay awake for nights thinking about her.

One morning, the drummer's wife came home from shopping, set her bag down, and said to Peter: "I have some news. I just cannot keep it to myself." And she related what she had heard from the mayor's wife.

"Lotte is engaged to Gerard, the town clerk's son. They will be married in only a few weeks time!"

"No!" cried Peter. He sprang out of his chair. "Is this really true, mother? Tell me that it's just a joke."

His mother laughed. "No, not at all. The mayor's wife told me herself. Isn't that nice?"

"Of course", said Peter, but he did not mean it one bit.

In the weeks that followed, Peter was very sad. He could not get Lotte out of his thoughts. He kept thinking time and again about how awful he felt that she should be married to that ugly Gerard. Then he would cry quietly to himself in his little room and play the tune which he had written especially for Lotte.

After a few months, Peter became less miserable. This was mostly because of the letter which he had received. Not just any letter, no, but a letter from the king who asked whether Peter would like to come to play at the palace. Only the once. The king thought that that would be fun. He had heard people tell of Peter and now he wanted to hear for himself just how beautifully Peter could play the violin. Peter was so proud that he packed his bags at once to go to the capital where the king's palace stood. Peter left for the palace early the following morning. The very next day he played in front of the king. How he played his very best! He had never played as well as he did then for the king. The king was so impressed that he wanted to hear him play every day.

Peter became very famous. In the afternoons he had to play at the king's palace. In the evenings he played in the concert hall. He played so finely and so clearly that soon everyone in the whole country knew who Peter was. Whosoever went to the capital to hear Peter's playing for themselves always found themselves repeating to everyone just how splendid it had been. Peter enjoyed it all himself. He found playing the violin more and more fun. He now had enough money and lived in a nice house, close to the king's palace.

His mother, the drummer's wife, enjoyed it more than anyone. She was terribly proud of her son. She went to the capital as often as she could to listen to Peter, and when she was not in the capital, she would visit everyone never ceasing to tell of her son's latest successes.

The day came when her husband, the drummer, died. His wife was very sad. Fortunately, she still had her son who sent her money every month and so she was able to go on living in her own house. Moreover, Peter wrote her letters almost every day so that she would feel less lonely. When she read Peter's letters she felt it was just as if he were there in the room with her.

The mayor's wife said: "What a lot of nonsense. Everyone has to read her son's letters. Everyone has to know what the latest pieces are that that fire-head has been fiddling away at. Humbug!" That she was jealous is for sure. The girls in the village felt differently, thinking Peter quite wonderful, and not only the village girls, but also the town girls – in fact all the girls in the country thought that Peter was marvellous. They went to the capital to ask for a lock of his hair. It was so beautiful that they felt it did look just

like gold. This was something on which the drummer's widow could agree. She still spoke of 'my golden darling' when she meant her son.

It was a lovely summer's day when Peter came home. He looked handsome. His hair and eyes shone. He looked like a hero. And so he was. His mother threw her arms about his shoulders. "My golden darling, my golden darling!" she kept on repeating.

The widow and her son talked for a long time about the past and the war, but especially about Peter's success.

"I'm so proud of you", said the drummer's widow, and so she was.

Peter had never been given a medal for being such a good soldier, but now that he was such a good violinist and so famous he had earned a good ten thousand-worth of them.

At that moment the drummer's drum let out a drum roll, without anyone having touched it. So it was that, although he had died, even the drummer was able to let everyone hear how proud he was of his son.

It might be that Peter and his mother imagined it all, then again maybe not, but that his father was also proud of him is absolutely for certain.

The princess and the swineherd

any, many years ago, in a small country, there lived a young and handsome prince, who wanted to get married.

There were plenty of nice girls in the kingdom, all of whom would gladly have become his wife. The prince thought them very nice, but he didn't want to marry any of them. He was secretly in love with the daughter of the emperor of a country not far from his kingdom. He was so much in love that he lay tossing and turning in bed all night, and could not sleep. He thought the emperor's daughter was the most beautiful and most lovely princess he had ever met, and thought it a pity that he had only seen her once.

Alas, the prince was very poor. His father had lived expensively all his life. He had a fine castle, surrounded by a large garden; he went abroad every year, and wore the grandest clothes. Besides, every week he gave a party, and he drank out of golden goblets. Now he was dead, there was not a penny left for the young prince. So he couldn't send any costly presents to the princess he loved so much.

One day he decided to send her the most precious things he possessed. They were the only two things of any value. The first was a red rosebush, which bore a single rose once every five years. That is very little, just one rose for a whole bush. But the rose smelt so sweet, that you forgot all your cares if you held it to your nose.

The second was a nightingale who could sing beautifully.

The prince put his two treasures in boxes, one for each present. He stuck silver paper on the sides of the boxes, so that it looked as if the boxes were made of silver. Finally he tied a lovely red ribbon round them. The princess will like that, he thought.

The prince sent the boxes to the princess. He hoped that the princess would now fall in love with him.

The emperor received the prince's envoy with the silver boxes, and took him to his daughter. She was chatting with her ladies-in-waiting.

"Look at that! Presents!" cried the girl. "Let me guess... I think there must be a white kitten in that box. And in that one a puppy with curly hair!"

She didn't wait any longer, but opened the first box. She saw the rosebush. It bore only one rose.

"Bah!" she cried, "I don't like real flowers at all. I only like silk flowers; they always stay fresh, and never wilt. Real flowers are too much trouble, you have to keep watering them. What a boring present. Throw that bush away at once!"

"Don't be cross, my child, just open the other box," said her father.

As soon as the box was opened, the nightingale began to sing. It was so beautiful, it brought tears to the eyes of the ladies-in-waiting.

"Horrible! I only like toy birds. I only want birds with a key in their back. At least they only start singing when I want them to," said the princess angrily. She threw the bird out of the open window.

"Tell your prince that I never want to see him," she screamed at the prince's envoy.

"The princess won't receive you," the envoy told the prince, when he got back and explained the princess's spoiled behaviour.
"Then I'll go to the princess's palace myself," said his master, "but I'll not go as a prince, I will disguise myself."
The envoy couldn't understand it at all.
The prince made his face dirty, and put on old clothes. He put on a tattered old hat, and carried a stick. He looked just like a swineherd. And that was exactly the idea.
The prince said goodbye, and set off for the princess's kingdom. He arrived a few days later.
In the castle everyone thought that he was the emperor's new swineherd. He was given a tiny room next to the pigsty, and had hundreds of pigs to look after.
The prince did his best. That was very difficult, for the work was heavy and dirty. He worked from early in the morning till late at night, but he still had some time left over.
In his free time he made himself a little pan, with bells on it. When it was put on the fire it played a little jingle.

One day the princess and her ladies-in-waiting were walking past the pigsty. They heard the tune, because the prince had just put the pan on the fire to see if it could make some pleasant music.

"The new swineherd has an extraordinary musical instrument," said one of the ladies. "He made it himself. Isn't he clever?" and all the ladies-in-waiting giggled.

"Ask him if he will sell it," ordered the princess.

The lady-in-waiting put on some clogs and went to the young man. She soon came back, and said: "He doesn't want any money for it, but he would like ten kisses from the princess." She had to laugh a little. Who on earth would sell something for ten kisses from a princess?

"What a rude young man. As far as I'm concerned he can get lost!"

Just at that moment they heard the merry bells of the prince's pan again. "You know what?" said the princess. "Offer him ten kisses from ladies-in-waiting, that should do." The ladies-in-waiting looked a bit put out, because that wasn't at all the thing. That's not what they were ladies-in-waiting for. But of course, if the princess gave a royal command, they had to obey it, so one of them went in and told the swineherd what the princess had told her to say.

"No," said the prince decisively. "I want ten kisses from the princess, and not from a lady-in-waiting. And if I don't get my kisses, the princess doesn't get her little pan. Certainly not, not even for a hundred kisses from ladies-in-waiting. Royal kisses I want, and nothing else."

The princess had to think that over, after the lady-in-waiting had told her the prince's decision, but then she said: "All right, he can have them."

The princess and her ladies waited till the prince came out. The ladies-in-waiting stood in a ring round them both, and the kissing began. The ladies counted: one, two, three, four... They were big smacking kisses. Eight, nine, ten. The princess got her little pan and went back to the palace with her ladies.

The swineherd went on working hard. The pigs had to be cleaned out every day, and his other duties filled the rest of his day. But he still had a little time left. In that time he made a rattle on which you could play the finest tunes. And they were all tunes that made you want to dance.

A week after the ten kisses the rattle was ready. All the ladies who came past the sty began to dance as they heard the swineherd's new musical instrument.

"I must have that instrument immediately," said the princess. A lady-in-waiting had told her what a wonderful sound it made. "But," said the princess, "no more kisses!"

"Oh dear," thought the lady-in-waiting, "now we have a problem." "He wants a hundred kisses from you," she said, "and if he doesn't get them, there will be no sale."

"That's unheard of, he's mad. What is he thinking of? I'll give him ten, and my ladies will give him the rest."

"He insists he wants a hundred kisses from the princess," said the lady-in-waiting.

"Oh well, what does it matter," thought the princess in the end. Actually, at the bottom of her heart she found the swineherd quite attractive.

"All right, then," she decided, "but you must help me a bit."

She called the other ladies, and the whole party went to the swineherd's hut. The princess said: "Screen me with your dresses, ladies, the emperor must not see us! Stand round us in a circle."

They did that, and the kissing began a second time. "One, two, three, four..." counted a lady-in-waiting. But a hundred is a lot of kisses, and gradually the ladies forgot that they were supposed to stand in a tight ring round the swineherd and the princess. They started to look at the pigs, moved a few steps back... one even picked a basketful of flowers. All that kissing was so boring. In the end there were only two ladies-in-waiting left counting the kisses: "sixteen, seventeen, eighteen..."

Meanwhile the emperor had come out on his balcony. What was that he could see in the distance? He pushed his glasses further onto his nose. He wondered what new game the princess was playing with her ladies. And wasn't that a young man among them? He couldn't see very well. "Twenty-four, twenty-five, twenty-six," he heard. He was curious. "I must have a closer look," he thought.

On tiptoe he walked towards the ladies. They didn't hear him coming, they were much too busy looking at the pigs, and picking flowers. Only one lady-in-waiting was still counting kisses. "Thirty-three, thirty-four, thirty-five," she counted cheerfully.

And then her father saw what the princess was doing! It was an awful shock! He went red in the face, and his glasses fell off his nose. "What's going on?" he shouted angrily. "Kissing, with a perfect stranger? With a swineherd? Leave my palace immediately! I never want to see you again!" he shouted to the princess. "And you, too, you filthy swineherd!" he went on. "You should be ashamed of yourself. Ugh, a swineherd who lets a princess kiss him! Away with you, both of you, get out of my garden!"

The prince washed his face. He put his grand velvet suit on again, and went to look for the princess. He found her under a tree, just outside the palace garden. She was crying.

When the prince stopped in front of her, she looked up. What a shock! Who was that? It looked like the swineherd, but now he was grandly dressed, like a real prince.

She immediately began to dry her tears, and smiled at the prince as sweetly as she could.

But the prince was not in love with her any more, however sweetly she smiled at him.

"You were not content with presents from someone who loved you," he told the princess. "You preferred a swineherd's toys. And you were prepared to do anything for a stupid pan and a silly rattle." And he ended by saying: "You are a spoiled little madam, and you are not worthy to be my wife!"

The prince left the princess alone under the tree, and went joyfully back to his own country. He was going to marry a very nice girl, and there were plenty of those in his own country.

And the spoiled little princess? She sat and cried for a while under the tree, till she realized that she had to do something, because even princesses can't spend their whole lives crying under a tree.

She looked for a job, because now she had to earn her own living. She became a lady-in-waiting to a princess in another country. And she spent her whole life being sorry she'd kissed the swineherd.

The ugly duckling

It was summer. The fields stood high with golden corn, the hay had just been mown, and everything smelt wonderful. Butterflies played round the flowers, and everywhere you could hear the buzzing of the bees.

Near a pond, in the shadow of some shrubs, a mother duck was sitting on her eggs.

She had been sitting there a long time, and she thought that her ducklings were taking an awfully long time to hatch. Sometimes she got really bored with all this brooding. Then she got up and looked to see if there was any movement yet. But no, the eggs still lay there motionless.

But at last it happened, and one by one the eggs hatched. And out came funny little ducklings, which looked round in amazement.

"Peep," cried the ducklings, and looked round wide-eyed. "Peep, how big everything is here in the outside world, and doesn't everything look wonderful."

"Just wait and see," said mother duck, "there is a lot more to see in the big world, a whole lot more than just this pond."

Mother duck fussed over her ducklings. She looked carefully to see if they were all there. But no, they weren't all there yet! One egg had still not hatched, and it was the biggest egg of all.

Mother duck sighed and went back to sit on the egg. She didn't really feel like it at all, she would much rather go swimming in the pond with all her ducklings.

"Hi, how's it going? Haven't you finished brooding yet?" asked an old duck, who always liked to know everything.

"This big egg just won't hatch. And I've been sitting on it so long! The other ducklings have all hatched. What do you think of them? Don't you think they are the most beautiful ducklings in the world?"

The old duck just chattered on, and didn't look once at the ducklings.

"What an odd egg that is, the one you're sitting on. Let me have a good look at it. It looks more like a turkey egg. That happened to me once. I

thought I had a duckling, but it was a turkey, and of course, it wouldn't go into the water. If I were you, I would leave that egg and have a nice swim with your other children."

But mother duck didn't want to do that, she wanted to hatch that egg out, too. The old duck thought it odd of the mother duck to go on sitting on the egg so long. She shook her head, shrugged her shoulders, and went away again.

At last the big egg hatched. A great big chick came out, all grey – and very ugly.

Mother duck was worried. "Could it be a turkey?" she muttered, and had another look at that odd big chick. The chick looked back and said: "Good morning, mother, where are all my little brothers and sisters? I'm glad to get out of that egg. It was getting far too hot inside there!"

The next day mother duck went swimming in a stream with all her ducklings. They all jumped into the water, the grey one too.

"Oh good," sighed mother duck, "you see, that's no turkey. He can swim, and in fact he can swim very well."

She took the little ducklings to join all the other ducklings on the pond. "Look at that," cried the other ducklings. "Lots of new ducks! What a lot, and there are already so many of us! But we don't like that grey duckling, we don't want to play with him." One fat duck even bit the grey duckling angrily in the neck.

Mother duck was very angry. "Just you leave him alone," she said. "And you mustn't tease him either, because he can swim very well."

"We think he's big and ugly, and we don't like him," said the fat duck nastily.

Another old duck came to have a look. "They're all darlings, it's a pity that one duckling looks so ugly," she said.

"He swims much better than his brothers and sisters," said mother duck. "And he may not be very pretty now, but that will come as he gets bigger." She caressed the duckling softly with her beak.

"You all go off and play in the water," she said to her children. The grey duckling was badly bullied. The chickens and ducks pushed him over, and the turkey chased after him, gobbling. It got worse and worse. Everyone bullied him, and his little brothers called him rude names.

The grey duckling was very unhappy. He ran away from all the other ducks.

"I'm so ugly that I make everybody cross, and frighten them," he sobbed. "I'll go away. I'll go and live somewhere else, somewhere where not everybody thinks me ugly."

And he did. He took a last look at his mother, with tears in his eyes. His mother had never been nasty to him, but all the other birds were. He was going! He walked a long way and in the end came to a big swamp. Wild ducks lived there. He found a place in the reeds, where he could sleep comfortably.

But he couldn't sleep for long, because two drakes began to bully him. The grey duckling grew frightened again, but before the drakes could really hurt him shots rang out, and both of them fell dead in the water.

There were hunters by the swamp. They stayed around shooting duck for a long time, and their dogs went everywhere looking for them. The duckling was very frightened, and hid as well as he could.

In the evening it grew quiet at last. The hunters went away and the duckling dared to come out in the open again.

He ran as fast as he could. He had to get away from that dangerous swamp. He ran through fields and meadows, but he had no idea where he should go.

After hours had passed and he was getting very tired, he came to a tumbledown cottage. The door was ajar, and the duckling crept cautiously in.

An old lady lived in the cottage with her cat and one hen. When the cat saw the duckling he began to spit noisily, and the hen began to cackle loudly. The old lady couldn't see very well any more, and thought that a beautiful duck had just walked in.

"Oh, what a lovely duck," she said. "Now at last I'll be able to have duck's eggs."

The duckling was allowed to stay. It suited him very well, because the cat and the hen didn't tease him very much. But after a few weeks the old lady kept looking to see if he had laid any eggs, but of course, there never were any. She began to wonder if her duck was really a proper duck. The hen and the cat grew curious, too. Why wouldn't this duck lay eggs?

"Can you lay eggs?" the hen asked the duckling.

"No," said the duckling, surprised.

"Can you arch your back?" asked the cat.

"No, I've never learnt to do that," said the duckling, even more surprised.

"Well, in that case you're not really a proper duck," said the hen and the cat.

The duckling went to sit sadly in the corner and cried. He was so comfortable there, and now it had all gone wrong again.

That afternoon the sun shone, and a cool breeze wafted through the house. Suddenly the duckling didn't want to live in a cottage any more. He would much rather swim.

He stretched his wings, and look, he could fly! In the few weeks he had spent with the old lady he had grown bigger and stronger, and now his wings could carry his weight.

He flew far away, and finally came to a lovely big pond.

Meanwhile the summer had come to an end. The leaves on the trees had turned a lovely red colour, and later fell to the ground. The duckling loved living by the pond.

In the evening he often saw magnificent white birds with beautiful long necks flying overhead. These birds were flying to warmer countries. He watched them till they were out of sight. They were swans! He sometimes got tears in his eyes as he watched; he thought they were so beautiful.

Winter came, and it was bitter cold. The duckling had to keep moving to keep warm. The surface of the pond slowly froze over. When he wanted to swim, he had to stamp hard with his feet, otherwise the water froze round them. But the water kept freezing more and more, and finally the pond

froze solid. The duckling was quite exhausted, and very cold. He couldn't even move, he was so cold.

He crept up onto the bank of the pond. Just in time, because there was already a thin skin of ice over the place where he had been swimming. He lay very still. He was so cold and tired, he couldn't move any more.

Luckily a farmer found him the next morning. The duckling had nearly died. The farmer took him home and showed him to his children. The children would have liked to play with him, but the poor ugly duckling was still very frightened.

He fled away from the children, as fast as his feet could carry him. Of course, he couldn't fly in the farmer's house. He tried to, but that was a big mistake.

By accident he landed in a pail of milk, and then in the flour barrel. Then he ran quickly outside and flew away.

The farmer's wife and the children tried to catch him again, but the duckling had already disappeared.

Again he flew a long way. He hid himself somewhere in the snow, and stayed there a long time. Luckily he occasionally found a few leaves to eat, but he was still hungry all day.

That winter lasted for ages. The duckling felt very lonely and unhappy. There was no one to play with and it was so cold all the time.

But one day the sun began to shine brightly again, and all the birds began to sing. The ground got warmer, and the duckling at once felt far more cheerful. Spring had begun.

The duckling was very happy. He felt good. During the winter he had grown bigger, and he had become much stronger, too. He could beat very hard with his wings. And he could fly much farther than he could before. And that's what he liked doing best – flying!

The duckling flew up in the air and flew on until he saw a park below him with a big lake. There was a lovely tree with large branches on the edge of the lake. Three magnificent swans floated near the tree. The duckling swam cautiously towards them. He was very afraid that they would chase him away again, because he was so ugly. But they didn't.

The swans were very nice to him, and let him swim with them. The duckling was amazed. How was it possible, when everyone teased him because he was so ugly? And these swans, the most beautiful birds in the whole world, were so nice to him!

The duckling climbed out of the water, and stood on the side. He looked down, and saw himself in the water. What a shock! He had changed completely during the winter. He was no longer the ugly grey young duckling... He had become a beautiful swan himself! He could hardly believe it. He kept looking at himself in the water again, because he was afraid he might have only dreamed it.

But no, the three swans could see it, too. They swam up to him and caressed him with their beaks.

And that wasn't all. People scattered bread into the water for him, and the children who stood on the edge of the lake, watching the swans, thought he was the most beautiful of all!

It made the little swan quite shy. He quickly hid his head under his wing, and then secretly peeped at them from underneath it. Again he looked at himself in the water. Was he really as beautiful as the children said?

He was very happy, everybody loved him, nobody bullied him any more, and he could live for ever after with the other swans. All that, when he had always been such an ugly duckling before.

Everything in its place

nce upon a time, a very long time ago, there was a great castle behind a forest. It was a beautiful castle with two towers and a high gate. Surrounding the castle was a deep moat. Reeds and water-lilies grew along the waterside.

Close to the castle gate stood an old, stately willow tree. Its branches hung over the water of the moat. The tree had stood there for years. No-one knew for exactly how long.

One day, a girl walked by the willow on the way to the castle. She was the goose-girl and she was just about to bring her geese back to their pen. She stopped for a moment to look at the tree.

"What a beautiful old willow", she said to herself.

Suddenly, she heard the sound of horses' hooves. The baron, who lived in

the castle, was just that moment returning from the hunt. He had a large number of friends along with him.

As he rode towards the girl he shouted loudly: "What are you doing there, you stupid child, just standing and staring? I'm going to push you in the mud. That's where you belong. Everything in its place!" He gave the girl a sharp kick with his boot.

The girl tumbled over and nearly fell into the water. She was only just able to grab hold of one of the willow branches. But then it broke off in her hand! She would surely have fallen into the mud were it not for being held back by a strong arm. It was the arm of the market trader. He had been on his way to the castle as well and was only just able to prevent the girl from falling into the moat.

The market trader stuck the broken willow branch into the ground. He said to the branch: "Grow quickly now. I hope that some day your branches will give that nasty baron a good beating."

The market trader then went off to the far side of the castle where the servants' quarters were to be found. He went inside and sold some of his wares. He heard a tremendous commotion coming from above. A party

was in progress. The baron was drinking a great deal together with his friends. There was wine and beer and everyone was drinking as much as he could. The market trader was called upstairs.

"Hey, trader, come and have a little drink with us for a moment", said the baron. He held an old sock in front of the trader's nose and filled it to the brim with wine. "But you'll have to drink up quickly otherwise your glass will leak it all out!" he shouted. Everyone laughed, excepting the trader, and the baron laughed loudest of them all.

In the end, the trader was allowed to return below. Up there is not where I belong, he thought. What a horrid baron and what horrible friends!
He quickly walked outside. He greeted the goose-girl and set off for the next castle. He was glad that he could once again be on his way. He had really taken a dislike to the nasty baron.
The unfriendly baron at the castle often held parties where there was a lot of drinking and gambling. Sometimes the baron and his friends would gamble whole farms! Naturally enough, this could not go on for much longer. And neither did it. After five years the baron had to leave the castle since he could no longer afford to pay his servants. Neither did he have money with which to buy food. He had gambled away all his money.

A very wealthy trader bought the baron's castle. He went to live in it very quickly. The trader was incredibly rich, so rich that he himself had no idea how much money he had. It was too much to count.
In the past he had been a market trader, but through hard work he had earned a very large amount of money, and he was not just any trader

94

either. No, he was the trader who had helped the goose-girl.

From the moment that he became owner of the castle, beer was never again drunk there and there was never again any gambling. The trader had seen for himself in the past how the old, unpleasant baron had gambled and drunk away all his money. He did not want to be so foolish himself.

The new lord of the castle very much wanted a nice girl to marry. Who could be a better choice than the goose-girl? In the meantime she had grown up. She was kindly and clever and very pretty. He asked her at once if she would marry him. The girl did not hesitate, for she found the trader very kind. They married one month later. It was a magnificent occasion and all the people from all around were invited.

The trader and the goose-girl had a wonderful life in the old castle. To begin with, they had to have the whole castle painted from top to bottom since the baron had not taken good care of it. Furthermore, it had to be well cleaned.

However, once that had been done, it was very jolly. The trader and his wife soon had children. That made it even jollier. There was always a game being played and laughter to be heard somewhere. The children ran about the whole castle where they played hide and seek which all went very well as there were everywhere lots of splendid hiding places.

The trader, the goose-girl, and their children were all very happy. Friends often came to visit them. Not that they then drank a great deal – the trader did not approve of such excesses. He felt that the baron had already done quite enough of that sort of thing.

Meanwhile, the willow branch next to the castle gate had grown into a large willow tree. "That is our family tree", said the trader. "I planted it myself and we shall take good care of it. Not a branch will ever be cut from it." And it never was either.

One hundred years later, there was not much left of the castle. The old trader and his wife had died. Neither were their children alive any longer. All that could now be seen were some of the castle walls. One of the towers remained, leaning at a strange angle.

Only the old willow, which the trader had planted, was still standing. Its trunk was very broad and its branches almost touched the clouds.

A grandson of the trader had had another castle built for himself. It stood not far away on the other side of the forest. This is where he lived with his wife and two children. He did not like the idea that his grandfather had been a market trader. He was rather ashamed of it in fact.

"That's not appropriate for a gentleman of my position!" he always said. He had become a baron. In the past, it was possible to become a baron if

you paid enough money for the title, and this is what the grandson had done. His grandfather, the market trader, had never wanted to do that. He did not think that it mattered whether you were a baron or a market trader, so long as you were honest and did your best.

"Everything in its place", the baron, his grandson, always said. He had decorated his castle very nicely and it had cost a lot of money. Everywhere there hung the most expensive paintings. He had old Chinese vases, as well, which stood on top of every dresser and every table.

Two paintings were hung in the servants' room. These were the portraits of the market trader and the goose-girl. It did not matter to the baron that they were his own grandparents. "Everything in its place", he said. For that reason the paintings belonged amongst the servants and not in a good position in the great hall. The baron only very rarely went to look at them.

One sunny morning, the castle warden and his pupils were walking by the old castle. His pupils were the baron's children. The baron was so rich that he could easily afford to have such a warden live in his castle and teach his children everything.

They walked past the old willow.

"That is our family's family tree", said the baron's daughter. She told the whole story which she had heard about her great-grandparents. "A rich market trader who married an ordinary goose-girl, isn't that lovely?" she said.

Her brother did not agree with her. "What a lot of nonsense. It should have been a nobleman's daughter." He was embarrassed that his great-grandparents had not been barons. "Fortunately, our father became a baron", he said. He walked to the old willow tree and broke off a branch.

"What are you doing?" cried his sister. "That is our old willow!"

"What does that matter?" said her brother. "So, you believe in all the old stories then, do you? Why, it's no more than just a very common old willow tree."

"That's not true. It's our family tree, and we have to look after it."

"Girls! ..." sighed the boy, and he asked his tutor: "Can you make a flute from this branch? You're so good at that."

"That will certainly be a very special flute", said the warden, "if it's made from a branch of your family tree!" He took his knife and began to carve into the wood.

The warden, the son, and the daughter walked on further and the warden told them about the plants and the trees of the forest. They returned at midday. The lesson was over.

The little flute, made from the willow branch, was now completely finished. "It's for you", said the warden and he gave the flute to the girl. "That tree is so important to you and, furthermore, you play much better than does your brother."

In the evening a great party was held in the castle. The baron, who enjoyed his wine, had had huge barrels brought.

"Welcome, welcome to my castle", he said to everyone at the door. Indeed, he needed to say this many times. Dozens, perhaps even hundreds, of barons, dukes, duchesses, and baronesses were invited. The castle was teeming with distinguished people. The castle warden was there too.

The party had been going for some time when, all at once, the warden called out: "Ladies and gentlemen, pray a moment's silence!", and he clapped his hands together.

It was a while before all was quiet.

"The baron's daughter would very much like to play a little something on her new flute! The flute is made from a willow branch. The same willow that her great-grandfather himself planted!"

The baron's daughter blushed scarlet. She had not wanted to play on her flute at all! But everyone looked so full of expectancy that she dared not

refuse. She went and stood in the middle of the room and began to play. It was then that something very strange happened. Outside, the wind began to blow very hard. It was almost as though the wind were saying something. Everyone understood what it was: "Everything in its place!" whistled the wind.

The baron's daughter kept on playing. She knew that it was no ordinary flute. The willow tree it had been made from was very special.

"Help!" cried out the baron. He suddenly flew across the room and out of the window into the chicken house. Everything in its place! He was not the only one. The mayor and his wife, who had also come, flew outside together. You could hear the splash as they landed in the moat. Everything in its place! And there went the banker. He floated over to the fireplace and landed with a crash in the ashes. Everything in its place!

The baron's daughter was suddenly seated at the head of the table and found herself wearing a gold necklace. She continued playing on and on as though her life depended on it.

The door of the bird-cage opened and the three parrots imprisoned there flew outside and were free. Once again, everything was in its place.

The girl stopped her playing and with that the spell was broken. The banker sat once more on his chair with a glass of wine in his hand. Even the baron was back in the room again, chatting with the mayor. The door to the bird-cage was shut with the parrots sitting inside. Furthermore, the girl's gold necklace had disappeared without a trace.

For a few moments everything in the castle had been in its place. That is how it should have stayed for ever, but that is not what happened.

No-one made the slightest mention of the girl's extraordinary flute. Neither was anything to be seen that was connected with the strange events in the baron's castle.

Was there truly no sign at all? Yes, there was after all something. Something had changed. The paintings of the goose-girl and the market trader no longer hung in the servants' quarters. After the party was over, they were suddenly found hanging in the great hall. It did indeed seem as if the trader and the goose-girl were secretly laughing a little bit in their portraits, as if they thought that what had happened was quite splendid. The baron tried to take the paintings back to the servants' room but, however he tried, he could not remove them from the wall. It would not surprise me if they hang there still.

The shepherdess and the chimney-sweep

Once upon a time there was a man who lived in a house on a hill. It was a fine white house with a big garden. Everyone in the village thought the house the grandest in the whole village.

Now this man was not only so rich that he could buy such a big house, but he was also very ugly. He was so ugly that not a single woman wanted to marry him. So he lived all alone in his big house. To keep him company he bought all kinds of vases, paintings, little figures, china plates, and all sorts of other things. His whole house was full of them.

On a chest in the sitting room was a porcelain shepherdess. She was perhaps the prettiest figure in the whole house. Her face was radiant, she was so pretty and friendly. She wore pink shoes and a lovely light blue dress. She had beautiful yellow curls, and great big blue eyes. And she had a little smile, as if to say: "Believe me, I'm even nicer than I look." You will understand then that all the other figures in the house were a bit in love with her.

One figure wasn't just a little bit in love with her, but a whole lot. It was a chimney-sweep, who stood on the same chest as the shepherdess. His face was all sooty, just like his clothes. He looked lovingly at the shepherdess, and she smiled lovingly back. The chimney-sweep was so much in love with the shepherdess that all he could do was think of her throughout the day.

Between them there was another figure. It was a Chinaman, sitting with his legs crossed. He looked a bit odd, because you don't often see the kind of clothes he wore here. People in China then wore quite different clothes from us. But that was not the only strange thing about the Chinaman. He kept nodding his head. Everyone was a little afraid of him,

so that when he nodded they trembled a little, every time.
And the Chinaman nodded a lot, even to the most horrid man in the whole house.

The most horrid man was not made of flesh and blood, but of wood. He was carved on an old-fashioned cabinet which stood quite close to the shepherdess's and chimney-sweep's chest. How ugly he was! He was an old devil with horns and a beard like a goat, and all round him, carved in the wood of the cabinet, were wild beasts. All day long he watched the shepherdess. He stared at her rudely, and grinned. He, too, was in love with the shepherdess and wanted to marry her, just like the chimney-sweep. He was in love with her pretty face and her yellow hair. Whenever she smiled, he grinned back at her. The little shepherdess was really very lovely in her pretty clothes and with her shy, sweet face.
"I want to marry you," said the old devil with the horns.
The Chinaman nodded, because he always nodded.
How worried the girl was! She didn't at all want to marry that scary man, she wanted to marry the chimney-sweep, who was big and strong, and far more handsome. He really was, even if his face was all covered in soot.

"But I want to marry her," said the chimney-sweep. "We are the same age, and we belong together."

The Chinaman and the little old devil didn't want any of that. For once the Chinaman didn't even nod. He almost looked as if he was shaking his head to say no.

"You shall marry," the Chinaman told the shepherdess, "but not a chimney-sweep." He nodded to the old devil on the wooden cabinet, and said: "We'll have the wedding tomorrow. I think you'll suit very well together."

"Why must I marry that horror?" cried the shepherdess, in tears.

"He's rich, his cabinet is full of valuable gold and silver plate. You will be very happy together with his other eleven wives. You won't be bored," answered the Chinaman.

"Eleven wives!" screamed the shepherdess, shocked. "He is even more horrid than I thought! I would rather die than marry him. I don't want him, definitely not. And besides, why should I? Aren't eleven wives enough for him? Why should he need a twelfth?"

But the Chinaman thought differently. "I am the oldest and also the wisest of all of us in this room, so you must just do what I say," he grumbled. "The wedding will be tomorrow, and that's that. And I don't want to hear another word about it."

He shut his eyes, nodded once, and went to sleep.

The old devil looked terribly mean. The grin on his face looked even more terrifying than usual. He said: "In a few hours you will be my wife, shepherdess." Having said that, he went to sleep, too. He started dreaming about his beautiful new wife.

Night had fallen. There wasn't much time left to do anything. The shepherdess and the chimney-sweep talked to each other quietly. There must be something they could do to stop the wedding next day.

"We must run away," whispered the chimney-sweep.

"But how?" asked the girl.

"Come with me, I know where we can go."

The shepherdess was just a little afraid. She had never been away from the chest. She didn't even know if she could really walk properly.

"Where are we going?" she asked, as the chimney-sweep drew her after him.

"We will escape up the chimney," she heard him say.

The chimney-sweep led the shepherdess to the corner of the chest. There was a ledge along which they could climb down.

"I daren't!" said the shepherdess, but her friend said: "It's not really dangerous, hold on to me tight." And they got down. At first slowly, but they jumped down the last bit.

"And now up the chimney," said the chimney-sweep.

He looked at the little shepherdess. "Are you sure?" he asked. "Are you sure you wouldn't rather stay here? You know just what it's like here, and you don't know where we are going to end up. Perhaps you won't like it outside this room."

"Yes," answered the little shepherdess. "I'm quite sure. I don't want to be the twelfth wife of any old horror. And besides, I want to marry you. And as long as I am with you I don't mind where I am."

"Then we'll do it," said the chimney-sweep, and held the door of the stove open for the girl.

They crept into the stove, and bravely began to climb. They climbed by putting their hands and feet in the cracks between the bricks. How slow it was! They kept going up, brick by brick, but there were an awful lot of bricks still left to climb.

"Are we nearly there?" asked the shepherdess.

Then in the distance they saw the opening at the top. It was a dark blue hole that got bigger, the higher they climbed.

"Nearly there," said the chimney-sweep.

At last they reached the roof. The chimney-sweep got up first, and pulled his little friend up the last bit. "We're there," he said.

It was nice and fresh outside. It needed to be, after that long climb up the chimney. They felt less tired already.

The shepherdess suddenly looked down, and saw how high up they were. That gave her a dreadful shock! She had always thought the chest she stood on was rather high. Now that was nothing compared with the roof! Everything looked so tiny down below!

"It looks quite different from what I expected," cried the little shepherdess.

"What you can see now is only a very small bit of the world," answered the chimney-sweep.

At first the shepherdess still thought it was all very beautiful. The brilliant crescent moon lit up the sky, so that you could see the trees in the distance. They could see other houses, with bright lights shining out of their windows. You could hear the sound of cheerful music coming from some of them, and here and there the shepherdess could see people moving about behind the windows. It all looked very pleasant! The

chimney-sweep and the shepherdess sat with their arms round each other's waists, looking out at the world.

But soon the shepherdess began to think that it wasn't all as nice as it had been at first. She grew a little afraid. It was very high up here, and the world was a lot larger than she had thought.

"I... I believe I'm a bit frightened! I would like to go back to the sitting room," she said.

The chimney-sweep thought it a pity, but he soon realized that this adventure was too dangerous for two porcelain figures.

"If we go back, we won't be able to get married," he said, "and then you will have to become that old devil's wife."

"But I wouldn't be happy here either," said the little shepherdess, "I'm too frightened. I think it's really much too dangerous here."

"Then we'll go back," said the chimney-sweep. He didn't really want to go back to his chest in the room, but his little friend was so unhappy, and wanted to go down again so much, that he had to agree.

The journey back down was even more tiring than the climb up. They scrambled and climbed down as fast as they could, because they wanted to get back to the chest again as soon as possible.

They jumped down the last bit, because they were so tired. Of course, they didn't make a lot of noise, but because it was the middle of the night, and everything in the house was quiet, all the figures heard them, the Chinaman and the old devil, too.

"They're running away," shouted the Chinaman, and nodded his head. He'd only just woken up.

"Follow them," screamed the old devil. "Grab them."

The Chinaman tried to stand up, but fell down flat on the floor. He broke into pieces, and lay shattered on the ground. His head rolled under the chest. Finally it stopped. It couldn't even nod any more.

The old devil was furious. His only friend had fallen on the floor. He thought the chimney-sweep and his little friend had done it. It was their fault! If they hadn't tried to escape, it would never have happened.

"Do you think I won't marry you now?" the little man cried. "Too bad for you, but the wedding will go right ahead."

The little shepherdess cried, but the vases and other figures in the room couldn't comfort her. Only the chimney-sweep stayed calm in the confusion. He knew that there must be a tube of glue in a drawer somewhere. He could mend the Chinaman with it.

To the shepherdess he said: "We will glue all the pieces back together and put him back on the chest. Don't be afraid, he will look just as good as he did before."

He picked up the pieces and began to put the Chinaman together again. When he got to the neck he did something a little bit different: he put a metal clamp in the Chinaman's neck.

There the Chinaman was again, as good as new. He could do anything he could do before, except... nod.

The chimney-sweep and the shepherdess put the Chinaman back on the chest and then went to stand very close to each other.

"That's not allowed, that's not allowed," shouted the old devil. "Get away from that chimney-sweep. You are going to marry me."

"I'm certainly not going to marry you, you mean old devil," answered the girl, and moved still closer to her friend. "I'm going to marry the chimney-sweep, and you have nothing to say about it."

"Oh no?" said the devil, and asked the Chinaman: "Do I marry the shepherdess?"

The Chinaman didn't nod. The devil asked him again, but again the figure didn't nod, because he couldn't nod any more. The metal clamp in his neck had seen to that. The old devil realized that now he wouldn't be able to marry the pretty shepherdess. His only friend, the Chinaman, didn't agree with him any more. Nobody liked him.

The chimney-sweep and the shepherdess stayed close to each other. They were both very happy together on the chest, because they had no more trouble from the old devil.

And so the two figures lived long and happily, till someone bumped into them and smashed both of them into smithereens. But they were really quite old by then.

The fir-tree

nce upon a time there was a little fir-tree growing among all the big trees in the forest. He was still quite small, and looked up at all the tall trees standing round him. How big they were! The little tree was rather jealous of them. He wanted to be as big as they were.

One day a farmer walked past. He saw the little tree, and said: "Oh, what a cute little tree!"

When the little fir heard that, he was very unhappy, and said: "Oh, if only

I was as big as the other trees. Then at least people wouldn't think me cute, and I could look out on the whole world from my top branches." He liked the idea of that. There must be so much more to see than just a lot of other trees with long branches. He was sure of that, but what was there really to see?

The little fir had never seen anything except the forest and the animals living in it. He didn't know what houses were, or cars, or factories, or toys, or chocolates.

The little fir went on dreaming.

"If I were very tall, the birds could build nests in my branches. And in those nests little birds would hatch out of their eggs," he said. Little birds coming out of eggs, that was good! It was a pity he was so small that in winter, when it snowed, he disappeared completely under the snow. Then the hare, who lived with his wife and children in his form not far from the tree, could easily jump right over him.

"See how well I can jump over you, little tree," said the hare. And you can be sure that a tree doesn't like it when a hare can jump over it! When the hare saw that the tree didn't like being teased, he teased him even more. He mocked the little fir-tree all through the year.

The tree became so unhappy that he couldn't hear the birds singing or see the flowers blooming, in fact he couldn't see anything pretty any more. He just kept on whining that he wanted to grow, that he wanted to be taller, as tall as the tree next to him. That one was so tall that sometimes you couldn't even see the top, it was lost in the clouds.

The little tree didn't seem to realize that he would grow all by himself. But he did. When he was three years old, he had grown so tall that the hare couldn't jump over him any more, but had to walk round him. How pleased that made the tree! At least those tiresome hares couldn't tease him now. No, now he teased the hare!

"What funny little creatures you are," he said, and boasted: "You will never be as big as me, and I am going to get even taller, just you wait."

After a few more years the tree had grown so tall that the hare had to put his head right back to be able to see the top. The fir-tree was not yet as tall as the trees next to him, but that didn't worry him. Now that he had grown this far, he was sure to go on growing.

Every year, once the summer was over, men with great big axes came to cut down the tallest trees. While the fir-tree was still quite small, he wasn't afraid at all; he was so little that they'd never cut him down. They only did that to the tallest trees. Why they did it, he had no idea.

Now that he had become a big tree, and was all of seven years old, he

started to get frightened. Perhaps they would think he was tall enough...
But luckily he wasn't cut down.

The branches of the trees that were cut down were all cut off. The shorn trunks were loaded onto carts drawn by horses. One by one they were taken away from the forest.

Where were they taking them? And what would happen to them there?

The fir-tree didn't understand it at all. Why should people want to cut down trees? Weren't trees much more beautiful when they were standing in the forest?

In the spring, when the swallows and storks came back from the hot countries where they had spent the winter, the fir-tree asked them: "Did you see any of the trees they took away from the forest?"

"Yes," answered an old stork. "I saw them on ships, on my way to Egypt. They had been turned into tall masts. They still smelt of fresh pine. Actually, one of those masts used to stand here just near you, and asked me to send you his best wishes," he said, and flew away.

The fir-tree didn't know what to think.

He was all right here in the forest, but one day they would come and cut him down, he'd already realized that. Would he then have to go on a ship as a mast?

At least that was doing something useful. All he did in the forest was just stand there. If he was on a ship he could make sure that the ship got somewhere. Because without a mast you couldn't have sails on a ship, and without sails to catch the wind for you, you wouldn't get anywhere.

The fir-tree thought about all these things, and decided that he had better

be cut down as soon as possible. Only then would he become a really important tree.

Christmas came. Again men came with their big axes and cut down the most beautiful trees they could find.

The fir-tree was not cut down. He was very disappointed. He had failed to be selected again. "Where are all those big trees going?" he asked the birds. He wanted to know if those trees were also going to be used for masts on ships.

"They are decorated with candles and silver balls, and then they stand in people's sitting rooms," answered the birds.

"Really and truly?" asked the fir-tree. He could hardly believe it. Decorated with lights? And silver balls? Surely nothing could be more magnificent than that?

"Quite true," answered the birds.

How jealous the fir-tree was. He, too, wanted to stand in people's sitting rooms with little lights on his branches.

After the winter came spring, and after spring, summer, and at the end of summer it started getting colder again, and winter returned. Again the men came with their axes to collect Christmas trees. A man came up with a big axe. He went to the fir-tree, and said: "You are rather a nice tree. I think you are nice enough to be in a sitting room. You are beautifully straight and you are big enough. I've no use for those little Christmas trees. I'll get a good price for you, I'm sure."

The little tree almost glowed with pride. He would go in someone's sitting room.

And yes, the man began to chop him down. That hurt a little, but the tree didn't find it too bad. He was going to be with people!

When the tree had been cut down, three strong men put it on a cart, together with a whole load of other trees, and later on they were taken to the market.

There the fir-tree stood, beside his friends, in the market-place. A fat man stood beside them, and called out to everyone who came past: "Beautiful Christmas trees for sale! Beautiful Christmas trees for sale! And not at all expensive," and every now and then somebody came to look at the trees.

A little boy came along. He came up to the tree, and said: "What a beautiful tree. I want that one!"

"I am indeed a beautiful tree," said the fir-tree happily, but the little boy didn't hear him.

Then the little boy's father came, too. "Do you think that's a nice tree?" his father asked the little boy.

"Yes!! Yes!!" shouted the little boy.

"Then we will buy it," said the man, giving some money to the fat stall holder.

The boy's father took the tree over his shoulder, and carried him to a big house not far from the market-place. The boy helped his father, but because he was still quite small, he couldn't carry much yet. So the fir-tree's branches scraped along the street. Ugh, they got all muddy and dusty.

When at last they reached the boy's house the tree was taken inside, and immediately two little girls came up, who cried: "What a lovely Christmas tree you've bought, father! We've never had such a fine big one before. May we decorate it now?"

They could. The girls carried in the box of silver balls and tinsel, and the tree was set up in the sitting room.

First came the candles, and then the girls hung up the tinsel and the balls. How lovely the tree looked. Last of all they put a star right at the top. The fir-tree thought it was wonderful. How proud he was. He could see himself in the mirror hanging on the wall. He had never in his whole life imagined that he could look so beautiful.

Suddenly the door opened, and at least ten children ran into the room. They ran up to the tree. "How lovely!" they all said.

He looked even more beautiful when father lit the candles. The fir-tree was so happy, happier than he'd ever been before. He was shining with light.

The children all went quiet. They thought the tree so lovely with its candles lit, with its balls and tinsel, and its lovely star on top.

Then suddenly a candle fell over and set light to a branch.

"Ouch!" shouted the fir-tree. "That hurts!" Luckily the children's mother was quick enough to put out the flames, but the fir-tree didn't think it nearly so nice now. He did his best to stand up straight, but he found it very difficult.

The children started dancing round the tree. The tree didn't like that at all, because there wasn't really room for it.

Whenever a boy or girl ran round the back of the tree, he shook from side to side.

"Careful, or I will drop the silver balls," said the tree, frightened, but no one heard him. The children just went on dancing and running around.

"Now you may take the parcels off the tree," said father.

The tree was terrified. The parcels were near the top, so that the children had to climb half-way up the tree to get them.

"Careful, careful!" he cried, but again no one heard him.

The tree felt very uncomfortable. People might think he was lovely, but he kept getting hurt, and the children kept running into him. Besides, one branch was already burnt, and the other candles could easily fall over, too.

He didn't like it any more at all.

Fortunately the children had to go to bed. "Get undressed and brush your teeth!" called mother. In a little while the room was quiet. Father blew out the candles, and read a book in a corner of the room.

The tree was very depressed. Was that all? Was it all over? Or would the party start again tomorrow?

The next morning father came back into the room. The tree thought that the candles were going to be lit again, but he was badly mistaken. Father

took all the candles, balls, and tinsel off the tree, and put them away in their box. He carried the tree itself up the stairs to the attic.

The fir-tree could have cried. He'd been in the sitting room for just one evening, and that hadn't been all that pleasant. And of course, it's not nice at all in a cold attic. There was no company. The fir-tree had no one to talk to.

The tree lay in the attic for several days. It was deadly quiet, and besides, it was bitter cold. The fir-tree began to think that he would never again hear another sound, when suddenly he heard a soft noise next to him.

"Psst!" he heard. "Where have you come from?"

It was a mouse. He had seen the tree lying in the attic, and wanted to have a chat.

"I came from the great forest," said the tree, "where the sun shines, the birds sing, and flowers bloom." How he'd like to go back. He didn't like it up in that attic.

The mouse had disappeared again, and the tree lay alone in the dark. He knew that he could never go back to the forest. After all, he couldn't walk. A few days later he suddenly heard someone coming up the stairs, and yes, there was father. He carried the tree outside.

There the tree saw that his needles had gone all yellow. And a lot of them had gone completely. They had dried up and fallen off while he was in the attic. He couldn't understand it. He'd never seen such a thin, bare, yellow tree as he was now.

"I'm going to chop you into logs, tree," said father, and began at once.

That hurt! It hurt much worse than when the man with the axe had cut him down.

But, well, he had known then that he was going to be in a sitting room, and now he knew that whatever was going to happen, he wasn't going to like it.

In the afternoon the children came home and everyone went to sit round the big stove.

"Can we have a fire?" they asked. It was very cold outside, so a nice warm fire sounded a good idea.

"Go and fetch some wood, it's in the garden," said their mother.

The children brought the wood from the garden. Everyone brought a big log. Father put all the logs in the stove.

The fir-tree was unhappy. Had he exchanged his happy life in the forest for this? Weren't the blue sky, flowers in full bloom, and birds singing, much nicer?

Father lit the wood, and it began to burn up quickly. Because it had been lying in the attic for some time, it had got very dry, and dry wood always burns well.

118

"Hey, that's nice!" said the children contentedly. "Now we are getting nice and warm. Isn't that good? First we had a lovely Christmas tree, and now its logs see to it that we aren't cold any more."

So ended the life of the fir-tree. Luckily the children were pleased with the warmth he provided for them, but the tree would rather have enjoyed the sun for a few more years, among the birds and the hares in the great forest.

Simple Johnny

nce upon a time there was a rich old baron who lived in a big house with lots of servants. He had enough money to buy anything he liked, and he did, too. He had a magnificent coach, a stable full of horses, and a castle full of the most beautiful furniture you could find in the world. His wardrobe bulged with grand suits, and the buckles on his shoes were of fine gold.

The only thing he couldn't buy with all his money was wives for his sons. He had three sons, and he would have liked to marry all three of them to nice girls, but especially to rich ones! He felt that was very important, because he thought that a rich young man should always marry a rich girl; poor girls might spend all his sons' money.

One day he heard that the king's daughter wanted to marry a man who was a good talker. And not one who just chattered, but one who could talk seriously about difficult subjects and affairs of the highest importance. The princess thought that was so important that she decided to hold a competition – a talking competition. And she would marry the man who could talk best of all.

In two weeks the princess would see all the young men who thought that they could win the competition. The baron thought that would be a chance for one of his sons; they could talk the hind legs off a donkey. They knew so many words, they would be bound to win. He liked the idea that one of his sons might marry the princess. Then his son would become king of the whole country! And moreover, the princess was awfully rich, of course.

Obviously he only meant to send the two cleverest of his sons. There was always his third son, Johnny, but he was no good for anything. It wasn't even worth his trying, it would be a waste of time, thought his father.

The baron sent for his two clever sons.

"Listen," he said. "In two weeks' time there will be a competition. It will be to find out who can talk best. The winner will marry the princess. Do you want to enter?"

"Of course," both his sons said at once. "We are the best talkers in the whole country. One of us is certain to win the competition." And they immediately began to read and to study. One son learnt all the laws of the land by heart, and the other the whole of the Latin dictionary. There were only two weeks to do it in, but they studied so hard that they were ready by the time the competition was to be held. They had read day and night, and hadn't slept at all, so anxious were they to marry the princess.

At last the day came: the day they had to go to the city where the princess would see all the competitors in the great royal palace.

"Good luck," their father said to his two sons. He gave one of them, the one who'd learned the Latin dictionary by heart, a pitch-black horse. The other, the one who'd learned all the laws, got a white horse. At the last moment the two brothers rubbed cod-liver oil on their lips. That was so that they could say all they had to say more easily. All the servants stood in a circle round them when they were ready to start. Suddenly someone else turned up. It was Johnny, the third son.

"Hey," he cried. "Where are you off to?"

"We're going to the city for the princess's talking competition," said the son who had learned all the laws.

"One of us will certainly be the best talker. I think it will be me," said the other." I know the whole Latin dictionary by heart."

"I want to go with you," cried Johnny. Everyone always called him Simple Johnny, because he never got anything right, and always looked like a simpleton. His clothes were all torn, and each time his father gave him new ones he threw them away. Besides, he wasn't keen on learning. He preferred carving little wooden dolls. He made them of any pieces of wood he could find in the forest. And he was fantastically good at it. He carved witches and horses, monkeys and elephants; whatever you wanted, Johnny could carve it for you.

"You can't go, the competition is only for clever young men," said his father. "Oh," said Johnny. "Just give me a horse; after all, I can try."

"No way," said his father. He wished his two clever sons luck, and the black horse and the white one went off with them on their backs.

Johnny said: "I'm still going. If my father won't give me a horse, then I'll go on my own goat."

He jumped on his goat, which was so old that his father hadn't wanted to keep it any longer.

The servants stood and laughed, because it was really a funny sight to see shabby Johnny riding off on a goat so old it could hardly move at all.

The two clever brothers rode their splendid horses as fast as they could to the big city. They thought of all the things they could say to make an impression on the princess.

Johnny wasn't in a hurry at all. He hobbled slowly along on the back of his goat, picking up anything he found on the way. The first thing he saw was an old dead crow, which he took along. A little further on he found a single clog. "That might come in useful!" Johnny told his goat, and took it along. A bit further on he saw a ditch at the side of the road, full of thick mud. He got off his goat, and filled his pockets with mud. You could never tell when it might come in handy…

An hour after his brothers Simple Johnny reached the palace on the edge of the big city. He tied his goat to a tree and went in.

"What do you want?" asked the sentry on the gate.

"I've come for the talking competition," said Johnny cheerfully. The man laughed. "You?" he asked. "You don't look at all as if you would be any good at talking."

"I'll have a go," Johnny insisted. The sentry said: "All right, go down that passage; the competition is being held in the main hall." He hoped that everyone would laugh at this odd young man. They surely would, because he looked so stupid!

Johnny walked down the passage, opened the door of the main hall, and went in. He joined a queue. All the young men standing there were going in for the talking competition. The princess was already hard at work judging, but so far no one had turned out to be suitable to be her husband. The princess saw that they were all doing their best, but she was still getting bored. There hadn't been a single man who could talk so well that she wanted to listen to him.

Johnny could scarcely move as he stood in the queue. It was so crowded; everyone wasn't squashed absolutely flat yet, but they weren't far off. After a while it was the turn of the son who had learnt the Latin dictionary by heart. He came forward, and wanted to start his speech. But he couldn't, because he had forgotten it all! He was so nervous that he couldn't remember a single word of Latin any more. And it was so terribly hot! The stove was glowing red hot.

"How hot it is," he said. And that is all he could utter.

"That is because my father is roasting chickens today," answered the princess. The young man would have liked to say something, but he couldn't. The words all stuck in his throat.

"This one's no good. Take him away," cried the king's daughter.

Then it was the turn of the other brother. "It's terribly hot in here," he started. He was frightfully shy, he was so nervous. The princess answered: "Yes, today we are roasting young chickens." The young man didn't know what to say to that. It was completely unexpected. What had a talking competition to do with roasting chickens?

"What? How?" he stammered. It was all he could think of.

And the reporters who were writing down everything that everyone said, wrote in their notebooks: "What? How?"

"This one's no good either. Take him away," cried the princess. She was annoyed, because no one could speak well. She was just wasting her time here. It would have been better to have done something amusing, like buying a new dress, perhaps.

One after another the young men had to demonstrate how well they could talk, but most of them failed completely. Each one was more nervous than the last. Occasionally they managed to come out with something, but certainly none of them was a really good talker.

At last it was Simple Johnny's turn. He had to go and stand in front of the princess. The stove was still red hot, and drops of sweat were pouring off the foreheads of everyone in the room.

"Princess, it's stifling in here," said Johnny.

"That's right, today we are roasting chickens," answered the princess.

"Oh yes?" said Johnny. "Then perhaps I might cook my crow in the same pan? It only needs a sauce, and it will be ready to eat."

The princess had to laugh when she saw everything Simple Johnny pulled out of his pockets. A crow, an old clog, and a handful of mud. Johnny put the crow in the clog and smeared mud over it.

"You are very clever and funny," the king's daughter told him. "You've got all the answers!" She was pleased that at last there was someone who could give an amusing answer to a question. None of the others had been able to.

The princess still wasn't quite sure if Johnny was a suitable boy for her to marry, so she asked him another question.

"Do you know that everything you say is written down by those reporters over there? It will all be in the newspaper tomorrow."

Johnny had an answer to that, too. He said: "Then I know what to do to make sure that tomorrow morning everyone will have to fight to get hold of a paper."

"I'd like to see that!" said the princess happily.

Johnny went to the head reporter, the boss of all the reporters. He pulled some mud out of his pocket and threw it in his face.

"That's good fun!" cried the king's daughter. "Nobody has dared do that before! I would like to marry you."

The three reporters didn't know what to think. They were so surprised that they dropped their notebooks.

The next day the princess and Simple Johnny got married. The whole country celebrated, because now at last the princess had found a husband. Later, when the king died, Johnny would be king. Because he could give such clever answers he had got himself a wife, and would later get a crown and a throne.

It was all in the paper the next day. The head reporter had written down exactly what Johnny had said and done. At first his readers couldn't believe it. Simple Johnny to be their next king – incredible!

Johnny's father was the most surprised of all. But he never again said anything bad about Johnny.

Ib and Little Christine

Somewhere in Denmark there is a province called Jutland. Jutland has been around for a very long time and people have been making their homes there for many centuries. There were farmers and woodsmen, and nice little villages scattered all about.

Right in the middle of Jutland, at the edge of a great forest with terribly tall trees, was a tiny little farmstead. You really had to look hard before you saw it since all the way around it there were trees and bushes. It was not so very big because the farmer and his wife who lived there did not have so very much money. They had to work hard on the little piece of land next to their cottage. The soil in which they planted their grain was not very fertile. So that they could afford to pay the rent on their cottage they also kept some sheep in a separate field behind the house.

The farmer was busy on the land in the spring and summer. He had to sow the seed and bring in the harvest. Nothing grew on the land in the wintertime. The farmer would then make wooden clogs. All winter long, the little stove would burn away in the living room. The farmer would sit next to it and make his clogs. He was very good at it and his clogs were the best in all of Jutland. All the girls from the area had thrown away their shoes because they thought that the farmer's clogs were much nicer and, moreover, the clogs were good and warm in the winter. So, what with the clogs, the sheep, and their little piece of land, the farmer and his wife earned enough to stay contentedly in their cottage next to the forest.

Ib, the farmer's only son, was seven years old. He liked to help his father. "May I carve out a clog?" he often used to ask his father. It was very difficult to make good clogs. More than that, it was dangerous because the chisel with which you had to work was terribly sharp. Therefore, it sometimes happened that the chisel hit Ib's fingers. This made a cut, and usually it bled a lot. But Ib would grit his teeth so as not to cry because he wanted more than anything to make clogs as well as his father did.

After a few years, when he was a little older, he tried even harder to do his best. He worked all day long until he could proudly show off the clogs which he had made.

"Look, these clogs are for Christine!" he cried.

Christine lived a way further off and was the only other child who Ib knew. He did not go to school as his parents could not afford it.

Christine lived with her father in a cottage just as small as Ib's. Her father was the skipper of a barge which he sailed along the great rivers of the country. Christine had hardly known her mother, as she had died when Christine was only two years old.

Now, a skipper is often away for weeks at a time, and Christine usually stayed with Ib and his parents when that happened. This is why they knew each other so well.

Christine was one year younger than Ib. She was a sweet girl. Everyone liked her because she was just a little bit different from all the other children. Ib and Christine loved to be in each other's company. They played together in the forest and knew exactly which berries were good for you and which would make you sick. When it was nice weather, they made sand-castles at the river's edge.

"Ib and Christine", the skipper asked one day, "I have to take a cargo of firewood to Seisheide; do you want to come along?"

"Yes, that would be fun!" they both shouted. Fortunately, Ib's father said that it was all right.

The next day came. All three of them went to the harbour, and the skipper put Ib and Christine on top of the great pile of wood which lay on deck. The journey was wonderful. The sails billowed out and the barge glided quickly through the water, since the wind was behind them.

"Lovely, isn't it?" said Christine to Ib. Ib thought so too, as he had never been there before. The children were looking in all directions the whole way because there was so much to see.

At Seisheide all the wooden logs were taken from the barge. That took a long time. As soon as the ship had been completely unloaded it was immediately loaded up again, this time with food. Strong men came on board, first with barrels filled with salted meat, then followed by crates full of fish, and lastly a whole piglet.

In the end, the barge was fully loaded. The skipper called out: "Cast off the ropes!" and then off they went. This was somewhat different from the outward journey: the wind was no longer behind them but quite against them, so the journey took much longer.

When the barge had gone about half of the distance, they tied up at a little harbour. They wanted to rest a while from the long trip, because they had been travelling all day.

"Don't get up to anything naughty, children!" called the skipper.

"We won't!" Ib and Christine called back. But that was not exactly what happened.

"Are you coming with me on deck?" asked Ib. "There's a piglet there. It looks really delicious." Christine did not in all honesty dare, but went along with her friend nonetheless. They walked to the place on the deck at the back of the barge where the piglet lay. It had just been killed and looked very tasty. Ib carefully touched one of its trotters.

"Be careful, Ib, it might fall", whispered Christine. She was truly frightened because if anything were to happen to the piglet her father would have to pay for it and he had no money for that. The piglet was not his, he simply had to deliver it somewhere.

"Don't worry, that piglet isn't going to fall off, I'm very careful", said Ib. "Just look at those fat trotters of his. I'll bet they're delicious. I wish I had a huge sackful of money! Then I'd buy so much lovely food that you could eat it for months and months."

Ib stood there looking at the piglet so hungrily that he could no longer stop himself and he carefully picked it up.

"How fat it is", he said. The piglet seemed so delicious to him that his mouth fairly watered.

"Put it down again!" said Christine. She did not think the careless way that Ib was behaving was fun at all. Ib was about to set it down once more when suddenly he stumbled.

"Look out!" shouted Christine, but it was already too late. The piglet flew out of Ib's hands and landed with a splash in the water. Ib was so shocked that he began to cry. This would be very bad for the skipper as he earned very little, and now he would have to pay for that piglet himself.

Ib heard Christine's father's footsteps. He was looking for the children.

"We have to get out of here!" said Ib to Christine.

"But where to?" asked Christine, frightened.

"Just come with me", said Ib and pulled Christine along with him by her hand. They ran along and jumped from the barge on to land. They started off at once in the direction of the forest. They ran farther and farther away from the river.

Christine could go no further, that was obvious. She kept on stumbling and was crying softly to herself. She did not say anything about it to Ib. Luckily, they came to a clearing. There were no trees but the ground was covered in little blueberry bushes. The children began to pick and eat the berries immediately. They tasted delicious.

It was a good thing that they had something to eat because they had completely lost their way. Ib knew this already but he hardly dared tell Christine.

That night they slept on the moss. They did not have any blankets, of course, and their clothes were not very warm so they felt pretty cold. It was also a good thing that it was not winter!

The next morning, Christine went for a little walk by herself and suddenly saw some water.

"Ib", she called, "come and look, there's some water here! We've found the river again!"

Ib rubbed his eyes. For a moment he did not know where he was, but when he saw Christine in front of him he remembered everything again. He walked up to her and together they pulled back the branches of some bushes. There was the water.

"That's not the river", said Ib. "It's a little lake." But what was this? There, between the hazel bushes stood a woman with dark eyes and an olive skin. It was a gypsy woman

She said: "Come closer, children, and I'll give you three magic hazelnuts."

Ib hesitated for a moment but he was too curious to run away. So he walked up to the gypsy and she placed three nuts in his hand.

"These are wishing nuts", said the gypsy.

Ib and Christine looked in amazement at the three nuts. They looked very ordinary to them.

"I wish ...for a wagon with two horses to be inside", said Ib.

"Better than that", said the woman to him, "there's a golden coach inside with seven golden horses."

"Give it to me", said Christine, and she took the nut from Ib's hand.

"Is there a scarf inside this nut like the one Christine is wearing?" asked Ib softly.

"That is by no means all there is", said the gypsy. "There are ten scarves inside, as well as dresses, hats and shoes."

"I want that one too", said the little girl. She put the nut in her pocket.

The third nut was black and ugly. Ib asked the old woman: "This one is really very dirty, what is inside it?"

"That which is the very best for you", replied the strange woman.

Ib and Christine were happy. They said goodbye to the mysterious gypsy woman and once more went on their way back home. They had walked for hours and had still not seen anything which they recognized. They began to feel hopeless. Being lost was absolutely no fun at all. Finally, just as it was nearly dark again, they saw a man approaching them from the distance. It was a woodsman. He knew Ib and brought the children home. The following day, Ib placed his little black nut between the door and the

doorpost and slammed the door shut. Crack, went the nut and it broke in two. Ib opened the door again and looked to see what was inside. What a pity, there was nothing inside the nut except for some black earth.

In that case there is sure to be nothing inside the nuts which Christine has, thought Ib. How could it be otherwise? How could you put that which is the very best for you inside just one nut?

A little while later Ib was sent to the boarding school in the town. Christine went to a big city in the west. There, she was to work for an innkeeper. The two children had to make their goodbyes to one another.

"I still have the hazelnuts", said Christine, and she showed them to Ib. Then she had to go because the coach was leaving for the city.

One day, Ib's father died. Ib had just finished boarding school and discovered that he had to return to the farm again. In the winter he was a clog maker and in the summer he was a farmer, just like his father. Fortunately, his mother was still alive and she and Ib lived together in the little cottage.

Years went by. Ib was content with his life as a farmer and clog maker and was nearly as good at it as was his father. He earned just enough to buy enough food every day for himself and his mother. He did not think about marrying.

One day, there came a knock at the door. Ib went to see who it was. When he opened the door he was a little startled. Before him stood a charming lady. Her dress was smart and looked terribly expensive. Ib stood there only in his shabby working clothes which were fine for his job but not attractive. Ib was a farmer, and that is what he looked like.

Ib took Christine's hand, for she it was, of course, but he did not dare to say too much. Eventually Christine said: "How are you, Ib?" Ib did not reply, but said "You look so smart and I look so shabby ..."

Christine reassured him and suggested that they go for a little walk. This they did and after a quarter of an hour Ib said: "Christine, if it should be that you don't find all those things in the city important then marry me soon and come to live here."

"You are right, dearest Ib", replied Christine. "I shall happily marry you and come to live here again. This is where I come from and this is where I feel at home."

They continued walking for a while, but then Christine had to go again. The coach for the city was leaving and Christine had to be back on time at the innkeeper's where she was still working. Ib waved after her. He thought it a pity that she had had to go away so soon and he hoped that she would return quickly to marry him.

Time passed by. Winter became spring, spring became summer, and that is how it went for a number of years. Ib and Christine wrote each other letters. At the bottom of each letter which they sent stood 'Faithful unto death'. They wrote of all kinds of unimportant things which is what they both enjoyed.

However, it suddenly all ended when Ib stopped getting letters from Christine anymore. That was strange since it never took her more than

two weeks to reply. Ib wondered what the matter was.

One day, the skipper, Christine's father, came by to visit Ib and his mother. He brought greetings from Christine with him. The skipper did not very well know what to say. He stuttered a little. In the end, Ib came to understand that the innkeeper's son wanted to marry Christine. He was a respectable young man who had a good job in Copenhagen. He earned a lot of money, more than enough to be able to take care of Christine.

"Christine isn't sure whether she wants to marry the innkeeper's son, because she has made a promise to you", said the skipper.

Ib turned pale. Christine had promised that she was going to marry him, but Ib did not want to make Christine unhappy and that is what he told the skipper.

"Write her a letter then", said the skipper.

Ib took all evening and all night to write the letter. He found it very difficult to do. In the end he succeeded and had said what he wanted to say. This is the letter which he sent to Christine:

> *I have heard from your father that you could be even happier if you were to marry the innkeeper's son. I am only a poor farmer, with me you will never be happy. Do not think of me, but do what your heart tells you. Although you had made me a promise, you do not have to marry me if that is not what you wish.*
>
> *Your friend forever,*
> *Ib*

Christine married the innkeeper's son soon afterwards. She led a life of leisure in the big city. As time went by, Ib became ever more quiet and worked ever harder. He missed Christine, but there was nothing to be done about it. He remembered the gypsy's hazelnuts; Christine had indeed been given her golden coach and beautiful clothes, and he a heap of earth. In fact, that was fair, he thought. The soil was what was best for him.

Two years later Ib was still working terribly hard on his little farm and trying to forget about Christine. That was not at all easy to do since he was really very much in love with her still.

The skipper received little post from his daughter. Christine and her husband had thought that they could live easily. But even if you have a lot of money, it soon runs out when you buy lots of very expensive things and often go out. And that is what Christine and the innkeeper's son had done. They bought smart new clothes, lived in the biggest house in the city, and gave a party every week. That could not go on forever and after a while all their money had been spent. Ib did not know about this since he did not hear anything any longer from his girlfriend.

One day, while Ib was working his field, his ploughshare hit against something hard. Ib took a spade and dug it out. First of all he had to wash off all the earth to be able to see what it was. But once he had done that he saw that all his efforts had not been in vain. He had found a heavy gold arm band. It was certain to be extremely old! Ib took the arm band to show it to the minister.

"Ib, this arm band is very valuable", said the minister. "Take it with you to the museum in Copenhagen. They're sure to want to have it to be able to show it to all the people."

Ib went to Copenhagen and sold his arm band. He was given a whole sackful of money for it as the arm band was thousands of years old. Even the people at the museum had never seen such an old arm band!

Ib thought of the gypsy's hazelnut once again. That's right, he thought, what's best for me lies in the ground. Perhaps the gypsy was right after all! It was awfully cold in Copenhagen but even so Ib went for a walk through

the city. Out of a small house came a little girl who was crying her eyes out. She ran towards Ib and fell on the ground in front of him. When Ib helped her up again, he saw that she looked just like Christine. The child was crying. Ib comforted her and asked: "Where is your mother?"

The child brought him inside the house. In the corner of a dark room Ib saw a woman lying in a bed. It took a few moments before he recognized her, but then he realized: it was Christine! She lay in an old ugly bed. She did not have a penny left and had been abandoned by everyone. Ib could see at once that she was dreadfully sick. Groaning and moaning, she pulled herself up and said: "Look after my child, I know that I am going to die!"

Ib was completely bewildered, but before he could reassure her Christine had died. Her large, frightened eyes looked up at him. Ib had a lump in his throat and wondered: had Christine recognized him? Ib did not know and he never would.

Christine was buried the next day. Ib did not want to stay in Copenhagen any longer, so he made his way back again to his little farm. He took Christine's little daughter with him.

After Ib had returned to his cottage at the edge of the forest it began to turn into autumn. The strong wind flung the dry leaves against the newly painted walls. It was a happy time again indoors. A little Christine was living there now.

She would often sit on Ib's lap. She was always so cheerful! It did seem as if she had forgotten that her mother had passed away. Ib felt happy when the little girl fell asleep on his lap.

Ib, little Christine, and Ib's mother, who was still alive, were never hungry. Ib dug up yet more precious things from his garden. He no longer needed to work since he had more than enough money, yet he kept on making clogs as that was the thing which he still enjoyed doing the most. Especially for little Christine, for whom he made beautiful little clogs.

And Christine? She stayed a sweet and cheerful girl who was very happy in her little cottage next to the forest. Ib was a caring father and Ib's mother a doting grandmother. Little Christine had never had such a good life. She would often go with Ib when he went to the city. Ib enjoyed that very much and together they had a lot of fun.

So it remained, year after year. Ib grew to be incredibly old and thus was alive to see Christine become grown, marry and have children of her own. She kept living at Ib's cottage always, and when she had a baby girl she called her Christine as well. So it was that yet another little Christine came to live at the farm with Ib.

Little Ida's flowers

Once upon a time there was a little girl called Ida. She lived with her parents in a very ordinary house in a very ordinary town. She looked pretty, and she was always happy. She loved playing out of doors, and she had lots of friends. When she walked home from school her friends would often say: "Are you coming to play with us, Ida?" Ida liked that, and usually she said yes, she would like to.

But sometimes she didn't go, but ran back home fast, because she had one special friend, a student, who occasionally came to visit.

He could tell wonderful stories. Little Ida liked him very much, and when he began to tell one she sat on his knee, so that she could hear the story better.

One day she came home from school quickly again, because the student would be there. He had been there yesterday, too, and he'd promised to come again today. Yesterday he had brought a lovely bunch of red and yellow tulips, but these had already wilted. The flowers on their stalks drooped limply over the edge of the vase. A pity, thought Ida, because she liked the student, and she thought he wouldn't be very pleased that his flowers had died so quickly.

Then she heard the bell ring; the student had arrived.

"Hello, Ida, how are you?" he asked when he came in.

"Well, thank you," said Ida.

"Why do my flowers look so unhappy today?" asked the student.

He had already noticed that his tulips had wilted.

"I don't know," said Ida. "They were perfectly all right yesterday."

"Did you know, Ida, that flowers are alive just like us?" the student asked. "They don't do anything in the daytime, but at night they enjoy themselves and go dancing." Ida looked at him in surprise. How could flowers go dancing? "Where do they go to dance?" she asked. It must be somewhere a long way away, because she had never yet seen a flower dancing a tango.

"To the big castle on the other side of the park," said the student. Ida lived on the edge of a big park, with tall trees and big lakes.

"I didn't know there was a castle on the other side of the park," said Ida, and looked at the student. "Is that really quite true?"

"Absolutely true," answered the student. "The king only lives in that palace in the summer; in winter there are only a few servants to keep things clean. There is a big moat round it with swans swimming in it, the ones you always give bread to."

"Is that where the flowers go to dance?"

"Yes, of course. Where else did you think all the flowers went? In summer the park is always full of flowers, but now they've all gone to the castle. As soon as the king and his courtiers leave for the city, the flowers leave the park and go to the castle."

The student told her more. He explained that in winter it was too cold for the flowers to stay in the park. That's why they left then for the palace.

"The two prettiest roses go and sit in the king's and the queen's places as soon as they have left. Then the roses rule over the flower people from the throne."

"How lovely," said Ida.

"It is, too," said the student. "The flower king is served by a lot of red coxscombs. And hundreds of other flowers dance. The blue pansies dance best. They dance waltzes with the crocuses and the hyacinths. The tulips and the tall yellow lilies sit on sofas and chatter about this and that."

Ida thought this a wonderful story. A castle full of flowers, that was brilliant. "Does no one chase the flowers out of the castle?" she asked.

The student knew the answer to that. "Nobody knows that they are there. Not even the servants. Because whenever people come along, the flowers hide behind the long curtains."

"That's funny," said Ida. "If I'm ever in the king's garden feeding the ducks, I'll have a look through the windows of the palace. Perhaps I'll see the flowers dancing."

"You're sure to," said the student.

"And the red flowers in our garden?" asked little Ida. She was getting more and more curious about that wonderful flower ball in the castle.

"Of course, all the flowers go to the king's castle."

"But how do they get there?" asked Ida. "It is a long way from here to the other side of the park."

"The flowers can turn into butterflies and fly there. Have you never seen butterflies that are red, yellow, and white, just like the flowers in the garden?"

Ida had seen them sometimes. How nice to know that the butterflies were really flowers. She had always wondered where they came from.

"But how do the flowers know when the king and queen have left the palace?" she asked.

"The flowers tell each other."

"How can they do that when they haven't got voices or mouths?"

"If people can talk, why shouldn't flowers be able to? They talk quite differently from people," answered the student. "Listen very carefully some time, you'll hear the flowers make very quiet sounds. That's how they talk to each other, just like people. And they use sign language, too. Have you never noticed how a flower sways backwards and forwards in the wind? That's when it's explaining something."

"What a lot you know," Ida said to the student.

He had to smile a little.

"Just go to the park and tell all the flowers that there is a big party up at the castle. After an hour or two all the flowers will have gone. You only have to tell one flower, and it will pass it on to all the others."

"I'll do that," said Ida.

"Now I must go home. Give my love to the flowers," said the student. He put his coat on and went away.

The next day Ida's uncle came to call. He didn't think much of the student.

"What's he been telling you this time?" he asked Ida.

"He told me how the flowers go to the castle in winter," explained Ida, "and there they dance the whole night through. And they can turn into butterflies."

"What nonsense," cried her uncle. "That's quite impossible."

146

How cross her uncle was. He had taken a dislike to the student, that was obvious.

"And I suppose he still keeps cutting out those stupid shapes for you? A witch on a broomstick with three ears, and a cat with two tails behind her? How does he think them up?" cried her uncle angrily. "I think it is quite wrong for that young man to tell you such nonsense. He's teaching you all sorts of things which just aren't true."

He had made Ida cry. "He is terribly nice, I tell you," she sobbed. "And he knows an awful lot about flowers and animals. Much more than you do!"

That night little Ida kept thinking about the student's wonderful stories. Could they be true, she thought. But perhaps he had been wrong, and her uncle had been right to be angry.

She wasn't quite sure if it would be any use, but she put some of her prettiest flowers in her doll's bed. If they have a good night's sleep, she thought, they will surely be quite fresh again. And then they'll get all their colour back.

Before Ida went to bed, she bent over the bunch of flowers her mother had put on the small table near the window. She whispered: "I know you

are going dancing tonight, but don't make it too late! Tomorrow is another day."

It looked as if the flowers nodded. Ida said goodnight to them a second time, put on her pyjamas and went to bed.

As she lay in bed she thought about the flowers' party in the king's great castle, on the other side of the park. It would be nice to see it some time. Imagine, a great hall full of flowers dancing! She fell asleep and dreamed all night. She dreamed that brightly coloured flowers and butterflies were dancing all round her.

In the middle of the night Ida suddenly woke up. It was very hot. She had certainly had strange dreams, but she couldn't remember what about. How were her flowers getting on, she wondered. Had the tulips gone to the party? Or had they been sensible enough to go to sleep?

She suddenly heard soft music coming from the sitting room. It sounded lovely. It was exactly the same music as the tune she had heard in her dream. What was going on?

Ida got more and more curious. She must find out what was going on downstairs. She jumped out of bed and ran down the stairs on tiptoe to

the sitting room. Quietly she opened the door. She looked into the room in astonishment.

A large white lily was playing the piano. It nodded in time to the music. The hyacinths and tulips were dancing happily with each other. Beyond them she saw some pansies, who were enjoying themselves. In the corner a group of dandelions sat talking, and now and then they laughed heartily.

"Hey," exclaimed Ida. "Those are mother's flowers. The vase on the table is empty! And those tulips, they're mine! How well they dance!" The flowers were talking to each other. Ida listened hard to what they were saying.

"We'll go on dancing all night," they were all saying, "because tomorrow we will wilt. But luckily we've got tonight to enjoy ourselves in. And that's because Ida always looks after us so well."

Ida was pleased to hear that. If the flowers themselves said she was looking after them well, that must be so.

Then she heard a white narcissus saying something to a big yellow carnation sitting next to it on the bench.

"I hope that Ida will remember to bury us in her garden, like she did with her canary. If she does that we will flower even better next year. If only she thinks of it. She is still so little! Little children forget so much."

The carnation answered: "Tell her doll, he's lying asleep in the drawer, he's sure to tell Ida in the morning."

The white narcissus quickly went to the drawer and gently woke the doll. The doll opened his eyes. It said hello to the flowers in a friendly way. The white narcissus said to him: "Tomorrow morning ask Ida to bury us in her garden."

"All right, all right," said the doll. "But now I want to dance with you. I've been lying in this drawer for so long, now I would like to stretch my legs a bit."

When Ida heard that the doll was going to dance, too, she wanted to as well. She wasn't tired at all any more, and felt just like dancing merrily to some nice piano music.

She ran back to her bedroom to put on her prettiest dress. It took some time, but in a little while she was satisfied, and put on her hat. The flowers will like that, she thought.

At first she hardly dared go in, because dancing with flowers is not a thing you do every day. She hesitated a little, and wasn't sure she really dared,

but then she opened the sitting room door all at once and went in. All the lights were out, but you could see the moonlight shining through the window. That made it very cosy.

Ida had thought that the flowers might go away when they saw her, or that they would be angry. But that didn't happen. It was as if they just didn't see that Ida was in the room. Ida danced until her feet were so tired that she couldn't dance any more.

Then suddenly the window flew open, and a whole crowd of lovely flowers and brightly coloured butterflies came in. They said hello to each other, and then the flowers all joined hands and started dancing round the room.

"Just play us a quiet tune, so that we can rest a bit," said a pansy to the big white lily.

An iris bowed to the pansy, and led her out to the middle of the room to dance with her.

Ida danced the whole night through, till at last the sun rose again. Everyone said their goodbyes. The doll went back to the drawer. The tulips went back to their bed. And mother's flowers went back to their vase. But Ida didn't see all that. She had gone back to bed when she saw the first

rays of the sun, and she slept away the rest of the night like a rosebud.

The next morning Ida ran to her tulips. They were still lying in the doll's bed, but they were all wilted. Ida grabbed a cardboard box on which she had drawn some pretty birds, and put the flowers in it. Then she pulled the doll out of the drawer, and asked him: "Haven't you got something to tell me this morning?"

The doll said nothing.

"Have you really got nothing to tell me?" Ida asked again. What had happened, hadn't the doll promised to tell her that she must bury the flowers?

"You are being naughty," said Ida angrily. "Have you forgotten that you promised the flowers to tell me that I should bury them in the garden?"

Again the doll said nothing. Ida put him back in the drawer as a punishment.

Then she had a wonderful idea. Her cousins Ralph and James were coming to play with her today. She would organize a proper funeral for her tulips!

As soon as Ralph and James arrived, Ida told them all about her flowers. "Will you help me with the funeral?" she asked her cousins. "A proper funeral, the way it should be done?"

"Yes, fine," said the boys. It seemed a splendid idea. They'd never been to a flower funeral before.

"I've got my bow and arrow," said James, "we can fire a salute."

"What is a salute?" asked Ida. She had never heard of one.

"I don't know," said James, "but there ought to be one. They always have one when they bury someone who was very important."

Ida thought it a good idea. If only her flowers were to get a proper funeral, everything would be all right.

The three of them went into the garden. They took the flowers with them in a basket. Ralph and James walked in front, with their bows over their shoulders. Ida walked behind, carrying the basket with the tulips. They walked slowly, looking very serious. You had to do that, said Ida, because you had to look solemn at a funeral.

They went into the park. There was a strip of grass near the big lake where hardly anybody ever came. That was the best place to bury the flowers.

Ralph and James started to dig a grave for the tulips. Ida watched. She left the digging to the boys, it wasn't girls' work, she thought. It only made your hands dirty, and besides, you got a pain in your back if you bent down for too long.

When the grave was ready, Ida took the tulips out of the basket. Carefully she laid them in the grave.

152

While her cousins shovelled the earth back, Ida said with a smile: "Grow again quickly, lovely little flowers, then next year the garden will be full of magnificent colours again."

The hole was closed up again. Ralph and James took their bows and arrows, and each aimed an arrow at the sky.

"Ready?" Ralph asked James.

"Ready," answered James.

In turn they shot their arrows off over the grave, where Ida's tulips lay. That was the salute. You really need guns for a salute, but they hadn't got any. Besides, they would have made a lot of noise, and flowers don't like that.

"That was a lovely ceremony. Now the flowers will grow twice as big next year," said Ida. She laughed happily.

"Come along, we must go back," said Ralph.

And the three children went home hand in hand.

The princess and the pea

Once upon a time there was a prince who lived with his father, the king, and his mother, the queen, in a large palace, standing a little way outside the town in a large park. It was a big castle, but the country where his father was king was large, too, so that was quite suitable.

There were hundreds of servants to serve the prince. He could travel wherever he wanted, and he did just whatever he liked. There was never any need for him to polish his shoes, mow the lawn, or go shopping, because everything was done for him. He only had to flick his fingers, and a long row of servants immediately started doing things for him. All princes lead a life that might quite rightly be called princely! This prince was no exception. All his wishes were promptly fulfilled. There was nothing left for him to wish for, although...

There was one thing all those hundreds of servants could not produce, and that was a girl for him to marry. The prince would very much have liked to get married, but as a prince you don't move around among people much, so he didn't meet very many girls. Moreover, he didn't just want an ordinary girl, he wanted to marry a real princess. A prince and a princess go together, he thought. And his father and mother thought so, too.

One day the prince decided he didn't want to wait any longer. No, he was going to do something about it; he was going to look for a real princess himself. He called for his coach, put on his best clothes, and travelled round the world to have a look at the daughters of all the kings. There were some princesses he liked, but they were either too young, or they were already married. The others he thought were too silly, or not pretty enough, or not nice enough.

Wherever he went, the princesses were waiting for him, because they all wanted to marry a prince from such an important country. And the prince

looked... and shook his head. No, not pretty enough, or too small, or too tall, or too thin, or too fat...

And on the prince went, to the next palace.

One evening the prince was reading in front of the fire, but couldn't quite concentrate. He had just come back from a journey round the world, and still he had not managed to find a suitable wife. It was beginning to make him unhappy. "Where on earth do I find a real princess?" he asked himself sadly. Surely it could not be that difficult?

It started to rain. The prince couldn't feel the rain, of course, because he was sitting by the fire. But he could hear it, especially when it started to thunder as well. So loudly, that the prince got worried, and looked out of the window to see if any of the ten turrets of the castle had fallen down.

He couldn't see a turret, but he did see a shadow in the distance. The shadow came nearer. It was a woman. She was small, and having difficulty walking in the storm. Quickly the prince called to his servants to open the door for the girl, and he walked into the hall to see if he knew her. A wet and bedraggled girl stumbled inside when the door was opened. As soon as she was inside, she took off her soaking wet cloak and shook the rain out of her curls.

"Who are you?" the prince asked the girl, after they had greeted each other.

"I am a princess from a distant country," said the girl. She told him that she had never been in such a storm, and she asked if she might perhaps sit by the fire for a little while. "Otherwise I will die of cold," she explained. "I was on my way to the town, where I wanted to stay with the baroness, but then one of the wheels of my coach broke. The coachman went to fetch help, but he took so long to come back, and I was getting so cold, alone in that coach... So I decided to go looking for help myself. It was dreadful! Almost as soon as I had started it began to rain and thunder. No princess should be out in such weather!"

The prince agreed, she could certainly not stay out in the rain. Her hair was soaked, and her curls clung to her head like wet rope. Water streamed from her clothes, so that there was a puddle where she stood, even when she had taken her cloak off.

In spite of her being so wet, the prince could see that she was a pretty girl. Now, if she were a real princess...

"Are you really a princess?" he asked the girl.

"Yes, really and truly," she said, "and wet into the bargain!" She smiled, and little dimples appeared in her cheeks. That made her look even nicer. The prince laughed, too, he rather liked the girl.

"Who's there?" they heard. It was the queen, who came to find out who it was her son was talking to.

"A princess, looking for shelter," answered her son.

"Is she a real princess?" the queen wanted to know.

"She says she is, and I believe her," answered the prince. He said that because he liked the princess very much.

"We'll find out about that," said the queen. "She'd better stay the night, because you don't send anyone on their way in this rain. Take her to the dining room, because dinner is nearly ready. I have something to do, so you will have to excuse me."

The prince and the girl went into the dining room. It was a beautiful room with a large chandelier hanging from the ceiling, with at least a hundred candles burning in it. In palaces there are always such dining rooms, because it is not considered the done thing for kings and queens to eat in the kitchen.

The prince and princess went to sit at a beautifully laid table, and were waited on. The princess was particularly hungry, perhaps because she had walked such a long way. She enjoyed her food, and meanwhile talked to the prince, who couldn't keep his eyes off her, he thought her so beautiful.

What was the queen doing all this time? She went to one of the ten spare bedrooms in the palace, and took all the blankets, sheets, and pillows off

the bed. There are lots of them on a royal bed. On top of the mattress she put a raw pea, which she had collected from the kitchen. It had been quite difficult for her to find one. Not because they hadn't got any, but because she had never been in the kitchen before. She always left that to the servants.

She called her servants. "Bring me the mattresses from all the other spare bedrooms," she ordered. They did that, and soon there were nine mattresses on top of the one which held the pea. The queen hadn't told the servants why, and the servants hadn't asked any questions either; servants don't do that. But they were rather surprised, because who wants to sleep on ten mattresses all at once? Surely one is enough?

"Did you enjoy your meal?" the prince asked the girl, when they had finished eating.

"Very much, thank you," said the girl. "Do you think I might go to bed now, I'm very tired after my long journey?"

That was all right, and the queen took the princess to the spare room, to the bed with all the mattresses on top of each other.

"How do I get into that bed?" asked the girl.

"There is a little ladder next to it," answered the queen. The princess climbed up the ladder and lay down in her bed. The queen wished her goodnight, and left the room.

Now you would imagine that the princess would go to sleep immediately. After all, she was so tired! But that didn't happen at all! No, the princess lay tossing and turning all night. She just couldn't get to sleep. If you listened carefully you could sometimes hear her sigh and groan.

The night passed, and dawn broke. The cock crowed, and everybody got up. One by one everyone came downstairs and sat down at the breakfast table.

The prince had had a good night, and told his parents so. They, too, had slept soundly that night.

"It is lovely to sleep in my own bed again," said the prince. It wasn't long since he'd come back from his long journey.

At last the girl who had claimed to be a real princess came into the dining room. Her hair was untidy, and she looked tired. She had rings under her eyes. She slumped down on a chair, looking exhausted.

"Did you sleep well?" the queen asked kindly.

"Actually," the princess began, "I don't like telling you this, but as you are asking, I'd better do so. I wasn't able to sleep a wink last night. There was

something hard somewhere in my bed, some sort of stone. I am black and blue all over. It was really dreadful!"

The king smiled cheerfully at the queen, the queen smiled cheerfully at the prince, and the prince smiled cheerfully at the girl. Because the girl who claimed to be a princess, really was a princess. That had now been proved. "Because," the queen explained, "only a real princess has such a sensitive skin that she can't sleep if there is a pea underneath nine layers of mattresses."

The princess, the real princess, never left the palace again. Because as soon as the queen had finished speaking, the prince said to her: "Please, will you marry me, princess?"

"Yes, prince," said the princess, and a few days later they were married. They gave a huge wedding party that went on for three weeks, and everyone in the country was invited.

Later the prince became king, and the princess became queen. Every night they slept in a great big four-poster bed, as soft as silk, without a pea in it. But they always kept a pea nearby, because on the bedside table there was a beautiful glass dome on a gold stand. Inside it there was just one pea. It was the pea which had brought them so much happiness.

The flying trunk

Once upon a time there was a rich merchant, who had worked hard all his life, and had earned a lot of money. He lived in a beautiful house with a large garden. He only had one son, and when he felt that his life was nearly at an end, he called his son to his bed.

"My boy," he said, "your father will soon be dead, and you will be on your own. You will have all my money. There is a lot of it, but don't waste it, because then it will be gone. You must promise me faithfully that you will use that money very sensibly. It's not for nothing that I worked so hard all my life; I wanted to leave you a rich man!"

"I'll be careful, father," said his son.

"Then I can die in peace," said his father. He shut his eyes, and never opened them again. Now that his son had promised him that he would live sensibly and take care of his money, he could die in peace.

But the young man didn't do as his father had asked. He sold his father's house, and had a grand new one built on a high hill outside the town. There he went to live with seven servants, and gave a party once a week. No expense was spared at those parties. Anyone could eat and drink as much as they liked, and everyone was welcome. Of course, more and more people came just to see what it was like, and he thought that was fine. He paid for everything!

As you can imagine, your money doesn't last long if you live like that, and that is what happened in less than a year. The merchant's son had to sell his new house, and all he had left in the end was a pair of bedroom slippers and a dressing gown.

There were no more parties, large or small. He hadn't a penny left. Of course, he asked his friends for help. Hadn't he always invited them to his parties? And hadn't they eaten and drunk as much as they wanted there, every time? Yes, now they would surely help him, at least until he had found a job to earn some money for himself.

But no, his friends left him all alone. Now that he couldn't give any more parties, they didn't like him any more. There was just one who gave him

something – an old wooden trunk. The young man didn't know what to do with it, because he had nothing to put in it. Even his clothes were gone. The butcher and the baker, who were owed money for all the food at his parties, had taken his clothes instead.

He decided to use the trunk as a bed, but when you are used to a featherbed with down pillows, you don't find it easy to sleep in a wooden trunk. The merchant's son got a sore back from the hard wood, and bumps on his head from hitting it on the lid. He went on trying, and in the end began to get used to his strange bed.

Then one day a funny thing happened. The young man discovered that his trunk, when he locked it, could fly, even when the lid was still open. He only had to turn the key in the lock. What luck! Now he could just fly away in his trunk if anyone came wanting money from him. And that happened from time to time. As soon as he saw anyone in the distance who looked as if they wanted money, he went and sat in the trunk, turned the key, and flew up in the air. He thought that was terrific! He flew high above the town, he saw the houses and churches whiz past him very small, he was just like a bird.

Day and night he flew, over forests and over seas, over villages and over towns, and after some days he came to an unknown land. He wondered where he was. He had never seen a country like this. Everywhere he saw strange towers with domes on top, looking like onions. And everyone was walking about in dressing gowns and slippers, just like him.

The young man hid the trunk in a wood, and walked to the town he saw in the distance. He saw golden domes and tall towers. The square white houses with narrow doors and windows were built higgledy-piggledy against the hills.

At first he was afraid that the people would think he looked very strange. But no, everyone here was wearing dressing gowns and bedroom slippers, so that was all right.

And then he suddenly realized: he had seen those domes before, in pictures in a book. He was in Turkey, and people were not wearing dressing gowns and bedroom slippers, but robes and mules, because that's what they called them. And that was not surprising, because it was so hot that you would be much too hot in a woollen sweater.

The young man came to a large square in front of a beautiful palace with light blue decorations.

"Whose is that magnificent castle?" he asked a woman he met. She looked quite different from the girls in his own country.

"That is the castle of our princess, our king's daughter. She is locked up in a turret there, because a sorcerer has foretold that she will be made

unhappy by a man who wants to marry her. She is guarded day and night by very strong and brave guards, so that no one can reach her."

The young man felt sorry for the princess. All alone in a turret, that was dreadful! He decided to visit her. He could do that, because he had a flying trunk, so that he didn't have to pass the guards. He could just fly to the turret!

He went back to the wood to fetch his trunk, flew over the town and came to the castle. He flew in through an open window. The guards hadn't seen anything, because they were looking out straight in front of them, towards the road.

The young man climbed out of his trunk, and found he had landed in the right room, where the princess lay asleep on a bench. He crept silently towards her bed. How beautiful she was!

She was so beautiful that the young man could not stop himself touching her hand. She did not wake up. The young man gathered up all his courage, and kissed her on her soft cheek.

Now she woke up. Two big, dark eyes opened wide. What a shock she got!

"Oh," thought the young man, "what should I say?"

"Don't be afraid, I am... uh, I am a Turkish god," he stammered. What on

earth had he said now? What made him say that? He was only a very ordinary young man.

He had to say something, to explain his visit. The princess really believed he was a god, and asked him all sorts of questions. The young man told her all kinds of exciting stories about fairies and sorcerers. The girl fell head over heels in love with him, and she decided to marry him.

"It is late now," said the princess. "You must go away. But come back tomorrow, my parents will be here then. They will be very pleased that I am going to marry a god, and one who can tell such good stories! My father will certainly enjoy them, and I'm sure that he will like you. See you tomorrow!" "Goodbye," said the young man, and the princess gave him a splendid sabre, decorated with thousands of diamonds.

The young man got into his trunk again, turned the key, and flew away, back to the wood.

There he started to think up a story he could tell to the king and queen. That was difficult! He had already told all the stories he knew to the princess. Fortunately he was able to think up another thrilling story, and the next morning he flew back to the town in a happy mood.

First he sold the sabre, and bought some fine clothes, because he had to look tidy. It is difficult to tell a story to a king and queen when you are wearing a sloppy old dressing gown.

Wearing a silver robe he flew to the princess's palace in his magic trunk. There were the king and queen, and, of course, the princess, waiting for him.

"Greetings, young man," said the king. How grand his clothes were. He wore a gold robe, which was much larger than the young man's; that could hardly be otherwise, because the king was much fatter than he was. The young man presented himself to the king and queen, and began his story. Listen carefully, because this is the story he told them.

"In the kitchen of a fine castle, in a country far from here, the kitchen things were all quarrelling. Each thought it was the most valuable and the most expensive of all.

Particularly the matches cried loudly that they were made of expensive wood, and that you couldn't do much without matches.

'Who lights the fire?' they asked, 'the fire to heat the water? Without us the fireplace would be worthless. And you, inkpot, what use are you if people can't light the candles when it gets dark? Without us people

couldn't even use you, because they couldn't see what they were writing. Suddenly a servant came into the kitchen. He seized the matches, struck one, and let it burn before he held the flame to a candle.

`You see how useful we are?' said the other matches. But once the candle was alight, the servant blew the match out. There was nothing left but a little heap of ashes.

`Ha,' said all the other things in the kitchen, `you may be very useful, but at least we live longer!'

`It is better to live long with a little happiness than to have a very short life with a lot of happiness,' they thought. Perhaps they were right."

"What a wonderful story," cried the king. "You may become our son-in-law. Let us arrange a wedding feast at once!"

And they did. They chose a day for the ceremony, and the king had the master of ceremonies come over to see that everything would be very special.

The young man had a brilliant idea. He bought squibs, rockets, and all kinds of fireworks that would go off in the most magnificent colours, in balls and stars, and with long shining tails. That night he sat in his trunk,

turned the key, and flew over the town. There he let off his fireworks. They banged and sizzled splendidly. Everyone came out of their houses to watch the fireworks. The whole sky was lit up with red and yellow and green stripes.

"How splendid," they cried. "Now we know for certain that the princess is marrying a real god." They all thought that an ordinary man could not produce such a grand fireworks display.

The next day the young man went back to the town. He had hidden his trunk in the wood. What would people say? Would they have enjoyed it, he wondered.

"It was marvellous," a girl told him. A man ran after him, bowing constantly. "What brilliant fireworks," he said.

How pleased the young man was. He was a hero! He'd never have dreamed he might be a hero, when his money was all gone, and all he had left was a dressing gown and a pair of bedroom slippers.

Everyone in the palace was impressed, too.

"Wasn't that lovely, those fireworks!" said the princess to her father. "It was indeed," said the king. "Now I'm quite sure that we've found a good husband for you."

The young man went back to the wood to get himself ready for the wedding ceremony. He wanted to go shopping with his trunk, because he needed special clothes for the wedding. And he had to buy presents, too, because that was the proper thing to do.

He went cheerfully back to the wood, and saw how everyone bowed before him. The girls strewed flowers, and everybody tried to get into conversation with him, because they thought that he must be someone very special. Because of all that, it took a long time for the young man to get back to the wood. He started to look for his trunk, but what was this? He couldn't see the trunk in the place where he had hidden it. He took another look, and realized what had happened. All he could see was a little pile of ashes, so the trunk must have been burnt! A spark from the fireworks he had let off must have fallen inside, and his magnificent trunk was completely burnt up.

Now he couldn't fly back to the palace any more. He couldn't go through the gate, because there were the guards. And they certainly wouldn't recognize him or let him in.

He went on looking for his trunk for a long time, but he really knew that he was not going to find it, and he didn't.

Poor young man! He was just an ordinary young man again, who was not marrying any princess. He tried to earn some money telling fairy stories, but his stories weren't as amusing as they had been earlier. He stayed poor for the rest of his life.

And the princess? She waited, and waited, and always hoped that her prince would come back. But he never did come back, and the princess stayed lonely and all alone. She had a long life, but a very unhappy one, and so what had been foretold really happened.

The tin soldier

Once upon a time, a very long time ago, a little boy lived in an ordinary house in an ordinary town. It was his birthday. He was four years old.

"Have I got any presents?" he asked his mother.

"Of course," said his mother, and gave him two parcels.

The boy opened the first parcel. When he had torn off the paper, he found a small box.

When the boy opened the box, he found some soldiers, tin soldiers, all painted in pretty colours. There were twenty of them. They looked brave, and had red coats and dark blue trousers. They carried guns, and had red and white feathers in their caps.

"How lovely," said the little boy. He took them out of the box, one by one, and stood them up in line. One didn't quite fit in the set. He only had one leg. When this soldier had been made, there was hardly any tin left, so that there wasn't enough for his second leg. But he still looked brave and proud, and the boy thought he was the nicest of all twenty.

In the second parcel was a cardboard castle. It actually looked more like a large country house. It was white and had a red roof, and it stood in a large garden with big trees. There was a pond in the garden with two fine swans swimming in it. The house had lots of windows.

"Thank you, mother," cried the little boy, and gave her lots of kisses. He was very pleased with his presents.

When he had a closer look at the castle, he saw there was a girl at the gate. She was the most beautiful thing about the castle. She had tied her hair in plaits, and her eyes were as clear as the water in the pond. She looked sweet, because she had large kind eyes, and a dimple in her little paper chin, and she was always smiling.

She was a ballet dancer, and wore a transparent dress, tied with a ribbon round her waist. She was very slim and very beautiful. Her hands were held in an elegant pose, and she stood on tiptoe on one foot. Her other leg was raised high, and partly covered by her dress.

The little boy began to play with his new toys straightaway. He put the castle with the dancer on the floor, and set up the soldiers by it. They looked as if they belonged there. The dancer could see the soldiers, and the soldiers could look at the beautiful ballet dancer.

The girl thought the tin soldier with one leg very handsome. He kept looking at her, and thought her the most beautiful ballet dancer he had ever seen. That was hardly surprising, because he had never seen a ballet dancer before. Besides, he thought that she only had one leg, just like him. It looked like that from where he stood. He couldn't quite see that she had raised one leg right up. And because of her one leg, he thought her still more beautiful.

The soldier wanted to get to know the ballet dancer. He had to pluck up his courage a bit, but one night he decided to visit her. That meant he had to avoid being put away in the box by the little boy, because he couldn't get out of the box by himself.

So when the boy wasn't looking, he quietly hid behind the box. At night the boy put the soldiers away in the box, but he forgot the soldier with one leg. He couldn't see him straightaway, and besides, it was time to go to bed, so he couldn't really look for him.

There was nobody in the room at night except the toys. All the cuddly toys began to play, and so did the clown standing in the corner of the room. A teddy bear was playing leap-frog with a cuddly monkey, and two rabbits were playing hide and seek.

The paper ballet dancer did not move. She stayed just where she was, with one leg in the air, and standing on the other, on tiptoe.

The soldier was a bit shy. He daren't go right up to the ballet dancer, because he thought she was so beautiful that it made him nervous. He thought, "I'll wait a bit, and then go up to her. If I think about it a bit longer, I will feel more daring." The soldier thought so hard about the ballet dancer, that he completely failed to see what was going on round him. So he didn't see that an ugly little gnome was standing a little way off.

That gnome was very much in love with the dancer, and very much wanted to marry her. But he realized that he had to get the soldier out of the way first. He was much uglier than the soldier. So he knew that he wouldn't stand a chance if the tin soldier was anywhere near. The dancer would certainly choose the soldier. "Hi, soldier, come here," shouted the gnome, but the soldier didn't hear him, because he was looking so hard at the dancer that he couldn't hear or see anything else.

"Soldier, I called you!" the gnome tried again, but again the soldier didn't answer.

174

All through the night the tin soldier didn't dare go up to the ballet dancer. The next morning the little boy came into the playroom again.

"Oh," he said, "I forgot to put away one of my soldiers." He didn't want to put the tin soldier in the box, because it was his favourite soldier. So he put him on the window sill, in front of the open window. Then he could always look at his best soldier.

Perhaps it was the wind, but it may even have been that the gnome blew very hard. In any case, the tin soldier suddenly fell out of the window. He didn't fall down one or two floors, no, the soldier fell right down five floors, because the little boy's playroom was at the top of a very grand and very tall house.

The soldier fell, and fell, and saw the windows flying past. He looked down and saw he was already quite near the ground.

Bang! He had hit the ground. Not on his head, fortunately. He landed with his gun pointing down. It had a sharp point, so it stuck in the ground.

The little boy had seen the soldier fall out of the window, and ran straight down all the stairs, and outside to look for his soldier. But there were so many people in the street that he couldn't find him. In a little while he

gave up and went back home. He cried because his favourite soldier was lost.

Suddenly it began to rain, and it just poured down! Within a few minutes there were floods of water on the street. Everyone tried to get home as fast as they could.

Two boys who had nothing to do, and who weren't worried by the rain, saw the tin soldier sticking in the ground. That was fun, a tin soldier with only one leg! They pulled him out of the ground and made a paper boat from an old newspaper. Then they put the soldier in the boat and put the boat in a stream of water.

The boat swung from side to side, but went faster and faster. It wasn't long before the soldier saw a drain in the distance, and the boat was heading straight for it!

"Help!" shouted the soldier, but there was no one to hear him, and the boat was already disappearing down the drain.

Underground the boat simply kept on sailing along. It was cold and dark in the tunnel the water flowed through, and the soldier couldn't see anything. He thought he would soon be dead. For how could a soldier in a paper boat survive a boat trip down a sewer? And even worse, rats and mice live in sewers, and they lived in this sewer, too. The rats and mice in this sewer didn't approve of a trespasser in such a strange boat, so they tried to hit the soldier with their long strong tails. The soldier grew more and more afraid and didn't open his eyes any more. Luckily the water ran very fast, so that the boat was able to get past the rats just in time. The soldier drew a deep breath, and dared to look round him again.

Suddenly he saw a small light in the distance. It was only a tiny point, as big as a pin-head, but still, it was light. The soldier began to feel more hopeful. The boat floated on and on, and the speck of light grew larger and larger.

Soon the soldier realized what the light was: it was the outfall of the sewer. Good, if he got back to daylight again, he would surely be discovered.

But suddenly the tin soldier had a shock, and not a small one. Where the tunnel came out was another great big grey rat with ghastly green eyes looking straight at him. The boat floated closer and closer, and the rat grabbed at it with its paws.

Fortunately the current was still too strong, and the boat floated quickly past the rat. The soldier heaved a sigh of relief. At least he had not been eaten by that dirty rat. He didn't know what would happen next, but that last rat seemed to him about the worst thing that could happen to him.

The tunnel came out in a little stream, and the soldier floated onwards in his boat. The stream ran past fields and meadows. That was a pretty sight.

The soldier couldn't get enough of it. The cows grazing there looked at him with their big eyes, because they didn't see a tin soldier floating past in a boat every day.

Suddenly the boat began to sway. What was happening? Then the soldier saw what it was. The boat was travelling straight towards a waterfall! The soldier tried to steer it to one side, but that didn't work. It wouldn't be long now before the boat would drop over the waterfall!

Closer and closer it came to the waterfall, and... yes, over it went! As it went right over the waterfall with the soldier in it, the water swirled all over the boat. The soldier fell to the bottom. He had lost the boat.

"This is the end," he thought, "now I'm sinking and then I'll be dead." But that didn't happen, because a great big fish swam round near the waterfall, and it saw the soldier sinking. It thought that he would make a tasty snack, and swallowed him down in one gulp.

The soldier couldn't see anything now he was in the belly of the fish. It was quite dark all round him. He couldn't hear anything either.

The fish swam a little further and saw another tasty mouthful. It swam up to it and swallowed it. But this time it wasn't a little fish, nor was it a tin

soldier. It was a hook, and the hook was fixed to a fishing rod, and a fisherman was holding the rod tight.

The fish had been caught. It was pulled out of the water and thrown into a large bucket.

There the fish stayed for a while. Only when the bucket was completely full of fish, was it put on a cart, and the cart set off. Bump, bump, it went. The cart rode along the road past the meadows and the woods till it came to the town. The fish were taken straight to the market, where they were laid out on a stall.

"I'll buy that fish," cried a woman, pointing to the fish with the soldier in it. She paid the stallholder and took the fish away. At home she opened up the fish to clean it. Her son was standing by watching.

"Hey, there's my tin soldier," shouted the boy. It was the same boy who had got the soldier for his birthday. What a coincidence! The boy danced around.

"I've got my soldier back, I've got my soldier back," he shouted happily.

The ballet dancer looked pleased, too. She was very happy to have her friend back, because she liked the tin soldier very much.

The ugly little gnome was not pleased at all. No, he was very angry indeed! He had done his best to keep the soldier out of the way of the ballet dancer. Now that hadn't worked.

The gnome had to think up a new trick, because as long as the soldier was around, the dancer just wouldn't want to know him.

That night, when the little boy was asleep, the gnome put on his jester's cap and went into his room. He whispered quietly in his ear: "Throw your tin soldier in the fire tomorrow. He is a very mean soldier, and if you don't look out, he will shoot all the other soldiers dead. A tin soldier with only one leg is dangerous!"

When the little boy woke up the next morning, he still remembered what he had dreamed. He opened his box of soldiers and took out the soldier with one leg. After hesitating for a moment, he threw the soldier in the fire. The little figure melted in the heat of the flames. Only the soldier's head was left.

Suddenly the door opened, and the boy's mother came in. As the door had opened, a draught blew through the room. The curtains flapped in the window, and the paper castle was knocked over and blown into the fire.

"Oh, no! My castle!" shouted the little boy, and wanted to pull it out of the fire.

"Don't!" said his mother. "You'll burn your fingers."

The little ballet dancer, who had been blown into the fire with the castle, landed just beside the tin soldier. So at last the tin soldier and the ballet dancer were together. Unfortunately not for long, because the fire soon reached the ballet dancer. The flames turned the paper dancer into a little heap of ash.

When there was nothing left to burn, the fire soon came to an end – just like this story.

The snow queen

nce upon a time there was an evil spirit. Nobody knew if he was a ghost, a troll, or perhaps a wicked magician, but that he was bad everyone knew. And not just bad, but malicious, and thoroughly mean. Listen to what he did.

He made a great big mirror, which made everything look ugly, and ugly things even uglier. His plan was to take that mirror up to heaven, and then fool all the angels by making them look at themselves in the mirror. Then all those beautiful angels would see ugly reflections of themselves. He hoped that they would be horrified.

The evil spirit set off on his journey to heaven. Slowly he flew upwards with his mirror, higher and higher in the blue sky. But he hadn't got very high yet when suddenly a storm broke. It wasn't really blowing that hard, but it shook the spirit. He clutched his mirror even tighter, but it was too late: it slipped from his hands and fell to earth. There it shattered into thousands of separate pieces.

If one of those tiny pieces got into someone's eye, they saw the worst side of everything from that moment. It was even worse if a sliver penetrated someone's heart. Their heart froze as cold as ice, and the sliver made sure that the person affected became really mean. If anyone got one of those slivers in their heart, they didn't even want to see their best friends any more.

In a narrow street in a small town two houses stood next to each other. Both of them had balconies. There were pots of herbs on them, and in each pot there was also a rosebush. Long shoots came out of the rosebushes, which wound past the windows and joined the bushes to each other. They made a sort of archway, green in winter, and red in summer when the roses were in bloom. In one house lived a girl called Gerda, and in the other house lived a boy. His name was Kay. The children were very fond of each other and often used to visit each other.

One lovely summer's day Gerda was sitting on a little bench under the rosebush. Kay came over to sit with her, close to his friend. They spent happy hours together. There was a lovely scent of roses. The two children told each other stories, asked each other riddles, and tended their gardens.

In winter Gerda's parents went away, and she stayed with her grandmother. Kay and Gerda couldn't sit on their balconies any more then, and Kay had to go up three flights of stairs to get to Gerda's grandmother's house.

Outside it was snowing big flakes. Gerda's grandmother had a story about them. "Those are the white bees," she said. "Their queen is there, too; she is the biggest. She is the only one who can fly above the big dark clouds. Sometimes she looks through the windows and then she draws frost flowers on them with her frozen breath. But be careful, because occasionally she steals children!"

At home Kay pressed his face against the cold pane. A great big snowflake whirled down on the edge of the balcony. The snowflake grew bigger and bigger, until it turned into a woman with a white veil of frost flowers. Kay stepped back a pace, because he was very shaken. The woman beckoned him with her sparkling eyes. Kay didn't go any nearer, because he was too frightened to move. The snow queen, because that's who she was, suddenly disappeared.

It was a very long winter. It snowed almost every day, and it stayed very cold, but after that long winter came spring, and at last it was summer again. The roses were in bloom again.

One day, when the children were outside on their balcony looking at a picture book, Kay said to Gerda: "Ow! I've got something in my eye. Ouch! And now there's something in my tummy. You must have done it! It's because you are wobbling the bench. This is a very stupid book, anyway. And aren't those roses ugly. And you are ugly, too!"

Kay had been hit by two slivers of the evil spirit's magic mirror. Now he saw the worst side of everything, and he was always angry and dissatisfied.

For the next few months Gerda was very unhappy, because Kay didn't say anything nice any more. He was always cross with Gerda, and didn't enjoy anything at all. Kay had changed, and Gerda didn't know why. It made her very unhappy, because it wasn't nice to be with her best friend any more. Actually Kay did nothing except be nasty to her.

Winter came again. It snowed every day and was very cold again. Kay was a little more cheerful. He thought snowflakes and frost flowers were beautiful. That was because his cold heart was well suited to the ice and snow. The sliver of the magic mirror had given Kay a heart like a block of ice.

One day he took his sled to the market-place. Lots of children met there to be pulled along by the farm carts. They did that every year in the town where Kay and Gerda lived; the farmers came to the big market-place so that they could pull the children on their sleds. They brought their carts, and sometimes big horse-sleighs as well. Of course, they only did this when it was cold enough, as it was that winter.

Kay didn't have to wait long. A big horse-sleigh stopped in front of his little sled. Kay couldn't see the driver's face, because he was wearing a thick white fur coat. Kay quickly tied his sled to the sleigh.

The horse-sleigh set off and slid straight out of the gates of the town, into the forest. How fast that horse-sleigh went! Kay thought it was wonderful. He was cold all right, but he'd never gone as fast as this in his little sled. But he was still a bit worried, because it went on so long. So long, in fact,

that he didn't know where he was any more.

"Stop! Let me go!" he called to the driver of the horse-sleigh, but he got no answer. Of course, he couldn't hear him, with the wind blowing so hard. It was several hours before the sleigh stopped. The driver got down and took off his hat. But what was this? It wasn't a man at all, it was a woman. It was the snow queen! That was the second time Kay saw her.

"Come and sit with me under the bearskin," she said to Kay.

Kay stood and looked at her, without moving. He thought she was very beautiful, but he didn't dare go up to her. Then the snow queen put her arms round him, and Kay forgot where he came from, he forgot Gerda, and the roses. He forgot his town, his school, the other children, and his home. He forgot everything. He could think of nothing except the snow queen.

The horse-sleigh started up again. It was dark now, but the snow queen didn't stop. The sleigh even seemed to be going faster and faster. Kay wasn't cold any more, because he had the snow queen's bearskin to keep him warm.

Gerda was very unhappy when Kay didn't come back. Even if he hadn't been nice to her lately, she missed him terribly. Every day she went to the big market-place to look for him, but of course, she couldn't find him. Could he have been drowned, she wondered. She couldn't think of anything else. That made her even more unhappy; she wasn't sure that her friend had drowned, but she couldn't think what else might have happened to him!

The new year came, winter passed, and it grew warmer. One spring morning Gerda went to sit on the river bank. She was hoping she might see Kay. She didn't know how that could happen, but she still hoped. She sat by the river for days on end, and kept staring at the blue water. She saw all sorts of things: fishes playing in the water, frogs jumping onto lily pads, but she didn't see Kay.

But what was that in the water, a little further on? She went closer. It was a little boat that had never been there before. Should she get in, she wondered. She hoped the boat might take her to Kay. She didn't know why, but she decided to get into the boat.

She put one foot in. The boat started moving immediately. Quickly she jumped right in, otherwise she would have fallen in the water. But now the boat was moving still faster. That was odd, because there was absolutely no current, and hardly any wind.

Gerda tried to get back to the bank, but whether she tried with her hands or with a stick, she was unsuccessful.

After some time she grew frightened. "Help! Help!", she cried, but no one heard her.

Luckily an island in the river appeared in the distance. Gerda hoped fervently that the boat would float to it. The island came nearer and nearer. It looked wonderful. Tall palm trees were swaying in the sun, and everywhere Gerda could see flowers: red ones, blue ones, yellow ones, and any other colours you can think of. She couldn't see what sort of flowers they were yet, but it wouldn't take long, because the boat headed straight for the island.

It took another quarter of an hour, but then the boat bumped against the shore. Gerda climbed out and was pleased to be back on dry land. The palm trees looked magnificent, and all those flowers! She walked between two trees to a small field, full of the loveliest flowers she had ever seen. She didn't know their names, but they were beautiful, that was certain. Suddenly she saw a little house on the far side of the field. It was built of red bricks; that blended well with the red flowers, so that it looked as if there was another large red flower at the far end of the field.

"At last," thought Gerda, "someone must live there. I will be back with people again," and she ran as fast as she could to the little house. On the way she trampled on a few flowers, but that didn't bother her. She knocked on the door.

"May I come in?" she called.

She heard footsteps behind the door, and the door was opened with a loud squeak. There stood an old woman on the doormat.

"Of course, come in," she said. "I can use a little company, I get terribly bored here. And those flowers aren't much company either."

When they were in the old lady's room Gerda told her all about Kay. The old woman nodded, but said nothing.

"And then I just had to jump into the boat, else I would have fallen in the water," Gerda explained. The old woman interrupted her. "Ah, my child, and your hair is all tangled. We must do something about that."

"Why should we suddenly have to do that?" thought Gerda. Funny that the old woman should be worried about her hair.

She didn't have much time to think about it, because here came the old woman carrying a large hair brush. Gerda wanted to say "no", because somewhere in her head a small voice told her that this was a special brush, but it was already too late.

The old woman was brushing her hair, and every time the brush went through her hair, Gerda forgot something.

By the time the old woman had got her hair tidy, Gerda had forgotten everything, just like Kay with the snow queen. Kay, her school and all her friends, her grandmother, and the house with the roses – she had forgotten them all.

"Where am I?" she asked.

"I don't know. You just turned up here," said the old woman, and sent Gerda away.

What was Gerda to do, all alone on the island? After walking about for an hour she had lost the little house, and couldn't find it again. She didn't meet a soul.

For days she wandered through the woods, eating berries and roots, because she couldn't catch any animals and she didn't want to anyway. There wasn't much left of her clothes either, and she became more and more desperate. "Where am I?" she sometimes shouted loudly, but that didn't help.

She searched and searched until she came to a small field. She had never been there before. There was something red in the distance, and she walked up to it. When she got nearer she saw that it was a big red rose. Suddenly Gerda remembered the rosebushes between her friend Kay's house and hers. She remembered the day Kay had disappeared, and at last she knew what had happened when she stepped into the boat and floated down to the island.

She had to look for Kay! But where? She didn't know. Gerda ran across the fields, and soon discovered that it wasn't an island at all where she had been roaming about, because it never came to an end. She kept

coming to new fields and new woods, and she kept getting lost again. She slept in the open air, and had to eat berries, because she couldn't find anything else she could eat.

So time passed. It was getting colder again, because summer was almost over. Now it was very difficult for Gerda to find anything to eat, and she hoped that something would happen soon. It would have to be soon, because it was nearly winter already.

Nothing did happen, and then it was winter. It was just as cold as the year before, and soon it began to snow every day.

Shivering from cold and hunger, one day Gerda met a raven, sitting on the branch of a tree. It was a friendly bird, and felt sorry for Gerda.

"Caw, caw, what are you doing alone in the snow?" croaked the raven. Gerda didn't understand it, but she caught the word "alone" all right. She told the raven everything that had happened, and asked him if he had perhaps seen Kay.

The raven nodded and said: "Perhaps. My sweetheart is a royal raven, and often visits the king's palace. She told me that the princess has married a young man. A poor young man, but handsome and clever."

"That must be him," Gerda cried. "I'm sure of it! Tell me what he looks like." The raven described the prince. It fitted, it must be Kay.

"It's him, it's him," cried Gerda. "Please, take me to him."

"All right," said the raven, "follow me. My sweetheart knows a secret door. We'll just slip into the royal bedroom. Then you'll know for sure if our new prince is your former playmate. And then you can ask him if he'll go back with you."

Gerda was so happy she forgot how cold she was. She was going to see Kay again! She followed the raven through fields and woods, and came to a place she'd never been before.

A few hours later they saw the palace. It was a magnificent building, with high towers, and surrounded by a moat. The raven took her to a secret entrance. Gerda crept into a cold tunnel and crawled along, till she saw a light.

She crawled out through the hole, and found she had come out in a fireplace. The prince and princess lay asleep in the next room.

Gerda tiptoed in. She pushed aside the lace curtain and looked at the prince and princess. But the prince wasn't Kay. Gerda began to cry. The princess woke up. "Who are you?" asked the princess.

By now the prince had woken up, too.

Gerda told her whole story. She hoped that the prince and princess wouldn't be angry because she had got into the palace by a secret entrance, and fortunately they weren't; they were sorry for her.

They had food and warm clothes brought for Gerda. They were very nice to her and thanked the raven for bringing Gerda to them. Gerda became a little impatient, because she wanted to go on with her quest. She wanted to find Kay, because she still missed him.

"I want to go on looking for Kay," she said at breakfast the next day. "Fine," said the prince. "We'll get a coach for you." The coach the prince and princess sent her off in wasn't just any coach, it was a magnificent golden coach drawn by beautiful and fast horses. Then the prince gave her a basket full of food.

"Thank you, and goodbye!" said Gerda, when the coach was ready. The prince and princess waved, and the coach set off, into the forest.

They didn't get far, because there were robbers in the forest. They soon spotted the golden coach, and a band of them ambushed it. They stopped the coach. A girl robber dragged Gerda out of the coach.

The leader of the band was a woman, too. She looked at Gerda hungrily. And hungry she was! She wanted to eat Gerda. Then the girl robber, who had dragged Gerda out of the coach, came along. She said: "I want her, she's my prisoner! You can't eat her!"

Gerda was taken away to the robbers' lair. She was terribly afraid. There were cobwebs hanging in the cracks of the walls. She was in a big dungeon, with a tiny window high up in one wall which let some light in. It wasn't much, so it was always rather dark, even in the daytime when the sun was shining.

Gerda was not alone. A big reindeer with large soft eyes was tied up to one wall, and there were two wood-pigeons in a cage hanging from the ceiling.

The girl robber said: "Tell me your story, or I'll hang you from the ceiling, too."

What a nasty girl, thought Gerda, but she told her whole story over again. When she told her about the big white sleigh, the pigeons went completely wild. They flew in utter excitement against the bars of the cage. One of them said: "Coo, coo, we have seen little Kay, he got into the snow queen's horse-sleigh. The horse-sleigh flew over our wood on its way to Lapland, where the snow queen has her ice palace."

The reindeer knew about Lapland as well. "Lapland is so beautiful," he sighed, "I wish I could go back there and play in the snow again every day, as I used to."

The girl robber felt sorry for her. It may not have lasted long, but it was long enough. "All right," she said to the reindeer, "I'll give you your freedom. You can take Gerda to her friend."

Gerda thanked her and jumped on the reindeer's back. The girl robber opened the door of the dungeon, and the two of them, Gerda and the reindeer, ran off into the cold forest.

"To Lapland," cried Gerda.

The reindeer ran through great forests and white plains. He was so happy that he ran on through day and night. He and Gerda hadn't much to eat, but that didn't worry them. They were both so happy to be free again. The reindeer ran as fast as he could, he wanted to get back to Lapland so much.

Weeks after they had set off, they came to a little house. It was very cold, because the closer they got to Lapland, the colder it became.

An old woman opened the door. "Come in," she said kindly. She was a wise woman, the reindeer knew that. He said: "Wise woman, I have brought you this little girl. Help her, and give her enough power to break the spell over her friend."

"She doesn't need me," answered the wise woman. "Because she is still so young, she has all the power in the world. She is so good that nothing and no one can oppose her. The castle is quite near. The queen is away at the moment. Take her to her friend quickly."

Gerda went out again and wanted to get back on the reindeer. She was colder than ever. But that was not surprising because she'd left her coat behind in the little house. She walked back to it and went inside.

As she picked up her coat, she saw a boy in the room. At first she didn't recognize him, but when she looked again, she saw that it could only be one boy in the whole world. It was Kay.

Tears sprang to Gerda's eyes, she was so happy, and she flew into Kay's arms.

Kay began to cry, too, and that made the piece of magic mirror jump out of his heart. And all the tears soon washed the sliver out of his eye, too. They were both very happy to have found each other again. And because the slivers of magic mirror had gone from Kay's heart and his eyes, he loved Gerda again, even more than before.

So, just like they used to, Kay and Gerda could read together, and tell each other stories, and ask riddles on their balcony under the rosebush. But the snow queen and the evil spirit of the magic mirror were so cross with each other, because Kay had escaped, that they began a terrible quarrel. And they are still quarrelling every day, even now!

The soldier and the tinderbox

Once upon a time there was a soldier who came back from the wars to his own village. He had been fighting long and hard, but now he was pleased that the war was over, and that he could do something else. He looked round contentedly. The birds were singing in the trees, the sun shone, and the world looked very cheerful.

One, two! One, two! With his kitbag and his sabre he walked along the road, feeling happy. He looked in all directions, listened to the birds, and admired the flowers along the way, when suddenly an old woman appeared in front of him.

The soldier had a bit of a shock. The old woman was so ugly that she must be a witch. And you have to be careful with witches, everyone knows that, and so did the soldier. But the old woman smiled at him in a friendly way, and she did not look as if she meant him any harm.

"Hello, soldier," she said, "you have a beautiful sabre, but your pockets look empty. I don't suppose you are a rich man?"

"No," answered the soldier. "I have just come back from the wars, and I haven't earned much money. And all I had, I have spent. But that doesn't matter, because I am young and strong, and I can work. I am sure I can earn myself a living in the big wide world."

The old woman smiled again. "Of course you can, you look bright enough to me. But I know something better. I can help you make a lot of money! Just look over there, in the distance, at that old tree. That tree is quite hollow, and it goes so far down that when you go inside it, you finish up in a passage. If I put a rope round your waist, then you can climb into the hollow, and call me when you want me to pull you up again."

"But why should I want to go down that tree?" asked the young man. He did not really feel like climbing inside a tree. What on earth is there to do in a hollow tree?

"To get money, soldier. As much as you like," said the witch. "When I let you down, you'll end up in a passage with hundreds of lights. In that passage you will see three doors. They are not locked, and there is a room behind every door. In the first room you will see a large chest, with a dog sitting on it. He may scare you, because his eyes are as big as saucers. But don't be frightened. Just put my apron on the floor, and the dog will sit on that. Then you can open the chest, and help yourself to as many copper coins as you want."

The soldier began to feel he might go to that tree after all, climb into it, and go down. Would he really be able to help himself to as much money as he wanted? He began to think of all the things he could buy with it. Nice food, beautiful clothes, and perhaps a little house. And all the girls in the town would queue up for him! The soldier began to feel very cheerful! But the old woman hadn't finished talking yet. "If you prefer silver, you have to open the second door," she said. "There is another chest, with a dog on top of it with even larger eyes than the dog in the first room. His eyes are as large as plates! That will frighten you even more, but if you put my apron down for him, he will sit on it obediently. Then you can take away as many silver coins as you like."

The soldier was really beginning to enjoy himself. He knew that silver was worth a lot more than copper, and he began to wonder what he could buy with all that.

But the witch had not finished yet. "There is still a third room," she went on. "Don't be scared: there is a dog there with eyes as big as wheels. He will look at you very fiercely, but if you put my apron down in front of him, he will sit on it and not do anything to you, just like the other two. If you open the chest in that room, you won't believe your eyes, because that

198

chest is full of gold coins! You can take as many of them as you can carry."

"That sounds all right to me," said the soldier. Gold was worth even more than silver. What a lot he could buy with that! He thought so hard about everything he would be able to do and buy, that his eyes almost turned into gold coins. He'd never have believed that one day he would be a very rich man!

"What do I have to give in exchange for all that money?" he asked the old woman. He thought it was rather odd that the witch simply wanted to make him a rich man. If it was as easy as she said, she surely would have gone for the money herself? No, there was something wrong there. But the old woman didn't want any money at all, she wanted something completely different.

"I'll be satisfied if you bring me the tinderbox," she said. "My mother left it behind when she last went down the hollow tree. You can make a fire with a tinderbox, and I want to light my stove with it, because the weather is turning quite cold!"

"All right, give me your apron and knot the rope round my waist, then I'll

let myself down the tree," said the soldier, who was now very keen to get started.

Everything happened as the witch told him. The old woman tied the rope round the soldier's waist and let him down. He found himself in the passage the witch had told him about. What a lot of lights there were!
He looked round and saw three doors. Slowly the soldier walked to the first door. Did he really dare open it? Would the witch be right, and would there really be a chest with copper coins in it? He opened the door a little, and slipped inside. The door squeaked terribly.
He nearly jumped out of his skin with fright once he was inside and looked round him. Although the witch had told him about the dog, this beast looked so dangerous that the soldier almost ran away. But when he remembered how much money he could earn, he suddenly did not feel frightened any more, and put the witch's apron down in front of the dog. And yes, the dog came down from the chest, and sat quietly on the apron. The soldier walked to the chest and opened it. The witch had been right, the chest was full of coins. There wasn't room for even one more. The soldier didn't wait, and filled his pockets with the money. And the dog sat obediently on the apron, looked at the soldier with his big eyes, but did nothing, nothing at all.
The same thing happened in the second room. This dog looked even more dangerous than the first one, with his eyes as big as plates, but the soldier thought of all the silver he could earn, and put the apron down on the floor. The dog sat on the apron, and the soldier filled his pockets with silver from the chest.

When he was back in the passage, he wasn't quite sure if he dared try the third door. He didn't mind so much about eyes as big as saucers or plates, but eyes as big as wheels, that was different.

In the end he did open the door; nothing is that dangerous if you can earn as much gold as you like.

The dog looked terrifying. Not only were his eyes as big as wheels, but they looked so mad and mean that the soldier's hair stood straight on end. The soldier put the witch's apron on the floor and… the dog sat down on it and didn't do a thing. He kept looking straight at the soldier with those terrible eyes, but that was all.

The soldier walked to the chest. Would it be true what the witch had said, he wondered. And yes, it was really true. The chest was full of gold coins. Large coins and small ones, thick coins and thin ones; the chest was filled to the brim.

Greedily the soldier grabbed as much money as he could manage, and took so much that he almost couldn't carry it. He even filled his boots with gold. When he had also found the tinderbox lying in a corner, he called to the witch that she should pull him up again.

When the soldier was back at the top, he asked the witch: "What are you going to do with that tinderbox?"

"That's nothing to do with you, soldier. Be content with all that money!" answered the witch, while she eyed the tinderbox greedily.

"But I want that tinderbox myself! Give it to me, or I'll do you an injury!" said the soldier, who was curious to find out what the tinderbox could do. It had to be good for something, otherwise the witch wouldn't have given him so much money to fetch it. With all the money he had found down in the hollow tree, you could buy a thousand tinderboxes, even ten thousand. No, there was something odd about that tinderbox, and the soldier got so angry, he killed the witch.

With his pockets full of gold, and with the tinderbox in his hand, he walked to the nearest town. There he asked for a room at the best inn.

And that he got, the finest room in the whole inn. There was a four-poster bed in it, and the taps on the washbasin were made of gold. How rich he was now! And scores of girls wanted to marry him! But the soldier didn't want to marry any of them, even if he enjoyed their company when they came to see him. Then he could show off how rich he was. Yes, the soldier enjoyed himself no end.

One day the innkeeper told him about the princess, the king's only daughter. She was very beautiful, he said, as beautiful as the white swan in the king's garden. "I would like to meet her," said the soldier.

"You won't be able to," said the innkeeper. "The princess lives in a castle so well guarded that no one can enter it: the walls are high, it is surrounded by a moat, and three hundred dogs make sure that nobody

can get near the gate. And if anyone should get as far as the gate, there are thirty soldiers on guard making sure that no one can get in. The king is guarding the princess so well, because it has been foretold that she will marry a common soldier, and the king does not want that!"

The soldier was rather disappointed. He so much wanted to go to the princess; he wanted to see for himself if she was really so very beautiful. Oh well, too bad, he wouldn't be able to.

The soldier might have been rich, but he spent so much money that one day he hadn't any left. That meant, of course, that he couldn't stay in his expensive room in the inn, because that cost a lot of money, and money he hadn't got.

He had to move to a dirty little attic room. It smelt, and it was also very cold, because there was no fire. His friends didn't come to see him any more, and the soldier was very lonely. One dark night he wanted to light a candle.

Fortunately he still had the witch's tinderbox. He tried to strike a light. The first two times he struck it, nothing happened. The third time he didn't get

a spark, but suddenly one of the three dogs with large eyes stood in front of him.

"Tell me what I must do, master, and I will do as you say," said the dog. "The other two dogs will do the same."

The soldier was thrilled to bits! The tinderbox was not just a tinderbox, it was a magic tinderbox. Now he could just wish for anything he liked.

"Money!" he shouted. "Bring me silver and gold, as much as you can find."

The dog went away, and came back a moment later with a whole load of gold and silver. So much, that the soldier could almost swim in it. He was rich again!

The soldier bought a beautiful house. That was easy now, because he only had to strike a light with his tinderbox and the dog would go off to get another load of gold. Soon his friends came to find him again, and the girls came to see if he would marry them.

Now he had everything he wanted. At least, almost everything. There was one thing he did not have and would like to have: the princess the innkeeper had told him about. The soldier couldn't help himself, he had fallen head over heels in love with her, even if he had never seen her.

One night he could stand it no longer. He told one of the dogs to go and fetch her. The dog had no trouble getting past the dogs and the soldiers guarding the castle, and brought the girl away from it. She was asleep on the dog's back, and still asleep when she arrived at the soldier's house.

"How sweet and beautiful she looks," the soldier said to himself, and he kissed the princess. Then the dog took her back to the castle.

The next day the king, the queen, and the princess were having breakfast. "I had such an odd dream," said the princess. "I dreamed that I was carried to a beautiful house in the town on the back of a dog. Then I was kissed by a handsome young man."

The king didn't really believe it was a dream. The princess had never had such a dream before. Just to be sure he ordered his servants to keep a sharp eye on her for the next few nights.

The next night the soldier again struck his tinderbox, and told the dog to fetch the princess again. Once more it worked. The dog was so expert that he managed to bring the princess to the soldier's house without anyone noticing. The king's servants could not follow him.

When the princess told them the next morning that she'd had the same

dream again, the queen was very angry, and had a little bag of rice sewn into her daughter's dress. She made a small hole in the bag.

That night the dog came to fetch the princess again. He couldn't know, of course, that grains of rice kept trickling out of the little bag, so that they left a trail all the way from the castle to the soldier's house.

The next day the king's soldiers came to arrest the young soldier.

"He must be hanged!" said the king. The queen agreed, so they decided that the soldier should hang the next day.

A whole crowd of people turned up at the market-place, where the soldier was to be executed. They all found that sort of thing very exciting.

Every prisoner who is about to hang is allowed one last wish before he is executed. The soldier could have one, too.

"May I smoke a last pipe, before you hang me?" he asked the king.

"Of course," said the king.

A pipe needs lighting, so the soldier got out his tinderbox. He struck it three times.

And again no spark came from the tinderbox, but the three dogs with the big eyes came! That was a clever trick on the part of the soldier!

The dogs ran to the king and queen and bit them to death.

"Long live the soldier!" cheered the people, who hated their fat king and queen. The king had always had fine palaces built with money belonging to the people. And everyone had to work hard, while the king sat in his palace, doing nothing all day. No, the people were quite pleased that there was an end to that situation. Now at least they would have a king who would care for the country.

"Long live our new king!" shouted the people. "Hooray!"

The soldier was crowned king, and married the princess. They had three beautiful children, who didn't have to be afraid of anything, because they had three dogs with large eyes to protect them. And the dogs did that, because they thought the three children of the soldier and the princess were the nicest little masters they had ever had.

The snowman

There was once a snowman. He was made up of a great big snowball for his body and a smaller one for his head. An old hat was placed on top. He had a carrot for a nose and two pieces of coal for black eyes. The boys from the neighbourhood had made him, and that had been a lot of work. It took them hours to roll the great balls of snow. In the beginning it had gone quite easily but once the ball was really big it became more difficult. The ball kept breaking in half when it was just nearly big enough. At last it finally worked. The boys put the balls on top of one another and then packed yet more snow on to the snowman to make him even stronger. And there he stood.

At first, the snowman enjoyed it, with all the children around him. However, after a time the children were called indoors by their mothers. They had to eat, do their chores, and go to bed. The snowman remained behind alone.

"I think it's wonderful when it's a little bit chilly", said the snowman. "Then it creaks inside me and that is such a nice feeling. I don't like that peeping Tom over there, though, not at all." He meant the sun which was just then busy setting.

"That peeping Tom only ever sits there watching me! It's driving me crazy. Look, here he comes again!"

The moon had risen. The snowman thought that the sun and the moon were the same thing. He could not stand either of them.

"How I'd like to go and play on the ice together with the boys who made me..." he sighed.

The old guard dog had overheard him. He said: "That peeping Tom, as you call it, is called the sun. He'll get you running all right! But watch out, because then you'll get smaller and smaller."

"I don't understand that", said the snowman. "He starts disappearing before my very eyes and then after a while he starts to appear on the other side. I think it's ridiculous."

"You'll see. If it gets warmer tomorrow, the sun will get you running for sure." The snowman still did not understand any of it, but he did not enquire any further.

The next day, a girl and her fiancé were walking by the snowman. The night had been freezing cold and that day was even colder than the day before. The whole world seemed to be made of ice: a thick layer of white frost lay all around. It was a beautiful sight. The snowman, too, was sparkling in the cold.

"What a lovely snowman", said the girl.

"It won't be there in a few weeks time", said her fiancé. "The thaw will soon be starting."

The girl gave the snowman's hat a pat and then both she and the young man walked on, chatting together merrily all the while.

"Who are they?" the snowman asked the guard dog.

"Oh, those are friends of mine", said the dog. "The girl gave me a bone once. She's my master's daughter. She'll soon be taking the young man's hand in marriage."

The snowman had never heard of marriage. "What's that then?" he asked.

"Marriage is something very important", related the guard dog. "A young man and woman then go and live together in a kennel. From then on she makes sure that he gets his bones to eat on time. But don't you worry about any of that, that's all much too complicated for you."

The snowman looked all around him but in the empty street there was not all that much to be seen. All the children had gone to school. The snowman took a look through the window closest to him. There, in the room within, he saw something rather strange. It was a sort of closet made of metal with a flame inside. He asked the guard dog what that thing might be.

"That is the stove. That's what I always lie in front of at night. The stove is

so nice and warm! She's my best friend."

"Is she at all like me?" asked the snowman.

"Like you? No, she's not a bit like you! You're cold and she's warm."

The snowman looked at the stove. She seemed so big and strong and stood so sturdily on her four feet. This was once again somewhat different to a snowman or a guard dog. Furthermore, she had such a lovely red tummy. It kept changing colour. One moment it was red and the next it changed into orange or even yellow with little blue points of light. The colours kept on moving without staying still for one moment. That was something else that was different, compared to a chubby old snowman who was not able to move himself at all!

"I have a strange feeling inside me", said the snowman. "I'd so much like to go in there and lean against the stove. It seems to me that that would be the nicest thing in the world. Do you think that would be possible? Would your stove's master let me in?"

The dog laughed and said: "Of course not, silly snowman! You wouldn't even get to the door because you can't walk. And even if you could, you certainly wouldn't be let in. Who wants a dirty, wet and, on top of

everything, cold, old snowman in his room? And even if they did let you in, it would mean the very end of you."

"The very end of me?" asked the snowman, shocked.

"Yes, you'd melt. That stove is so warm that nothing would be left of you. All your snow would change into water."

"But I do so want to go to the stove!" said the snowman.

It had become a big problem for him. He longed terribly for the stove.

"You are a strange snowman", said the dog. "What kind of snowman is it that falls in love with a stove?" What he said was true because the snowman was terribly in love. He could think of nothing else other than the beautiful stove which was so near to him, over there in that room. So near and yet the snowman could not get to her. The snowman became very sorrowful and his spirits were not improved even when the children came out of school and straight away started to play with him again.

The following day, the weather changed. It became warmer and the sun began to shine. It was the beginning of spring. The snowman quickly began to lose weight. One by one, his eyes and nose fell to the ground.

Then, his head rolled off. Even his body was melting. He became ever smaller, until there was nothing left of him anymore. Only a stick remained on the spot where the snowman had stood. That stick had been stuck inside the snowman's body to make him stronger.

"Now I understand why the snowman felt so in love with the stove", said the guard dog. "The snowman had firewood in his body, and what firewood wants most of all is to lie burning inside a stove!"

The children could play outside later in the evenings again because it stayed light for longer. The stove went out because it was warm enough as it was. And there was no-one who longed for the snow or a snowman anymore.

The housewife and the pixie

There was once a young woman who had read so many books and so much poetry that she had become very learned. She knew all the world's cities, she spoke seven languages, and she could recite the most difficult books from memory. She knew so much, in fact, that she wrote her own poems on the most difficult of subjects.

Furthermore, she was a very good speaker. She knew more than enough difficult words and was more than happy to use them. She could have been a church minister, or a doctor, or a lawyer. Being mayoress was also something that she might have liked to do.

However, the young woman in this story was not a mayoress, neither was she a church minister – she was a housewife. That came about because she was married to a gardener who spent the whole day in the garden. He trimmed the bushes, planted seeds in the ground, and watered the flowers and plants. He did not have any time for housekeeping, so his wife had to do everything. She had to keep the house clean, do the dishes, cook the food, make the beds – in short, everything that a housewife has

to do. That does not mean that she never again wrote any poems. No, she had never been able to stop doing that. She wrote whole notebooks full. This she mostly did in the evenings once she had done all the housework. One morning, she decided that the world was at its best when she was dressed in her Sunday clothes.

"How funny", she said to herself, "I'll write a poem about it", and off she went to sit behind her desk to write a poem. She forgot all about the pan of milk which stood boiling on the stove. This kept happening more and more often and the gardener did not like it at all.

The schoolmaster, Mr. Kisserup, came to call on her one Sunday. He was the housewife's cousin. The housewife had just had him listen to her poem about her Sunday clothes.

"Enchanting", said Mr. Kisserup. "Madam, you are very talented. I think, madam, that you write truly wonderful poems. Madam, you must become a famous writer."

He always said 'madam' to his cousin. He felt that it suited his position and sounded gentlemanly. A schoolmaster was polite with everyone, even

with his own family.

The gardener, who had heard the poem again for the hundredth time, said: "What nonsense. Do me a favour and tell her to stop writing all these poems. Let her get on a bit more with the pans and a bit less with the pens. Otherwise, I'll be eating burnt potatoes every day, and I've had enough of burnt potatoes because of all these poems thank you very much." He was, of course, quite right. She had burnt the dinner again only the night before.

"I will not let myself get annoyed", said the housewife, but she clearly found that very difficult indeed. "Everyone who listens to you must think that you never have anything else to think about except food. And that's not the way it is because flowers are the most important thing to you." She was terribly cross because she felt that the gardener should also be saying how good her poems were.

They were so good, in fact, that it was not at all so awful that the potatoes were burnt as a result. Yes, that is what the housewife thought but the gardener did not agree one bit. He did not like poems so very much.

The gardener thought his garden was the best thing that there was.

"You're quite right, flowers are the most important thing in the whole world", he said to his wife. "But I've just remembered that I still have to give the plants some water. I'll just pop into the garden for a moment."
He got up and walked out of the room, off to his garden.
The schoolmaster talked a while longer with the housewife. He went on about the Sunday clothes poem and they had a whole conversation on the subject.
The housewife and the schoolmaster were not the only ones who were talking in the house. In the kitchen, a little pixie sat talking with the black cat. The pixie had a red pointed cap, a beard, and a moustache. He looked just like pixies always do, in fact.
The pixie did not like the housewife all that much. In particular, the housewife did not believe that he existed. That was terribly stupid of her since the pixie really did exist. It was also very strange for her not to know because she must have read something about pixies once, mustn't she? She had read so much! In that case she should have known that pixies like him were real.
As well as that, he was the housewife's house pixie. He lived in her house

218

and saw everything that happened. Yet still the housewife would not believe that he really existed. The pixie felt that this should change. The housewife should give him something tasty to eat for once, a nice glass of milk, or some wild strawberries, or a piece of cheese, for example. That is never what he did get, of course. Not even at Christmas.

The pixie found it all terribly annoying. His father and his grandfather had both been given tasty things to eat from the housewives who then lived in the house. They had been given a saucer of porridge every day and at Christmas a piece of Christmas pudding, and those housewives had not been half so well-educated as this one!

Because he was cross with the housewife, the pixie helped the cat as often as he could by lifting off the milk pan's lid. The cat was then able to drink as much milk as he wanted, and the pixie was always then given a sip.

"She thinks that I'm a figment of the imagination; she doesn't think that I really exist", said the pixie to himself. "That is completely untrue since here I am, and if I'm here then I'm here. That's what she has to believe too." He became more and more cross until at last he was so cross with the

housewife that he decided to start pestering her as much as he could.
He blew on the fire in the stove. The flames went so high that the porridge
was over-cooked and burnt.

"So, we've got that one out of the way again", said the pixie contentedly.
"Now I'm going to go and make a few holes in the gardener's socks. Then
the housewife can just go and sew them back up again. This time there
won't be any poems, just socks. That'll do her the world of good."

The cat meowed: "And what about me?"

The pixie said: "For you there is a whole jug of cream in the larder. I've left
the door open. Have what you like, but save a little bit for me."

However, the pixie was not nearly finished yet. "I'm going off to the
schoolmaster's house. Then, I'm going to put eggs in his slippers, one in
each slipper. Yesterday I pestered the guard dog. It woke up the whole
neighbourhood."

"I'm going to eat up my cream", said the cat and he went off to the larder.
The pixie went into the living room and listened to what the housewife
and the schoolmaster were talking to one another about. The pixie made
sure that they could not see him.

"Mr. Kisserup", said the housewife, "I wish you to read something that I have never yet allowed anyone to see. It is a collection of my finest poems. It is called 'The Thoughts of a Lady of Respectability', on which I have worked long and hard. I am, actually, rather proud of it as I have written all those poems by myself."

From a secret drawer in the bookcase she took a little notebook and handed it to the schoolmaster. He opened it, full of curiosity.

"It all looks very serious", said the schoolmaster.

"Yes, it is", said the housewife, and she named a few of the poems. "Voices in the Silence, The Hopes of a Housewife ..."

"Wonderful", said schoolmaster Kisserup. "Wonderful", he said again.

"An amusing poem has also been included. That is because I am also sometimes cheerful. Perhaps I will become a real poetess some day. As you see, sir, I cannot stop my pen from flowing. I must write poetry, I simply must!"

The schoolmaster was fascinated to find out which poem it could be. He did not need to ask, as the housewife carried on talking.

"The poem is called Little Pixie", she said. "Naturally you are familiar, sir, with the superstition that every house has its own pixie? I believe it is as follows: if I am the house of poetry, then the little pixie must live inside. He is then master over me, and has me in his power."

The schoolmaster nodded. This was quite true, he felt, even if what the housewife had said was terribly complicated.

"But speak of this to no one as it is a secret!" said the housewife. The schoolmaster promised at once that he would never do such a thing.

"Would you like, sir, to read the poem out loud?" the housewife asked the schoolmaster. "Then I can hear for myself how lovely it is."

Kisserup began to read aloud. "Little pixie", he began.

The pixie on the other side of the door pricked up his ears. What was this? It was about him! He listened even harder and heard the whole poem. How he was master over the housewife, that he lived in her house of poetry, and lots more besides. He did not understand very much of it but he did hear how nice it all was.

In fact, the poem was not about anything at all and was not intended to be so very nice, but the pixie was not all that clever.

He became happier and happier. He stood up straight as a poker which made him a whole two inches taller. He began to feel much more distinguished and thought himself to be a very important pixie indeed.

"How unfair I have been to the housewife", he said. "How could I ever have let the milk boil over? How could I ever have made holes in the gardener's socks? How could I ever have given cream to the cat?" He vowed to himself that he would never pester the housewife ever again.

"I'll take a little cream myself now and then if I feel like it, but the cat gets nothing anymore."

The cat had seen it all and said to himself: "How like a person that pixie has become! The mistress has only to say something nice and the pixie changes like a weather vane. That mistress of mine is awfully clever!"

The housewife was not at all so very clever, the pixie only seemed very much like a person, and people are, often enough, stupid.

That was the story of the housewife and the pixie. If you do not understand it then just ask someone to explain it to you. Whatever you do, do not bother asking the housewife or the pixie as they do not understand any of it themselves …

The Sandman

All children like a good story. They like to listen to someone telling them one, particularly if it is funny or exciting. And the best storyteller of all is the Sandman.

The Sandman only tells his stories in the evening, when the children are so tired that they go to sleep. As soon as they are in their beds the Sandman comes in, wearing his silk slippers, so that nobody can hear him. Then he sprinkles sand in the children's eyes. That is no ordinary sand, but sleeping sand. He always carries it around with him, by the sackful. Sleeping sand is very fine, and you can hardly see it. But it is a little bit itchy, so the children start rubbing

their eyes straightaway. They have trouble keeping them open. Then the Sandman blows gently at their necks, and they fall asleep.

Only then does the Sandman start on his story. The children are asleep and are very quiet. That is nice for someone who is telling a story, because it is rather a nuisance when people keep on saying "and then?", and "go on", when you are in the middle of one.

The Sandman has two books with him. One is full of lovely pictures, and he tells a story to go with them. He can do it so well, that the children think they actually see the pictures, even if they are fast asleep. In the other book is nothing at all. That book is for children who have been naughty. They don't dream of beautiful stories, but they are restless all night, because they can't go to sleep. The Sandman only tells his stories to good children.

Once upon a time there was a little boy whose name was Peter. Peter was never really naughty, so the Sandman came to tell him a story every night. One week he kept him particularly busy, more than ever before. I will tell you what happened to the Sandman and Peter that week.

Monday

Tonight it was rather difficult to get Peter into bed, because he didn't want to go to sleep one little bit. The Sandman had to sprinkle sand into his eyes three times, and had to keep blowing at Peter's neck. But at last he managed it, and Peter lay in his bed and slept.

The Sandman said: "First we'll make things look a little prettier here!" and at that moment all the plants in the flower-pots began to grow very fast. Peter always watered his plants himself every day, because he liked them. But even if he watered them every day, they grew very slowly. Now they were suddenly as big as trees! There was some tasty fruit on them, too. The Sandman gave Peter an apple from a large tree, which ten minutes ago was only a little plant. The apple was delicious.

Suddenly the Sandman heard crying. It came from the drawer where Peter kept his schoolbooks and exercise books. The Sandman went to open the drawer. The crying came from an exercise book. There was a sum in it, which had been worked out wrong. The pen lying next to it was trying to correct the sum. That didn't work, because it needed a human hand to put it right. There also seemed to be something wrong with the book in which Peter had done his writing exercises. The pages flipped backwards and forwards, from back to front.

"The letters are too slanted," complained the book, and that was true. All

224

the letters Peter had written were slanting too much, and floated above the lines.

"If you lot don't stand up straight, you'll all get a good hiding," said the Sandman to the letters.

"Oh no, don't," cried the letters.

"Come on, then, stand straight!" said the Sandman. "It isn't as difficult as you think!" And sure enough, one by one the letters stretched themselves out and went to stand tidily on the lines. In a little while the whole book looked neat.

"Now the sum," said the Sandman. He tapped against the sum book and in a flash the right answer appeared.

"That's how it should be," said the Sandman.

The next morning when Peter woke, he looked in his sum book. What a bad mistake that was in the book! And when he opened his exercise book he really got a shock. All his letters were higgledy piggledy again! Had he been dreaming it all?

Tuesday

The Sandman had great plans for tonight. That's why he came a little earlier than usual. He sprinkled sleeping sand into Peter's eyes, blew at

his neck... and Peter was soon so tired that he went to sleep.

"How quiet it is here," said the Sandman. He looked round him, and at once everything in the room started to talk. The bed, the chair, the table, the wastepaper basket. There was a painting in a golden frame above the table where Peter always sat to do his homework. It showed a landscape with trees and flowers. In the distance a river flowed down to the sea, and further along you could see the turrets of a castle.

When the Sandman looked at the painting, it began to come to life. The river really began to flow, and the trees swayed in the wind.

The Sandman picked Peter up, and carried him to the painting. He put him in it. Peter's legs disappeared in the long grass. He walked further into the picture. The sun shone on his fair hair, and the birds were singing. Peter walked towards the river, and saw a boat tied up there. He stepped into it. The water splashed against the boat. In the distance six beautiful swans came swimming along. With their beaks they picked up the rope that was fixed to the front of the little boat, and pulled it up the river. It sailed past a large wood.

Peter could hear the birds sing about the witches and wizards who lived in the wood, and he saw how the rabbits hurried into their rabbit holes when the boat came near. It was a lovely trip. When they left the wood behind them, there were beautiful gardens on both sides of the river. Peter saw little princesses in them. Their faces were like the girls in his class.

When the little boat sailed past the castle, Peter saw the soldiers guarding it. They saw Peter, and saluted him, because Peter had now also become a knight. He wore a helmet, and had a long sword that glittered in the sun. After the castle came the town, and in one of the houses Peter saw his nanny standing in front of the window. She had always looked after Peter, but she had left because she was getting married. Peter was very sad about that, because he loved her very much.

The nanny was singing a lovely song:

I often think of you, my dear,
My memories are very clear.
'Twas difficult to go away,
New duties meant I could not stay.
I'm married now, in my new life
I'm first and foremost now a wife,
And soon I'll be a mother, too;
I'll call him Peter just like you!

And with those words in his ears, Peter lay down in his bed again, and slept until his mother woke him.

Wednesday

Tonight Peter went to bed in good time. The Sandman had seen to that. Peter was sound asleep, but suddenly he heard it pouring with rain outside. The rain beat against the windows, and the wind howled in the chimney. Then the Sandman opened the window. The rain flooded into the room. Everything got wet.

Outside a large ship was waiting for them.

"Shall we go sailing, Peter?" asked the Sandman, and he took Peter by the hand. How it happened he didn't precisely know, but suddenly Peter stood on the deck of the ship in his best clothes. And it was an interesting ship, because everywhere there were large cages full of hens and turkeys. Peter wasn't sure why all those hens were there, but it was fun, all that clucking around him. The ship set sail at once, and sailed out of the street, round the church, and out of the town. Once they had left the houses behind, the Sandman and Peter could only see the wide sea, and

there wasn't another ship in sight. There were waves on the sea, and the wind was blowing hard.

High above them Peter saw a flight of storks, returning from Africa because spring had come. The birds had spent the winter in Africa. There, in the far south, it is much warmer than here. Now it was spring again they had come back. They'd had a long journey, and were tired after their long flight.

One of the storks was so tired, that he couldn't go on. He was the youngest of them all. He had no strength left to fly any further. He fluttered down, and thought he was going to land in the water, but his feet touched the mast of the ship. Just in time he curbed his speed, and landed on the deck. For a little while he just stood looking round, until a sailor picked him up, and put him in a chicken run with the chickens and turkeys.

The chickens looked at him in surprise.

"What is that strange bird doing in our run?" they said to each other. The stork stood in a corner. He didn't quite know what to say.

"Where do you come from?" said a fat turkey.

"From Africa," said the stork.

"And you expect us to believe that?" said the turkey.

The chickens and turkeys began to shout at the stork and call him names.

"Go away, you ugly thinlegs! You don't belong here!" they called.

Peter felt sorry for the stork. He went to the run and opened the door. The stork stepped outside at once. He was not a bit frightened of Peter, and he felt a little rested by now. Peter gave him a handful of food, so that he would recover his strength even more. The stork flew away to join his family again.

"Why did he let him go?" asked the chicken. "Why not us?"

"Because storks don't taste so nice," said the turkey. "And that is nothing to be proud of!"

When Peter woke up the next morning he thought: "I'll ask if we can have chicken soup today."

Thursday

"Don't be frightened," said the Sandman to Peter, when he was fast asleep in his bed again, "but today I will introduce you to a mouse." He held a little grey mouse in his hand.

"Peep," said the mouse. "I've come to invite you to the wedding of two little mice from the wardrobe. They love each other so much, they want to get married tonight. Are you coming?"

"How can I do that?" said Peter. "I would never be able to crawl through a mousehole! Surely I am much too big for that?"

"Don't fuss, I'll see to it," said the Sandman. He'd hardly finished talking, when Peter began to shrink, and to shrink, until he was about the size of his own big toe!

"You'd better borrow your toy general's uniform. Then you will be suitably

dressed for the party," said the Sandman. Fortunately the toy general didn't mind lending his uniform to Peter at all. He understood very well that Peter could not go to a wedding in his pyjamas.

Peter was soon dressed. There he stood, in the general's uniform. He looked splendid, and very distinguished. Just right for a wedding.
"Get into your mother's thimble, and I will take you to the party," said the little grey mouse. Peter got in, and off they went.
It was quite a long journey to the wardrobe. It took a while before they arrived.
Then Peter saw the mousehole, and the thimble drove inside.
They found themselves in a long passage; on both sides they saw little girl mice, who were waiting for the arrival of the principal guest. Behind them were the gentlemen, who had decked themselves out as well as they could.
At the end of the passage was a hall. In the middle stood the bride and bridegroom. The bride was wearing a beautiful dress. It was a long gown, green and blue, and embroidered with little sprigs of flowers. Peter saw at

once that it was made of a piece of his mother's new curtains.

It became more and more crowded in the hall, until the mouse minister came in. He called out: "No one else may come in, the ceremony is about to start!"

Everyone clapped. The mouse minister made a speech, and he finished by saying: "And now I declare you mouse and wife." Everyone started to dance. The mice were married! "Good luck to them!" cheered all the other mice, and Peter cheered heartily with them.

The party went on all night. It was already getting light when the bridegroom called out that the party was over.

Peter climbed into the thimble again, and was taken back to his own room. The Sandman used his magic to turn him back to the same size he was before.

And the toy general? Poor man, he'd been rather cold all night in his underwear!

Friday

"Do you know how many people come and ask me for a visit?" the Sandman asked Peter. It was night, and Peter had only just got into bed.

"Particularly people who have done something wrong come complaining to me that they can't sleep a wink. They are very fed up that they can't sleep, even if they are very tired. They don't tell that there are trolls sitting on the edge of their beds every night. Those trolls are really their bad deeds, and they don't want to be forgotten."

"What are trolls?" asked Peter.

"Trolls are small, scary, evil spirits," answered the Sandman. Peter shivered. Trolls, no, he would rather not have them sitting on the edge of his bed every night. He could think of things he'd rather have!

"I would love to go to another wedding," said Peter.

"That can be arranged, because two of your sister's dolls are getting married." And the Sandman told him about Olaf and Karen, two dolls who had spent so much time together on a shelf that they had decided to get married.

Peter looked around him. He saw a candle on the table, and his tin soldiers standing around it. They had spruced themselves up beautifully for the party.

The bride and bridegroom were sitting at the table, and all the other dolls were standing around them.

The Sandman was wearing a black suit. He made a solemn speech, and conducted the marriage ceremony. The ball-pen had written a song for the occasion, and everyone in the room started to sing it. The dolls, the tin soldiers, but also the cupboard, the table and the chairs joined in the singing. Peter sang loudest of all. This is the song they sang:

We're singing a happy song
About Olaf who's brave and strong;
He's married sweet Karen today,
Together they'll always stay.
And all of us here in this room
Wish good luck to the bride and the groom.

Nearly everyone had brought a present. Nothing to eat, of course, because they didn't need to eat anything. No, they were given lots of nice things for the new house, where they were going to live.
"Where do you want to go for our honeymoon?" Olaf asked Karen.
The bride didn't know. She had never been outside. She didn't know what there was to see in the world. So they consulted the swallow and the hen. The swallow had travelled far and wide, and told them about far-away countries, where it was warm and the sun always shone.

The hen didn't quite agree: "They don't have such lovely cabbages there as we have here!"

"But it is always lovely and warm there. Here it is always raining!"

"We're used to that," said the hen, "I don't even notice it any more."

"I agree with the hen," said Karen. "I rather like it here. We will just go for a stroll round the garden, and if it gets cold, we'll put our scarves on."

"All right," said Olaf, and he kissed his bride.

Saturday

Peter had gone to bed early again. He had done that on purpose, because he liked the Sandman coming to see him. Peter wanted to hear him tell a story tonight.

So many things had happened this week, but the Sandman hadn't really told him a good story yet. He told the Sandman that.

"Not a hope, I haven't got the time," said the Sandman. "I still have a lot more to do!" He opened his book, and showed Peter a picture. "What do you think of this?" he asked.

In the picture were two Chinese men, leaning on the parapet of a crooked

little bridge, and looking into the water.

"Don't forget that it is Sunday tomorrow. I have a lot to do still. I have to go to the church to see if the church goblins have polished the bells properly. But that is not the most tiring job; I also have to pick all the stars out of the sky and polish them. And I have to number them, because if I hang them back in the wrong place, then all the ships everywhere will sail in the wrong direction. All the captains always look at the stars to see which way they should go."

There was a sound as if someone was clearing his throat from the portrait on the wall above Peter's bed. It was a portrait of Peter's grandfather.

He said: "You listen to me, Sandman. I have been watching what you were doing with my grandson, and what you told him, but now you've gone too far. Picking stars out of the sky! You can't pick stars at all! They are enormous planets, just like the earth, but usually even bigger."

The Sandman was quick to answer. "You are old, but I am older still, and wisdom comes with the years. I was around at the time of the ancient Greeks and Romans. They used to call me the god of dreams. I was always welcome and visited everyone. Emperors, but slaves, too. Now it is the same: I visit kings and queens, and just now I am with your grandson, Peter. I get on very well with him. I would be pleased if you didn't spoil it for me."

The Sandman was cross. He tucked his books under his arm, and ran out of the room. He didn't even say goodbye to Peter.

"Good gracious!" said grandfather. "Can't I even say what I think to my

own grandson, in my own house, and on my own wall?" And then Peter woke up. The sun was shining again, and Peter had to hurry, or else he would be late for Sunday school.

Sunday
"Here I am again!" said the Sandman, as soon as he came into the room. He saw that Peter had turned his grandfather's portrait round. Now grandfather couldn't interrupt the Sandman, because he was looking into the wall.
"Will you tell me a story now?" asked Peter. "Just an ordinary good story about a princess and a wicked stepmother, or a magician and a witch?"
"No," said the Sandman. "Nothing of the sort! I want to show you something today. Or rather, show you somebody. You see, I have a brother who is also called the Sandman. And sometimes they call him Death. He is not nearly as scary as people think. In picture books he looks like a skeleton, but in real life he wears a beautiful velvet cloak. He tells stories, too, just like me, but he only ever comes once. He takes someone with him on his horse, and then he tells them a story. He only knows two,

one lovely story, and the other a horrid one. Look, there he goes by on his horse!"

They looked out of the window. There they saw someone flash by on a horse. He kept on picking people up. He simply plucked them away, and put them in front of him or behind him on his horse.

The Sandman went on: "If someone sits in front on the horse, he will hear the beautiful story. If he sits behind my brother, then he will have to listen to the horrid story. If you have been good, you can sit in front; if you have a bad record he will put you behind him on his horse."

"I don't think I need to worry about that Sandman," said Peter.

"It would be quite unnecessary," agreed the Sandman, "as long as you make sure that you have a clean record."

"At least that is a sensible thing to say," said grandfather. He had heard everything, in spite of his portrait having been turned round. "What a pity the Sandman doesn't like to listen to anyone else!"

When Peter woke up the next morning, his grandfather's portrait was hanging the right way round again, and it looked as if grandfather smiled at him, and winked.

That is the story of the Sandman. If you behave well, he may take you out somewhere next week! Or perhaps he will tell you a story, about magicians and far-away countries, or about good children and naughty ones.

Big Claus and Little Claus

Once upon a time there were two people called Claus: Little Claus and Big Claus. Their names had nothing to do with how tall they were, because they were both as tall as each other, and just as strong. One was rich and the other poor, that was the difference. Big Claus had four horses, Little Claus only one. They lived in the same village, which was why it was easier to call one of them Big Claus and the other Little Claus, otherwise people would get them confused.

Little Claus and Big Claus both had a piece of land that had to be ploughed. In the old days, before tractors were invented, this had to be done with a plough drawn by horses. Little Claus and Big Claus had a very good solution for that: from Monday to Saturday Little Claus ploughed Big Claus's land with all their horses, and on Sunday he could borrow Big

Claus's four horses, and he ploughed his own land from dawn to dusk with all five.

"Gee up, my horses, hurry, there's work to be done!" Little Claus cheerfully urged his horses on. It was Sunday, so the work in Big Claus's fields was finished for the week, and now Little Claus could get started on his own field.

The church bells rang, because it was Sunday, and everyone was going to church. The whole village came past in their Sunday best. They looked at Little Claus, and they thought: "What's he doing, working on Sunday?" They didn't think much of that, because Sunday was a day of rest!

"Come on, my horses! To work!" shouted Little Claus, happily. "Tear the ground open, then everything can soon grow properly again."

Big Claus went to church every Sunday, and he came past in his black suit, carrying his Bible under his arm.

"Faster, my horses!" called Little Claus, just when Big Claus came past.

"What are you saying, Little Claus?" asked Big Claus. "You mustn't say that, because only one of those horses is yours!"

"I won't do it again," promised Little Claus.

The next Sunday Little Claus was busy ploughing again. "Gee up, my good animals, let's start!" he called, again just as Big Claus came past.

"I warn you not to talk to my horses as if they were yours!" said Big Claus crossly.

"I am sorry," said Little Claus. "I really won't do it again. I will try and remember, but it is very difficult. It is just a habit of mine."

Big Claus walked away, and Little Claus went on working. But soon he needed to encourage the horses again and called: "Gee up, my dear horses!"

Big Claus had hidden behind a tree, because he wanted to see if Little Claus would keep his promise. With his face red with anger he came from behind the tree, and cried: "This is the last time! This is the end!" and he picked up a large piece of wood and killed Little Claus's one and only horse dead with one blow.

"How could you do that?" called Little Claus. "Now I haven't got a horse at all."

He was very sad, because he loved his horse. It had always helped him so well in his work, and had always been gentle. And what would Little Claus do now, without any horse at all? How could he plough his field? But Little Claus didn't have much time to waste on being sad. He had to earn money, because otherwise he would have nothing to eat. So he stripped the hide from the dead horse, and hung it up to dry in the wind. When the

hide was properly dry, he folded it, put it in a bag, and went into town to sell it there.

Because the road to town went a long way round a large wood, he decided to walk straight through the wood. That would save a lot of time. But it would have been better if Little Claus hadn't done that. The trees were so close together and it was so dark that he soon lost his way. And then it began to rain, too! First gently, but soon it rained harder, until the rain came down in buckets.

The wind blew hard. The branches swayed backwards and forwards, and Little Claus was so very cold! First he tried to shelter under a fir-tree, but even there he didn't stay dry for long. Quite soon he started walking again, because he was wet already. At last he found his way out, but it was too late by then to go all the way to the town.

What luck, at last he saw a light in the distance. It was a farm. Little Claus walked towards the house, and knocked on the door.

"May I come in?" he asked the farmer's wife, who opened the door.

"No," said the farmer's wife, "my husband won't allow me to let anyone into the house when I'm alone, and he's away tonight."

"Then perhaps you won't mind if I sleep in the haystack?" asked Little Claus. The farmer's wife thought for a moment, and then she said: "That's all right. But I won't let you come inside the house," and she banged the door shut.

Little Claus walked through the yard, and between the haystack and the house he found a little shed.

"That looks rather more comfortable to sleep in," he thought, and opened the door. It was dark inside, but he saw light coming through a crack in the wall. He looked a bit closer, and saw that he could see right into the living room of the house.

He saw at once that the farmer's wife had been lying. She was not alone at all. She was sitting at the table with the verger, and they were eating the most lovely food you can imagine: succulent meat, a crusty loaf, a large cake for dessert, and some bottles of wine, of which quite a few were already empty.

Then Little Claus heard a wagon drive over the gravel. The farmer was coming home! And the farmer hated vergers, and this verger in particular. This verger worst of all!

The verger and the farmer's wife knew that, too, of course. The farmer had often made that clear to them. That was why they were now enjoying a day together, while the farmer was away. But they couldn't know, of course, that the farmer would come home early because of the rain, so they had a frightful shock when they heard the wheels of the wagon crunch over the gravel.

"Quickly, into the oat bin!" cried the farmer's wife, and she opened the lid of the bin. The verger climbed in.

"Oh dear! What shall I do with all the food?" said the farmer's wife to herself. She picked everything up and looked around her. "The oven," she thought, "I'll put everything into the oven!" And so she did. She put the wine behind the door in another room.

Meanwhile the farmer had put his wagon away and started towards the house. But suddenly he heard something in the shed. What was it? Had one of the dogs been shut up in the shed? Or a fox, who couldn't get out again? He'd better have a look. He went in and at once saw Little Claus.

"What are you doing here?" asked the farmer.

"Your wife wouldn't let me in the house. So I thought I might sleep here."

"That sounds rather uncomfortable," said the farmer. "Come inside, then you can have a bed to sleep in." Little Claus and the farmer went into the farmhouse.

When they were indoors, Little Claus explained that he was on his way to town, but because of the bad weather he had got lost in the woods. Meanwhile the farmer's wife put a bowlful of porridge in front of them. The farmer started eating the porridge hungrily, but Claus didn't really like porridge. He kept thinking of all that lovely food the farmer's wife had hidden in the oven, which he'd seen through the crack in the wall.

He had pushed the sack with the horse's hide he was trying to sell under the table, and by accident he bumped it with his foot. The dry hide inside rustled.

Little Claus said: "Be quiet."

He kicked the sack again, and again the hide crackled.

"What have you got in that sack?" the farmer asked.

"My hobgoblin," answered Claus. "I always have to take him with me, because he gets so unhappy if he is left all by himself at home. Now he is saying we are silly to eat porridge when the oven is crammed full of gorgeous food."

"What's that?" shouted the farmer. He went straight to the oven and opened the door, and there were all the delicious dishes his wife had put there.

The farmer thought that Little Claus's goblin had put all that lovely food there, and naturally the farmer's wife didn't say that she had hidden it. She took the porridge bowls away and put the party food on the table instead.

Claus kicked against the sack again, and again the horse's hide crackled.

"Does he know something else?" asked the farmer.

"Yes, he wants to know why we are not having wine with our meal. The bottles are in the corner behind the door."

The farmer's wife went to fetch the wine. They had quite a happy party in the farmer's house. The wine made the farmer very merry. He told Little Claus that he could consider himself very lucky to have such a good hobgoblin.

"But," he said, "how I'd like to have just such a goblin as yours!"

They spent the whole evening at the table, eating, and drinking wine. Suddenly the farmer said: "Could your hobgoblin conjure up the devil?"

"Of course he can," said Little Claus. He kicked against the sack.

"My goblin," he went on, "will do what you ask, but you will have to be careful. The devil will look like a verger."

"Like a verger?" The farmer shuddered. "Then he must be really horrid. I can't stand vergers! But I would like to see the devil."

"I'll ask," said Claus. He kicked the sack, and when it crackled he listened carefully.

Then he said to the farmer: "If you open the oat bin in the corner of the

room you will see the devil. But be careful, don't let him out."

"Give me a hand to hold the lid," said the farmer, while he walked to the bin. Little Claus held on to the lid, so that it would only open a little way. The farmer looked into the bin, and saw the verger's face. He closed the lid again with a bang. "I saw him!" he shouted. "And he looks exactly like our verger. Horrible!"

The farmer needed another quick glass of wine. He said: "Sell me your goblin. I don't mind how much money you want."

"I can't do that," said Little Claus. "He is my hobgoblin. I can't sell him."

"But I really do want him," said the farmer. "I will give you anything you want, and I promise to take great care of him. He may always sit by the fire, and I will take him with me when I go away, just like you do."

The farmer went on begging for a while, and at last Little Claus said: "All right, you may have my goblin for a bucketful of gold coins. But that bucket will have to be full, mind!"

The farmer bought the goblin. But he said to Little Claus: "You will have to take away the oat bin with the devil, because I don't want to keep the devil in my house. Just imagine what horrible things might happen! No, I definitely want to get rid of that devil."

Little Claus gave the farmer the sack with the horse's hide and was given a bucketful of gold coins, the bin containing the verger, and a wheelbarrow to take everything home.

The next morning he put the bin and the bag of money on the wheelbarrow, and left to go back to his own village. After an hour's walk he got to a river.

Right in the middle of the bridge he stopped, and said, loud enough for the verger to hear: "I'm really quite mad to go on lugging this bin all the way. I will throw it in the water. That way we'll be rid of the devil, too."

He got hold of the handles, but the verger inside the bin called out: "I'm not the devil! I am the verger! Let me out, and I'll give you a bucketful of gold coins!"

"That's a good idea," said Little Claus. He let the verger out of the bin, and together they went to the verger's house. The verger gave him a bucketful of gold coins, and said: "Get off with you! You've had your bucketful of

gold coins. Now leave me in peace!" And he slammed the door shut.

Claus was very pleased with himself. He had two bucketfuls of gold coins, nearly a whole wheelbarrow full. He said to himself: "That's a good price for a horse's hide!"

When he got back home, he tipped the wheelbarrow over in the middle of the living room. The coins rolled in all directions and made the whole room glitter. "How surprised Big Claus will be when he hears how rich I am," he said to himself.

He sent a small boy to Big Claus to borrow a corn measure. That would make it easier to count all his money.

Big Claus was curious to know why Little Claus wanted a corn measure. "What does he want to count with it?" he fretted. Suddenly he knew how he could find out what Little Claus wanted to count. At the bottom of the corn measure he smeared a little bit of tar, so that things would stick to it. He gave the little boy the corn measure to take to Little Claus. A little while later, when Big Claus got it back again, he saw some gleaming coins at the bottom of the corn measure.

"Money," muttered Big Claus. "Little Claus has money! How on earth did he get that?"

He walked across to Little Claus's cottage and went inside. "How did you get all that money?" he asked.

"Oh, that's nothing special," said Little Claus. "I sold my horse's hide and got two bucketfuls of gold coins for it."

"That's a good price!" said Big Claus. He went home, picked up a big piece of wood, killed all his four horses, stripped off the hides, and hung them up to dry.

"Now I can earn eight bucketfuls of gold coins!" he said.

The next morning he took the hides to the first leather merchant he met. "I'm not giving more than one gold coin for those hides," said the man. And he was not the only one who said that; all the tanners and leather merchants Big Claus tried gave the same answer. No one wanted to pay him much money for them.

"You are all thieves and cheats!" shouted Big Claus furiously. "I must have two buckets of gold coins each for them!" The tanners got so angry that they kicked him out of town.

"I'll get even with Little Claus," said Big Claus to himself. "I'll murder him!"

Meanwhile in Little Claus's cottage something sad had happened. His grandma, who lived with him, had suddenly died in the night. Little Claus was very sad, even if he had quarrelled with her nearly every day. He put her in his own bed, and sat down to sleep in his chair, hoping he might bring back some life into her that way.

That night Big Claus crept into Little Claus's cottage. He walked across to the bed and hit the old woman on the head.

He thought he had murdered Little Claus.

"There," said Big Claus, "he won't bother me again."

Little Claus had kept very quiet, but he had seen what happened. "Just as well my grandmother had just died, otherwise it would have been me," he said.

The next morning he went to work. He borrowed a horse and wagon from his neighbour, dressed his grandmother in her best clothes, and put her on the back seat. Then he dressed himself in his best suit. When the first cock began to crow, he started off.

In a little while he came to an inn. Everyone knew that the innkeeper had lots of money. Little Claus had thought up a good plan. He left his wagon at the side of the road and went into the inn.

"Good morning," he said to the innkeeper. "Lovely weather today!"

"Hello, Little Claus," said the innkeeper. "You are out early today."

"That's right," said Little Claus, "I've got to take my grandmother to town. We are very thirsty."

"Where is your grandma, then? I can't see her."

"She's still in the wagon," answered Little Claus. "She can't walk very well, so she is not coming in. Perhaps you can take a cup of coffee out to her? She is very deaf, so if you want to talk to her you will have to speak up."

"I'll see to it," said the innkeeper. He poured out a cup of coffee and took it outside.

"Here is your coffee, grandmother," he said to the old woman in the wagon. But the dead grandmother didn't answer, of course.

"Your coffee!" said the innkeeper louder. Again the old woman didn't answer.

"Coffee!" shouted the innkeeper furiously. He was rather a short-tempered man.

When he still didn't get an answer he became so furious that he threw the coffee in the woman's face. She fell over backwards, and stayed like that.

Just then Little Claus came out. He had been watching from a window. "What have you done now?" he called to the innkeeper. "My grandmother is dead! You have murdered my grandmother!"

The innkeeper was shocked. "I didn't mean to do it. But she said nothing at all, and then I got rather cross."

"Rather cross? Rather cross?" shouted Claus. "That is surely no reason to murder her? If I go to the police you'll get twenty years in jail!"

Now the innkeeper became very nervous. "Twenty years?" he squealed. "Please, Little Claus, we have always been such good friends. Can't we come to an arrangement?"

"What do you suggest?" asked Little Claus.

"I'll give you a bucketful of gold coins, and I'll see to it that your grandma gets a beautiful funeral."

Little Claus pretended to think the offer over carefully, but he already

knew the answer! "Well, all right then," he said at last. "Give me the gold coins."

An hour later he left with a bucket jingling with coins. Moreover, he knew that his grandmother would have a decent funeral.

As soon as he got home, Little Claus sent the little boy nextdoor to Big Claus. "Ask him if I can borrow his corn measure again," he said. The boy went to Big Claus's house, and told him what he had come for. "Does Little Claus still need a corn measure?" asked Big Claus. "But I killed him last night! So that's impossible!"

"He's still alive and kicking," the boy told him.

"That I want to see," said Big Claus fiercely. "I'll come with you." And he went to Little Claus's cottage with the little boy. Little Claus was waiting at the door.

"Do come in and have a look, my friend," said Little Claus, "then you can see how much money I have earned thanks to you."

He showed Big Claus in, and pointed at the large pile of money in the middle of the living-room floor.

Big Claus was flabbergasted.

"How did you manage that?" he asked.

"Well," began Little Claus. "You killed my old grandmother last night, when she was in my bed. I sold her body for a bucketful of gold coins to the pharmacist. You are a mean and cruel fellow, but I am still grateful to you. It's meant a lot of money for me, as you can see."

Big Claus ran home, grabbed his axe and hit his own grandmother, who was having a nap, as hard as he could on the head. Then he went to the pharmacist with the body.

"I've come to sell you my dead grandmother," he said to the man. "How much money will you give me for her?"

"That depends how your grandmother died," said the pharmacist. Big Claus answered, "Oh, I killed her with an axe, this morning."

"What are you saying?" said the pharmacist. "Did you kill her so that you could sell her to me? Do you know you can go to jail for that. If you don't go away fast, I'll call the police."

Big Claus got away fast. He went to Little Claus's cottage.

"You have tricked me again!" he said furiously to Little Claus. "Now you've gone too far."

He picked up a big sack and put Little Claus inside it. "I am going to drown you in the river!" he said. He tied the sack up good and tight.

It was a long walk to the river. Moreover, the sack with Little Claus in it was very heavy indeed. Big Claus found it more and more difficult to carry that heavy sack. Fortunately he came to an inn. He put the sack with Little Claus in it against a wall, and went inside to have something to eat and drink.

While Big Claus was inside, Little Claus tried very hard to get out, but Big Claus had tied the sack up too well. He couldn't manage it. Little Claus had almost given up hope, when an old cowherd came past with his beasts. The man was very bent, and could hardly walk.

Little Claus said from inside his sack: "How awful to be so young, and then to die."

The cowherd said: "I wish I could swap with you. I am an old man, and I've just about had it. I wouldn't mind in the least if I died now."

"Open the sack, then," said Little Claus, "then you can swap with me."

The cowherd untied the sack and freed Little Claus.

"If you sit in the sack," said Little Claus, "then you'll soon be gone."

"Thank you, dear boy," said the old man. He climbed into the sack, and Little Claus tied the sack up tight with the rope.

"Will you look after my cows?" asked the man from the depths of the sack. "I'll do that," said Little Claus, and he did exactly as he had promised. He walked off with the cows, back to his cottage.

When Big Claus had finished eating and drinking, he came out again. He'd had a big omelette, and he felt quite fit again. The sack seemed a lot lighter, he thought. But he'd had such a good meal; that must have been why it seemed much easier to carry Little Claus. He heaved the sack over his shoulder, took it to the river, and threw it into the water with a big splash.

Pleased with himself he set off back home. He whistled a merry tune, until he saw someone walking along in the distance. It looked a bit like Little Claus! When he got closer, he saw that it really was Little Claus.

"How is that possible?" said Big Claus. "I have just thrown you into the river!"

"That's right," said Little Claus, "but I didn't drown." Big Claus couldn't make it out at all.

Little Claus explained to Big Claus what had happened. "These are no ordinary cows," he told him. "These are underwater cows. Come with me to the inn, and I'll explain it all to you there."

They did so, and a little later they sat at a table, each with a pint of beer, while the cows grazed quietly.

"May I thank you from my heart?" said Little Claus. "You did me a great favour by throwing me in the river! I am now fabulously rich, thanks to you. When you threw me in I started to sink at once. I thought I wouldn't be able to breathe, but I was able to keep on breathing quite normally. At the bottom the sack was opened straightaway by a sweet and very beautiful girl.

"She said: `There you are at last, Claus. I have been waiting for you for hours. I have a fine herd of underwater pedigree cows for you.' Only then I realized how beautiful it was under the water. The river is actually a great big roadway for underwater people. Wagons and carts ride backwards and forwards along the bottom. There are fruit trees with apples and pears along the sides. Everything belongs to everybody in underwater land."

Big Claus had been listening with astonishment to Little Claus's story. "Why did you come up again, if it was so marvellous down there?"

Little Claus answered: "It is quicker to move the cows overland. The river twists all over the place. Also, I am not quite used to walking underwater yet."

Big Claus could understand that. But he was rather curious what it would be like, down there in underwater land.

"I would like to have a look down there," he said. "I have lost my horses and my grandmother because of you, and you are incredibly rich. Wouldn't it be fair if this time you threw me into the water? We have surely done enough quarrelling, don't you think?"

"Surely," said Little Claus, "I think so, too. Let's go back to the river, then I'll throw you in."

Big Claus paid for the beer, and asked for a big sack. The innkeeper thought that a little bit odd, but fortunately he still had one. The two went on their way. They walked steadily on, and it didn't take long before they got to the river.

"Goodbye, Little Claus. I am very obliged to you for doing this for me," said Big Claus to Little Claus. He crept into the sack. Little Claus tied the sack up with a rope, as tight as he could. When he had finished, he put an extra knot in the rope, just to make sure.

"Off you go, Big Claus!" he shouted. "Give my love to that pretty girl down there." He flung the sack into the water. It started to sink at once.

"I wonder how many cows Big Claus will bring back with him," grinned Little Claus.

Then, whistling merrily, he set off home, to count his money, and to buy a new horse. He lived a long and happy life, with lots of money, and with a gentle horse for his friend.

The emperor's new clothes

Emperors always have to look good. They can't just walk around in an ordinary suit, but they should always wear the most magnificent clothes. And once upon a time, when there were many emperors around, that was, of course, especially so. Then you could tell if someone was an emperor by the clothes he wore.

There was one emperor, in a country far away, who thought clothes were the most important thing of all. He did not have to have the most expensive and nicest food, and did not mind about going away on holiday every year. The only things that were important to him were his clothes. He spent all the money in his treasury on them. He loved new materials and every day he bought new clothes. In the end he needed half his palace just to store them all!

Dozens of people were busy every day making new clothes for the emperor. The most expensive velvets and the most beautiful furs were transformed into the most magnificent clothes. Trousers, which were called pantaloons because they were so fine and so expensive, long trains, and a mantle with a border of ermine. Even his underpants were embroidered with beautiful patterns.

The emperor had different clothes for each hour of the day. At breakfast he wore a pair of red velvet pantaloons and a white silk shirt. In the afternoon he was dressed in a splendid pale blue suit with a train, and in the evening he wore black brocade to go the theatre. Moreover, on Sundays he wore different clothes again.

Life in the capital city was good. There was a market every day on the big square in the middle of the town. It was always busy there. There was fish for sale, vegetables, and all kinds of things to eat, but the most important were the dress materials. There was one merchant there every day selling velvets, another sold the most expensive embroidery thread, and a third sold magnificent mantles and trains. They did not have to worry that no

one would buy their wares, because the emperor bought almost all he could find in the way of materials and clothes. And that was a lot, because he was a very rich emperor.

One day two swindlers came to town. They had heard that there was a big market there, and they hoped they might make some money. When they heard that the emperor was so fond of nice clothes, and especially new ones, they thought up a plan.

They said they were the best weavers in the whole country. They told everyone they met: "We make the most beautiful materials you can imagine. The colours are magnificent, and the patterns are brilliant. Anyone who wears clothes made of them will only want to wear our clothes for the rest of their lives. But," they warned, "only clever people, who are good at their work, can see the clothes. Stupid people, who are not fit for their trade and who haven't got a sensible thought in their heads, can't see them. So our clothes have a little bit of magic as well."

"What?" shouted the emperor, when he heard the stories about these two weavers. "Are there two tailors in the country who can make clothes only clever people can see?"

258

"Yes, that's right," said the emperor's valet. He had heard the story in town, and had run straight to his master.

"Go and fetch those weavers at once! They must come and work in my palace!" The emperor sent his messenger to look for the two weavers. The messenger went to town and it did not take him long to find them. They were still in the market square boasting about what they could do.

"Come with me to the emperor's palace," said the messenger to the two weavers. "You can have as much money as you like, if you work for the emperor." The swindlers went straight to the palace. They knew quite well how much money they could earn there. They winked at each other. So far their little plan to swindle the emperor was working out very well!

When they arrived at the palace, they were taken straight to their room. It was a magnificent hall, full of weaving looms, large reels of thread, and a bedroom each.

The emperor called for the two tailors at once. He had been waiting impatiently for their arrival. "Make me the most magnificent clothes ever made. In two weeks there is a grand imperial procession. Then I will have to be dressed in the very best. If you are really such good tailors as you say, I will pay you well," he told the weavers in a stern voice.

"Yes, please, your Majesty, we will do our very best. But we need gold, silver, and silk thread, Majesty," said the two swindlers. "And we would like to be all alone in our workroom, because our method of making clothes has to be a secret. We will let you know when we have finished weaving a yard of cloth. That will take a while, because the beginning is always the most difficult."

The emperor gave them a large bag full of gold coins, so that they could start work at once.

"Thank you, emperor," said the swindlers. "This will be enough to start with, but we will need more in a little while. The clothes we make just don't come cheap."

The two swindlers put two large weaving looms in the middle of their room. Every day new sacks of costly thread were delivered. There was nothing to be seen on the looms, because the reels remained empty. Not a fraction of thread was used. But every time someone came into the room to bring more thread, or anything else, both sat down behind the weaving looms, and pretended to be very hard at work.

"Obviously I'm not clever, and not good enough for my work," thought one of the servants when he came in to deliver another bag of gold coins. He couldn't see the clothes the tailors were weaving at all. But of course, he didn't want anyone to know he was stupid, so he just pretended, and told the tailors the material was beautiful. "What lovely colours! How did you do it? The emperor will be so pleased!" When he had gone, the two swindlers burst out laughing, and carried on with the game of chess which they happened to be playing. They had nothing else to do!

Every night one of the swindlers sneaked out across the border to sell the sacks of thread they had been given. They got a lot of money for it, because all that silver and gold thread was very expensive.

"I would like to know how the tailors are getting on with their work," said the emperor after a few days to his prime minister. "Will you go and have a look for me?"

The prime minister went to the workroom. He knocked on the door. Quickly the two swindlers went to sit in front of the weaving looms. They moved their hands quickly along the reels and shuttles.

"Come in!" they called. The prime minister opened the door and saw the two weavers sitting there. He looked at the weaving loom, and pushed his glasses a bit higher on his nose. He shut his eyes, and opened them again. He squeezed them shut again, but it didn't help: he could not see a single thread of cloth. "I can't see a thing!" he thought to himself. That frightened him. "Nobody must know that I can't see a thing," he thought, "otherwise they will all know I am no good at my job."

"Splendid!" he said out loud. "What beautiful colours, and the patterns in the material are so lovely. I am sure the emperor will like it."

So it seemed as if he could really see the cloth. He said goodbye to the tailors, went back to the emperor, and told him the same he had said to the tailors. "Such beautiful clothes you have never seen before!" he said. "The colours... the cloth... Never before have I seen anything like it. It is really wonderful!"

After another two days the emperor was wondering if his clothes were nearly ready. He sent a high official. He was quite sure that this man was clever and good at his work. He would be able to see how the weavers were getting on with his new clothes.

"Just go to the tailors and tell me how far they have got," said the emperor.

The official went to the swindlers' workroom and knocked at the door. Quickly the two men put their game of cards away. One sat down by a loom, the other grabbed a needle.

When the official came in, both men were busy at work. One was weaving thin air, and the other was busy sewing thin air. "Good gracious," thought the official, and started to quake. "That cloth is quite invisible to me, so I am not good enough for my job! How awful, the prime minister could see the cloth all right! So he is fit for his job, but I am not!"

"It is magnificent!" he said aloud to the two swindlers, and hurried out of the room. Just in case they discovered that he couldn't see a thing!

To the emperor he told a story of beautiful cloth, magnificent colours, splendid patterns, and fantastic embroidery. The emperor was satisfied. "I will have the most beautiful clothes in the world," he thought.

A few days later time began to run out. It would not be long before the imperial procession would be held, and then the clothes had to be ready. "I'll have a look for myself," decided the emperor. With a few servants he went to the workshop, and opened the door. At first sight the two swindlers seemed to be busy at work, passing invisible reels of thread to each other, and weaving invisible cloth.

The emperor became nervous, because he couldn't see a thing. "Am I not a good emperor?" he asked himself. "Or am I stupid?" No one must find out. Otherwise he might be deposed, and perhaps people would be so angry with him, that he would be exiled from the country. Then he would never be able to buy expensive clothes again! And that wouldn't do at all.

"Splendid! Magnificent! Wonderful! Fantastic!" he called out. "Such splendid clothes have never been made before. I am sure everyone's eyes will be popping, when I wear these."

"Look," explained the tailors, "this cloth is of the most expensive Chinese silk and magnificent brocade. Don't you think the peacock feathers on it are beautiful?"

"Yes, I do," said the emperor. "I've never seen anything like it." He was right, of course. He really had never seen anything like it. Even more so, he still couldn't see anything now!

The emperor's servants all said: "It is a masterpiece, magnificent! These weavers are artists!" Of course, they couldn't see anything either, but they didn't want to lose their jobs. They earned good wages, and moreover, they were also allowed to wear beautiful clothes, because the emperor didn't just want to dress up well himself, everyone round him had to look good too.

"You will really have to wear these clothes for the annual procession," said one of the servants.

"Of course," said the emperor, "these wonderful clothes deserve nothing less." He went on: "The two weavers will each get a medal and be made Supreme Imperial Weaver. That is the highest distinction in the land."

The swindlers bowed deeply to the emperor. "Your clothes will be ready tomorrow, your Majesty," they said.

The night before the procession the two swindlers were busy working. They left the door of their room open, and worked throughout the night, by the light of sixteen candles. Their fingers moved rapidly backwards and forwards. Their feet worked the treadle of the weaving loom. They sewed, weaved, and embroidered, and everyone passing the room looked in and said that the clothes were magnificent. And how hard the weavers were working; you could see that it was very difficult to make such beautiful clothes.

"Tomorrow the emperor will look as he has never looked before," said the prime minister, who was passing by again.

"I am sure of it," said one of the two tailors. "No one will know what they are seeing!" And that was true, too.

The cock crowed, and people rubbed their eyes. Today would be the big day of the imperial procession, and everyone knew about it. What would the emperor look like in his new clothes?

"The emperor's clothes are ready!" called the two swindlers. From all sides people came running along. The prime minister, the high official, dozens of servants, and the emperor himself.

"Oh!" said everyone, and: "Ah!" They could not stop saying how beautiful they thought the materials were.

"Splendid!" said the emperor. "These clothes are amazingly beautiful.

How magnificent, how very magnificent!" The whole court agreed with him.

"Would you please be so kind as to undress yourself, then you can put on your new clothes," said one of the tailors. The emperor did so.

"Do you see these beautiful pants of Chinese silk? With laburnum flowers embroidered in real gold thread. The buttons are of the finest gold you have ever seen," said the tailors, as they helped the emperor into his invisible pants.

"Here is your shirt. That is made of the finest linen from a distant country. The embroidered border is in scarlet, and is made with thousands of stitches."

Again the emperor was given a piece of clothing he could not see. No, worse, he could not feel it either. That meant he must be very stupid indeed.

"Splendid, magnificent!" the servants kept on shouting, and: "Fantastic, magic!" called the emperor, louder than anyone.

After a while the emperor was completely dressed. Well, not exactly, because he had nothing on at all. But the tailors had said that anyone who could not see the clothes was stupid, so no one dared tell the emperor.

Finally the swindlers buttoned the train onto the mantle. The emperor looked in the mirror. "Such splendid clothes I have never had before. I am very proud of them," he said. "Now I am ready for the procession. Let's go! I can hear the trumpets already. Won't everyone be surprised at my new clothes!"

Two servants bent down to pick up the train. They had to carry it, because that was their job. They could not see the train, but they held up their hands, just as if it was there.

The emperor came outside. Holding his head high and his chest thrust out he walked slowly along the red carpet. The chamberlains carried the train which wasn't there.

People couldn't believe their eyes! They couldn't see a single thread! But everyone knew that if you couldn't see the clothes, you were stupid, or not good at your work. Then you might lose your job, and nobody wanted to risk that.

"Splendid!" shouted the people. "Wonderful!" And: "How beautiful." Everyone pretended it was marvellous. No one dared say that he couldn't see a thing, because if you lose your job, you never know if you will get another.

But children don't go out to work, so they don't have to worry if they will lose their job. And suddenly a cute little boy said: "But the emperor hasn't got any clothes on at all! He is in his altogether!"

It didn't take long for everyone to whisper: "The emperor has no clothes on..."

"I've really got nothing on," thought the emperor, "they are quite right, but no one must know." So he went on walking with his head held high and his chest thrust forward. His chamberlains still held up the train that wasn't there. The prime minister, walking behind the procession, was still saying: "Aren't the emperor's clothes splendid!" But no one believed him any more. The further they walked, the worse it became. The people no longer believed that the emperor was wearing any clothes. And however proud the emperor looked, the people began to laugh harder and harder. They nudged each other, and pointed at the emperor, who was walking in the imperial procession in his altogether.

The emperor went on walking proudly, however difficult he thought it, until he was back in his palace and no one could see him any more. Then he sat down in a chair, holding his head in his hands. The two swindlers had, of course, long since flown.

In the end the emperor thought he had learned his lesson. He sighed deeply, walked to his clothes cupboard, and took out his very best suit of

clothes. As a consolation he would wear that for the rest of the day, and tomorrow, too. Because it would take a long time for people to forget that their emperor had walked through the town in an imperial procession in his altogether! That would be a jest for many years to come...

The story from the Jutland dunes

The story which I am now going to tell you comes from the Jutland dunes in Denmark, but that is not where it begins. It begins in Spain, far away to the south. It is much warmer there than in Denmark. Their spring is just as warm as a lovely Danish summer's day and in the summer you need to find some shade, otherwise it is far too hot. The most unusual plants and trees grow there, like eucalyptus trees and palms as well as olives and oranges. Amongst all the beautiful greenery, you will also find many reminders from the past. From the Moors, for example, who were a people who lived in Spain hundreds of years ago.

Spain is both very far away and close all at the same time. A great, deep sea lies between Denmark and Spain. If you were to board a ship in cold Denmark, it would not take long before you were in Spain. There will not be any Danish sand dunes to greet you since they do not have dunes in Spain, and everyone seems happy all the time. You will hear a lot of music and even more laughter.

Life in Spain seemed very much like a long, wonderful dream for two certain young people – a boy and a girl. They grew up in this beautiful country and wanted to stay there for the rest of their lives. They married there and had everything which their hearts desired. Both were the picture of health and they lived in a magnificent house. This they could do with ease because they came from a good and wealthy family.

They had every reason to be contented and that they were. Nonetheless, there was still something which they missed, and that was a child. Try as she might, the young woman could not become pregnant. She prayed every day for a child for she so wanted to continue the family name. It must not be allowed to die out.

Only a little while later and the young couple were much happier: the young woman became pregnant! She had succeeded at long last! Every day was a celebration.

"How wonderful life is!" said her husband, and his wife nodded. They

268

were terribly happy with each other and, with a child waiting to be born, they felt as if they were walking on the clouds.

Shortly afterwards, there came a message that the young man was expected at the royal court. He quickly journeyed to the capital where he met the king in his palace. "I have the honour of asking you to represent our country in Moscow", said the king to the young man. This was splendid news! He had become the ambassador for Spain in Russia! Joyful at his great news, he travelled back to his expectant wife.

He proudly told of the king's request. "I'm from a good family and have the knowledge appropriate to become an ambassador", he related. "In Moscow, with my salary, we can live in a beautiful house as befits an ambassador of Spain!"

His wife did not so like the idea of leaving beautiful Spain for Russia. On the other hand she was proud of her husband. The couple bade farewell to their family and friends and embarked on their journey. They went on board a grand, Spanish ship to Stockholm. From there they were to take a Swedish ship and sail on to Finland where they would travel overland to Moscow.

The journey began smoothly. A strong south wind filled up the sails and drove the ship in the direction of far off Sweden. However, after a few days the wind slackened and for days there was a dead calm. One Sunday, a south-westerly wind blew up at last, which quickly pushed the ship towards the north-east. They were half way between Scotland and Jutland and could carry on with their journey.

Jutland has changed a great deal since the new Spanish ambassador to Russia came there. The marshes have been drained and the heaths have been changed into farm land, but there is also much which has remained the same. Whoever travels through Jutland today can well imagine how it must have looked then. Even now, there are still vast heaths with a great many burial mounds, marshes, and meadows. That is how it is today, and so it was then when this husband and wife sailed by Jutland on their way to Moscow.

September was almost over. It was a sunny Sunday morning and a fisherman and his wife had just come out of church and were walking across the churchyard. It was an empty space where not a single tree or

bush grew; little mounds showed where someone lay buried. There were hardly any gravestones since most of the dead had been commemorated with wooden crosses. Wood is much easier to obtain in Jutland.

"The minister gave a very good sermon, today", said the fisherman to his wife.

"Yes", she replied, "a good sermon helps to cheer us up a bit." They had reached a simple grave with a little wooden cross upon it. There lay their son who had died one month before. "Our son would have been five tomorrow", said the woman. She did not want to be sad but, nonetheless, she still had to wipe a tear from the corner of her eye at the thought of it. A gust of wind behind them stirred up the grains of sand for a moment, but it was only a little flurry and soon enough there was nothing else but the lovely warm sun. The fisherman and his wife knew that this was a sign. One single gust of wind meant that a storm was brewing. Gales in any event, and perhaps even thunder and lightning with driving rain. They quickly went home and changed from their Sunday best into their normal working clothes. They raced over the dunes down to the beach and with all their strength pulled the little boats out of the water.

White foam capped the waves and the wind became ever stronger. By the time that evening had fallen, and the fishermen had gone back to their homes, the wind had become a gale and had begun to howl. The howling of the wind was even louder than the roaring of the sea.

The fisherman and his wife lay in bed, trying to sleep. Even for them, so used to this kind of weather, it was difficult to get to sleep. Once they did, they slept so lightly that they were awoken at once when a knock came at their door sometime around midnight.

"Neighbour, wake up!" called a voice, loudly. "A ship has run aground on the sandbank!"

Within one minute the fisherman and his wife were standing outside fully dressed. The wind tore at their clothes and the rain streamed down their faces. With enormous difficulty they climbed down over the dunes. Once they had reached the beach it was much worse. The sand whipped up about them. Great clouds of salty sea spray rained down on the fisherfolk, soaking their clothes and hair.

In the distance, they saw a beautiful two-masted ship. It lay stranded on the farthest sandbank and its tall masts quivered and creaked in the wind. All at once, a great crack sounded, as if two huge millstones were turning against each other, and the ship was lifted up and over the distant sandbank. It moved landwards and then hit the innermost sandbank. There, it tilted over. The mast broke and boiling waves crashed over the deck. The ship was no more than five hundred yards from the coast yet the fishermen could not reach it. They would never survive the passage through five hundred yards of such a seething sea. All that they could do was wait. Now and then it seemed as though they could hear the terrified calls of the great ship's crew. They saw how the crew laboured in vain to save the ship. Suddenly, a gigantic tidal wave rose up, washing over the deck and no-one was seen again. No-one? No, two tiny figures leapt hand in hand into the sea and were at once consumed by the dreadful waves.

Only a few minutes later, the body of a woman was thrown on to the beach by a great wave. Was she dead? She had to be. No-one could have survived those five hundred yards, being turned this way and that by such a furious sea and afterwards being tossed on to a beach. Three fisherwomen bent over the woman and saw a little bit of movement. They quickly pulled her further up the beach and carried her to the nearest fisherman's house. There, they laid her on a bed and covered her over with woollen blankets.

It was not hard for the fisherwomen to see that this lady came from a distinguished background. On her fingers were beautiful rings and her clothes, although streaked with mud, were nonetheless quite splendid.

The lady came to her wits and began to babble some words. She spoke in Spanish and so the women could not understand what she was saying. She was probably ill, too, for she had a high fever and her whole body was trembling. She clearly had no idea where she was or what had happened to her. This was just as well, in fact, since the fisherwomen found it hard to believe that she could have been travelling alone, and whatever had happened to her travelling companion it was certain that he or she was no longer alive.

For whatever had been washed ashore, be it driftwood or the crew from the wreck, there had been no survivors.

The next day, the lady was racked with terrible pains. She muttered something but no-one could tell what she was saying. An hour later the fisherfolk were able to understand what it had been. The Spanish lady gave birth to a son. The son of the new Spanish ambassador to Russia and his wife.

She should have given birth in a splendid four-poster bed. The child should have come into the world amidst great celebration but it had all turned out differently. The son of the new ambassador was born in a lowly, Danish fisherman's cottage in the province of Jutland.

He was not even given a kiss from his mother, for as she gave birth to him she also breathed her last breath. He had been fatherless before he was born and by the time he first opened his eyes he was already an orphan.

The unknown lady could not have left her child anywhere better than with the poor fisherwoman. She it was who only the day before had stood thinking of her little son at his graveside in the churchyard. Her little boy who would have been five years old that very day.

Back in Spain, no-one knew what had happened to the ship. No message had been received from either Moscow or Stockholm and it was quickly

deduced that the ship must have been lost with all hands on the way. The town where the young couple had lived went into deep mourning.

The fisherman and his wife were happy in their little cottage at the edge of the dunes. The fisherwoman had a son who had been born on the same day that their own little son would have been five years old. They called him Jurgen.

The boy grew quickly. He learned to speak Danish and was brought up as a fisherman's son but it was obvious that he was different. His hair was dark and his skin was a light brown. As well as that, he looked so distinguished. So distinguished and special that his friends were rather jealous of him. However, apart from that he was just the son of the fisherman and his wife.

Jurgen had a good childhood. He had all the freedom that a child could wish for. He could play on the beach or in the dunes and, in summer, in the sea. He collected shells. He used to make drawings of the very best ones in the sand.

When the tide came in his pictures were washed away. He did not mind as he then made new ones. Jurgen was a bright boy and not at all stupid. He remembered all the stories that were told to him at once. He had only to hear a song once to be able to sing it later by heart. He was skilful as well. You had only to give him a knife and a piece of wood and he could make for you whatever you asked him.

Jurgen was a boy with many talents. As the ambassador's son he could have taken them a long way.

One day, another ship became stranded. Dozens of crates of flower bulbs washed ashore. The fishermen were not quite sure what to do with them. Some ate them but they were not very nice, giving them stomach ache. Most of the bulbs remained lying on the beach and were slowly buried under the sand. Would the young Jurgen travel, or would he, like those flower bulbs, get no farther than the sands of the Jutland beaches?

Jurgen never felt the slightest bit bored with his life in the dunes. In fact, it was not boring at all as there was always something to do. The weather was different every day. Sometimes it was stormy and rainy; the next day could be sunny again. Beautiful bushes grew in the dunes which bore delicious fruits. Brambles and berries were everywhere.

Once every year, one of the fisherman's brothers would come on a visit to the little village by the dunes. He was an eel trader and lived in Fjaltring. He travelled through all the villages in the district with his cart full of eels. The whole village looked forward to his visit for the eel trader was full of fun. Moreover, he was a good storyteller. Well, in fact, he only ever told the one story but he did tell it in a wonderful way.

One sunny Monday morning, the eel trader came by again. He rode up on his cart and rang out his bell. Jurgen ran to greet him.

"Hello uncle!" he called out, when still a way off. "May I ride on the billy goat?" This was allowed, and Jurgen bravely climbed on to the goat's back and led the beast to the market square.

That evening, after the eel trader had sold a great many eels to the fisherwomen, he returned to the cottage of the fisherman and his wife. Half the village came with him, too, for they did not want to miss hearing the eel trader's story. There was scarcely room enough since Danish fishing cottages were only very small in those days. The eel trader had brought a large bottle of brandy wine with him and gave everyone a small glassful. Even Jurgen was given a little. The eel trader kept insisting that

everyone should have a little brandy wine first in order to hold down a big fat eel. Why? His story would explain.

When everyone was quiet he began his wonderful story.

"In a tributary of the Skærumå River swam a mother eel with her eight daughters. She was a little cross with them because they would not stop complaining. They wanted so much to go swimming in the great river further down.

'Very well', said the mother. 'But only if you don't go too far. If that nasty eelman comes with his stick then you will all be killed.'

The eel maidens promised that they would be careful. Yet they were really much too young. After half an hour, but three of the eight returned in tears. Sobbing and sniffing, they told how the other five had been trapped by the nasty eelman.

'They will come back', said the mother eel with certainty.

'Oh no, for he beat them to death even while we swam there!' cried the daughters.

'And yet they will come back again', said the mother.

'Oh no', said the eel maidens, 'for he has cut them into pieces and fried them!'

'Yet they will come back, I am sure of it', said their mother.

'Oh no', said her daughters, 'for he drank a glass of brandy wine along with them.'

Then the mother eel began to sob. 'In that case they will never come back again! Brandy wine will bury an eel.'

And that", ended the eel trader, "is why you should always drink a glassful of brandy wine when you're eating eels!"

The story of the eels and the brandy wine was more than just a story for Jurgen. He wanted to do the same as the eel maidens: to travel a little farther! It might be dangerous but he was willing to take the risk. He dreamed of sailing. Not just a little way to catch fish but to see the world! Sailing far away on a beautiful sailboat to lands where no-one had ever been!

He began to speak of this often to his mother. She replied just like the mother eel had done. "That is much too dangerous", she said.

Still, Jurgen wanted to travel, and if he was not to be allowed to go to sea on a big ship then he would stay in Denmark – if he might only be able to travel a bit!

His wish was soon fulfilled. The fisherman and his wife received news that a great-uncle had died. He had been a well-to-do gentleman who had lived near to Copenhagen. Jurgen was to go and attend the funeral with his parents. They left at once, as soon as the bad news came.

The fisherman, his wife, and their son crossed over the dunes in a north-easterly direction. They crossed the Skærumå, the river where the mother eel and her daughters had been, and came to a magnificent castle, the old

fortress of Nørre Vosborg. The fisherman told his son the most wonderful stories about how the castle came to be there and why. Jurgen thought it was quite splendid. He had never been so far away and everything was a surprise to him.

A while after reaching the castle, the three of them travelled on by horse and cart. The road along which the horses pulled the cart was little more than a rutted track. The travellers felt every bump and jolt. The horses became tired and stopped now and then to munch on a tuft of grass. As a result, the journey did not go much faster than if they had been on foot.

The heath looked like one huge purple carpet with here and there a splash of green. Jurgen thought it would be wonderful just to roll around in the heather. When he mentioned this, a fellow traveller told him that the heath was crawling with adders. If you were bitten by such a snake, the wound would have to be cut out immediately or else you would die. In the past, told the stranger, it was much worse. In those days wolves had made the heath a dangerous place.

The journey across the heath took two whole days. Jurgen would have been happy for it to have lasted much longer. He enjoyed travelling and

thought it was a shame when they arrived at last. They were set down in front of the house where their distant relative had lived. It was a crowded and important occasion. Relatives had come from all over the country to be at the funeral.

It was, in fact, quite cheerful inside the dead man's house. There was absolutely no sadness. The many relatives told each other splendid stories. They ate delicious fat eels, drinking them down with little glasses of brandy. You needed to do that to bury the eel!

A minister gave a short sermon. The whole family sang a few psalms together. Afterwards, they listened to the speech given by the brother of the man who had died. He told how good the man had been and of everything that he had done for his family and country.

Jurgen explored the house and the area. He walked across the field where all the coaches stood and patted the horses. After three days, he felt completely at home in his new surroundings. He found it even more fun than in his own little village by the dunes. There was lovely heathland and everywhere grew deliciously sweet blueberries. Here and there stood fine old houses. Clouds of smoke billowed from the chimneys at night. They

were just like black sheep looking for their white brothers in the sky. The great-uncle was buried on the fourth day and all the relatives returned once more to the places where they lived. Jurgen travelled back with his parents to the little cottage by the dunes. The whole journey long he talked of nothing else but the heather and the beautiful countryside. He loved adventures so much, he wanted so much to travel! Jurgen did not stop even after they had been back at home for quite a time. He told them how he had dreamed about fabulous journeys across the sea.

"Mother, may I go sailing?" he would often ask. Every time, his mother would reply: "No, my boy, that is much too dangerous."

However, Jurgen kept on asking. He was very stubborn and would not accept anything that easily from his mother.

In the end, his mother agreed. Jurgen was just fourteen and now asked every day whether he might go sailing.

"Very well", said his mother, "but only if you promise that you will be careful."

"Yes mother!" cried Jurgen joyously, and off he went on his travels.

Jurgen travelled around the world as a cabin boy. He met different peoples and heard different languages. He came to know the burning heat

of the south and the icy cold of the north. He met friendly and unfriendly people and talked with everyone. Sometimes he sailed over a sea which was so still that it looked just like a mirror. Other times there were storms and he was buffeted back and forth in his bunk at night. The food he was given was almost always bad. Furthermore, he was often badly treated as the cabin boy. He was often beaten whether he deserved it or not. This made his blood boil but he was sensible enough not to let his anger show. He also went to Spain. Indeed, it came about that his ship put to harbour in the town where his parents had lived. Jurgen knew nothing of his background and nothing about his family. Everything was new to him.

On the last day of their stay in the Spanish town, Jurgen was allowed to leave the ship to help with loading. It was the first time in his life that he had seen a town. He thought it was beautiful! Everywhere were houses with big and little windows, arched and square doors, sometimes with turrets. There were also magnificent churches and pretty shops! People were everywhere and everywhere there was hustle and bustle. Jurgen loved it. Together with the sailor who he had to help, he went inside a large church. Jurgen was shabbily dressed but no-one minded. The poorest of people were walking about the church. The church had splendid marble pillars and in the middle stood a golden altar. What a shame, thought Jurgen, that they would have to leave again!

The cargo which had to be moved was as heavy as lead. Jurgen was tired of it. When he could go on no longer, he rested a while in front of a stately house with pointed turrets. A porter in his livery pushed him away with a stick. How could he have known that this boy in the shabby clothes was his master's grandson? The grandson had not the faintest idea himself.

Jurgen went back on board and his hard life began all over again. Long days, short nights, and many beatings. It took weeks before they were back again at the Danish fjord from which they had come. Jurgen journeyed back to the cottage by the dunes as fast as possible. Bad news awaited him.

While Jurgen had been at sea, his mother had died. She had suddenly become ill and died after a high fever lasting two weeks. He was now alone with his father the whole winter. That winter it was very cold. It snowed a lot and you had to wrap up very warm so as not to freeze instantly.

Jurgen thought it strange that such huge differences existed in the world.

Here it was so bitterly cold and in Spain it was warm. All the same, he liked to be at home. However much he had Spanish blood – and you could see that! – his home was Denmark.

Jurgen helped his father in the spring once the fishermen could start working once again. He had grown a good deal and was strong and agile. He could work the whole day without a break and could swim like a fish. He decided to sail again, together with Morten, his friend next door. They signed up to a large cargo vessel. The journey would take them to Holland via Norway.

Jurgen could get on well with Morten. They rarely argued, but when they did sparks would fly. Jurgen was sometimes hot-tempered; something which he had inherited from his Spanish father and mother.

One argument in particular became very overheated. While they were sitting down to eat, Morten pulled the bowl towards himself at exactly the moment that Jurgen had wanted to do the same thing. Jurgen reddened and stood up. He pulled out his knife and held it in the air. Morten said: "Oh, so that's the sort of person you are!" Jurgen then realized that he had been angry about nothing. He sat down and went on eating.

After the meal he said to Morten: "Punch me if you want to, I deserve it. I should never have let myself get so angry."

Morten calmly replied: "Let's not talk about it anymore." Both went back to their work.

Morten and Jurgen remained good friends. They were both young, healthy, and strong. Jurgen was clearly the strongest and the most athletic of the two. Later, once they were back again in the cottage by the dunes, they talked about their travels. They even spoke about the incident with the knife.

"Jurgen can almost explode sometimes", related Morten. That was true. Spaniards – and Jurgen was one – can sometimes nearly explode. There is no better way of putting it.

Else was a girl from the village. Jurgen had known her his whole life. They had played together often as little children. They looked very different. Else had light blonde hair and blue eyes, while Jurgen had black hair and dark eyes with which he could look very fierce. Moreover, Else was a very quiet girl. She was not quick to anger. She did not understand how it was that Jurgen could now and then be so hot-tempered.

One day, when Jurgen and Else were walking hand in hand through the dunes, Else stood suddenly still on top of a snow white sand dune covered only by a little patch of moss. She said: "I think you're a sweet boy. I'd so like for us to go on living in the same village for always. But I cannot marry you for I'm engaged to Morten."

Jurgen felt as if the sand dunes were shifting from under his feet. He said nothing and only nodded. All at once he knew for certain that he hated Morten. He thought about it and realized that Morten had stolen from him the most important thing of his whole life. He had loved Else without ever knowing it. He now saw everything clearly.

He started to hate Morten more and more. He remembered all the little arguments they had had. In his head they became terrible fights. Every time he could say something unpleasant to Morten he did. Some of the fishermen noticed that there was something going on between Morten and Jurgen, but Morten noticed nothing himself. He had put up with hearing nasty remarks from his friend more than once in the past.

Jurgen's father became ill. It seemed that he was suffering from the same thing as his wife. After two weeks of sickening in his bed, he died. He left the cottage to his adopted son. It was only a small inheritance, but it was still something which Morten did not have.

"You certainly won't be sailing off again now", said an old fisherman to Jurgen. Yet staying at home was not something Jurgen thought about. He had to travel, he wanted to go to sea again! The eel trader had an uncle in Old Skagen. This man was a merchant and had a great ship.

"He's a good man", said the eel trader. "You'd do well to go into his service."

Jurgen thought the plan a good one as he did not wish to remain anywhere near the dunes. The marriage of Morten and Else would be taking place in only a few weeks time and he did not want to be there.

"It doesn't make much sense to go travelling now", said the old fisherman. "Now that you have a cottage of your own you would be better staying here. Perhaps Else would then still marry you."

Jurgen thought about this a while and called on Else. He asked her: "If Morten were to have his own house, with whom would you then want to marry?"

Else said: "Morten will never have a house of his own."

"But if he were to have such a house?" asked Jurgen again.

"Then I would marry Morten", said Else decidedly, "for I love him."

Jurgen considered Else's words the whole night and then he decided on something. That something was stronger than his love for Else. In the morning, he went to Morten and sold him his cottage. He did not ask very much for it. Morten was astonished that Jurgen would sell him his house so unexpectedly. In fact, so was Jurgen. In his heart he was furious with Morten but he sold him the cottage, nonetheless!

When Else heard what Jurgen had done she came to him at once and

gave him a big kiss. Jurgen had made sure that she and Morten could be happy!

The next day, Jurgen set off for the eel trader's uncle's house. He took his knapsack, shut the door behind him, and climbed over the dunes to the beach. For days he walked along the beach towards Fjaltring where the old man lived. It was so hot that his nose suddenly started to bleed. Warm drops of blood fell to the ground. He held his handkerchief to his nose and waited for the bleeding to stop.

The sun was high in the sky when he reached the ferryboat which would take him across the Nissumfjord. He stepped on board and asked the ferryman to make good speed. He wanted to arrive in Fjaltring as soon as possible.

When the boat had gone half way across the fjord, Jurgen heard two voices behind him. Two cavalrymen stood by the ferry's jetty and shouted: "Come back in the name of the law!"

Jurgen did not know exactly what the two men meant. He thought that it must be very important. He took one of the oars and helped the ferryman to row back to the jetty.

Before he knew it the two cavalrymen had tied his hands behind his back with strong, rough rope.

"It's a good thing that we were still able to catch you!" said one of them. "That trick of yours is going to cost you your life."

Jurgen soon understood the dilemma he was in. He had been accused of murder! Morten had been found behind the dunes with a knife in his back. Everyone in the village knew that Jurgen had his eyes on Else. Furthermore, they had heard that Jurgen had threatened his friend with a knife once before.

Jurgen was innocent, of course, but it seemed as if he had killed Morten. On top of everything, his knapsack contained a handkerchief which was covered in blood! The cavalrymen took him to prison at once. He had already seen the prison once from the outside when on his way to the funeral of his great-uncle. It was the old fortress of Nørre Vosborg. He was put in a dungeon, a dark and airless hole with patches of moss growing on the walls. No-one listened to him whenever he tried to defend himself.

The only light to enter the dungeon came from a tiny air vent. The cell had a heavy wooden door shut by an iron bar. No-one could ever have escaped from there. A wooden bed was all the cell contained. This is what

Jurgen had to sleep on, which he managed to do. He knew that he was innocent and once you know that, sleep is not so difficult.

Luckily, Jurgen did not have to stay in the dark dungeon very long. After a little while he was taken to Ringkøbing. His cell there was just the very smallest of rooms, too, but at least it was somewhere else. It was certainly terribly cold in his dungeon cell. He was at his wits' end because there was nothing he could do except wait and see what would happen to him. Who had killed Morten? Who was it who had caused his unjust imprisonment?

At night, Jurgen was awakened by the storm howling outside the dungeon walls. The sound made him think about when he lived in his cottage at the edge of the dunes. He was miserable.

It took a whole year before the true murderer was discovered. The police had arrested a criminal known as Niels the Thief. The reason was clear: Niels stole anything that could be stolen.

Shortly before Jurgen had left, Niels the Thief had met with Morten. They had drunk a few glasses of beer in a little inn next to the Ringkøbing fjord.

It had not been enough to make them drunk but it was enough to make talking easier.

"I have a fine farm", Morten told Niels, "and I shall soon be marrying the prettiest girl in the district. I have money enough for her dowry."

"And where do you keep your money then?" asked the thief.

Morten pointed to his pocket. "Where it belongs!" he called out.

Niels did not know that Morten was exaggerating and he followed him back. Niels killed him close to his cottage at the edge of the dunes. He did not find any money, of course, but the crime had already been committed. He was able to escape arrest for a whole year but, finally, the truth came out. At long last, the police found Niels and as soon as he had been arrested he told them everything.

Jurgen was freed! How happy he was! After a full year in a dark cell he was once more able to enjoy life. The sky was such a wonderful blue and the birds sang so beautifully!

He had not been treated fairly, of course. Therefore, he went to the mayor and demanded money. He had sat imprisoned for one year and all for nothing! The mayor asked him whether it was not enough that his

innocence had been proven. All he received was a handful of ducats to help him travel on.

In Ringkøbing, where the young man had been imprisoned, there was also a merchant – the very same one to whom Jurgen should have introduced himself a whole year before. He was there on important business.

"How happy I am that you are free again", said the merchant. "Wouldn't it be best for you to put all your troubles behind you? Let us then start afresh. The day after tomorrow we shall journey to my house in Skagen where you can rest a little."

The journey to Skagen was just like a dream to Jurgen. He enjoyed everything that he saw as they crossed over the heath.

After four days travelling, the two men arrived. The merchant had a beautiful farm in Skagen and a few other properties as well. The whole village came to greet them as they turned into the road to the farm. Jurgen shook hundreds of hands.

The merchant's spacious house was very welcoming. The most delicious smells came from the kitchen, as well. The company went to sit at the table at once. The very best china dishes were already laid out filled with

lovely fish. There was plaice and sole fit to make a king's mouth water. This they drank down with an excellent white wine.

Jurgen was so happy that everyone had been so kind to him! This was precisely what he needed after spending a year in prison. The merchant's daughter, Clara, was particularly kind to him. It made Jurgen feel rather shy. He found it all rather difficult. He had discovered a year ago that Else, whom he loved, had wanted to marry Morten and not him! For that reason it was, perhaps, not such a bad thing that Clara would soon be going on a journey. She was off to Norway to stay with an aunt.

She departed a few days later. He saw that there were tears in her eyes. He did not know what to say and so just gave her back a kiss.

For the first few months after Clara's departure, Jurgen helped with the fishing catch. Mackerel, in particular, was being caught. It all went very smoothly: you had only to throw out your net and in swam the fish by themselves. It seemed as if the whole sea was filled with mackerel.

Autumn came. It rained nearly every day and later it even started to snow. There was often thunder and lightning too. Some evenings it gave Jurgen a very strange feeling. It was as if he could remember the stormy weather

at his birth. Fortunately, the merchant's house was always cosy and warm.
The merchant was wealthy enough to have the stove always burning. In
the evenings, Jurgen would listen to the wonderful stories which the
merchant could tell. Jurgen knew for certain that he had never been so
fortunate in his life. He did miss Clara, however. Luckily, it was not to be
so long before he saw her again.

"In April, you may travel with my ship to Norway to deliver some cargo",
said the merchant. "You will then be able to take Clara back with you."

That night, Jurgen dreamed that Clara had returned. He was cheerful the
whole day. So cheerful, in fact, that the merchant's wife said to her
husband: "That young man is back to his old self again; it's marvellous
just to watch him!"

"And", said the merchant, "you haven't lost any of your charms! Since
Jurgen has been with us, you look radiant again, just as when we were
first engaged."

The ship set off one sunny day in April. Jurgen stood on deck. After two
weeks sailing they came to the Norwegian coast and slowly sailed to the
harbour. Jurgen saw Clara standing there even from a distance. She
waved and he waved back wildly. He was so happy to see Clara again.

They ran to each other and hugged as soon as the gangplank had been put in place. The two young people danced on the quayside.

"How was your aunt's?" asked Jurgen.

"Fun," said Clara, "but not as much fun as at home."

Two days later they went back on board the ship. Half a day passed before the winds were favourable but the great sailing ship then set its course for Denmark. They were returning home!

The ship had been travelling a good three weeks when the Danish coast was sighted. The journey home had taken somewhat longer than the outward-bound trip.

"Another two hours and we'll be there", said Jurgen.

Clara thought it a pity that they were home already. She had everything she wanted just being on board the great ship with Jurgen.

"Will you always stay with me?" she asked.

"Yes", replied Jurgen.

At that instant they heard a very loud cracking noise! Creaking and splintering, a plank broke loose from the ship's hull. How it was possible with such a calm sea no-one knew, but what did that matter? The ship was sinking! Great waves of water poured in. Dozens of sailors risked their lives to close the hole and everyone with a pair of hands to spare helped to pump out the water. To no avail.

A second plank broke and then a third! The ship began to list to one side. Jurgen put his arm around Clara and leapt with her overboard. He was not going to wait until the ship sank.

Jurgen was a good swimmer. It did not matter so very much that he could only use one arm. The sea was cold but Jurgen kept swimming. Every few minutes he slowed his swimming pace so as not to use up too much energy. Now and then a wave would break right over them. Then they were raised up for a moment and Jurgen saw that a sloop was heading towards them. "Keep going, Jurgen!" he thought to himself, and he kept on swimming in the cold water.

The water was clear and deep below Jurgen and beneath him he saw a shoal of mackerel swim by. As he passed some sea-birds, they flew up into the sky. At a few hundred yards from the coast the rescue boat had almost reached them. "Just a little longer!" he thought. "A little longer!" On he swam, even though he had now become terribly cold. All at once,

the sea became rougher. Clara and Jurgen were tossed in all directions by the waves. The wind howled as Jurgen fought with all his strength to stay above water. The sloop was nearly there!

Then, it happened. Clara and Jurgen were picked up by a wave the size of a house and were smashed back down again. Just under the surface was a sunken ship's figure head. Jurgen's head hit against it with a great crack. Everything around him went black.

Jurgen and the girl dropped down into the deep but were fished out again at once by the fishermen in the sloop. They pulled the young couple into the boat with all hands. Jurgen's arm was clasped stiffly about Clara. The fishermen had difficulty in freeing her from him.

Clara did not move. She did not breathe and her heart did not beat. She had drowned. Jurgen had swum with a dead woman. Jurgen, himself, was alive but he had a deep head wound. His hair was caked in blood.

The fisherman brought the sloop back to harbour as quickly as they could. There stood the merchant awaiting news. When he heard that his daughter had died he was beside himself with grief.

"And Jurgen?" he asked.

"He lives", replied the fishermen. "But do not ask how. His head is deeply wounded."

Luckily, a doctor was ready and waiting on the quay. He cleaned out Jurgen's cut with a jug of fresh water and cut off the hair surrounding it with a pair of scissors.

"It doesn't look good", he said. "You must prepare yourself for the worst." He bandaged the wound and gently laid Jurgen in a warm bed.

Jurgen never recovered. He remained alive but had forgotten everything that had ever happened to him. Now and then, he saw faces before him or else he dreamed at night about his cottage by the dunes. He could no longer speak and no longer think.

Do you still remember how one summer's day flower bulbs were washed up on to the Jutland beaches? Most of them were left there and were buried under the sand. Something like that happened to Jurgen too. He was strong, clever, and he could have made much of himself. Alas, that is not what happened. Nonetheless, you might remember that when Jurgen forgot everything he was never again unhappy.

Remember, too, that life is far from being like this for everyone. Jurgen lived hundreds of years ago. Nowadays, it is much easier to take hold of your opportunities!

That was the story from the Jutland dunes. If it has made you sad then I apologize, but not all stories can end happily!

The woman who was good-for-nothing

The mayor stood at the window. He looked smart in his waistcoat and cravat. From his waistcoat pocket dangled his gold watch-chain. His cufflinks were also made of gold. He was the mayor and everyone had to be able to see that. It was a pity that the mayor had cut himself shaving that morning. There was a little cut just under his left eye. Alum had not helped to staunch the bleeding, so the mayor had stuck a piece of tissue paper on his face. The effect was much less stylish, but even a mayor is human.

A boy walked past the mayor's window just as he was considering the urgent business of his town. The mayor knew the boy. He tapped on the window pane and pushed the window open a little way.

"Come here, young man!" he called. The boy turned round quickly – he was a little nervous – and politely greeted the mayor. He took off his cap. His clothes, though clean, were old and shabby. His trousers had been patched ten times or more, his shoes were old and dull.

"What a fine, little fellow you are", said the mayor. "You always look smart, even though your clothes are clearly worn out ..." He thought to himself that 'smart' was, of course, not really the right word, but for such a poor boy it was not at all bad. He smiled and briefly patted his stomach. "But your mother, eh?" he continued, "the washerwoman, you haven't been very lucky with her, have you?"

He assumed that the washerwoman, the boy's mother, was at that moment busy with her washing. Soaping it, scrubbing it, wringing it out, hanging it up – precisely the thing for such a poor woman. Luckily, he never had to do such things himself. What a dreadful thought that was.

"Your mother has asked you to fetch something again, I'll be bound", said the mayor.

"Yes", said the boy and he knew what the man meant.

"How much do you have with you this time?"

"A pint", said the boy very softly.

"Come, come! And yesterday a pint as well. That's two pints altogether. Well, I hope that your mother does her job well", said the mayor. "Fortunately, my mother was not such a drunkard. Tell her that she should be ashamed of herself. She's a good-for-nothing!"

The boy looked at the ground and said nothing. The mayor shut his window again and so the boy continued on his way to the river.

It was autumn and a strong east wind had blown up. Nils, for that was the boy's name, had difficulty standing upright. He was cold as the wind blew through all his clothes. His hair stood up on end and was bleached by sun and sea-water.

Nils turned the corner and arrived at the river. Huge boulders rose out of the water. His mother stood up to her knees in water, rubbing clothes against the boulders to get out the dirt. There was a strong current, so she had to watch out that her washing did not all float away downstream.

"I'm glad to see you", said the washerwoman. "Now you can give me a hand." She shivered. "I'm freezing cold. Have you got anything with you?"

The boy nodded and gave his mother the bottle. She grabbed it and took two large swigs.

"That does a person good", she said contentedly. "Lovely and warm. I suppose it's much better to have a good meal, but drink is much cheaper and it feels the same. Do you want a sip too, Nils?" she asked sweetly. "Just one little sip – no more, because you're really much too young."

Nils took the bottle and sipped. The drink prickled in his mouth. He did not really like it very much but it did make him feel nice and warm.

His mother shivered. "As long as it doesn't make me ill", she said shakily.

"But that won't happen because I'm used to a lot. I work my fingers to the bone to help you up in the world."

An old woman approached them. She was poor as well and was all wrapped up in old shawls. Her left eye had a terrible squint and so she covered it with a curl of hair. However, the curl only drew even more attention to the squinting eye and because she walked with a limp, the whole town called her Crippled Karin with the Curl. She was a friend of the washerwoman's.

"Slaving away again, I see!" called Karin. "You need something warm. A blanket perhaps, or a steak, but no alcohol. I don't think it's at all good that you drink so much."

Karin then told what she had overheard the mayor say to Nils. She had been standing around the corner while the mayor was busy talking to the boy about his mother and how she drank so much and how she should be ashamed of herself.

Karin became angry again as she repeated it. She said: "That man gives a party every week himself with gallons of wine and beer. He should be

careful about what he says! If a poor person has just a little drink they call it drunkenness! When they themselves wobble across the street with red noses and their cravats half undone, well, then they say that they've just been having an enjoyable evening out! They should consider their own behaviour for once!"

"I see", said the washerwoman with tight lips. "So the mayor has said that my son has a good-for-nothing as a mother. That's very nice. He may be right but he should still keep his mouth shut in front of a child! Telling my own son that I'm a good-for-nothing!" The washerwoman bristled with fury. She was so angry!

"You were once a servant girl for that family, weren't you?" asked Karin. The washerwoman nodded. When the mayor had been a little boy she had scrubbed the floors in his parents' house.

"The mayor is giving a party again tonight. In a month's time he will have been in office for seven years and new elections are to be held. He very much wants to win again", said Karin. "He didn't really want to go on with the party because his brother has just died. But, still, all the wine had already been bought and the pies had been baked."

The washerwoman turned pale. Her whole body shook and her voice trembled as she said: "Is his brother dead?"

Karin gave her a strange look. "Are you so upset about it?" she asked. "Ah, but of course, you'll have known him from the past. Was he a nice man?"

"Nice? Nice?" cried the washerwoman. "He was the best man that I have ever met!" Her shoulders shook and wisps of hair stuck to her cheeks.

Crippled Karin put her arm around the washerwoman.

"Is everything all right?" she asked gently.

"No," said the washerwoman, "my head is spinning. Oh God! Don't let me be ill. I feel so sick and cold – I think I have a fever."

"I'll take you home", said Karin. "You're much too ill to carry on working."

"What about my washing?" asked the washerwoman.

"I'll take care of that. Your young son will keep an eye on it for a bit while I take you home."

The washerwoman said: "I've been standing in water all day and haven't eaten a thing. Perhaps I really should go and have a sleep." She sobbed.

Her son began to cry with her out of sympathy. He went and sat on the jetty, letting his legs dangle above the water. The two women went off towards the town, at first straight ahead for a way, then turning by the tree

on the right hand side into an alley. They did not get far for the washerwoman collapsed right at the mayor's door. Crippled Karin could no longer hold her up as she walked with such difficulty herself.

The mayor stood at the window, glass of wine in hand, and had just entered into a conversation with some friends.

"At present", he had just been saying, "things are going badly with the workers. They can no longer do anything, are often ill, and drink themselves into the ground."

At that same moment, the washerwoman collapsed before his very eyes.

"And there you have an example", said the mayor, smiling cruelly. "It isn't even midday and she's drunk again. Her young son is very nice and polite but I don't know what will become of him. One cannot go far with a good-for-nothing as a mother."

Luckily, one of the mayor's servants went outside with a glass of warm milk. The washerwoman took a sip and perked up enough to stand a little. Enough to stumble on to her cottage, with the help of Crippled Karin, and then fall into bed.

"Thank you, Karin", she said softly. She closed her eyes and at once fell into a deep but restless sleep.

Karin turned back towards the river jetty and there washed what still had to be washed. She was not really very good at it, so the washing was not dazzlingly clean. However, it was really very kind of her to help the washerwoman, even so.

That night, Crippled Karin sat with the washerwoman in her impoverished little room.

The mayor's kitchen maid had, all without the mayor's permission, brought over a pan of fried potatoes with a little bacon. It tasted very good to Karin, the washerwoman, and the boy.

Nils went to bed early that night. He slept in the same bed as his mother but in the opposite direction with his head at the footrest. An old tablecloth was wrapped around him. Things were getting better for his mother. The good food and a little sleep helped her greatly to recover.

"Thank you for everything, Karin", said the sick woman, hoarsely. "There is something I must tell you when Nils is asleep. I believe that he's sleeping already. He doesn't know all that has happened to me. I hope that he will not be put to the test as I was. That would mean a lot of trouble for him. Do you swear to tell no-one what I tell you now?"

Karin solemnly promised. The mother sat up straight and began her story. "I was a servant girl in the house of the mayor's parents. His brother was at that time still a student and a real tearaway. He wouldn't have been scared of the devil himself, he came home late at night – he enjoyed life. Even so, he was a good young man and never did anyone harm his whole life long. I swear it on my life. When I had been in the family's service one year, I fell in love with him and he with me. He was rich and I poor, but we were so in love that none of it mattered. Without telling anyone, we became engaged. It was our secret. He did tell his mother whom he loved dearly. She, being understanding and kind, agreed to it. We were happy for a time, but then he had to travel for his studies. As he left he gave me a long kiss and slid a gold ring on to my finger. We were then truly engaged but he was gone."

The washerwoman sighed deeply before continuing. In thinking about her history she became sad again, just as she had been before.

"Once he had definitely left and gone, it turned out that his mother was not so kind after all. I was asked to see her and she told me that the distance between me and her son was enormously great. A rich young man with a poor servant girl was quite obviously impossible. Her son would only become unhappy if he were to marry beneath his station. I, too, would become increasingly unhappy because the differences between us would be too many for us to be equal in our marriage together. And so it went on, for at least half an hour. I was too crushed to speak up against her. I didn't dare. Moreover, I was so young that I believed her. I felt awful, terrible. Only when I lay in my bed at night did I sense that we could have been happy because we loved each other so much. But it had been ended. I gave the gold ring to her and in so doing was forever separated from the student."

The washerwoman had not finished talking. She went on: "The next day, the mother called me to her again. She had invited over Erik Wennker, a glove maker. He was a widower without children and he asked me to marry him on the spot. The mother advised me to think very seriously about this proposal. It hurt me so much! I did not love Erik Wennker at all. I kept on crying and my work suffered. Why was it that a poor girl could not marry a rich boy? Why was it not enough that two people loved each other? It was with the greatest difficulty that I composed myself and once I had, who did I meet in the street but Erik. I knew at once with certainty that we did not belong together but I had no choice and asked him if he still wanted to marry me.

'If you wish to marry a girl who respects you, but who can never truly love you, then I will accept your proposal', I said.

'Love will come in time', he said and with that we became more or less engaged.

We married a week later. The minister blessed the marriage. My mistress was very happy and wished us much happiness.

Once we were married, everything went very well. As time went by, Erik became ever more famous and had ever more work. Expensive shops in Copenhagen bought his gloves and he had to take on three boys to make all the gloves that the people wanted. And you helped us wonderfully with the housekeeping."

Crippled Karin nodded. "You were a good mistress to me. I shall never forget how well you treated me."

"Yes", said the washerwoman. "When you worked for us we were well-to-do. Everything was so good! I never saw the student again. Or rather, just one time, but he didn't see me. That was at his mother's funeral. From a great distance I saw that he was grief-stricken by it. His hair was a mess, his cheeks were grey, and his eyes red from crying. He hadn't seen me, or if he had he hadn't recognized me. He wouldn't be able to recognize me at all now, now that I've become so ugly. He wasn't there when his father died. I believe he was too busy. He was a lawyer in Copenhagen and had many important cases to deal with."

The washerwoman continued her story. She told of the good times she had had together with Erik, but also about the time that things took a turn for the worse. "One evil day, everything went wrong. We had bought a new house and the agent told us it needed rebuilding to the cost of one thousand thalers. The builders had been at work for two weeks when it turned out that it would cost us two thousand thalers. Erik knew rich bankers in Copenhagen and was able to obtain a loan without difficulty, but the courier who was to bring us the money was robbed on the way and so Erik had to take out another loan. He couldn't really afford it. A little while later, when the sale of gloves began to get worse, he went bankrupt. We had to sell everything and let you and the servants go. Luckily, Erik was able to start up again with the help of his friends, but then he became ill. He lay in bed for months. Nils was born at the same time. Naturally, we were very happy about it, but raising a child costs money too and so I had to go and find work as a washerwoman to make ends meet."

The washerwoman needed to use a corner of her threadbare sheet to wipe away her tears when she told of how Erik died. "Erik became ever

more ill. He could scarcely speak anymore and one day he stopped being able to altogether. He always felt cold, at the same time suffering the most dreadful fevers. And then he died. Unexpectedly, nonetheless. We were never really able to say goodbye to one another."

She told of how hard she had had to work to keep herself and her son from starving. How she washed and scrubbed her fingers to the bone by working as a washerwoman. How she had sometimes had to walk for miles just to find the cheapest food to eat, and how she had always been happy that she still had her little boy, whatever pain and difficulty it might cost her.

Karin said nothing and asked nothing. It was not necessary, for the washerwoman's story was crystal clear and she knew much of it herself. So many troubles, it was just not fair that such things should happen to people. The washerwoman had fallen asleep.

The next day, the washerwoman awoke after a night filled with strange dreams. She felt well enough to go back to work but that was a mistake. As soon as she stood in the water her whole body began to tremble. Still,

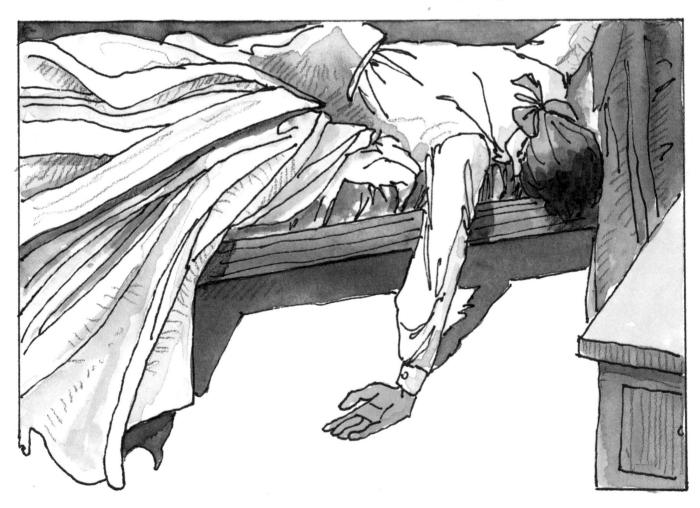

she went on working until she fainted. She plunged full length into the water, her face just above the surface. Her hair floated in all directions, her eyes slightly open to the sky.

This is how Crippled Karin found her friend when she came to tell her that the mayor was expecting her. She took terrible fright and immediately pulled the washerwoman on to dry land.

"Wake up, wake up!" she cried as loudly as she could, but it was all too late. At her wits' end, Karin slapped her friend across the face but that did not help either. The washerwoman was dead.

The mayor, smartly dressed as he always was, heard the bad news a few minutes later.

"So, the old washerwoman has drunk herself to death." He shook his head and smiled broadly. "That'll save the good people a heap of money!" He had received a message from Copenhagen. His brother's will had been found and what did it say but that his whole fortune had been left to the washerwoman, his lost love. Seven thousand silver thalers, enough to build a beautiful house and never to have to work again.

"The little boy will get all the money now", said the mayor to his wife that evening. He took a sip of delicious wine and continued: "I shall ensure

that he is brought up by decent people. People who are some good and who can give the boy a future!" The mayor had Nils come to see him. He promised him that he would be cared for.

"Perhaps it is better that your mother has died. She was a good-for-nothing!" said the mayor. Nils shuddered when he heard that, but said nothing.

The washerwoman was buried the following day in a pauper's grave. The mayor was not there, but Nils was glad of that. However, Crippled Karin was there, as well as all the poor people from the town. Nils threw the first handful of soil on to the coffin. Karin planted a rose stem on the top of the grave.

"Goodbye mother", said Nils softly, once the grave had been filled in. He was quiet for a moment and then asked Crippled Karin: "Is it true, Karin, that my mother was a good-for-nothing?"

"No," said Karin, "that isn't true." They walked away from the grave and went to sit on a grassy knoll.

Karin continued: "Your mother was good. She loved her fiancé very much and when he left she was never able to forget him. Although she thought at first it would never be possible, she did love your father very much and was always faithful to him. And since the day you were born she loved you more than all the treasures of the earth put together. Not many people have such a mother, Nils. She had a good heart – never forget it – and more than anything she wanted you to be happy. And if she is still somewhere, then that is still what she wants. I'm sure of it, for I knew her and loved her very much."

Crippled Karin became Nils' guardian and she bought a nice house on the outskirts of the town. There she and Nils lived until he was grown. Afterwards, he went to study in Copenhagen because he was a clever boy. He gave the house to Crippled Karin.

Nils became very happy. He used his fortune to buy a house in Copenhagen and to hire a servant. After his studies, he was given a good job at the harbour in Copenhagen.

Every year, he returned to the town where he had spent his youth. There he called on Crippled Karin and visited his mother's grave. A beautiful rose-bush stood there which flowered long each year.

When he sat by the grave, staring at the rose-bush and thinking about his mother, he would think: My mother was a good person. She was poor and

thanks to her I am now rich, not only because I have a great deal of money but also because I know how much I meant to her.

And every time that he thought this to himself, the rose-bush would sway to and fro in the wind.

The shadow

Each year, thousands of birds fly south where they spend the winter. It is warm in the south and the sun shines almost all the time. The people who live there are somewhat browner than those who live in the north.

Just like birds, there are a lot of people who travel south in the autumn, too. Just like the birds, they like to spend the winter there as well, but they have to be careful. It may be nice and warm but it can also be too warm. When you stay too long in the sun you become burnt all over: you turn as red as a beetroot and your skin hurts.

There was once a learned man who found the north too cold and so moved down to the south. He thought that he would be able to walk about there just as he was used to doing in the north, but that did not turn out to be the case. After only a few days, he found the sun far too hot and preferred spending the daytime indoors. He kept the shutters closed. He behaved in just the same way as those people did who had lived there their whole lives. They stayed inside during the daytime because it was much too hot outside.

The learned man, he was still a young man, felt it was a great shame. This was not why he had come to the south! The first few days that he was there, the town appeared to be deserted. He felt himself getting smaller, just like his shadow. When the sun is higher in the sky, your shadow does become a little smaller.

The learned man soon did as the town residents. In the afternoons, he tried to sleep a little. This sort of afternoon sleep is called a siesta there. Yet in the evenings, the town came alive. Everyone went outside and talked with each other on the street. Even little children were outside late. They were allowed to go to bed later as they had already slept in the afternoon. Café terraces were open where you could have something delicious to drink or eat. Later still in the evening, everyone lit candles and sat outside until far into the night.

The town was just as sleepy in the daytime as it had been lively during the evening.

Only in one house, right opposite the young man's, was it always quiet. There were, however, many plants on the balcony. Some were flowering. Someone had to be giving them water and so someone had to be living in that house. That was surely true because the learned man had once seen that the balcony doors were open. From the house came the soft sound of music which the learned man found very beautiful.

One day, he asked his landlord: "Do you know who lives in the house opposite?"

"No", replied the man. "No-one is ever to be seen! All I know of the person who lives there is that he plays the piano very badly! It's as if he's practising one piece over and over again and can't get the hang of it."

One particular evening, the learned man felt terribly tired and went to bed early. Because it was still warm, he had left the balcony doors wide open and had pushed his bed right up to them. After sleeping for a couple of hours, he was suddenly awakened. He sat up straight and looked outside where he saw something strange. It seemed as if the flowers on the balcony opposite were giving out light.

Amidst the flowers stood the most beautiful woman. She shone just like

the flowers. The light was so strong that it hurt the learned man's eyes. Even so, the learned man wanted to keep looking and opened his eyes wide. He got up and walked on to his balcony. There was nothing to see anymore: the woman had disappeared and the flowers were as before. The balcony door was slightly open, however, and the sound of a piano came softly from the house. Who lived in that peculiar house and how did its resident enter? There was only a long row of shops on the ground floor. Some evenings later, the young man was sitting out on his balcony again. A single candle was alight behind him which caused his shadow to be cast completely over the house opposite. The learned man's shadow stood, as it were, amidst the flowers and moved when the learned man moved. Exactly as you might expect from a shadow.

It would be fun, thought the man, if that shadow were just once to go inside and take a look.

"Shadow, just take a look inside that house opposite! But if you do, you must come back to tell me what you've seen!" He nodded to his shadow which nodded back politely. It would have been difficult for a shadow not to do so.

The man sat a while enjoying the warm evening and then stood up. He walked inside and shut the balcony door. Something strange happened behind him but the man did not see what it was. Luckily so, for had he seen it he would have taken fright. His shadow also went through a door but not the one to his own house! He remained at the house opposite and went to take a peek inside the strange house with the balcony plants! The learned man got into his bed and slept deeply. You do not need a shadow for that.

The next day, the learned man set off to do some errands. It was then that he discovered that his shadow had disappeared.

"That's odd", he said to himself. "How can one lose one's shadow?" Yet, wherever he looked, whether to the left or to the right, his shadow was not to be found. Well, now, thought the man again, perhaps my shadow did indeed go looking inside that house. I hope he comes back to tell me what he has seen.

The learned man did not very much like his shadow's disappearance. He felt a little lonely. Not that his shadow had been useful to him but, even so, it still gave him an empty feeling now that it was gone. Moreover, he was scared that people might say something about it.

That evening, the learned man went to sit on his balcony once more until late at night. He had again placed the candle on the table behind him, but no shadow appeared on the balcony on the other side of the street. He stood up, sat down again, waved his arms about, moved his head from side to side, but nothing helped. His shadow had gone away.

Nonetheless, you know how it is in warm countries – everything grows much faster there. To his great relief, the young man noticed that he was beginning to grow a new shadow after only a few days. Three weeks later, it was so large that the learned man dared to mingle amongst people again. No-one would notice anything odd about him anymore.

The learned man decided to return to his own country. He had had enough of the sun's heat. He sold his house with the balcony and went to live again in his own house in the north.

He had been at home for two months, when there came one evening a light tap at the door. The learned man barely heard it as he was studying his books. However, he had sharp ears and so he called out: "Enter!" The door did not open and no-one entered. So the learned man walked to the door and opened it himself.

A very tall, thin man stood on the other side. To all appearances he was dressed in the clothes of a gentleman.

"Good evening", said the learned man, and asked: "Who are you?"

"I had expected this from you, sir", said the visitor. "I knew that you

wouldn't recognize me! Now that I have put on some weight and am dressed, you no longer know me."

"Why ever should I know you?" asked the learned man, a little crossly.

"I am your very own shadow, sir!" cried the strange visitor. "A normal person recognizes his own shadow, does he not? You thought, of course, that you would never see me again. I do not know how you have been since we saw each other last. I have done very well. I have become rich." The shadow played with his gold watch chain as he spoke. He wore splendid rings set with diamonds on his fingers.

"What is the meaning of all this? I don't understand it."

"Ah, that you don't understand is not so strange", said the shadow. "What happened was quite extraordinary. I am not commonplace and neither are you, sir. I stood on my own two feet only after you asked it of me. I must tell you: it all went exceptionally well. I simply wanted to see you before you die, because people do die, after all", he smiled.

The learned man nodded. He could find no words to say.

The shadow continued: "I so much wanted to see again the country where I was born."

The learned man remained silent. It was all very confusing. He was standing in the doorway talking to his shadow! Well, perhaps it would be best if he were to ask him inside. A shadow, when all is said and done, is a person too.

"Shadow, please come in", he said. The shadow did as he was asked and entered the living room. He chose the best chair he could find there and sat down contentedly.

"I see, sir, that you have a new shadow", he said. "Did it cost you a lot of money? I can pay you back, of course. Just tell me how much you had to spend."

"Please, let us not talk about money", said the learned man, a little irritated. "I would very much like to hear what there was to see in that house opposite me!"

"I should be happy to tell you, sir, but you must promise me that you will never tell a soul that I was once your shadow. Annoying questions would then be asked. Everyone would want to know at once whatever you had been up to in your life and I so dislike speaking badly of people."

The learned man, while hearing the shadow's last sentence, made no

comment. "I promise that I shall tell no-one that you were my shadow. I give you my solemn word."

It was only then that he saw what a curious man his visitor was. He was dressed from head to toe in black as if he were in deep mourning. He wore a ring on each of his fingers. They were gold, silver, with diamonds, and others set with all other kinds of stone. From his waistcoat pocket hung a gold watch chain. For a shadow he did seem to be rather vain. Was he, perhaps, becoming a little bit human?

The shadow smoothed out his beard, crossed his legs, and went on: "I shall tell you everything. Poetry lived in the house opposite with the balcony. I stayed in that house for three weeks. I learned more there than someone who has spent their entire life reading all the poems he can find."

"Aha!" cried the learned man. "It was Poetry! Now I understand. Poetry usually lives alone, certainly in a town. I only ever saw her for a moment. She shone like a star. So, you broke loose from me and went inside?"

"That I did, sir", said the shadow. He rather snappily added: "But if you'll forgive me: I am an independent man. You made me so. Furthermore, I enjoy considerable wealth and have always behaved correctly. For those reasons, I deserve esteem and respect. I would, therefore, be very much obliged if you were to call me 'sir' as, indeed, I call you."

For a moment, the shadow looked smugly at the learned man who was quite astonished. However, he soon resumed his story. He said: "I entered and found myself in the salon. That is where you, sir, had so wanted to look. But that was not possible as there was no light there. I went on to the next room. It was completely dark there, too, but shadows, by nature, are used to the dark and so I was able to find my way. I passed through a good ten rooms, some of which were small and some like great halls. I then saw the lady of the house, Poetry, in the distance. I was unable to get too close to her or the light would have destroyed me."

"What did you see, sir?", asked the learned man.

"Everything", replied the shadow, confidently. "I saw everything and that's why I now know everything."

"But how did it look, sir?" pressed on the learned man. He did not quite understand and was, in any case, feeling impatient.

"I thank you for calling me 'sir'", said the shadow. "But a respectable man such as yourself surely knows that decent people have patience. Permit me to tell my tale without interruption. I find it very annoying."

It was now the second time that the shadow had corrected the learned man. He did not make any comment. He did not need to either because the shadow continued further.

"As I have already said, I did not go into the full light. I stayed in the gloom

where a shadow can still survive. From there, I saw everything and now I know everything. I was at the Gate of Poetry."

"But how was it, sir, that you could see everything? Were there books on the shelves containing all the world's truth?" asked the learned man.

"No, no", said the shadow, "just listen to me, please. It wasn't in books, it was just there. However it was, it made a great impression on me. Had you been there, sir, you might not have noticed much. I did. The truth all around me made me into a human being. I began to put on weight and realized at once that I was someone and not merely someone else's follower. I began to think over things. I didn't do that when I was stuck to you. At last, I came to know who I was."

The shadow took a small sip of the tea which the learned man had poured for him.

"I left that house to return to you as a person. You, sir, were no longer there; you had returned again to the cold north. I was ashamed. I had no clothes, no shoes, and didn't know the time. So, I hid and only came out when it was dark. I crept along walls and peered inside everywhere. I saw what no-one else could see and what no-one should see, in fact!

Even when I was still your shadow I had seen bad things happen. For that

reason I asked you not to speak a word of our past. I will then not need to tell anyone about it and will not have to answer any questions. I recall that before your exams you had written some difficult formulae on your hand to get a good grade. I still well remember how you copied pages from other books when writing your first book. And you, sir, have surely not forgotten the bottles of wine you used to drink at night. You told your parents that you would never touch a single drop of alcohol! Do you still remember the tax inspector who you cheated? And the borrowed books which you never returned? Ah! I should stop. You remember it all very well yourself, sir.

The evil which I saw in the weeks after becoming a person was a very different sort of evil. I heard the bad things that people said about their friends and families. I used that information: I wrote to those families, neighbours, and friends about what I knew of them. Those people became fearful of me. Naturally, they didn't want all that I knew about them to be put in the newspaper! To get what I wanted, all I had to do was to say it and it happened. I also received a lot of money. More and more of it, because I knew where and how to get it.

I am now fabulously rich. I have a beautiful house. This is my address.

Good evening to you, sir!" The shadow handed his visiting card to the learned man. He stood up and, without saying another word, walked out of the room. The learned man presently heard his front door open and shut and then he was alone again.

The learned man thought over the shadow's story for weeks afterwards. Yet man forgets everything in time and six months later the young man had almost forgotten that his shadow was leading its own life.

Seven years on, the shadow returned.

"How are things with you, sir?" asked the shadow, once seated on the best chair with a cup of coffee.

"Oh", said the learned man, "I'm still trying to teach people the difference between good and evil. But there's not much point. People don't want to listen."

"That's strange", said the shadow. "I don't take any notice of people and they all listen to me. I don't think that you understand people or the world. Why don't you go on a long journey, sir? Wouldn't you like to see some more of the world? I am going on a journey this summer, why not accompany me? We shall get on well for we've known each other our

whole lives. Come with me as my guest. You don't have to worry about money. I have, quite literally, more than enough of that. I'll pay for everything."

The learned man said: "I cannot accept your offer, sir."

"Why not?" asked the shadow, and he said: "Travel does a person good. In any case, you'll be my shadow, so you'll be doing something for me as well."

"That, sir, I shall never do", said the learned man. "It's madness to speak of such things."

"So is the world!" said the shadow, and he left.

In the weeks thereafter, things did not go so well for the learned man. He sold very few of his books, gave ever fewer lessons, and so no longer earned so much. He slept badly at night, dreaming of bailiffs coming to strip his house bare and of living a life of poverty. The worst thing of all, though, was that people did not believe in truth. They were becoming worse and worse and he could do nothing about it.

"You don't look at all well. You should see the doctor", said his housekeeper to him. "Why do you work so hard? You look like a very shadow of yourself."

A cold shiver passed through the learned man when he heard that. A shadow of yourself! He already existed but was far richer than him!

The next day, the shadow stood on his doorstep again.

He said: "You must stop working for a while. Go to the coast, sir! The sea air will do you good. I'll take you with me and pay any costs. You have only to keep me entertained and make a good report on the journey and everything will be fine."

When the learned man shook his head, the shadow quickly went on

further: "I do it not just for you, sir, but mostly for myself. My beard does not grow thick enough. Sea air is so healthy that it's sure to help. Be a sensible fellow and come with me."

The shadow had to spend a little more time persuading the learned man, but in the end he succeeded.

They left a few days later. The shadow was now the master and the learned man the shadow. They lodged in a charming house next to the coast. The sea was beautiful and the air was indeed healthy. Both of them were quite contented.

The shadow and the learned man ate together, walked together, and talked with each other a great deal. The shadow had no difficulty with his role as the master. He knew exactly what he could do as the master and that is how he behaved. The learned man respected this, as he was a friendly man.

One day, the learned man proposed that the shadow and he no longer need call each other 'sir'. "We've known each other so long!" he said.

"That is true", said the shadow. "We've known each other for a very long time. Even so, I don't feel that it's such a very good idea. I loathe it when

people don't call me 'sir'. I think it's because I'm reminded of when I was enslaved to you, sir. As a shadow, I always felt so subservient! Now that I've become a gentleman, I also like to be referred to as such. It has nothing at all to do with you, sir. It's just my feeling."

"I can quite understand", said the learned man.

However the shadow went on further: "Do you know what: we'll go along with your proposal half way. When I speak to you I'll drop the 'sir' while you go on using it to me. You'll have half your wish and it'll stop annoying you so much!"

So it came about that the shadow was called 'sir' by the learned man, while he was treated like an ordinary person by the shadow. It was strange, yet he had been given half his wish, after all.

The next day, the shadow and the learned man lay on the beach where they met with a real princess. She was a beautiful young woman with fine golden hair. She had also come to the coast for her health. She had a serious complaint: she could see too well! She saw every detail at once. You may think that that would be fun, but fun it was not. If you can see everything, you become desperately unhappy.

Within ten minutes, she had seen that the shadow and the learned man were different to all the others on the beach.

"That tall, thin man", she said to a lady-in-waiting – she meant the shadow, "he's here to make his beard grow. But there's something odd about him. He has no shadow!"

The princess was, however, an inquisitive young woman. She rather liked the shadow in a strange way. Therefore, she had one of her ladies-in-waiting invite the unusual man for a stroll. The shadow thought it a very good idea. It was not long before the princess and the shadow were walking along the edge of the dunes.

"How is it that you have no shadow?" the princess asked the shadow.

"You have truly remarkable eyesight!" cried the shadow. "No-one yet has remarked on my rather unusual shadow."

"Unusual shadow?" asked the princess. "Why, you have none at all."

"Indeed I do", said the shadow. "I have brought up my shadow to clothe himself like a person. I don't much like ordinary things and my shadow is certainly quite extraordinary! It's very expensive to keep my shadow, but a gentleman with position knows best how to spend his money." Could he

be right? the princess wondered. Could the air here be so healthy that I am now cured of my condition? I do not think that I shall return home just yet. This stranger's company is much too pleasant!

That evening, the princess met with the shadow again. A grand ball was being held in the great house by the beach.

"May I ask you for this dance?" asked the shadow, politely.

"But of course!" said the princess.

She knew at once that she had never ever had such a good dancing partner. The shadow almost glided across the ballroom floor. It was wonderful.

While they danced, the shadow told her about the country from which he came. "I come from a warm country in the south. You'd hardly believe how lovely the weather is there. Nearly as warm as the tropical room in your palace", he said.

The princess had never spoken to anyone who knew that she had a tropical room in the palace. That was remarkable! He must be the most learned man in the world. She did not know, of course, that the shadow had peered into the palace and had looked at all the secret places.

It did not take long before the princess fell head over heels in love with the shadow. She wanted to tell him but she was wise. She thought about it carefully at first. He dances very well, she thought, and he knows a great deal, but whether he is the right marriage partner I cannot be sure. If I married him he would be king and that is quite something!

She decided that she would compose some difficult questions for the shadow. She wanted to test him. She started at once.

"Buy a pile of books for me", she ordered her chief lady-in-waiting, who did as she was asked. Night after night the princess sat reading. She read about immortality, about nature, and about philosophy. Each time she saw the shadow, she would ask him a difficult question.

"Why does the earth travel round the sun?" she asked the shadow. The shadow then gave a long speech about two spheres being attracted to one other, about eclipses, and about space.

"Why does a person have a personality?" asked the princess, and the shadow explained and explained.

The princess was nearly satisfied, but a third time to be sure, she thought. They had finally reached the coast. She wanted to ask one more question before marrying the foreigner.

"Why is a person a person?" she asked. The shadow did not know. This was a terribly difficult question! Yet he was clever and laughed.

"That question is so simple!" he cried. "Even my shadow knows the answer to that!"

So the princess called to the shadow's shadow who was sitting quietly in a corner.

"Why is a person a person?" the princess asked the shadow, who was really the learned man.

"Because he thinks that he is a person! And so that is what he is!" said the learned man. He had thought long about this and had written a whole book on the subject.

The princess was now completely convinced. How clever he is, how clever! she thought. If even this man's shadow knows the answer to such a difficult question then he really is the cleverest man in all the world!

The princess saw that a great many women wanted to dance with the shadow. Another woman will soon take him for a husband, she thought. Therefore, she quickly went up to the shadow and asked him to marry her. The shadow was very clever. He did not say yes at once, although he very much wanted to do so.

"May I think it over for a day?" he asked.

"Of course, of course!" said the princess. She had fallen so in love with the shadow that she forgot completely that she was the princess and he the commoner. The next day, the princess asked again and the shadow replied: "I shall be happy to marry you."

The princess said: "Let us keep our engagement secret until I am back at my palace." The shadow was in complete agreement. "I shall tell no-one!" he promised. "Not even my own shadow."

The shadow and the princess journeyed the following day to the palace. The learned man went with them, of course, since he was the shadow's shadow. The princess and the shadow stared at each other the whole journey long, tightly holding each other's hand. They were in love, the princess a little more than the shadow. They reached the palace after half a day, a beautiful old castle surrounded by a moat.

Once the shadow and the learned man had been left alone for a moment, the shadow said: "You'll have heard the news already, of course. I'm to be a powerful man. Soon I shall be king of this country and shall reign over the people. I'll not forget you, of course, as I've known you all my life. You

may always live with me in the palace. You may ride in my golden coach and I'll give you a good salary every year.

I do have one condition. You may never tell anyone that you were once a person. You are my shadow and that is what everyone will call you. That is also how you'll be treated. I'll make sure that not too many of my subjects walk over you, but that is bound to happen now and then. When I'm sitting on my balcony with the princess and she stands up, it's quite possible that she might stand on your head. You'll just have to learn to live with it."

"That's going too far", said the learned man, determinedly. "I'm not having anything to do with this. It's pure deceit! I am a person and you are my shadow!"

"That's a great pity for you", said the shadow. "No-one will believe you. And would you mind watching what you say? You forgot to call me sir just then. I am almost a prince, a royal majesty! One more time and I'll call the palace guard."

"I'm not listening to you anymore", said the learned man. "I'll go and see the princess to tell her the truth."

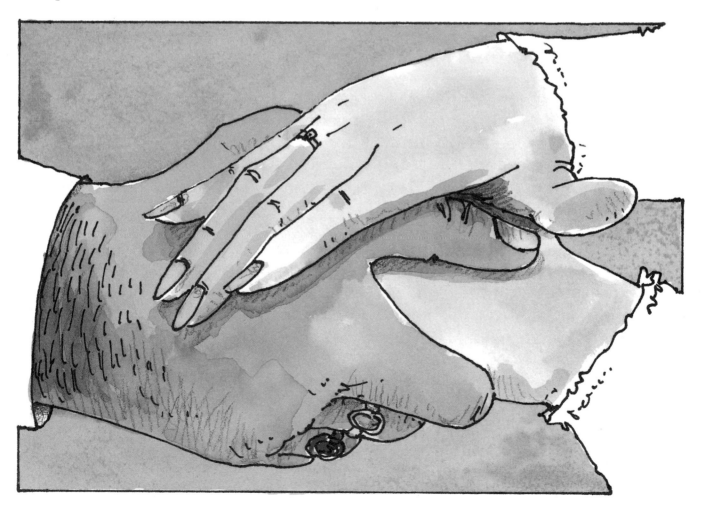

"I'll be seeing her before you do", said the shadow. "I am her fiancé. In the meantime, you'll be going to prison." He called the palace guards who, of course, listened to him. He was practically the crown prince. The learned man was handcuffed and taken to the dungeons.

"Is something wrong?" asked the princess when she entered the great hall a few moments later. "You look so pale and you're shaking all over. Don't get ill, now that we're to be married."

The shadow said: "My shadow has suddenly lost his wits! Probably he is unable to cope with the idea that he will soon be a royal shadow!"

"How dreadful", said the princess. "You've had him locked up, I hope?"

"Naturally. I think that he could be extremely dangerous in his present condition", said the shadow.

The whole town was lit up in celebration that night. Everywhere there were lamps hanging and torches burning. All the people came out of their homes to wish the princess and crown prince well.

The shadow and the princess were married in the palace's great ballroom. They gave each other a wedding ring and kissed. They were now man and wife, prince and princess. Outside, fireworks crackled. Inside, corks were popping from huge bottles of champagne. Everyone danced and made merry. The party was complete when the princess came on to the balcony with her new husband. All assembled shouted: "Hurrah! Hurrah! Long live the prince and princess!"

Everyone enjoyed the wonderful celebrations. Well, almost everyone. The learned man did not notice any of it. The princess had had him executed just before the wedding without a word to the shadow about it.

The Quagmire King's daughter

Perhaps you do not think that storks tell their chicks stories as people do their children. Yet even stork parents know a great many stories to tell to their small sons and daughters before they go to sleep. Naturally, each father or mother will tell a different kind of story. It always depends a little on who they are, where they live, and what they do to earn money or to find food. The stories which a stork tells are almost all about water and frogs. That is what storks like most of all.

Furthermore, storks who live in the cold north tell their chicks how lovely and warm it is in the south, in the country of Egypt, while the storks who live in the south, and who walk around breathless from the heat, tell their children about the wonderful coolness of the north. Of course, it makes a difference how old the storks' chicks are. Older chicks can be told different, more complicated stories than can younger ones. Little chicks are content with any story as long as it is exciting, but bigger chicks very much want the story to mean something or else for it to be about their own family.

There are, however, a few storks' stories which everyone knows, young or old. One of the very oldest stories is, of course, the story of Moses, a little boy who was placed in the river because his mother could not look after him and because she hoped that someone would find him who could. He was indeed found, and by a real Egyptian princess as well, the daughter of the king. So it was that he was raised to manhood in the royal palace. He became a very important and famous man, but no-one knows where he lies buried and so no-one can visit his grave.

There is another such old storks' story, a story which every stork mother and father has told to their chicks who have then told it to their own chicks so that no-one really knows just how old it is. It is, perhaps, one thousand years old and every stork who has ever told it has made it just that little bit better. The storks who first told the story lived every summer in a nest on the roof of a Viking's house. Viking was the name given to the warriors of that distant, cold land. The house was right next to a place

known as the Wild Quagmire. That lies all the way to the north where hardly anyone comes. The Wild Quagmire is enormously big. Some say that it used to be a sea and that the sea floor rose to the surface. It stretches for miles in all directions and is completely encircled by a sort of swamp with many shallow ponds. The swamp is overgrown with mosses, wild raspberries, and small stunted birch trees. The trees never become any bigger because the weather is too cold for it.

A kind of mist always hangs above the swamp, and people say that even ten years ago wolves were still living there. Therefore, it should be clear why this piece of land was called the Wild Quagmire.

If you were to see it, you would be well able to imagine how dreadfully desolate and also dangerous it looked one thousand years ago. Although, in fact, it cannot have been all that different. At that time, just as now, there were reeds with long, waving plumes growing everywhere as tall as a grown man and, just as now, the birch trees had a silver bark and delicate leaves on their branches which blew to and fro in the wind.

The animals were not so very different then either: the flies had the same transparent wings as now and the storks walked about on their long, red

legs, and they were clothed in their black and white feathers.

What happened at that time to unlucky people who accidentally found themselves in the swamp was precisely the same as would happen to people today: they sank in the mud and disappeared without a trace. Nothing was ever heard from anyone who had been lost in the swamp because they had gone to the Quagmire King who was master over the kingdom beneath it. Some people call him the Swamp King, but because the storks call him the Quagmire King that is what we shall do too, for it is the storks' story which will now be told to you.

No-one knows exactly how the Quagmire King ruled and perhaps it is better not to know. Right next to the swamp stood the Viking house made of heavy wooden beams built on top of a cellar made from stone. The house had three floors and a tower. On top of the tower's roof is where the storks had built their nest. The stork wife now sat there on her eggs, quite confident that they would hatch on time and be healthy chicks.

One evening, the father stork was away for much longer than his wife was used to and she began to feel a little worried. When, at last, he did return he was terribly agitated and upset.

"I must tell you something very dreadful", he said to his wife.

"Oh please, could you not!" cried out his wife at once. "Don't forget that I'm brooding here on our eggs? If you were to give me a shock it could be very bad for them and they might not even hatch!"

"But I must tell you", he said. "The daughter of our Egyptian host is here. You know, from the house where we go when it gets too cold here. Don't we do that every year? We always fly that great distance, but she, the daughter, has also dared to make the journey and has arrived here. But now she is lost and that was not what was meant to happen!"

"You don't mean that princess?" asked his wife. "Please don't take so long. You know how nervous I get just sitting here brooding!"

"Very well, I shall explain", said her husband. "You know, of course, that her father, the king, is seriously ill? The king's wisest men now say that only one particular flower from the Wild Quagmire can cure him. So, she dressed herself as a swan to fly here, together with two of her ladies-in-waiting. They are used to this, however, for they fly here every year for a beauty preparation. This time the princess has gone with them, but now she has been lost!"

"You always need to use so many words just to say something simple",

grumbled the mother stork to her husband. "You shouldn't tell it all so slowly and let me get all flustered – it'll make the eggs cool off!"

"I've looked very hard everywhere around", the father stork went on, taking no notice of his wife's complaining. "This evening, while I was hunting frogs amongst the reeds, precisely three swans came flying by. I don't know why, but I felt that something was amiss. I had the strange feeling that I only saw the swans' skin."

"That's as may be", said his wife, "but you were going to tell me about the princess, not about a few swan skins."

"If you stand up for just a moment", said her husband, "then you will be able to see that in the middle of the swamp lies a kind of lake. In that lake is the trunk of an alder tree, and that is where the three swans went to sit. They shook out their feathers a bit and took a look around. Then, one of the swans took off her swan's skin and I recognized the Egyptian princess immediately, clothed only by her long, black hair. I heard her ask the others to take care of her feather dress, and then I saw her dive into the lake to pluck the flower which she fancied she saw there. The others promised to do as she asked but, as soon as the princess had dived beneath the water, they flew off, taking her feather dress with them.

What were they up to? I wondered, and I think that the princess was thinking exactly the same thing. But it soon became clear, for the ladies-in-waiting called out from the sky: 'Dive all you like, for you will never fly again. You will never again see Egypt, for here you will stay in the Wild Quagmire!' They then tore the princess' feather dress into a thousand pieces, so that it seemed as if it were snowing, and away they flew into the high, blue sky until I could see them no more!"

"But that is just dreadful!" cried the mother stork. "What cruel women! But go on, do!"

"The princess burst into sobs and as soon as her tears fell upon the alder trunk, it suddenly began to move. The tree trunk turned over and then I saw that it wasn't a real tree trunk at all: it was the Quagmire King in disguise. The poor girl was terribly frightened and tried to flee into the swamp. Yet where she tried to run cannot support even a light-footed stork such as myself, and so she sank underneath at once. The alder tree disappeared into the ground as well, for it was he who was pulling her down. The water bubbled for a moment and then everything was gone! The princess is buried in the Wild Quagmire, and no-one can now bring

her father the flower which might cure him. I know that you wouldn't have been able to watch, mother stork, had you been there too."

"You shouldn't tell me such terrible things in my condition", complained his wife. "It could damage the eggs. That princess can look after herself very well and I'm quite sure that someone will help her."

"I shall go and look every single day", promised the stork, and he kept to his word.

Many weeks passed without event, but one day, as the stork was flying over the place where the princess had disappeared, he saw that a long, bright green shoot was growing from the bottom of the lake. Once the shoot had reached the water surface, there emerged a leaf from it which quickly grew bigger. A bud soon appeared as well, and one morning, with the sun's first rays, it opened. Inside was the very sweetest little child, a girl. It appeared quite as if she had just stepped from her bath and she looked so like the lost princess that, at first, the stork thought that that was who it was, but that she had become smaller again. Yet, when he began to think it over, it seemed to him more likely that she must be the

child of the princess and the Quagmire King. Why else would she be lying in a water-lily?

I cannot leave that poor child to lie there, thought the stork. Yet, what should I do with her? Our nest is full and there is not room enough for even one more. But wait. The Viking's wife very much wants a child and she has none. Everyone does say that we storks bring people their children, and so why shouldn't I do exactly that, for once? I shall take this little one to the Viking's wife and make her happy.

Without further ado, the stork picked up the little girl, flying with her to the Viking's house, and with his beak he pecked a big hole in the paper which hung in the window, serving as a kind of window-pane. He laid the baby in the arms of the sleeping Viking woman, returned to his family, and told the whole story to his wife.

The chicks heard everything too, of course, but were now old enough to listen when their parents had something to discuss with each other.

"I told you before that the princess wasn't dead, didn't I? She's sent her child to the world above where she'll be well cared for at any rate", said the mother stork. "And now, stop worrying so much about that princess

and spend some time on our chicks, for it won't be so long before we must leave for the winter. I get the shivers already, now and then. The cuckoo has already left and the quails talk of nothing but the wind. They say that the wind will soon turn and then we will be able to leave, too. I think that our chicks will manage the great journey extremely well."

In the meantime, the Viking's wife had awoken and was overjoyed with the child which she had found in her arms. She could not stop hugging and kissing the child but the child seemed not to like this at all, crying without stopping until it had cried itself to sleep. Even then, it was more lovely than any other baby could have ever been.
From the day that the baby arrived, the Viking's wife walked singing round the house almost all the time for, because of the child, she had been given the feeling that her husband and his warriors would soon be coming home. She and her servants at once set about making the house clean and welcoming.
Beautiful carpets embroidered with pictures of the Viking gods were brought from the cellar, the dust beaten out, and hung on the walls. The

old shields were cleaned and polished, brightly coloured cushions were placed on all the benches, and logs were piled high next to the great fireplace. The Viking's wife worked hard too. So much so, that at the end of the day she was completely exhausted and fell at once into a deep, contented sleep.

However, when she awoke the next day she was horrified: the little child had gone! She leapt out of bed and, because it was still dark, lit an oil lamp. She saw something sitting at the foot of the bed, yet it was not a baby but a terribly ugly toad which gave her the shivers. She picked up a broomstick with which to kill the creature but it looked at her so imploringly that she let her arm fall back. She could not bring herself to harm an innocent animal!

The toad gave out a rather sad, little croak and the Viking's wife went to the window to open the shutters. The sun's first rays entered the house and shone on to the toad. Then it was that something very strange happened: the toad's great mouth became smaller and shrank to the size of a child's. The creature stretched out its legs and, before the Viking wife's very eyes, the ugly toad changed into the lovely child which the stork had laid in her arms.

"What's wrong with me?" the woman asked herself. "Was this just a bad dream? For that is my child which lies before me." So saying, she picked her up, kissing and cuddling her. However, the child did not like this at all. She kicked and scratched and even bit her, just like a cat.

The Viking did not return that day, and when the woman watched for him the following day he did not come either. The Viking was, indeed, on his way, but a strong wind was against him and he could only sail slowly. The storks were very pleased with this strong wind but it did mean that the Viking took much longer to return home.

After a few days, the Viking's wife realized what the matter was with her child: she was bewitched! So it was that during the day she was a pretty little child, if badly behaved and bad-tempered, while at night she changed into a sorrowful toad, its eyes filled with sadness. It was as if there were two little children within the one child, and so it was, in fact. In the daytime, the child had the beauty of her mother, the princess, but the cruel character of her father. Yet, at night, her outward appearance would change into that of the Quagmire King while the sweet nature of her mother could be seen in her eyes. How was the evil spirit which held sway over the child to be defeated?

The Viking's wife, who loved the child dearly, did not know.

In any event, she could tell nothing to her husband, who any day might sail in with his ships. Were he to know what was wrong with the child, he would surely abandon her somewhere to die, as was the custom with their people. That must never happen to her child, decided the Viking's wife. Her husband would only ever see the child during the day.

The morning that the Viking and his men came sailing into harbour, huge flocks of storks grouped together on the roofs of the Viking's house and the roofs of the sheds and stables beside and behind it. There they had slept the night before and now they were quite ready to start their journey south.

"Is everyone ready?" called the leader. "Women and children pay attention, we're going!"

"I'm not so big yet", said a stork youngster. "That'll make flying easier. How exciting it is to be travelling!"

"Stay together!" warned the father stork, and mother stork added: "And don't flap your wings too much. It'll only use up energy and you'll need it all to fly such a long way." So away they flew, off to the warmth of Egypt.

The next morning, the blast of horns sounded everywhere to tell the people that the Viking and his men were approaching. They brought with them gifts from the faraway lands to which they had gone. They had won many battles and everyone in the lands where they went had been frightened of them. A celebration banquet was held that night in the Viking's house next to the Wild Quagmire.

A whole barrel of mead was brought inside, a sort of drink made from honey which people there often drank. The great fire was lit in the middle of the hall, animals were slaughtered, and the delicious roasting smells wafted through the whole house. The fire crackled and the smoke wound its way through the hole in the attic roof. Everyone had dressed in their finest clothes and everything looked splendid.

A great many guests had been invited and many magnificent gifts were handed out. All arguments and unpleasantness were forgotten, everyone drank and was merry. Men threw half-eaten chicken drumsticks to other men as a sign of friendship.

The Viking's men also had a singer amongst them so that their brave deeds could be retold and preserved for their children and grand-children. The singer, who had also been on the journey as a warrior and so well knew what to sing, had made up a song which told of all their brave deeds and adventures. Each verse was followed by this chorus:

"Though die I must, and die you must, and die as we all must,
Live on the honour we have earned, kept in our children's trust!"

Everyone sang along with the chorus, beating out the rhythm on their shields, which had helped them so well in battle, or simply hammering the wooden table with a bare bone. It all made an awful lot of noise.

The Viking's wife sat in the banqueting hall. She was dressed in her finest and wore a long, flowing dress made by hand from silk and around her neck was the most beautiful golden necklace from which hung many

jewels. The singer did not forget, either, to mention her beauty in his song, which was very long, and, of course, he also told of the priceless treasure which she had given her husband: the child.

The Viking was indeed most happy with the pretty child. He had seen her only for a moment that day and thought her very lovely. He rather liked the fact that the child was wild and angry. He hoped that she would some day make a brave warrior who would not so much as whimper if someone were to shave off her eyebrows with his sword, as was the custom of his people. No, she would not grow up to be just any woman. Even in so short a time, he had seen that at once!

A new barrel of mead came to the table, for there was a lot being drunk and warriors could drink a great deal. In those days, there was a saying which went: 'A cow knows when she has had her fill, but a fool does not know when to stop!' It was something which all the warriors had heard but to which very few listened.

The celebration lasted for a very long time and the Viking's wife became particularly tired, really much preferring to go to bed. Yet the guests stayed on since they found the food and drink far too good, and there was

still so much that it took ages to be finished. It was indeed a merry gathering that honoured the return of the Vikings! However, in those days it was normal to give parties which would last all night, where there was a lot of noise, and where no-one knew what he was doing anymore by the end. It was also normal, once the party had ended, for the servants to run their fingers through the warm ash of the old fire and to lick off the fat from their sooty fingers.

That same year, the Viking went away again on another journey with his warriors, even though the autumn storms had almost started up again. He said that he would only go to the other side of the sea. His wife and her pretty child stayed behind. The Viking's wife watched the ships until she could no longer see them through the thick mist hanging over the sea. She then slowly turned around and walked, deep in thought, back to the Viking's house. Her thoughts were particularly odd and she did not really dare to speak them out loud for she had come to realize that she loved the ugly toad with the sad eyes just as much as she did the kicking and biting child who she could only quieten with great difficulty. She was shocked by her own thoughts and did not quite know what she should do! It was now almost winter and the thick autumn mist, which the Vikings called 'the devourer' because it ate through the leaves on the trees, hung over the land almost every day. When it finally dispersed it was only to be replaced by snow beginning to fall. The snow floated down over the land in a million little snowflakes and covered everything in a layer of whiteness so that, eventually, the whole world appeared to be white. The sparrows came and flew up to the tower of the Viking's house, which the storks had used for their home, and said to each other what a terrible mess the previous owners had made of it.

Those previous owners, the storks, were now in Egypt, the country by the River Nile where the sun always shines and where it is usually as warm as it only ever is on the very best summer days in the north. While all the leaves had fallen from the trees in the north, leaving them looking thin and sad, flowers bloomed everywhere in Egypt in fabulous colours, and a flock of storks sought out a nice spot where they could rest after their long journey. Together, they built nests atop the many ruins there from which they could look out over the pyramids which stood out very clearly in the sharp sunlight. Ostriches raced each other in the desert where the pyramids stood, and lions stretched out lazily in the sun, wondering what they were actually doing there.

Yet, most beautiful of all to the storks in their 'second country' was the River Nile. There was very little water in the great river at that time

because there had been no rain, but that was to the storks' advantage for the river bottom was covered in frogs! The younger birds, who were there for the first time, could hardly believe their eyes, and yet it was really true. "This is how it always is in our warm second country", explained the mother stork.

"Are we going further or are we staying here?" asked her children who wanted to know.

"Further on there is nothing", answered their mother. "Nothing except great, dark forests which only an elephant could break through. There are a lot of snakes, but they are much too big and dangerous for us. Danger is on all sides, for if you went the other way, into the desert, you'd get sand in your eyes and were you to find yourself in a sandstorm no-one would be able to help you. No, we'll stay here. Here, everything is perfect – you can eat as many frogs and grasshoppers as you want and there'll still be enough left over."

So it was. The storks stayed and their children, especially, ate as much as they wanted. The grown-up storks were content with the high perch where they could rest, preen their feathers, and greet friends who flew by. Furthermore, they could keep good watch over their children.

This was necessary, too, for the girl storks had half hidden themselves in the rushes and peeked out, secretly, at the boy storks. They knew what was going on, of course, and strutted about proudly. They had arguments and even picked fights, hitting each other hard with their wings and pecking each other so sharply with their beaks that they bled. Others, who did not so enjoy fighting, tried to win the girls' attention by walking as gracefully as possible, or by eating up more frogs than they could really stomach. Some even let a little snake dangle from their beaks, pretending all the while that they had not noticed it.

After only a few days, the first storks had become engaged and were making wedding plans. They told no-one, but everyone could see it because together they started building a nest. However, the marriage did not always go ahead, for in the warm south everyone gets a little hot-tempered and has a lot of fights. The half-built nest would then be left until another pair finished it. Such a pair of young storks were happy not to have so much left to do.

From their quiet perches, the old storks contentedly watched all the commotion their children made. If the children were happy then so were the parents. Life was good in this beautiful country. You did not have to do anything, it was lovely and warm, and food was just there for the taking at the bottom of the Nile.

However, life was not so good for everyone there. In the palace of their Egyptian host, as the stork called the King of Egypt, everyone was filled with sadness.

The powerful king lay on his couch in his splendid bedroom, on the walls of which hung paintings from the most famous painters in the land, but he was so ill that he could not so much as turn to see them.

The king was not dead but, in all truth, you could hardly say that he was living! All his friends and family sat about him and his servants cared for him as best they could. Yet the flower from the swamp in the north, the only flower which might cure him and which had to be plucked by his daughter, whom he loved above all others, would never be brought to him. For his youngest and dearest daughter, who had flown over the seas as a swan to fetch the flower far to the north, would never again return. "She is dead and lies in her grave", had said the two ladies-in-waiting on their return, the same ladies who had flown with the princess.

They had made up an entire story. "The three of us were flying towards the Wild Quagmire when, beneath us, a hunter shot an arrow into the sky which pierced the heart of our dearest friend, the princess. Dying, she glided down below as she sang a song of farewell and then sank into the lake in the swamp. We found her body and, taking it from the lake, buried her at a pretty spot on the bank in the shade of a weeping birch. We took revenge on the hunter who killed her and set the thatched roof of his cottage on fire, burning his house to the ground and the hunter with it.

The tall flames lit up your daughter's grave; your daughter who will never return to Egypt, the land of sun and riches."

However, the stork, who had seen both ladies-in-waiting in the Wild Quagmire, knew that they did not speak the truth and was terribly angry. "I'd like to peck a hole with my beak right through those wicked women!" he growled.

"And break your beak for sure", teased his wife. "You should think more about yourself and your family for once. Just let that princess take care of herself!"

"Tomorrow I'm going to sit on the eaves of the house where the wise men are meeting to talk about the illness of the king, our Egyptian host", replied the stork, stubbornly. "Perhaps they'll find out that the ladies-in-waiting have lied." He was disappointed, however, for the next day many were the wise words spoken but the stork understood very little and the ill king in the palace was not made better by them. They, too, knew of no way to bring the princess back. Even so, let us listen to them.

Some years before, the wise men had already spoken about a way to heal the king. "The king is ill", they said, "and he will surely die. Yet life comes forth from love, and so love can save life."

The stork, who sat nearby, thought this very beautiful and told his wife who did not understand a word of it.

"It's probably because I have so much on my mind at the moment with all those children I have to keep an eye on", she said.

The wise men had also talked about different kinds of love, between friends and family, or between lovers. The stork listened the whole day,

standing on one leg without moving, but he did not understand very much of it. What he did understand was that it would be very terrible for the people if their king were to die. Therefore, he quite certainly had to be made better.

The wise men had also read in their books that the king could only be cured if he came into the possession of a rare flower. After much more searching, they had also found the phrase 'from life comes forth love'. They did not understand much about it, it sounded like a magic spell, until one day, a young wise man shyly said that perhaps something should come after it: 'only love can save life'.

It then became clear to all: the princess, whom the king loved most above all others, could save her father!

The princess, of course, wanted nothing more than for her father to get better and promised to do anything that was asked of her.

Some nights later, she dreamed that she should pluck a lotus flower far to the north in the Wild Quagmire.

Shortly afterwards, she had dressed herself in a swan skin and had flown to the Wild Quagmire. That is what the wise men and the storks knew, but

what had happened to her since and where she was now was known to no-one. They could only wait.

"I think that I'll take the swan skins away from those wicked ladies-in-waiting", said the stork. "Then, at least, they won't be able to return to the swamp to do any more evil."

"But where will you keep the skins?" asked the mother stork, who only half agreed with him.

"We'll take them with us for the princess and hide them in our nest on top of the Viking's house", replied her husband. "The princess needs only one skin, of course, but for safety's sake two skins are better."

"Do as you like", said the mother stork. "I never have any say. I'm just here to hatch the eggs until I get bruises! And after that, I have to watch over all the children because you're too busy with other things."

In the meantime, the child at the Viking's house had been given a name. She was called Helga, but it was really too gentle a name for such a tempestuous little child.

The years passed by. Each spring that the storks returned to the Wild Quagmire the little girl had grown taller and prettier. Before they knew it,

she was sixteen and beautiful, but inside she was as hard as steel and more wild than all the Vikings put together.

However, the Viking, who did not know that his daughter changed every night into an ugly, but sweet and sorrowful toad, did not think it at all bad that she was so wild. He was proud that his daughter was so pretty and could ride so well. She could also swim and dive better than a whole lot of boys and she was the best archer of them all.

The Viking's wife was strong, as were all women then, and she could put up with a hard life, but compared to her daughter she was weak. The girl did so many dangerous things that her mother was frightened every single day that something would happen to her.

There was but one moment each day when the wild child would become calm and that was at dusk. When twilight came, she would sit quietly in a corner and listen to her mother. Yet her fair appearance would soon shrivel up as she became an ugly toad.

In her toad form, the girl was also much larger now than she had been as a baby, so that she looked more like a sad, shrunken dwarf. As a toad she was unable to speak and only croaked sorrowfully to herself, so much so, that the Viking's wife took her on her lap to comfort her. The Viking's wife sometimes wished that her daughter had the toad's form in the daytime since, although she looked the very prettiest of girls, the woman was only ever afraid for her.

"If I hadn't picked her up from that water-lily myself, I'd never have believed that she'd once been so small", said the stork to his wife. "Now she's as big as all people are, and she looks just like the princess who we shall never see again. She couldn't have been able to look after herself, in

spite of what you thought! Every year, I have flown a hundred times or more, here and there, over the swamp, without ever seeing a trace of her. Those swan skins which we brought here with such difficulty could just as well have been left behind. Now they just lie in our nest and if a fire broke out they would be lost!"

"And our nest too", said the mother stork, dryly. "I always wanted you to think more about our family and a bit less about that princess. Watch out that one of us doesn't get an arrow through the heart from that wild Viking child! Do you know that I hardly dare go below when she's outside? At least in Egypt I can walk about quietly and safely. Here, I can only sit on this tower worrying about that child! If only you'd left her there in that water-lily, then no-one would have been bothered by her!"

Without waiting to reply, her partner sprang into the air, flapped his wings a few times, and then he sailed away with his legs gracefully stretched out behind him.

"What a handsome fellow he is", sighed his wife with pleasure, "not that I shall ever tell him!"

The Viking and his warriors returned that autumn after a long raid throughout the south. As with every journey, the ships brought not only gifts with them but also prisoners. This time, however, they had a very special prisoner with them; a young Christian priest who said all manner of terrible things about the Viking gods, even that they did not exist!

Especially amongst the Viking women, there had been much talk in those last few years about this new religion which seemed to be growing ever bigger in the south. Whenever the men returned from their travels, they told of how temples had been built everywhere to this god and they took all kinds of beautiful things from them which the Christians had made.

The Christian priest was locked up in a cellar deep beneath the Viking's house. Helga had heard about him, too, but she had not wanted to listen and wanted most of all for the priest to be punished severely.

Her wish was granted, for her father wanted the priest to be sacrificed, and Helga began at once to make her knife razor-sharp, for in her human form she was terribly brutal.

That night, when she changed, as every night, into an ugly but sweet toad, the Viking's wife told her how much sorrow was brought to her by her beautiful daughter whom she still loved more than anyone in the world.

"Never", said the Viking's wife, "have I told anyone how much sorrow I have because of you. I know that you have been bewitched and that there is nothing that you can do and therefore you have my pity. I love you as only a mother can, yet your heart stays hard and cold and knows no love. How did you come to be in my house? Where did you come from?"

The toad's ugly body trembled, as the Viking's wife spoke her words, and huge tears filled its eyes.

"Terrible times will be coming for you", predicted the Viking's wife. "You will know sorrow and so shall I! It would have been better if my husband had abandoned you. Perhaps the cold might have sent you into the deep sleep which never ends."

The woman cried when she had said this and walked to another room. She did not know whether she was angry or sad.

The toad stayed sitting all alone in a corner of the room and now and then sighed deeply. Tiredly, it then began to move and hopped towards the door which it clumsily opened. It took a torch with it and walked down the steps to the cellar. There, it came to where the priest was imprisoned. He was sleeping, but awoke when a cold, wet hand touched him. The priest was horrified when he first saw the toad, but then it cut him free of his bonds with its knife.

When he saw that the toad wanted to free him, he muttered a prayer of thanks and asked the toad who it was.

The toad could make no reply, of course. It winked at the priest and showed him the way to the stables, along pathways and dark passages. Once there, it pointed to Helga's favourite horse and the priest leapt at

once into the saddle, but before he could ride away the toad sprang in front of him on to the saddle and together they rode into the dark night. The toad held tightly on to the horse's mane and led the beast along roads which the priest would never have found by himself. So it was that they soon came to the heath. The priest no longer saw how ugly the toad was, he was only deeply grateful that he had been able to escape his prison and he sang a song of thanks.

Suddenly, as the sun began to rise, the toad started to tremble in front of him on the horse. It tried to stand and leap from the horse, but the priest stopped it and continued singing. However, while the horse galloped ever faster, the astonished priest saw the ugly toad in his arms change into a beautiful young girl! The priest brought the horse to a halt and stepped down, followed by the girl. Yet, as she sprang from the beast, she took out her sharp hunting knife and hurled herself towards the man, who thought that he was dreaming.

"I'm going to kill you!" she screamed and a terrible fight began. The priest was not easily defeated and was helped by an oak tree which stood right next to where they were fighting. The girl's feet became tangled in the tree roots, causing her to fall and lie dazed on the ground.

The priest took water from the nearby spring and let some droplets fall on to the girl's head while ordering the spirit which had bewitched her to be gone. This is how he baptized her, as is the custom with Christians.

When the girl came to her senses again, she looked amazed and speechless at the man as he made the sign of the cross on her forehead. She shut her eyes and let her head fall to her breast. Then, full of love, he began to speak about the good deed which she had done when she had freed him in her toad form and so saved his life. He would now attempt to free her from the evil spirit which had bewitched her. He himself did not have so much power, but God could do it, he said.

The horse scraped its hooves over the ground as the priest was speaking and pulled at the brambles, letting the berries fall into Helga's lap for her to eat and so recover her strength.

Afterwards, she allowed herself to be gently lifted on to the horse. The priest made a cross from two branches which he held high above his head. So it was that they rode on through the forest which became ever thicker and where there were no real paths.

They continued onward for what seemed forever, and the smell of the forest, the blackberries which they ate, and the water which they drank gave them ever more strength. However, it was the priest's fine words about faith, hope, and love which kept them going most of all.

Just as the sea can make even the hardest stone smooth from the rolling of the waves, so was the priest also able to soften Helga's hard nature with his words. It went very slowly, and you could hardly tell it was happening, but Helga's nature was changing.

When they had almost reached the edge of the forest, they met with a band of robbers.

"How does that pretty girl come to be with you, then?" they called out to the priest. Grabbing the horse's reins, they pulled off Helga and the priest. The priest only had the knife he had taken from Helga with which to try and defend himself. One of the robbers had an axe which he tried to use against the priest but, although he was just able to dodge the blow, the weapon glanced against the horse which, fatally wounded, fell to the ground. Helga knelt in horror by the dying beast while the priest tried to defend her. Yet he was unable to do so against so many and one of the robbers killed him with one blow of his hammer.

The robbers then grabbed the girl, but at precisely that instant the sun dipped below the horizon and she changed into a toad. The man who had held her fast suddenly found that he had the leg of a toad in his hands and, in shock, let it go. He could not believe his eyes!

The robbers, frightened of witchcraft, fled immediately while Helga disappeared into the forest to hide herself.

In the middle of the night, she crept back to the clearing again and looked at the priest and the horse with tears filling her toad's eyes. She knew that they were both dead and that there was nothing anymore that she could do. However, she did not want wild animals to find the bodies and so she began to dig a grave for them. Yet a toad's hands are not made for digging and they began to hurt and bleed. Helga saw that she would not be able to dig a grave which was big enough and so instead she covered the bodies

of the horse and the priest with branches and laid stones on top.

Once she had decided that the burial mound was safe enough, night was almost over and the sun rose. All at once, there stood the beautiful young girl, Helga, with bloody hands and, for the first time in her life, with tears in her eyes.

She was scared of the change which she felt within herself and ran to a nearby beech tree. She climbed it like a cat and stayed nervously in the tree top for the rest of the day.

Only when evening began to fall, and she felt that she was about to change into a toad once more, did Helga let herself slide down the trunk of the tree. As soon as she touched the ground, the last rays of sunlight disappeared and there Helga was again as a toad with bloody feet but with eyes which shone softly and kindly. They were no longer the eyes of a toad but the eyes of a gentle, good girl. Yet only a moment later they were filled with tears again as they saw the cross which the priest had made and which still lay next to the burial mound. The toad took the cross and placed it on the grave. Whilst thinking about the priest, she took a bare branch and drew signs of the cross all around the grave in the earth. As she did this, she saw with astonishment that the webs between her fingers were falling away. She walked to the spring and as she washed herself could see how her toad skin was peeling away to reveal the pretty girl underneath again, which she had only ever been in the daytime. However, she was so terribly tired that she fell asleep at once next to the spring.

Her sleep did not last long, for at about midnight she was awakened and when she looked up she saw her horse which she thought had died and lay buried. Large as life it stood before her, and next to the beast stood the priest.

He looked at her for a long time and the girl trembled, remembering all the fine words which the priest had spoken. She realized that it was love which had saved her and which had put an end to her double life.

The priest began to speak, softly but clearly: "I have returned for but a short time from the kingdom of the dead, but the day will come when you, too, will travel through the deep valley to the shining mountains. But first you must go to the Wild Quagmire and the place where you were born. That will be your task."

He placed her on the horse and gave her a golden casket from which came a sweet-smelling scent. The priest took the cross from the grave and leapt behind her on to the horse which rose up and began to fly through the sky!

They flew over forests, heaths, and lakes until they reached the Wild Quagmire which they circled again and again. The priest held his cross up high and began to sing, Helga singing with him uncertainly because she did not know the words. As she sang, she waved her golden casket to and fro from which came such a strong and delicious perfume that below in the swamp everything began to burst into bloom. From the water's depths, everything which could grow began to shoot upwards, so that a carpet of beautiful water-lilies came to cover the surface of the lake. On that carpet lay a pretty, sleeping woman who Helga thought at first to be herself. It was her mother, who she was seeing for the first time, the wife of the Quagmire King, the princess from the land of the Nile.

The priest and Helga carried the sleeping beauty to the horse which, though dead, was strong enough to carry all three of them because of the raised cross. As soon as they reached land, the priest and the horse disappeared in as mysterious a way as they had come. Helga and her mother remained behind.

"It is as if I see myself", said the mother and she put her arms around Helga. "My child", she repeated again and again, "my child, my beautiful lotus flower! I came here from Egypt in a swan's skin. I took it off and sank into the swamp where the current carried me off and I fell into a

sleep of dreams. But the alder trunk was still next to me and all at once it opened. The old king who sat inside was as black as mud. He stepped out and clasped his arms about me. At that moment I thought I was going to die, but suddenly I saw a bird fly up from my breast which sang a very pretty song. I saw it glide up to the surface of the water but it was attached to me by a very long, green cord. It sang a song of longing for freedom and sunshine. Then I thought of my country and of my dear father who I wanted to save, and I loosened the cord and let the bird go to my father. Afterwards, I slept and dreamed no more until singing and a delicious perfume awakened me."

The stork flew by as mother and daughter stood there together and understood everything.
He turned back to his nest, took up the swan skins, and threw them at the feet of the two women. They put on the skins immediately, and flew up from the ground.
The stork came flying next to them. "We are different, of course", he said, "but we speak each other's language and I very much wanted to ask you

something. Tomorrow, I'm taking my family south, to Egypt. Perhaps you know us. We go there every year. I wanted to ask you if you'd like to fly with us, perhaps. Then, you won't get lost as we know the way."

"The flower for which I journeyed will fly next to me", said the princess, looking at her daughter. "Yes, I very much want to go home. Early tomorrow morning, wasn't that what you said?"

However, Helga wanted to see her foster mother just one more time, for she had always been so good to her. All at once, she remembered everything and it seemed to her as if she it was who loved the Viking's wife most of all!

"Everything will be all right", said the stork, "for I live on the Viking's house so we'll all be going in the same direction. How surprised my wife and children will be!"

Everything was quiet at the Viking's house.

The Viking's wife was asleep at last but she had long lain awake from worry about Helga who, like the priest, had been gone for three whole days. The horse was missing from the stables and the priest's bonds had been cut loose, so Helga must have helped the man. The Viking's wife wondered if the priest might perhaps be able to free Helga. She fussed

and fretted until, finally, she slept. An early autumn storm was starting to blow up and, in her dream, the Viking's wife could hear the waves crashing against the shore. She dreamed that Helga sat on her lap as a toad and she felt that the world would end. At that moment she saw the priest and she kissed her toad-child. The toad skin fell from the girl instantly and there she stood in all her beauty with her gentle eyes. She kissed and thanked her foster mother and, with a powerful flapping of wings, flew away in the form of a beautiful swan.

The sound made the Viking's wife awaken, but even then she continued to hear it still and she walked to the window. On the roof of the Viking's house sat hundreds of storks with many more flying round about. However, two swans sat together on the edge of the well and looked at her with great, wise eyes.

The Viking's wife remembered her dream at once and felt, suddenly, terribly happy.

The swans clapped their wings together and the woman realized that they were saying farewell and she waved back.

At that moment, there came an enormous roar of beating wings. The storks had all taken to the air, starting on their journey south, and behind them flew two great, proud swans. They flew high above the clouds, over the mountain tops, and crossed many countries. The princess felt suddenly very happy as she flew in her swan skin over the Red Sea and there, far below, saw Egypt. Although very tired, she flew even faster and all the storks flew with her.

"I can see the frogs already!" called out one of the youngsters.

"Don't talk such nonsense", scolded his mother. "No-one can see a frog from so high up, even if it were as big as a horse! A little patience and you'll see them and then you'll also see our relatives here."

"What are they called again?" her youngest child wanted to know. He had hatched a little late and could not remember all the names.

"Marabou, ibis, and crane", said his mother, patiently, "but we're the most graceful branch of the family. The Egyptians spoil the ibises terribly but they've lived here a long time, too. They even put herbs inside their bodies after their death because they believe that ibises are sacred! I think you're better off filling yourself with frogs and grasshoppers, and that's just what we're going to do!"

"You've all done very well", said the father stork. He and his wife were

extremely happy that even their youngest, who hatched too late, had managed the journey.

"The storks are here", whispered people in the ill king's palace. He would only get better if his daughter came back with the lotus flower. Yet she would never return again.

Suddenly, the sound of wings was heard within the deep stillness of the palace, and two swans flew brazenly into the king's room.

As soon as they touched the floor with their webbed feet, they removed their swan skins and at once there stood two beautiful women who looked the very image of each other. They bent over the sick man and called him "father" and "grandfather".

As soon as Helga had bent over the old man, the colour came back to his cheeks and he felt new strength, for he sat upright as quickly as a young man and threw his arms around his grand-daughter.

Learned men at once set about writing down the story of the king's illness and his miraculous cure, and artists were asked to paint everything that had happened on the palace walls.

The storks were also happy, but most of their attention went to the frogs.

Nonetheless, the mother stork boasted to everyone about the part which her brave husband had played in the whole story. All the storks were very proud that one of them had done such things.

Meanwhile, the wise men tried to explain, by all manner of complicated means, how it all could have happened.

The father stork still listened in to them, but he did not understand very much of it.

It had been a long time since the people in the king's house had been able to go to their beds as peacefully and happily as they did that night. Only Helga lay awake, looking at the stars which seemed prettier, bigger, and brighter there.

She thought of the Viking's house where the Viking's wife had been so good to her while she had given her nothing back in return. Even so, she had still been comforted and stroked when, every night as a toad, she had longed for love.

She also thought of the priest who had risen from the dead and flown back with her to the Wild Quagmire to help her undo the enchantment. She owed it to him that she was now so happy with her mother and grandfather, as well as having a whole people who honoured her because she had saved their king's life.

However, to the stork, who had helped her so generously, she hardly gave a thought.

She looked up and she saw the ostriches playing in the garden. She was amazed that such strange birds existed with wings which looked half-clipped. She asked about them the next day and then heard the story

which the Egyptians have told for centuries about the ostrich.

Long, long ago, the ostrich was one of the most beautiful of all birds. One day, he was invited by two vultures to fly with them the next day to their home which was by the river and where he could drink as much as he wanted.

The ostrich accepted the invitation and they left early the next morning. They began by flying up very high but the ostrich, who in those days could fly better than any other bird, flew much too high and so came too close to the sun.

He did know that it was dangerous, but he was so proud that he could fly so high up that kept on climbing up and up until the heat of the sun scorched his wings and he fell back down to earth, without any strength left at all.

So it remained, for ever since then ostriches have not been able to fly and their strange wings are a warning to everyone who is too proud of themselves.

Helga thought deeply about this story and became serious. She realized that it also applied to her and the next spring, when the storks were preparing to leave again, she called on the stork who had brought the swan skins to her and her mother.

She gave him a golden bracelet on which her name was written and asked if he would give it to the Viking's wife so that she would know that Helga was well and that she was thinking about her foster mother.

"That's heavy", grumbled the stork. He went on, "Why do people wear such heavy things? But I'll do it to prove to people that storks really do bring good luck."

"You can't just live off good luck", mocked the mother stork. "When are we going?"

"Early tomorrow morning", replied her husband, and so they did.

The nightingale was also off to the north, and Helga, who in the time she had been a toad had learned to speak bird language, asked him if he would now and again sing at the priest's grave. The nightingale promised and was gone.

One day, a party of Arabs came from the east, astride beautiful horses, and with camels loaded with gifts. It was a prince with his servants who had come to Egypt to marry Helga. They arrived at the Egyptian king's palace and the celebrations began. Helga was dressed in beautiful clothes of silk and satin, and wore fabulous jewels.

She sat at the head of the table next to the handsome prince but paid little attention to him. Instead, she looked straight ahead at the sky which was full of stars.

Outside, came the sound of flapping wings.

The storks had returned and Helga watched the pair of storks who she

knew enter their old home. The storks knew that celebrations were being held and they also knew that, out of gratefulness, the king had had their portraits chiselled into the palace's great white wall on to which Helga's bedroom looked out.

"Is that it?" scoffed his wife. "They were better off giving you a real gift."

"Why? We now belong to history. Even when we are no longer here, people will still see us and talk about us", said her husband, wisely.

As soon as Helga saw the storks she went outside and stroked their long necks. The mother stork rather liked it in spite of herself!

Helga looked above her to the stars and suddenly saw the image of the priest who slowly waved to her. He had come to see her celebrations.

"Nothing on earth can compare to the beauty and the wonder of heaven", he said.

Helga asked if she might look at heaven, just for a moment, and the priest was given permission to take her. What Helga saw was a sort of dream world of light and music, but in the shortest time she had to leave again and was brought back down to earth by the priest.

Helga stood again on the balcony. Her bridegroom and all the guests had disappeared and she became frightened. She walked into the hall, but the servants there were unknown to her.

When she tried to enter her bedroom she found herself in the garden instead, and she found that it was a completely different garden to the one that she knew.

She had only been in heaven for a few seconds, but on earth a whole passage of time seemed to have gone by!

She then saw something which she recognized: the storks! She called to them in their own language and a father stork looked up and walked gracefully towards her.

"How is it that you, a strange woman, knows how to speak our language?" he asked her.

"Strange woman?" she asked back. "But it's me, Helga. We were just talking to each other here not three minutes ago!"

"Then you must surely have been dreaming", scoffed the stork.

"Of course not", she said, and she reminded him of everything that had happened in the far north at the Viking's house and in the Wild Quagmire. The stork thought long and deeply. "What you've told me is an awfully old

story. I still remember it from my great-grandmother. I think that it was about an Egyptian princess who was born in the land of the Vikings, who disappeared on her wedding night, and who never returned. But that all happened many hundreds of years ago, you know. If you want to know more then you can read about it on the palace walls. The whole story is there. You're there, yourself, right at the top, in white marble."

The stork was right. Helga saw what he had described, realized the truth, and knelt down to pray. The sun then rose and, just as once the toad skin had fallen away from her to reveal a beautiful young woman, so now, in the light of the morning sun, a beautiful young woman began to rise up towards the shining mountains, as the priest had called them. At the place from which she ascended was found only a shrunken lotus flower ...

"I'd never expected an ending like that", said the stork. "But it is a very lovely story!"

"What will our children think about it?" asked his wife.

"They'll think it's lovely, too," said her husband, "but what is much more important is what they will learn from it!"

The janitor's son

A janitor who looked after a large town house lived in the basement with his family. It is rather odd living in a place which is half underground and has small, low windows, so that all you can see is people's legs as they pass by.

The general lived on the upper floors of the house with his own family, and he had quite a different view of the world. When he looked out at the people in the street, he saw nothing but the tops of their heads. To him, people were mainly hats: black hats, brown hats, straw hats, bowler hats, and of course ladies' hats too, often with a few flowers or some fruit on them.

There was a little courtyard on the other side of the house, and the janitor and his family from the basement could go through a pair of French windows to a stone terrace outside. Beyond the terrace was grass, and in the middle of this lawn stood an acacia tree which sometimes flowered, if it felt like flowering. The general and his family could reach the lawn by way of a long stairway which led straight down from their balcony.

Sometimes the nursemaid who looked after the general's little daughter used these stairs. She would come down and sit under the acacia tree, dressed as if she were going out for a walk, and do her work, which was to make sure little Emilie, the general's daughter, didn't run away and get lost, and was well cared for and properly brought up. Emilie always wore

beautiful dresses, the kind of thing that ordinary girls wore only for their Sunday best.

The janitor's little son often played in the garden too, running barefoot over the lawn, tumbling head over heels, and doing all he could to attract the little girl's attention. He succeeded, too, and little Emilie often stretched out her arms to him because she wanted to play as well.

The general and his wife, watching from their balcony high above as the nursemaid looked after their little daughter, said to each other that Emilie was "*Charmante!*" But their charming little girl was struggling vainly in the nursemaid's strong arms, for the nursemaid had orders from the general to make sure his little daughter never came into contact with the janitor's son. Of course one could hardly forbid the boy to play outside, but the general's young wife in particular thought it would be a terrible thing for the two children to romp and play together. So the nursemaid kept strictly to her orders, and made sure the children didn't even talk to one another.

This summer the acacia was obviously in a good mood, for it did its very best and was covered with beautiful flowers. The janitor's son was in a happy mood too. He was always cheerful, he ran around all day, and he looked healthy and brown from the sun.

Compared with him, the general's little daughter seemed delicate and a little sickly. She didn't go out of doors often, and when she did come into the garden the nursemaid took very good care to keep her out of the sun. She always stayed in the shade of the acacia tree with Emilie, so that the little girl kept her pale complexion. Emilie's skin had been fair from birth. Sometimes the general's wife went out driving in their carriage with her daughter. Then the little girl used to wave to George the janitor's son from under her mother's sunshade, and even blew him kisses. When her mother noticed that she told Emilie to stop it, for she was too old for such things now.

One morning the general's letters were delivered to the janitor, who told George to take them upstairs. As he climbed the stairs, George heard a great deal of noise up above. The general's little daughter was crying and the nursemaid was screaming. The noise came from the nursery, and George ran upstairs to it. He opened the nursery door, and saw what the matter was at once: the curtains were on fire. He raced into the room, gave the burning curtains a strong tug, tore them down and crumpled up the fabric tightly to put out the fire. If he hadn't acted so quickly the whole house might well have burned down.

The general and his wife were dreadfully alarmed. They sternly asked Emilie if she had anything to do with it, and she said she had only lit a

single match, but when she lit it the curtains suddenly went up in flames, and she ran away because she was afraid her parents would be cross. The general and his wife thought that "those people in the basement" must have given their *charmante* little daughter the idea of doing such things. That was hardly fair, because George had never set the general's house on fire, and indeed he had actually saved the house from going up in flames.

However, of course Emilie got a good scolding, and George was given a shining silver dollar for his money box. When he added the dollar to what was in the money box already, he was finally able to buy the box of paints he had been saving up for so long, so that he could add red and blue and green and other shades to his drawings.

For George had done hundreds of drawings. Whenever he could lay hands on a pencil and a bit of paper, the boy would produce a drawing in no time at all. He gave Emilie the very first picture he painted with the box of paints. It was a picture of the general's carriage.

The general thought that was very nice of George; he looked carefully at the drawing, and announced that the young artist obviously had talent.

George's own family down in the basement heard him say so too.

The general's carriage, the one George had drawn so well, had two coats of arms on the sides, so that anyone could see the general's family was extremely distinguished and important. The bigger and more beautiful coat of arms belonged to the general himself and his family. It had been theirs for ages and ages, and the general was very proud of it. The other coat of arms belonged to his wife's family, but her father had been obliged to pay a great deal of money for it.

The general was old and his hair was beginning to turn white, but he held himself proudly upright, and was still a very good horseman. He had a great many decorations, so many that no one could imagine how a single man could ever have won them all. However, the general had joined the army when he was very young, and for as long as anyone could remember he had gone out on army exercises late in the summer every year. He still had many tales to tell of things that had happened on those military exercises, when the soldiers pretended to be fighting each other.

On their way back from one of these expeditions, a soldier under the general's command had taken the prince who was now king "prisoner", so

that the prince had to ride into town behind the general along with the other men captured during the exercise. This was a story the general told over and over again, and of course he also repeated the never-to-be-forgotten words with which he, the general, had given the prince back his sword: "It was my soldier and not I who took your Royal Highness prisoner. I could never have brought myself to do such a thing!" To which the prince had replied with the memorable remark that the general was "incomparable".

However, the general had never had to fight in a real battle. When there was war in the land, he was sent abroad as an ambassador, and he learned to speak such good French while he was abroad that he almost forgot his own language.

In fact the general did everything well: he could dance elegantly, he was an excellent horseman, he had made a good marriage with a very young and beautiful girl from a rich family, and then he and his wife had their beautiful little daughter Emilie.

Meanwhile, the janitor's son often gave Emilie his drawings, but she hardly ever looked at them, and sometimes even tore them up. However, of course that was because she was so pretty and so rich.

Her mother used to call her "Rosebud", and she told the general their little daughter had been born to marry a prince. She wasn't to know how differently everything would turn out, but people always have difficulty facing the truth even when it is staring them in the face.

One evening the janitor's wife told her husband that their son had been sharing his sandwiches with the general's daughter. He hadn't eaten any of the cheese or meat on the bread himself, but the little girl had enjoyed her share of the sandwiches. "If her mother gets to hear of it I expect she'll send the poor child straight to the doctor!" said the janitor's wife, laughing sarcastically.

It was true that George had given the girl half his sandwiches, and he would have given her half his heart too if she asked for it, because he thought she was so sweet and pretty. He was a good son to his parents, and a good pupil at the evening classes where he took drawing lessons so as to become even better at drawing and painting pictures. Emilie did very well at her school too. Nowadays she talked French almost all the time with her nursemaid, whom she called her *bonne*, and she was learning to dance as well.

When George was going to be confirmed he needed a new suit. His mother had the material cut out by a tailor and then sewed it herself. The suit was ready in plenty of time and looked very fine. George was confirmed, and his godfather, an elderly grocer's assistant, gave him a gold watch to mark the occasion. It was an old, second-hand watch, but it was still a fine present, and George was very pleased with it. Little Emilie and her family gave him a hymn-book bound in leather, and the little girl had written George's name in it, and underneath the name she added: "From your little benefactress". That was what her mother had told her to put, and when the general read it and looked at his daughter's handwriting he thought it was *charmant*.

"It's really very kind of such distinguished people," said George's mother, and George had go upstairs, still in his new suit and holding his hymn-book, to thank the distinguished family who lived on the floors up above. The general's wife was sitting in a chair, moaning. She had a headache, as she always did when she was bored. She felt very sorry for herself, and offered George a limp hand, wishing him every good fortune, and above all no headaches. The general, wearing a dressing gown, was pacing up and down the room, deep in thought. After he had marched over the Persian carpet a great many times, he stopped in front of George, took his hand and pressed it firmly. "You are not a child any more," he said. "Try to be a good man, and always show respect to those whose station in life is above you. Later on, when you grow old, you will always be able to say that the general himself told you that."

This was a longer speech than the general ever made in the usual way, and when he had finished he began pacing up and down again and thinking. He looked very distinguished.

But after George had gone back down to his family in the basement, he thought of everything he had seen up above, and most of all he thought of Miss Emilie. How beautiful and delicate and ladylike she was! The only way to draw her would be in a gleaming soap bubble! And she smelled so deliciously of roses! He was happy to think he had once shared his sandwiches with her, and she had enjoyed them very much. Did she still remember that too?

Well, of course she did! That was why she had given him the beautiful hymn-book. He had never really played with her, because the nursemaid she now called her *bonne* had always said they mustn't play together. However, George thought of the lovely little girl upstairs as his dearest

friend. Once, when the doctor's carriage stopped outside the door because Emilie was sick, and the doctor came back every day after that to visit his little patient, George was very worried. However, he was even more alarmed when he heard his mother say, "They'll never keep that child. She's always been far too sickly."

Luckily the janitor's wife was wrong. Emilie recovered, and George did some beautiful drawings for her, pictures of great foreign buildings and palaces, just as they really looked. Emilie was so pleased with the drawings that George gave her a great many more in the following weeks, all of them showing handsome great buildings, so that she could imagine what it would be like inside them.

He drew a Russian palace, and he drew Greek temples with marble pillars and steps all around them. He drew a Norwegian church decorated with wooden carving from top to bottom. But the best drawing of all was of a beautiful castle which he called "Emilie's Castle", because he felt sure she would live there once day.

He had put some of all the things he liked best about the other buildings into his drawing of Emilie's Castle. It had the carved wooden beams of

the Norwegian church, the marble pillars of the Greek temple, and the golden domes of the Russian palace.

It was a castle to delight a child's heart, and underneath each window he wrote what the room behind it was for. One by one, he wrote, "Emilie's bedroom", "Emilie's drawing room" and "Emilie's music room". The picture was a very pretty sight, and a great many people came to look at it. "*Charmant!*" said the general.

At the corner of the street where the general lived stood a great house which belonged to a real count. This count, who was old and who had a castle of his own, was even more distinguished than the general, but they were good friends, and one day he had a visit from the general, who came to ask the count what he thought of a couple of drawings he had brought with him. The count, who collected pictures and knew a great deal about them, looked at George's drawings and thought his own thoughts.

A little later George was summoned to see the head of the art college where he went to evening classes.

"We must have a talk, my boy," said the head of the art college. "You have a great deal of talent, and what's more, there are people who are willing to help you. The old count who lives on the corner of your street has been

talking to me about you, and he showed me a number of the drawings you've done which aren't part of your work here. Those drawings could be improved on, so you may attend our daytime classes twice a week as well as coming in the evening. I'd say myself that you have the makings of an architect rather than a painter, but the count doesn't agree with me. In any case, however, the first thing you must do is go straight to the count to thank him."

The house on the corner was very old and very large, and looked a little strange. The walls around the windows and doors were covered with carvings. All kinds of strange animals were carved in the stone, and the place looked very old-fashioned. However, in spite of all the elephants and crocodiles on the front of his house, the count liked modern times and the art of the present day best.

George was very happy when he came home from visiting the count, and next day his mother went to see the count too and thank him. She was in great good spirits when she came home as well. "If you ask me," she said to her husband, "the more important folk are, the more simply they behave! Take the old count – he's so friendly and straightforward! He talks just as we do, and if you ask me that's beyond the general and his wife! He thinks it would be better if we didn't send George to learn a trade, because he has so much talent for drawing."

"That's all very well and good," said the janitor. "So he has a lot of talent, but how will he develop it without help?"

"I'm sure the count will help! He said so clearly."

"Well, it was the general who went to see the count in the first place," the janitor pointed out. "So we must be grateful to him as well."

"That's true," replied his wife. "In any case, I'm very glad everything is going so well for George, and Emilie is better again too."

Yes, luckily the little girl was much better, and George did well at the art college.

In a year's time he won a silver medal for being the best student, and he was to go to Italy to complete his studies.

"Oh, if only we'd sent him to learn an ordinary trade!" sobbed the janitor's wife when she heard that. "He could have been a carpenter or a bricklayer like anyone else, and then at least he'd have stayed at home. What will a boy like that do all alone in Rome? You mark my words, we'll never see him back again!"

"This is a great thing for him, though," her husband defended George, "and he's likely to learn a great deal in any case."

"Oh yes, those are very fine words," said his wife, "but you mind just as much as I do!"

Of course she was right there, and the parents' sadness over their son's departure was not made any less by the way everyone kept telling them what a fine thing it would be for George.

Before he went away, George went to say goodbye to a number of people, and of course they included the general's family. The general himself received him, because his wife was sick with her headache again.

For the second time, the general told George the amusing story of the prince who had been taken prisoner during the military exercise, and then he shook hands with him and wished him luck.

So did Emilie, and she looked sad, but not half as sad as George felt.

Time flies, particularly when you're very busy and using every minute of it. And that was what George was doing, so that the days and weeks and months didn't seem so long. Only the evenings dragged on, when he sat

in his little room thinking of all the people he had left behind both in the basement and on the upper floors of the house. Of course he had letters telling him what was going on in and around his home. Some of them were very sad letters, like the one that came when his father suddenly died. His mother wrote to say how she was grieving, but Emilie, she added, had been very kind, and came to comfort her every day and had helped her with everything. There was no need for George to worry about his mother, because she was to stay on in the house and become the janitor herself.

Although Emilie didn't know it, the story of her life was being carefully recorded. Her mother had written in her diary all about Emilie's first court ball, for however often the general's wife had a headache, she conscientiously wrote her diary every day. Ever since Emilie was a little girl her mother had written about the plays and parties she went to, and she stuck all the admission tickets into her diary as well, and all the invitations, at least when they came from distinguished people. She liked her diary and was proud of it. It was getting thicker and thicker all the time, and looked as if it were going to grow even faster now that

invitations were arriving for Emilie too. The general's wife wrote down the details of what Emilie and she had worn to the court ball: her own red and black dress and her daughter's white dress, and how pretty Emilie had looked with her blue eyes and her pretty mouth, and a wreath of flowers in her hair. All three of the princes had danced with her.

This first ball was followed by several more. Emilie had never been very strong, and she sometimes felt very tired, so it was a good thing that summer was coming, and she and her parents were going to stay at the old count's castle for a while.

There was a beautiful garden around the castle, laid out in two different styles. Part of the garden was in the French style, with hedges clipped into pretty shapes, fountains and little waterfalls, and marble statues everywhere. Opposite the French garden was the English garden, which looked rather like a wood where no one pruned the trees, so that they could grow just as they liked, but the grass in between the trees was regularly mown short and rolled. When you walked over it you could feel the springy ground under your feet.

"The old and the new stand side by side here," said the count. "Soon the

whole castle is going to have alterations made. It will be a great improvement. I'll show you the designs at once, and this afternoon I'm going to introduce you to the architect who drew up the plans. I've asked him to dinner."

"*Charmant*!" said the general.

"I feel as if I were walking through Paradise," cried the general's wife, enraptured. She thought the two gardens were very beautiful.

"Well, it's only my park!" smiled the old count. "Or really I ought not to call it my park. It's more like old Else's park, because she looks after everything here. You can see all the animals she cares for: the chickens, turkeys, geese, peacocks and doves, and the ducks on their pond."

The general thought it was all *charmant*, and they walked on to discover what other charming sights there were to be seen.

That afternoon Emilie and George met again in the count's park, after several years when they had not seen one another.

George seemed to be standing there in front of Emilie all of a sudden, and she thought he had grown very handsome. He had an open, honest face, and you could see in his eyes that he knew what he wanted. His black hair gleamed in the sun, and he had a pleasant smile. They both felt a

little embarrassed, particularly because the old woman Else who looked after the park was there too.

Else had taken off her clogs specially for her guests, and was going about in her stocking feet. The chickens cackled, the rooster crowed, and the ducks waddled along, taking no notice of anything.

However, George's little childhood friend Emilie stood looking at him with a touch of pink in her face. Her eyes shone, and said more than words could do. She greeted him in as kind and friendly a manner as was possible between people who weren't members of the same family and had never been to a ball together. George and Emilie hadn't even danced with one another yet.

The general shook George's hand and called him, "My young friend George". The general's wife even made him a bow, and Emilie almost gave him her hand, but she didn't quite dare.

The group walked on, and as they walked the general spoke of "young Mr George", and "a delightful meeting with an old friend".

The general's wife went so far as to say that George looked like a real Italian with his black hair, and he spoke excellent Italian too. She herself sang Italian songs, but she couldn't speak the language.

George sat next to Emilie at dinner that evening, on her right. He had a great many tales to tell, and everyone listened. Most of the time only the general and the count joined in the conversation. Emilie kept very quiet, but she listened to everything George had to say with her eyes shining.

A little later Emilie and George were in the rose garden. No one could see them, because there was a large rosebush between them and the rest of the party. At first they said nothing, but just looked at one another. However, then George said, "I'm very grateful to you for all you did for my mother. She wrote and told me how kind you were to her, and how much you helped her when my father died. And I know you were with her too when she was sick, and stayed with her until she died peacefully." He took the girl's hand and pressed a kiss on it, and after what he had said the kiss didn't seem at all strange or impertinent. The flush of pink came into Emilie's cheeks again, but she held his hand tight and looked at him with her big blue eyes.

"Your mother was such a good woman," she said. "She thought a great deal of you, and she was so proud of you. She let me read all your letters, and then you were always so kind to me too – you gave me a great many drawings."

"Which you often tore up!" smiled George.

"I was only a child at the time," Emilie defended herself, "but I always kept my castle, the castle you drew me."

"And now I'll build you a real castle, just like the one in the drawing," George promised her.

All at once he felt he was a very happy and fortunate man.

While George and Emilie were in the garden, Emilie's mother and the general were sitting indoors talking about their late janitor's son. They both thought the young man behaved very well, and seemed extremely clever and able.

"In my opinion he might well become a teacher," said the general thoughtfully.

The general's wife reacted a little oddly to this remark. "That mind!" said she, and nothing more.

In the course of the summer George, who was now known as Mr George, came to the old count's castle several times, and whenever he went away again the company felt that someone was lacking, and they missed him.

"How talented you are, much more talented than ordinary people like us!" said Emilie one day, full of admiration. "Did you know that? Do you realize that you are a very special person?"

George was very happy, and a little proud too that this dear, beautiful girl admired him so much. We may wonder what he would have thought if he knew that the general often said, "Young Mr George can't possibly really be a janitor's son. However, his mother was certainly a good woman."

The time flew by, summer came to an end, the leaves fell and then it was winter. There was much talk in the city about Mr George. The newspapers wrote about the young architect several times, praising his work. George

met some very important people, and often visited their houses. Once he even met the general at a court ball.

One day in winter the general and his wife found they had a problem. There was to be a ball in the general's house, and the question was whether Mr George could be invited. He was certainly a famous architect these days, but he was still the son of the general's late janitor. "Can a general allow someone born of such a humble family into his house?" the general's wife wondered out loud.

"If the king doesn't mind asking him to a court ball, I don't think there ought to be any difficulty in it for a general," said her husband, and he bravely decided to invite George. It looked as if he actually grew a little taller when he said that, he was so proud of his kind condescension.

So Mr George received an invitation, and he accepted, just like several princes, counts and barons, all of them equally distinguished. They all danced very well, but unfortunately for them Emilie sprained her ankle during the first dance, so then she couldn't take part at all, and could only sit by the wall and watch the others dancing.

The architect decided to stand beside her as she rested her foot.

"You'll be building her a whole city yet!" said the general with a smile as he passed them. He was very friendly to Mr George.

He received him in an equally friendly way when Mr George asked if he could speak to the general a week later. First the young man thanked him for inviting him to the ball, and for his kind reception there, but then he said there was something else he wanted to ask. That something was quite a different matter: it was something ridiculous, something absolutely out of the question, something that, in the general's opinion, was not fitting or proper. For George had come to ask the general's permission to marry his daughter Emilie. The general couldn't believe his ears when he heard what the young man said. It was so outrageous and impertinent that he flinched back in alarm!

He almost stumbled over his own legs in pure horror. "What was that you said?" he stammered. "What do you want? How dare you ask such a thing! I never want to see you again! Leave my house at once and never show your face here again!"

The general left the room walking backward – he had learned in the army

never to turn his back to the enemy – locked the door from the other side, and leaned against it, panting for breath.

George, left behind alone, shrugged his shoulders and then left the room. Emilie was waiting for him out in the passage.

"What did my father say?" she asked, her lips trembling.

He took her hand and held it firmly. "He began shouting, and then he went out of the room in a rage and left me standing there. But don't cry. He will change his mind. You wait and see: a day will come when your father feels more kindly disposed to me."

Emilie did feel like crying, and had difficulty keeping back the tears that sprang to her eyes, but George's eyes radiated courage and confidence.

Meanwhile the general went to his room quivering with fury. He was muttering aloud to himself, and kept on saying how shockingly impertinent and coarse and outrageous he thought it for George to dare ask such a thing. "A man ought to know his station in life!" he said angrily. "Imagine my daughter, the daughter of a general who's won fifty medals or more, marrying the son of a janitor, an ordinary, poor, common man! Such a thing ought to be forbidden by law! A person who even thinks of it deserves punishment!"

Of course the general went upstairs too, to tell his wife about the scandalous incident. She was in bed with the bad headache she had more and more frequently these days. She listened to the general in surprise and shock, and summoned Emilie at once. Emilie came into the room with tears in her eyes.

"My poor dear child!" said her mother. "How deeply insulted you must feel that someone like that dares ask you to marry him! We all feel deeply insulted. Go ahead and cry, my darling. I was just the same when I was married! So have a good cry, my dear, and you'll feel better!"

"I can't do anything but cry," sobbed the girl, "until you and Father give me permission to marry George. I'm not crying because I feel insulted. I'm crying because I love him!"

"Child!" The general's wife almost screeched the word. "Child," she went on, in a rather quieter voice, "you don't know what you're saying. Oh, my poor head! Can you really wish to do something so terrible? Can you want to bring such great misfortune on yourself and all of us? I would die of shame and grief. Emilie, your mother would die, and then you wouldn't have a mother any more! You can't want that, can you?"

There were tears in the eyes of the general's wife, because she thought a great deal of herself, and didn't like to think of her own death.

However, that very evening they read in the newspaper that Mr George had become a professor, and was going to give lectures at Copenhagen University.

"What a shame his good father and mother aren't here to know about it," said the new janitor to his wife. They had come to live in the basement of the house and look after it, and they knew that the new professor had been born in the same house, and grew up there.

"If we ever have a son, dear husband, he must become an architect and professor too," the janitor's wife decided.

So the people who lived in the basement of the house spoke kindly of George, and even on the upper floors a few kind words were said of him. The general thought so distinguished a person as himself could afford to do that. The kind words he said were about the drawings George had done as a boy.

The conversation had turned to this subject because at a dinner where the count was present too someone began talking about Russia. He described the Russian palaces, saying how beautiful they were and how

difficult it must have been to design them. At that the count remembered the drawings George had done for Emilie in the old days. He had done a great many, but there was one the count remembered better than any of the others, and that was the drawing called "Emilie's Castle", with writing under the windows saying where Emilie slept, where she played music, where she ate, and where she received people who came visiting.

Yes, the count remembered that drawing very well, and now the boy who did it had become a professor! Everyone agreed that George was a very able man, and he would surely be a famous architect by the time he died, but why not have him build a real version of Emilie's castle before that time came?

"What a strange idea of the count's!" said the general's wife to her husband, when the old count had left. The general did not reply. He left the house and went out riding. He always did that when he wanted to think in peace and quiet. His servant, who was riding behind him, saw that he kept shaking his head as if he had a difficult problem to solve. Emilie's birthday this year was even busier than the year before, although

such a thing seemed almost impossible. She was sent so many bouquets of flowers that she could hardly count them all, and didn't know who had sent them. She had piles of letters, and books and other presents. Some very important people called to see her and wish her a happy birthday, even including two of the princes. Emilie was woken early in the morning by a kiss from her mother on one cheek, and a kiss from her father on the other cheek, and the celebrations went on all day.

It was all very lively and cheerful. People laughed and discussed balls and parties, books and politics. Someone began talking about the famous people everyone knew, and of course the name of the famous architect who was now a professor was mentioned.

"He's building his own immortality," said one of the princes, who liked to use fine phrases. He meant George designed so many beautiful buildings that people would still remember him after his death, for instance whenever they passed a building of his. Another of the birthday guests felt sure Mr George would soon be very rich, and on intimate terms with all kinds of important people in the best circles.

"The best circles?" repeated the general that night thoughtfully, just before he went to bed. "What did that mean?"

"I can tell you exactly what it means," said his wife, "but I won't. We have no need to discuss the matter, but I would be very surprised if I'm wrong."

"Then I'm surprised too," said the general, "because I have no idea what you mean." And he began thinking hard again.

Well, let us leave the general alone to think in peace, and go back to Emilie's birthday.

You could smell the fragrance of flowers everywhere in the house, and the table was covered with the presents Emilie's friends and acquaintances had given her.

There was no present from George. It hadn't been possible for him to send one, but he didn't need to, because Emilie saw things that reminded her of George all over the house. She had only to look out of the window at the acacia tree, and she saw herself again, struggling with her nursemaid because she wanted to play with George, but she wasn't allowed to do so.

She had only to go upstairs to the old nursery to remember how George had torn down the burning curtains and put out the fire. And she could still remember the taste of the sandwiches the little boy next door had once shared with her.

She opened a drawer and took out the drawings he had given her: the drawings of the Norwegian church and the Russian palace. All kinds of memories came back into her mind.

She remembered how she went down to comfort the janitor's wife when her husband died, quietly and without saying anything at all to her parents, and how a little later she held the woman's hand while she was dying herself. And she remembered what her last words had been. She had said, "Blessings on my son George." The mother's last thoughts had been of her son, and Emilie's last thoughts before she went to sleep that night were of George too, so in that way he had really been at Emilie's birthday all day.

The next day there was another party in the general's house. This time it was the general's own birthday. It was an amusing coincidence that he had been born the day after his daughter, though of course many years earlier. Once again presents arrived, and one of these presents was a fine and very expensive saddle for a horse.

The general knew only one man who had a saddle like that, and he was one of the princes. Who could have sent the saddle? The general was very pleased with his present, and he read the note that came with it at least ten times, but he was still none the wiser. The note simply said, "From someone you do not know."

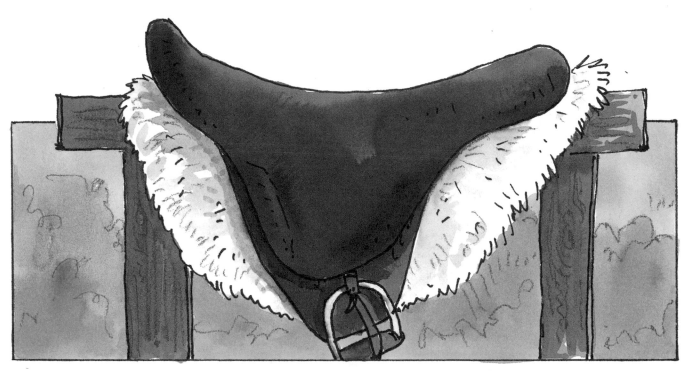

"What does it mean, someone I don't know? And why would someone I don't know send me a present?" the general wondered aloud, several times. "I know everyone!" He thought hard, and imagined himself at a great ball, looking into the faces of all the guests there to see if there was anyone he didn't know. "Oh, of course!" he said to himself then, laughing. "It's from my wife! She wanted to tease me a little. *Charmant*!" However, he was wrong, and his wife didn't want to tease him at all. Her headache was much too bad for that. She might once have teased him, perhaps, when she was younger, but that was so long ago. So the name of the person who had sent the present remained a mystery.

A few days later there was yet another party, a fancy dress ball, not at the general's house this time but given by one of the princes. The general came dressed as another and very famous general. He wore a Spanish costume, with a shining sword at his side, and he walked very upright all evening, trying to look even taller than he was.
His wife was dressed in black velvet and looked very grave. Her dress had a high neck with a big white pleated collar around it. It was summer, so she was very hot in her costume, but she didn't mind that, for she was the very image of a general's wife in an old painting, and she thought she looked very fine.
Emilie was dressed as a butterfly, with a dress made of lace and tulle, the kind of dress that ballet dancers often wear. She had made two wings and fastened them to her shoulders. She was unusually merry and lively, so lively that she seemed to be hovering in the air and didn't need wings at

all, but she wore them just to show everyone what her costume was. It was a splendid party, with decorations and flowers everywhere. Anyone could tell the prince was very rich. There was so much to see, and the guests were so beautifully dressed, that you could easily have watched them for hours.

A man dressed in black, with a costume like a domino tile and with acacia flowers in his cap, danced with Emilie.

"Who is that?" the general's wife asked her famous husband.

"That's His Royal Highness," replied the general without hesitation. "I am absolutely sure of it. I recognized him at once when he shook hands with me. Only the prince presses your hand like that."

However, his wife still wasn't sure, so the general went up to the domino in a very stately manner, and wrote in the palm of his hand the letters YRH?, meaning, "Your Royal Highness?"

The general hoped the domino would nod, so that they could know for sure he was the prince, but the domino shook his head instead. So the general had been wrong, but the domino did give him a little clue: "Think

of the note that came with your saddle," he said. "Someone you don't know."

"But if you gave me that saddle, surely I must know you!" cried the general in surprise.

The domino gestured with his hand, as if to say it didn't matter, and he disappeared among the other guests in costume.

"Who is that domino you were dancing with, Emilie?" the general's wife asked her daughter.

"I didn't ask his name," the girl replied.

"Because you know it already!" remarked her mother, without stopping to hear any more, and she said to the count, who was standing beside her, "Your protégé the young architect is here, Count. He is dressed as a black domino with acacia flowers in his cap."

"That may be so, madam," said the count, "but don't forget that one of the princes is dressed just the same."

"I recognized him from the way he shook hands, and I know for certain it's the prince!" said the general again. He didn't believe the domino,

although the man had shaken his head. "I always thought that saddle came from him! I'll invite him to dinner."

"An excellent idea! Yes, do," said the count. "And if it's the prince I am sure he'll come."

"And if it's the man you think it is," said the general to his wife, "I am sure he won't."

He went over to the domino, who was just talking to the king, and respectfully invited him to dinner. The general smiled as he did so, for he was sure he had invited the prince. But then the domino took off his mask. It was George after all!

"Does your invitation still stand?" he asked.

The general, who was not exactly a short man, seemed to grow even taller. At least, that was how it looked when he took a couple of steps back and then forward again. He was on tiptoe, and might have been doing a little dance, and he looked as serious as only a distinguished general can.

"I never go back on my word," he said sternly, as if he were facing a soldier. "I invited the professor, and my invitation stands." He made a stiff bow, looking sideways as he did so at the king, who of course had heard everything.

So there was a dinner at the general's house, and the only guests were the old count and the famous young professor.

Well, at least I'm inside this house, thought George, and we'll see what happens next.

It all went much better than he had dared to hope. There at dinner in the

house of the distinguished general and his equally distinguished wife, George managed to win everyone over.

The black domino the general had invited came as himself this time, as a professor. He spoke and behaved like a very clever and able man, and it was a pleasure to listen to him.

He had many very interesting things to say about all the foreign places he had visited, and all the famous buildings he had seen while he was studying in Italy.

The general said *"Charmant!"* from time to time during the dinner, and his wife even went so far as to tell people later how the young professor had been to dinner with them, and what a very pleasant person he was. One of the people she told was a lady-in-waiting at court, who said she would like to be invited too next time he came to dinner.

So the lady-in-waiting had her way. She came to dinner, and George came to dinner, and not only was he *charmant* but it turned out that he could play chess very well, and chess had always been a hobby of the general's. "He can't have come from the basement," said the general, repeating what he had said about George once before. "There must have been some mistake, because I know for sure that the boy had good, honest parents. Such cases have been known!"

The general thought that as the royal family had invited the professor into their houses, he could do the same, but he still wouldn't contemplate the idea of letting George marry his daughter. However, he was the only person in the city who felt that way, for everyone else knew that George and Emilie were soon to be married. And no one was greatly surprised when George was appointed to a high position in the city council at the same time.

Now even the general began to feel doubtful. Because he always thought so deeply, he could say some very deep, clever things at times, and he said one of them now. "Life is like a play," he said, "and the play may be a comedy or a tragedy. If it's a tragedy with an unhappy ending the main characters die, if it's a comedy with a happy ending they get married. Well, let's have a comedy this time!"

So George and Emilie were married at last, and they had three fine sons. When they were little the three boys liked to ride hobbyhorse all through the rooms of their grandfather and grandmother's house. And the general, who had been a very good rider himself in the old days, told them all about his time in the army, and of course he never forgot the story of the prince who was taken prisoner and called the general "incomparable". Whatever his grandchildren said or did, he called them, "*Charmant!*", for that was the greatest compliment that he could pay anyone.

Their grandmother still had a headache very often, but as soon as her grandsons came running into the house she felt better at once, and she smiled.

Yes, George the janitor's son did well in the world and was to do even better, or it wouldn't have been worth the trouble of writing this story.

The little elderberry woman and the boy

Once upon a time there was a little boy who came home one afternoon with soaking wet feet. No one could understand how this could be, because the weather was lovely and it had not rained in days. The little boy's mother was very concerned, because her son was coughing and shivering terribly.

"I'm going to put you to bed," she said to her son, and that is exactly what she did. Once he was lying in his warm bed, she made him a big pot of elderberry tea. She knew that elderberry tea is very good for you if you have a cold.

Suddenly there was a knock at the door. It was their neighbour. He lived on the floor above and would often pop in. He was old and a little lonely, as he had neither wife nor children. Every chance he had to pop out and do something was a great delight for him. The little boy thought it was great fun whenever he called.

"Hello!" exclaimed the boy. "Are you going to tell me another story?"

"Drink up your elderberry tea and I'm sure you'll get to hear a fairy tale," said his mother.

"I hope I know another one," said the neighbour. Then he quietly asked the boy's mother: "How did he actually come by those wet feet?"

"I've no idea," she said. "It hasn't rained for days."

The little boy was keen to hear the old man tell a story. He made himself comfortable and asked: "Are you going to tell me a story now?"

"First you must tell me how deep the gutter is in the street you walk along on your way to school."

The boy thought about this for a moment. He said: "It comes over my boots when I stand in the deepest part."

"So," said the neighbour, with satisfaction, "at least we now know how he came by his wet feet."

The boy was insistent: "Are you going to tell me a story now?"

"Of course I am," said the old man, "I did promise, after all. But I don't think I know any fairy tales that I haven't told you before."

"Then make one up!" the boy persisted. "My mother always says that you can make up a fairy tale out of everything you do."

"That I can," said the man, "but those are not good fairy tales. Good fairy tales come from the heart. When you tell them, they come out by themselves. There's nothing more you need to do. If I make up a fairy tale, then I must do the best I can. And then a fairy tale is bad from the very start! You must wait until something comes up."

"Is anything coming up yet?" asked the boy impatiently.

The neighbour closed his eyes. "Not so fast, not so fast," he said. "Don't worry, a fairy tale will present itself!" And all of a sudden he opened his eyes. "There's one!" he exclaimed. "A fairy tale! Hiding in the teapot."

The boy looked at the old teapot on the table. Something strange was happening. The lid was lifting a little. Lovely white elder flowers came into view. Strong stalks pressed the flowers upwards and pushed up the lid of the pot. Stalks were also sprouting from the spout. The elder grew and grew; long branches grew on every side with hundreds of flowers on them.

The elder had soon become a bush and not long after a tree – the whole room was full of elder. The scent was lovely!

In the tree sat an old woman. She had kind eyes and a friendly smile. She was wearing a lovely green dress that was the colour of elder leaves trimmed with white elder blossom. The dress billowed around her. The boy could not see whether the decorations were made of real leaves or of material. Whichever, the woman looked lovely.

"What's that woman's name?" the boy softly asked his neighbour.

"She has different names," said the man. "The ancient Greeks and Romans called her a wood nymph. We just call her Little Elderberry Woman. Look at her closely and also look at that lovely elder. Long ago just such a tree stood somewhere on the edge of the town. It stood in the corner of a little courtyard. Below it was a bench. One day two old people came to sit on that bench. They were a very old sailor and his equally old wife. They were talking about their golden wedding: soon they were going to have been married for fifty years. But however hard they tried, they could not remember the exact date; after all this time it had slipped their minds. They really racked their brains, but the date would simply not

421

come back to them. Little Elderberry Woman sat above them in the tree and said softly: "I know exactly when you should celebrate your golden wedding!" The old people under the tree did not hear her. They were talking about the old days, about the good times they had together. They had known each other even as children.

"Do you remember," the sailor asked, "how we used to play together in this courtyard? We made a garden out of sticks."

"Yes," said the woman. "We didn't have real plants then. Do you remember how one of those twigs took root? It was an elder twig that grew into a big tree. And that's this very tree we are sitting under now!"

The man remembered. He went on: "And I also remember that there used to be a water butt in that corner in which I sailed little boats I had made myself. But not for long, because I went to sea myself fairly soon!"

"It was longer than you think, you know," said the woman. "First we went to school. We used to be in the same class. We always used to copy from one another, do you remember?"

"Yes, we used to be in the same class," said the old sailor. "You were always copying from me, I seem to remember. I never did from you."

"Oh yes you did," said his wife. "But whatever, it hardly matters now. Then you went to sea. Sometimes you were away for months on end. I thought that was terrible. I very often used to cry for you in those days. If I didn't hear anything for a long time, I would think that your ship was wrecked and that you were lying at the bottom of the sea somewhere. And if I knew that your ship was about to put in, I often used to get up in the middle of the night to look at the weather vane on the church. If the wind was blowing in the wrong direction, your ship couldn't come into harbour. And sometimes the wind was set fair, but then there was not a ship to be seen as far as the eye could see. Someone had made a mistake and you were still on the other side of the world."

The old woman sighed. "It's all so long ago ..." She glanced at her husband, cleared her throat and went on: "What I shall never really forget is that day it rained so much that I thought the Flood was on its way. I was just scrubbing the doorstep of the people for whom I worked as a housemaid when the postman gave me a letter. It was a letter from you, which had been halfway round the world and which had taken ages to arrive. I opened the letter and read that you were in Brazil, and that it was really nice and hot there. You wrote that coffee beans grew there – and while I was reading, I suddenly felt an arm around my middle and someone tried to kiss me."

"I remember it very well!" exclaimed the man. "I can still feel that slap you gave me."

"How was I supposed to know it was you? I had a letter in my hand saying that you were in South America!"

"And I didn't know that I had brought my own letter home with me on my own ship," said the man.

"You were so handsome then," the old woman continued. "You still are, of course, but in those days you had everything. You were slim and strong – those were the days."

"And you were beautiful in those days too. We married shortly after! Do you remember?"

"Well, if I think very, very hard!" said the woman, with a laugh. "And then came our children. Nils, Marie, Peter and, finally, Hans Christian."

"How lucky that they have all become strong, healthy, and good people. Everyone has respect for them and at the same time everyone likes them. And then they had children and we became grandparents. Our grandchildren have had children too. I'm sure that it was this time of the year that we married."

"That's right," said Little Elderberry Woman in the tree above the couple. "You have been married exactly fifty years today." The little woman had clambered a little way along the branch. Her head was now in between those of the old people, but they weren't listening to her.

It was not long before the old couple's children, grandchildren and great-grandchildren arrived. They all knew perfectly well that today was the big day. They had been to congratulate the couple early that morning, but the old sailor and his wife had soon forgotten. They remembered perfectly things that had happened fifty years ago, but they had already forgotten what had happened that very morning.

The elder tree smelt lovely and the setting sun shone down on the old couple so that they both looked rosy-cheeked and very healthy.

A great-grandchild announced that there was to be a big party. A wonderful festive meal had been prepared. In the tree Little Elderberry Woman nodded in approval.

"Hip, hip, hooray!" everyone shouted, but Little Elderberry Woman loudest of all.

The neighbour fell silent; his story was at an end.

"But," said the little boy, "that wasn't a fairy tale, was it?"

"That's quite right," replied the old man. "I have an idea. Let's ask Little Elderberry Woman whether she knows a good fairy tale."

They had no need to ask. Little Elderberry Woman climbed out of the elder tree. In a lovely, soft voice she said: "The story about the golden bride and groom was certainly no fairy tale. But listen carefully, for now I'm going to tell you a real fairy tale. And it all really happened! Because the best fairy tales of all have really happened, otherwise this lovely elder would not have been able to grow out of the teapot."

She lifted the boy up and held him close to her. At once elder branches wrapped themselves around him. He saw only Little Elderberry Woman, and elder branches, and blossom, around him – it was as if the two of them were sitting in a leafy glade.

It was lovely! Little Elderberry Woman had suddenly turned into a little girl, the same age as the boy, but she was still wearing the same dress. In her hair she wore a garland of lovely elder flowers and on her breast a living flower as a brooch. Her eyes were big and light blue. The boy thought she was so nice and so beautiful! He kissed her and she kissed him – they were both happy.

Soon afterwards they stood up and left the leafy glade hand in hand. They walked through a glorious flower garden. Wherever they looked, they

could see lovely coloured flowers and plants in the grass. But what they could also see was the boy's father's walking stick. And what was so strange was that the stick was tied to a pole! The two children went and sat on it and in a flash the stick turned into a lovely horse that stood up, gave a little snort and set off at a trot, with the girl and the boy on its back. It trotted round and round the field.

"Now we're going far, far away!" said the boy. "We're off to the castle!"

The horse trotted on and on, but only round and round the field. The girl pointed things out to the boy as they passed. "Can you see that house? A farmer lives there. Three calves were born on his farm today. Two are black and the third is red. All three of them are healthy. And can you see that elder bush there? That's where the chickens scratch and scrape. Aren't there a lot of them! And doesn't the cock strut about! But we're not stopping here. We're going on. Now we can see the church on the hill. Can you see the age-old oak trees around us? They are lovely trees and it's a shame that one of them will die soon. There's the smithy. The smiths are pounding away on the glowing iron with their heavy hammers. Aren't they strong! And now we're going to the castle."

The boy could see everything the girl was talking about. He thought it was fantastic riding around on the horse. He saw so much, but still they had not left the field. "I'll just draw something for you," said the girl, and she brought the horse to a stop.

On the flagstone path she drew a garden with a piece of chalk. In the garden she planted the elder flower she had been wearing as a brooch. At once the flower began to grow. The cutting soon grew twigs and in a moment or two the bush was as big as the elder tree the two old people had been sitting under.

The boy and the little elderberry girl walked hand in hand. Suddenly, the girl flung her arm around the boy's middle and off they flew.

It was spring when they set off and at once it turned to summer. After the summer, which was very hot, it turned to autumn, and finally came the winter.

The boy saw more than he had ever seen before. Towns, villages, forests, rivers, churches, too many to mention.

"You will never forget what you see," said the girl. "The scent of the elder, of the roses, and of the hay – you'll remember them all." Perhaps she was

right, because the boy found it all so lovely that it was making a big impression on him.

"Isn't springtime wonderful!" said the girl. They were standing in a forest full of mighty beech trees. The first leaf buds were just opening and wood violets and lilies-of-the-valley were growing everywhere. "Why can't it always be springtime in the forest?" exclaimed the girl.

In the summer they flew past old castles, whose towers and battlements were reflected in the moats. Lovely white and black swans drifted back and forth on these moats.

The corn in the fields looked like an enormous yellow ocean and everywhere you looked the world was covered with flowers of the prettiest colours. They saw buttercups, and cuckooflowers, flowering rushes, daisies, and poppies. The smell was so incredible! "How could you forget this?" cried the girl.

In the autumn the sky seemed higher than during the rest of the year. In the forest the leaves turned a variety of lovely colours: yellow, orange, dark red, and brown. In the distance you could see great ships sailing on the sea, their sails billowing in the wind. Strong men did their best to catch fish from the stormy sea, and in the village the women and girls sang as they brought in the harvest.

In the evening in the houses old women tell tales of trolls, gnomes, fairies, and elves, as they have been told for centuries past. They are exciting stories, loved by all the children.

And then it turned to winter. Thick snowflakes turned the landscape white as a sheet. "It's so lovely in the winter!" exclaimed the girl. All the trees were covered in thick frost as if they had turned to coral. Everywhere the snow crunched, and behind all the windows stood great Christmas trees with coloured baubles and fairy lights.

428

Little Elderberry Woman, who had become a girl, thought it was all so lovely that she wanted to show the boy everything and this she did. The boy grew up into a strong young man. He went out into the big, wide world and travelled to every corner of the globe. He saw lands where palm trees grew and where large trees with oranges and coffee beans stood.

When the boy signed up as a sailor, the girl took the elder flower from her breast and gave it to the boy to keep. They said goodbye to each other and the ship sailed away. Carefully, the boy put the flower safely inside his hymn-book. Every time he opened the book, it fell open at the page with the elder flower. So he often thought about his sweetheart.

The boy looked in his hymn-book nearly every day. It was just as if he saw Little Elderberry Woman; through the flowers of the blossom he could see the pretty face of his sweetheart. It was just as if the blossom was whispering: "It's lovely here in the springtime, in the summer, in the autumn and in the winter! Come home soon to enjoy everything with me!" Hundreds of memories passed through the boy's mind, because he had forgotten nothing of what his sweetheart had told him and shown him.

Many years passed by. The boy, who had become a sailor, was now an old

man. He sat with his wife – who was also very old – hand in hand under the flowering elder tree in his garden. They were talking about the good old days and they knew that soon they would be celebrating their golden wedding. They had forgotten exactly when it was.

The little girl with steely blue eyes sat in the tree and said: "I know when it is! Your golden wedding is today!" She took two flowers from her garland and gave them a kiss – suddenly the flowers began to glisten like gold. The girl laid a flower each on the heads of the man and the woman, so that it looked as if they were wearing crowns. The old sailor and his wife sat under the elder tree as king and queen. The man told his wife the story of Little Elderberry Woman, as he had heard it as a small boy. There was much in the story they had done themselves. That is what he liked best about it.

"And that's how it is," said the girl in the tree. "Some people call me Little Elderberry Woman; others say wood nymph. Really I'm nothing more than a memory. I sit in the tree and grow with the tree. I have a good memory, so I can talk about everything I have seen and done." And she asked the man: "Do you still have your flower?"

The old man opened his hymn-book. He had kept it with him all his life,

on all the journeys he had made – to the warm south and the chilly north. The elder flower was still there, as fresh and fragrant as the day it had first been placed there. The woman nodded. The two old people sat there in their golden crowns in the red light of the setting sun and ...
The fairy tale was done!

The boy who had caught cold after he had come home with wet feet was lying in his bed again. He did not know whether he had had a dream or someone had told him a story. On the table stood the teapot in which his mother had made elderberry tea. It is very good for colds. There was no elder bush growing from the pot and no branch full of blossom sticking out of the spout.
"I've been to hot countries!" cried the boy. "And I've seen the spring, and the summer, autumn, and winter! It was fantastic!"
His mother laughed. "You must have slept well. You should have done after two cups of hot elderberry tea." She tucked him in again. "You slept for hours while I was talking to the neighbour. But we couldn't decide whether it was a fairy tale or a story that he told you."
"Where's Little Elderberry Woman?" asked the boy.
"I think she must be in the teapot," said his mother, with a chuckle. "And that's where she's going to stay for now!"

The red shoes

Sometimes it can be rather fun to walk about on your bare feet. In the summer, for instance, when the weather is warm; on the beach, or on the soft grass of a meadow. But if you have to go about on bare feet because you don't have any shoes, it is no fun at all. Because sometimes it can be cold even in the summer, or it may rain, and then there is often mud on the road, and it will squeeze up between your toes. That is a horrid feeling, and besides, your feet get very cold, even if it is summer. The little girl in this story had no shoes at all. Her father died when she was still very little, and since his death her mother had been so poor that there was never enough money to buy shoes. That is why Karen, that was the little girl's name, walked about on bare feet in the summer, and on clogs in winter. But those clogs had once been her father's clogs, and they were much to big for her, so they hurt her feet. She couldn't walk very well in them, and she often had big blisters on her feet. The worst was that it did not look as if things would change for the better. Her mother had got very ill from all the hard work and worry, and what little money they had all had to be spent paying for the doctor, and for medicine. But nothing helped, and one day Karen's mother died, too.

Their nextdoor neighbour, who had always helped Karen and her mother, was sorry for the girl. She did not want Karen to go to her mother's funeral on bare feet, so she made her a pair of shoes. Of course, she wasn't a proper shoemaker; she had never made shoes before, and they were not a particularly good shape. She made them of bright red material, left over from when she had made some curtains one day. But Karen thought they were beautiful, and she was very grateful to her neighbour.

She thought it was just a little bit odd to go to her mother's funeral with red shoes on her feet, but she had no others, and so she wore them anyway. And it felt rather nice, much better than walking over the gravel paths in the church-yard on bare feet.

After the funeral, which didn't take very long, as Karen walked away from the grave with the minister, a coach stopped right beside them. It was a

432

beautiful, shiny, lacquered coach drawn by two magnificent horses, and in it was an old lady. She had heard that Karen's mother had died, and because she was very rich, she wanted Karen to come and live with her. She promised the minister that she would look after her well, and Karen was allowed to ride with her in the coach.

Karen thought that the old lady had taken her with her because she liked her red shoes so much, but that turned out not to be the case. As soon as they had arrived at her enormous house, the old lady told her butler that he should burn those awful shoes! Karen was given new clothes, because she had to look respectable. She was sent to school and learned lots of things: reading, writing, drawing, arithmetic, sewing, and knitting.

Everyone who came to visit the old lady thought Karen was a sweet girl, and they often said that to her, too. This made Karen a little vain, and when she looked in the mirror in her room, she often told herself that she was really quite pretty!

One day the queen paid a visit to the town. Everyone was very excited, and people came trooping to the town hall, where the queen would be welcomed. Of course, Karen was there, too. She stood right in front, so

that she could see everything well. The queen was not alone: she had brought one of her little daughters, a real princess, with a pretty white lace dress, and... beautiful, shiny, red leather shoes! Those shoes were, of course, much nicer than the shoes Karen's neighbour had made for her when Karen's mother had died, but now Karen was quite sure that there was nothing in the world more beautiful than red shoes. And she hoped that one day she would have just as beautiful a pair of shoes as the queen's little daughter.

Because Karen always did her best, the day soon came when she would be confirmed into the church by the minister. The old lady, who was very religious, thought Karen should look very special for this occasion, and so they went together into town to buy new clothes, and shoes, too. In the shoemaker's shop there were at least a hundred pairs of beautiful shoes, but Karen only had eyes for one pair, all by themselves in a big glass cabinet. They were magnificent, shiny, red shoes. The shoemaker told them that they had been made for a nobleman's daughter, but when she had tried them on they did not fit.

"Are they made of patent leather?" asked the old lady.

Her eyesight was very bad, but she often forgot to put on her glasses, so she couldn't see the shoes very well.

They were indeed patent leather shoes, and Karen was told she could try them on. They fitted exactly, and the old lady bought them for her. But she didn't realize that the shoes were red, because she would never have allowed Karen to go to church to be confirmed with red shoes on her feet. And perhaps she would have been right, because when Karen walked along the aisle right to the front of the church everyone looked at her feet. It seemed as if even the paintings on the walls, portraits of long-dead noblemen and ministers, followed her with their eyes, and looked disapprovingly at her red shoes. But while the minister said all kinds of difficult words to Karen, and welcomed her as a member of the church, Karen could not concentrate very well. All she could think of was the shiny shoes on her feet. She did hear the people in the church sing, and the solemn tones of the great organ, and the minister's long sermon, but nothing really got through to her; she kept thinking of her shoes.

Later that day some people came to visit the old lady; they told her that Karen had been wearing red shoes to church, and that was really not how it should be. The old lady was very angry with Karen, and told her that in future she would only be allowed to wear black shoes for church.

The next Sunday Karen obediently put on her black shoes, and showed them to the old lady. But as soon as the old lady had taken her glasses off, Karen ran upstairs, and quickly put her red shoes on instead.

Together the old lady and Karen walked to church. An old soldier met them in front of the church. He bowed deeply to them and offered to clean the old lady's shoes. It had been a long walk, and the shoes were rather dusty, so the old lady accepted gratefully. Karen, too, put one of her shoes in front of him.

"Those are very good, strong, dancing shoes," said the soldier, "they should last a long time!" He tapped the soles approvingly.

Karen and the old lady went into the church, and just like the last time everybody, including the noblemen and ministers in the paintings, looked at Karen's red shoes. Karen herself had to kneel at the altar, and drink wine from a golden chalice, and sing, and pray, but again she could not concentrate: she only looked at her feet.

When the minister had finished speaking and the service was over, everyone left the church again. The old lady got into her coach, and Karen was about to follow her, but just when she had put her foot on the running-board the old soldier turned up again, and said: "Just look at those beautiful dancing shoes!"

Karen thought it was rather nice of him to say so, and to please him she made a few dancing steps. But suddenly she found she couldn't stop again! It was just as if her feet had taken charge of her. She danced away from the soldier, away from the coach, right round the church. She danced so far away that the coachman had to climb down from his box to fetch her back. But even when he had caught her up and grabbed hold of her, her feet in the red shoes kept on making dancing steps, so the coachman picked her up and carried her into the coach. But even there Karen could not stop her feet dancing, so that the old lady even got kicked in the process! The coachman, the old lady, and Karen herself then tried to get her shoes off, and only when between the three of them they had succeeded did her feet come to rest and the dancing finally stopped. As soon as they came home, the shoes were put into a safe place inside a cupboard, and the old lady told Karen never to wear them again. Karen obeyed, but she couldn't resist having a look at them every day. They were so beautiful!

Some time later something very sad happened. The old lady hadn't been feeling so well for a while, and now she really became ill. The doctor came straightaway, and when he had had a good look at her he said that there was nothing he could do for her: she wouldn't live much longer. Of course, the patient had to be nursed very carefully, and everyone was sure that Karen would do that, because the old lady had taken her in and always looked after her so well.

But Karen had had an invitation for an important ball, which was held in the town every year, and she had been looking forward to it for weeks. And now she had to stay at home to look after the old lady. She looked at the old lady, who after all would soon die, and from the old lady at the red shoes. Surely she could put them on for just a minute? She couldn't resist trying them on – surely that could not be wrong? But as soon as the shoes were on her feet they began to dance. For a moment Karen tried to keep her feet still, but she couldn't manage it, and so she went off to the ball, dancing all the way.

The people who saw Karen dance looked on full of admiration. But they made one mistake, for it was not Karen who was dancing, but the shoes, and Karen was simply carried along with them. If she wanted to turn right, the shoes went to the left, and if Karen wanted to go forward, the shoes danced backwards.

Karen enjoyed the ball tremendously. She had never been to one before, and she danced with everyone. She didn't even think of the old lady, who had taken such good care of her, and who was now all alone at home, while Karen was having fun at the ball.

But suddenly something odd happened. While Karen couldn't get enough of the ball, her shoes, who had such a power over her feet, danced out of the hall with her! They danced down the stairs and out of the building, out of the street and out of the town, and even further, into the woods. It was now very late, and it was dark outside, and very cold. When Karen had reached the woods, she suddenly saw a face looking at her through the trees. But the face she saw wasn't the face of the moon, but the face of the old soldier with his long beard, who nodded approvingly, and said: "What a beautiful pair of dancing shoes you have there!"

Suddenly Karen felt very frightened. It was night, she was all by herself in a large wood, and her feet just wouldn't stop dancing. She was so frightened that she wanted to throw her shoes away. But she couldn't manage it! She couldn't get the shoes off her feet. It was as if they had grown onto them. She simply had to dance, and dance she did, without stopping.

She danced through the morning and the afternoon, the evening and the night, when it rained, and when the sun shone, when it was warm, and when there was a sharp frost.

She danced through the streets of the town, across the fields and meadows round it, in the park, and even in the church-yard. She had to dance for so long that she was tired out, but even when she wanted to rest on a moss-covered gravestone for a moment, her shoes wouldn't let her. She had to go on dancing all the time. She came to the church, and almost danced into it, when suddenly an angel stood in front of the door. The angel held a large, shimmering sword in front of him, and looked at her seriously and severely. "You wanted to dance, and dance you shall," said the angel threateningly. "You shall dance until you are old and wrinkled! You shall dance past every door, past the houses of poor people and rich people, and past houses where there are children who are as vain as you. They will see you, and you will be an example of what can happen to you if you are vain, because you will go on dancing until you die!" "Have pity on me," begged Karen fearfully, but she couldn't stand still and wait for an answer from the angel, because her shoes had carried her off again, away from the church and the church-yard, to the fields around it, dancing all the time.

One day it happened that Karen danced past a house she knew very well, because she had lived in it for many years. When she danced past it, the

door suddenly opened. Four dignified men in black suits came out, carrying a coffin covered with flowers. At the same time Karen heard the solemn tones of the great church organ. She understood then that the old lady she had let down so meanly when she was so ill had died. She knew she was alone in the world now. But she could not even stop to go to the funeral, because she had to go on dancing, from the sunny day into the evening and the dark night. The shoes she had first admired so much, but hated now, carried her on. And they did not always keep dancing on the road or the grass, but they dragged her straight through shrubs with sharp thorns, so that her legs got horribly scratched.

On her way through the middle of the forest she finally came to a small, lonely cottage, where she knocked on the door and called: "Please will you come out and help me? I want to ask you something, and I can't come inside, because I have to dance."

"Then you probably don't know who I am," answered a voice from inside the cottage. "I am the executioner! I have to chop off the heads of murderers and other bad people!"

"You needn't chop off my head," said Karen, "because I haven't murdered anyone. But I am a bad person, and I have only been thinking of myself.

Could you please chop off my feet with my shoes?"
The executioner came outside, and Karen told him how meanly she had let down the old lady, who had always been so good to her, when she was ill and needed her. She also told him that as a punishment she would always have to dance until she died, as the angel had said.

The executioner felt sorry for Karen, and thought it might be punishment enough for her if she didn't have any feet any more. So he chopped off her feet, and they danced away, across the fields, carried off by the red shoes. Then the executioner made her some new feet and a pair of crutches cut from supple willow wood. He let her stay with him until her feet had healed. When that had happened, Karen thanked the executioner for everything, and said goodbye. Slowly and awkwardly she walked away on her wooden feet, supporting herself on her crutches.

She walked back to the town, and decided to go to church, because she thought that she had been punished enough now. But when she was nearly at the church, she suddenly spotted the red shoes again, dancing some way in front of her. Sadly she turned round and went to her room. The following week she did nothing but cry and feel sorry for herself, and

the next Sunday she decided she had suffered enough to be allowed back into the church. But at the gate of the church yard the red shoes were again dancing ahead of her, so that once more she went home disappointed.

Then she went to the minister and asked him if she could work in his house. She promised that she would work hard and didn't need to earn much money, as long as she had somewhere to live, with good people.

She was told she could come. She worked hard, and listened attentively when the minister read to her or talked to her. The minister's children loved her and always told her everything about the things they were doing. But if they talked about beautiful clothes and having fun, Karen did not say anything, but shook her head sadly.

One morning, when they asked her to go to church with them, Karen looked at her crutches with tears in her eyes, and remembered the red shoes. She stayed at home, all by herself, and began to read her hymn book. The wind blew the sounds of the church organ towards her, and she began to feel a little less lonely. She decided to work hard and listen well to the minister, and to stop feeling sorry for herself. And when a few

weeks later the minister's children again asked her to come to church with them, she agreed hesitantly, and slowly, leaning on her crutches, went with them. And this time she didn't see the hated red shoes dancing ahead of her, and gratefully she went into the church. She heard the organ play, and the people sing, she saw the paintings of the noblemen and ministers of bygone days, and she listened attentively to the minister's sermon. The sun shone through the stained glass window, straight at Karen's seat, and suddenly her heart was so full of peace and happiness that it broke.

Her body stayed behind, but her soul slipped away, along the sun's rays, to a place where no one ever spoke of red shoes, so they never bothered her any more.

The poet who was born too late

There was once a young man who fell in love with the sweetest girl in the world. He wanted very much to marry her and, luckily, she felt the same. However, two people together need twice as much money as does one alone. Unfortunately, the young man had no money at all. He was studying to be a poet and hoped to be finished by Easter. So, he studied very hard indeed but he earned nothing.

To become a poet is extremely difficult. You are always deep in thought because you have to keep on coming up with new subjects so that you can write poems about them. This young man found that terribly hard. He felt that it was all because he had been born too late. Before his time, there had already been thousands of poets who had long ago used up all the subjects on which he wanted to write a poem.

"The poets who were born a thousand years ago had it easy," he sighed. "They could choose from all the subjects they wanted. Even poets born a few hundred years ago were lucky because they still had enough things to write nice poems about. But where can I find something nice to write about now?"

So he took his books for the hundredth time and searched desperately for one tiny, little subject which the poets who had lived centuries ago had failed to notice.

The young man worked terribly hard. All day long he sat in his small room thinking about everything in the world which might be beautiful and interesting. Yet, everything that he came up with had already been written about once before, hundreds of years ago. The young man worked so very hard that he became ill. He went to ten or more different doctors but no-one could cure him.

At his wits' end, he went to visit a fortune-teller because everyone had said that she knew more than however many doctors did. He hoped that she would be able to tell him how he was to become a famous poet.

The fortune-teller lived in a neat and tidy, very ordinary, little house. The young man thought that it looked rather boring, not at all as he had imagined it. The house did have a garden surrounding it but not a single plant or flower grew there, and so he wondered to himself what a beehive was doing next to the front door. A small piece of ground in the corner of the garden was piled high with potatoes. There was also a sloe bush with berries which were not yet ripe.

What a boring garden, he thought, it could look a lot more attractive. So it was that he began to fantasize about beautiful gardens, the fortune-teller thus helping him with a subject before he had even seen her. It had, therefore, been a good idea to go and visit her.

"I know exactly what you've come for," said the fortune-teller, who was also a mind reader. "You can't think of anything to write a poem about. But even so, you've already found something small to be starting with."

"I'm still too late," sighed the young man. "I was born much too late to find a good subject. In the past it was much easier. If only I'd been alive a few centuries ago!"

"You should really consider," said the fortune-teller, "that it wasn't so very easy then at all. Very many people were poor. If you didn't have much money, then you had to think, above all, about how you were to survive. You didn't have any time to write nice poems! We now live in very good times, for even a poet who doesn't know what to write about, like yourself, need not die of hunger and even wears nice clothes. In the past, even famous poets were sometimes so poor that they had to walk around in worn out rags. And they didn't have any money to buy bread with. They often died from hunger and the cold. You should think this over carefully: there are enough things for you to write about, but you first have to want to see them. Here, just try my spectacles on and see things as I see them. Complaining won't get you anywhere."

The young man was still not completely convinced but he put the fortune-teller's spectacles onto his nose and walked with her to the corner of the garden where the potatoes were piled. The fortune-teller pushed a potato into his hand and all at once the young man heard a song. It was the potato itself which sang its own story. It was a long tale.

The potato sang about its great-grandparents, the first potatoes which had come to Europe. They were badly treated and it had taken a very long time before people realized how important they actually were.

"We were shared out amongst the people in every city because the king had ordered it. Yet people had never seen a potato up until then and they thought us peculiar things. Moreover, they had absolutely no idea what to do with us. Some people threw a whole sackful of us into a deep hole all together, others put us in the ground one by one, but much too far apart from each other. They thought that potatoes would appear above ground

446

like fruit trees from which you have only to shake off the ripe fruits. The potatoes which had been planted in the ground well tried their very best. They grew up and had berries, but the berries are poisonous. People tried to eat them but only had stomach ache. No-one thought to look under the ground and so they all thought that potatoes were absolutely useless. No, we potatoes have not had it easy. Yet, we stayed the course and now everyone knows how useful we are."

"And now you have said quite enough," said the fortune-teller. "Let's take a look at the sloe bushes."

Still wearing the fortune-teller's spectacles on his nose, the young poet could also hear the sloe bushes talking. "We still have relatives in the land which the potatoes come from," said one of them, "but they live further to the north. The Norsemen arrived there long ago, after having had to sail a long time through storms and icy cold. Once they had passed the parts of the land covered only by ice and snow, they found beautiful bushes covered in dark berries which only ripened if there had been a frost. We are those bushes the sloe bushes. And because they thought us such a lovely green, they called the land 'Greenland'.

"That does sound very romantic," admitted the poet.

"Come along quickly then," said the fortune-teller. She took him by the hand, brought him to the beehive, and let him peer inside through the opening. It was seething with activity inside the beehive. There were bees everywhere beating their wings as hard as they could to let a little fresh air waft through their honey factory. More and more bees came flying up to enter the hive where they shook off the pollen from their legs, while others flew out again. The queen bee also wanted a breath of fresh air, but if she were to fly out of the hive all the other bees would follow and it was still too soon for that. Therefore, four bees stood guard around her so she could not fly off, even secretly, for one minute.

"How sad," said the poet. "She must be terribly unhappy."

"And now," said the fortune-teller, "look over the fence at all the people going by."

"There's a lot of them," said the poet taken aback. "And they, too, all have their own story. There is much too much to think about or to write down. I'm going to stop with all of this!"

"No!" said the fortune-teller. "On the contrary, you must go on. You have

to go up to all those people and talk with them. If you listen to their stories, then in no time you'll have more subjects for your poems than you'll ever need in your entire life. Just go to them. But give me my spectacles back first."

The young man took the spectacles off his nose and gave them to the woman. However, it was to his disappointment that as soon as he did this he no longer heard or saw anything anymore.

"Now I still see only boring things," he sadly told the fortune-teller. "There's nothing any longer to write poems about."

"In that case, you still won't be a poet when you've finished your studies at Easter," she predicted.

"When will I be one?"

"Not at Whitsun and not at Christmas. Probably never."

"But how can I then live the life of a poet?"

"Just begin on New Year's Eve," said the fortune-teller, "for that is the evening when all poets read their poems out loud. Make no poem yourself, but listen to their poems and then go and write about them yourself. Make jokes about them, or say what you don't like about them. Write everything that you want to write and you will have money enough to buy all the mince pies that you and your wife can eat."

What is she talking about? thought the young man as he walked home. Yet, on the way, he decided that the fortune-teller might well have been right. Once at home, he began to write about other poets and their poems because he himself could not become one.

Just as the fortune-teller had foretold, he earned a lot of money, so much in fact that in no time he had become richer and more famous than all the poets about whom he was writing and of whom he had at first been so very jealous.

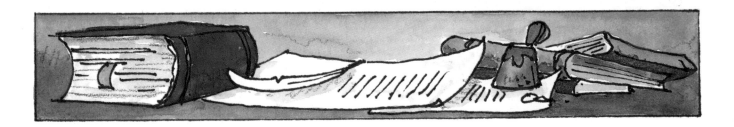

The thistle's tale

In a far and distant land there was a magnificent castle with an enormous garden round it. It was full of rare trees and colourful flowers, and it had winding paths bordered with grass running all through it. The nobleman who owned the castle often allowed people to visit his garden, because he was very proud of it. Elegant ladies and gentlemen strolled along the paths and were amazed at the garden's beauty. It was so wonderful that people even came from outside the country to see it. And every time they were astonished by the splendour of the flowers and of the trees, arranged neatly in rows in the green grass.

Outside the garden, near the gate at the roadside, there was a large thistle. It had branched out in all directions, and almost looked like a thistle-bush. No one looked at the thistle, and that was quite reasonable: foxgloves, lady's mantle, and poppies are much nicer to look at!

Only a chubby old donkey sometimes looked at it. He often came along the road with his master's milk cart. Then he stretched out his neck in the direction of the thistle, and softly brayed:

Oh my, oh my, you do appeal!
I want to have you for my meal!

But his harness held him back, so he had no opportunity to nibble a bit of the thistle, who was actually rather indignant about it all. Why on earth would he want to eat her? She was surely too beautiful? She was trying so hard to grow to a good height. And she did not do that to be eaten by a silly donkey.

One warm summer the nobleman had a lot of guests. A large family had come from Scotland to spend the summer at his beautiful country estate. The father and mother slept in the White Hall, and the seven daughters in the Blue Hall, which looked out on the garden. One of the girls was the prettiest and nicest of all seven. She'd had so many proposals of marriage, that she had quite lost count of all the young men who wanted to marry her. But every time she said no, because she thought she was far too young to marry. First she wanted to spend more time with her parents and sisters. She could always get married later, she thought.

The girls spent the whole day in the garden, in the company of the nobleman's seven sons. They played croquet, or walked slowly along the paths between the flowers. Each girl picked a flower, and put it in the buttonhole of one of the young men. Most of them chose poppies, but the prettiest girl found it hard to choose a flower. She walked through the whole garden, but she didn't see any flower pretty enough – until she came to the thistle.

"Do please pick me a thistle flower!" she said to the young man by her side. "There is a thistle in the coat of arms of Scotland! It is a beautiful plant!" And the young man, who was the eldest of the seven brothers, did what the girl had asked him. He was happy to do anything, as long as he could be in her company. He climbed over the gate and picked a flower from the thistle. Then he gave it to the girl. She tucked the flower into his buttonhole. "Ouch!" he cried, because the thistle had pricked him.

All the other boys were jealous of their brother. They would have been happy to exchange their poppies for a thistle, if that could have won them the girl. The eldest brother was so proud! But proudest of all was the thistle! One of her flowers was now inside the walls of the garden! And what's more, it was in the buttonhole of the nobleman's son!

"I am far more important than I ever knew!" said the thistle to all her flowers. "I should be inside the gates and not outside them. Oh, why was I born on the wrong side of the gates? I should be in the garden, because I have managed to have one of my flowers installed in a buttonhole!"

Every time a new flower unfolded its petals, the thistle told the story of the flower which had gone such a long way. But after she had told the story a few times, she heard some very good news. The girl and the young man were going to get married!

"I was responsible for that!" said the thistle excitedly. "That is because I surrendered the flower she put in his buttonhole!" Every new-born flower had to hear this story, and knew from birth how well one of its sisters had done.

"I rather expect they will transplant me to the garden soon," thought the thistle. "Or perhaps they will put me in a tub. That may be a little cramped and stifling, but it would be a great honour for a thistle!"

After a few days the thistle told everyone that she would shortly be moved to a tub. "There is one ready for me," she said. And she told the same to all her flowers. "Soon you will be potted," she said, "and then you will surely be picked to be put in a buttonhole."

But nothing happened. No one came with a spade to dig the thistle up and transplant her to a tub. No one came to pick a flower to put in a buttonhole. Only bees came from time to time to collect some pollen They left the flowers just where they were.

"Thieves!" scolded the thistle, but the bees didn't pay any heed; they often heard such remarks when they were at work. "I'll sting you to death!" shouted the thistle. The bees hummed softly, as if they were laughing, because they knew that the thistle was bluffing – she couldn't sting the bees!

The thistle's flowers waited and waited for the time they would be in a tub at last. That was what they had been promised, and they believed what their mother had told them. After a while they dropped their heads in disappointment, and their colour faded, even if the sun shone happily every day. Fortunately there were always new flowers.

"You are just in time!" the thistle told them. "Any moment I expect them to move us through the gates."

Around the thistle grew little daisies and plantains. They liked to listen to the thistle, and admired her greatly. They believed anything she said.

Meanwhile the milk cart came past every day, and each time the donkey made another effort to eat the thistle. The milkman took care that he didn't, by holding the reins tight.

The thistle got prouder and prouder by the day. Since that day the girl had said that there was a thistle on the Scottish coat of arms, she thought it must have been one of her ancestors who appeared on it. That meant that her family was very important and had a great past. How splendid, how marvellous!

Even that long, warm summer came to an end. The trees began to scatter their leaves all over the garden. The gardener spent hours every day clearing fallen leaves. All in vain, of course, because whenever he had finished, he had to start all over again. That didn't matter. He sang:

> *Whenever I have done it all,*
> *Another lot of leaves will fall!*

The young fir-trees on the edge of the wood began to look forward to Christmas. That was still a few months away. "And I'm just left to stand here," complained the thistle. "It's as if nobody is interested in me. Me! And I was responsible for getting those two young people engaged! And they got married last week! They didn't even invite me to the wedding..." She sobbed a little, or perhaps it just looked like that, because thistles can't really sob. In any case she was very unhappy.

Weeks went by, and it got colder, and colder. Every day the thistle was tormented by a raw wind, which robbed her of all her colour. She only had one flower left, which already looked rather dried up. There was nobody left she could tell her story to, because she wasn't getting any new flowers now.

But then at last the thistle received a little bit of attention. The young couple came into the garden, hand in hand. It was snowing, and it was very cold, so both the young man and the girl were wearing thick coats. They walked up to the gate. The young woman looked over the top, and pointed at the thistle. She said: "Look, the thistle is still there, but there aren't any flowers left."

Her husband said: "Yes, there's just one! But it isn't much more than a skeleton."

"It's still a beautiful flower," said the young woman. "It almost looks as if it's made of silver, it has lost so much colour. Let's frame it."

The young man climbed over the gate to pick the thistle's flower. She pricked him, just to punish him; she wasn't going to have anyone call any of her children a skeleton!

The young man took no notice of the thistle's prickles, and carefully he picked the flower.

That's how the thistle's flower came into the garden, into the house, and finally into the sitting room. There the girl put the flower in a frame, and

hung it on the wall, next to a beautiful wedding portrait of herself and the young man.

The thistle was happy now. One of her daughters had ended up in a buttonhole, and a second in a frame! She sang:

> My first was in a buttonhole,
> My second a gold frame;
> A thistle who's not satisfied
> Does not deserve such fame!

The donkey stood on the side of the road and looked at her. "Would you like to end up inside me? Now, that really would be an honour for you!" he brayed.

The thistle was not listening. Why should she take any notice of a donkey, now that she was the queen of the thistles?

"If my children are happy, then so am I. What more could I want?" she thought.

"That is a beautiful thought," said a gentle voice. It was a ray of sunlight, which had crept through the clouds to have a quick word with the thistle. "But you'll have a good place yourself, too!" said the ray.

"Where?" asked the thistle. "In a tub, perhaps? Or in a frame?"

"Even better," answered the ray of sunlight. "In a fairytale."

The piggy bank that couldn't rattle

Toys were scattered all over the playroom. There were wooden blocks all over the floor and in the corner stood a forgotten toy train with a doll on top. On one side of the room stood a big chest of drawers, which was bulging with toys. One drawer was full of dolls and teddy bears, and there was a model aeroplane on top. In amongst them all were paper folders and colouring pencils.

Right on top of the chest of drawers stood a piggy bank. It was made of clay and in places its pink paint was beginning to peel away. In its back the little pig had a slot you could drop coins into. Someone had made the slot a little wider with a knife so pound coins could go through. There were three of them inside. Otherwise the piggy bank was full of other coins. It was so full that with the best will in the world you could not cram another coin into it. If you shook it back and forth it couldn't even rattle any more, it was so full.

The piggy bank stood on top of the chest of drawers and looked down on all the toys in the room. It knew that with all the money it had inside it

could buy everything it could see in the room, and that made it feel good. It was very proud to be so rich. Everyone should look up to a pig of such distinction, it thought. This was actually quite true, because its position in the room was higher than anybody else's. But the pig did not think this was enough, because it thought that this meant it could lord it over everybody.

All the other toys in the nursery were a little afraid of the pig. The dolls, the bears and the train knew how rich the pig was and respected it. They had no money inside them and knew that the pig was crammed full of it.

The pig thought it was wonderful that the other toys knew how rich it was. On the other hand, the toys paid little attention to it because they were far too busy with other things.

"Shall we play mothers and fathers?" asked the doll in the corner of the room. Her neck had been broken once and Mother had repaired it, so it was all right now. All the toys in the room thought this was a splendid idea. The doll's pram tried to cheer (but could only manage a little squeak) and the firecracker cracked loudly in approval.

The toys decided that they should really invite the pig to join in their game. They did not dare simply ask it, so they wrote it a letter. But the pig thought this sort of thing was beneath it and wrote back saying that it was quite happy to watch from the chest of drawers, provided it did not have to join in. The toys thought this was fine.

"We all have our pride," said the doll's pram. "Everyone has his place; there are workers and there are men of standing."

The toys decided to put on a real show. They set up a big theatre in the middle of the room so that the pig would have a good view of it all.

The plan was to start with a play and then to talk about all sorts of important things. But the toys did not keep to their plan, because they thought it was more fun to start with the talking. When the curtain went up they all started to talk at once.

The hobbyhorse gave a long talk about training and purebred horses. It really was a wonderful speech and everyone listened carefully. It was fully an hour before the horse was finished. Everyone clapped loudly and then the next speaker came up to speak. It was the doll's pram, which spoke about railways and steam power. It knew what it was talking about because it had wheels itself! Once again the audience clapped loudly. The third speaker was the clock. It talked about politics, and it knew all about it because it knew what time it was. The walking stick listened closely and every now and again made clever remarks. It was old and had seen and done many things.

Everyone watched and listened carefully and clapped loudly. The walking

stick did not think the audience was clapping loudly enough.

"Clap louder if you like it!" he cried.

"I never crack for old people, only for the young, especially couples!" said the riding crop.

"I crack for everyone!" said the firecracker.

And so the show went on. All the talking was at an end, because no one had any questions. It was time for the play to begin and so it did. It was not a very good play, but the actors did their very best. They all kept their painted sides to the front. This they had to do because they had only been made to be looked at from one side. The other side was dull and grey and that was no good to anyone. A big doll in a white dress was the princess and she acted the best of all. She also had a big advantage, because she could cry. She made it look so real that even the audience had tears in its eyes. The doll whose neck had been broken also did well. She really put everything into her part as the wicked stepmother. It was a pity she could only say "Mama!", but then nobody's perfect.

The piggy bank thought the whole thing was marvellous. It was very impressed by the play put on by all the toys. It clapped at the end of every

462

act and called: "Encore, encore!" which means "I want to see that again, and again!"

But that was not all. The piggy bank found the doll in the white dress so very beautiful that it decided to remember her in its will. If she should die, she was to be buried with the piggy bank in its family grave! This was, of course, a great honour for a simple doll.

When the play was over they decided to start talking about all sorts of things again. It had been such fun the first time! This time they talked about the meaning of life. A difficult subject, of course, so everyone thought, but dolls know a lot or think they do. For hours one speaker followed another. They all thought hard about what the piggy bank would think of them. All the toys wanted to be remembered in the piggy bank's will, because it was such a great honour. On the other hand, it would be a long time before the piggy bank was dead, thought the toys.

But it all turned out very differently. All of a sudden the piggy bank fell onto the floor with a loud crash and shattered into thousands of pieces. Ten pence, five pence and fifty pence pieces rolled all over the floor. One of the three pound coins rolled the furthest, because it really wanted to go out into the big wide world.

The pound coin got what it wanted, as did all the other coins. They were spent on new toys and the old piggy bank ended up in the waste basket. The doll with the white dress was thrown away too, because she was very old and now there was more than enough money for a lovely new doll, who had eyes that could really open and close. So she was buried in the piggy bank's family grave, though she did not have the lovely funeral she had expected.

The next day there was a new piggy bank standing on the chest of drawers. It too was made of clay and was painted a lovely shade of pink. It had not a penny inside it, so it couldn't rattle either. Really, it was not all that different from the first piggy bank that couldn't rattle. This new piggy bank could make a fresh start. And with this new beginning this fairy tale is at an end.

The old street lamp

ar, far away there was once an old street lamp that had always done its best and taken great pride in its work, but which was now about to retire. This was going to be its last night standing on its spot and lighting up the street. It was a bit sad and not at all looking forward to the morning, because then it would be sent to the council depot, where wise men would decide whether it still shone brightly enough to stay in use for a little while longer.

Maybe they would send it to some small village somewhere, where hardly anyone ever goes out at night, or it might find itself on a deserted factory site somewhere. Even worse, the wise men might decide to have it melted down. Then it would be made into something else and the lamp was quite afraid that it would not remember anything of its life as a street lamp.

Whatever happened, it would never see the lamplighter again, nor his wife. In all the time that it had been standing there, the man and his wife had actually become a small part of the street lamp's family. It would miss them a lot.

When the street lamp was first put up, the lamplighter had still been young and strong. They had both started on the same day. What a long time ago that had been! To begin with the lamplighter's wife had not been very friendly. More recently, now that the street lamp, the lamplighter, and his wife had all grown older, even she would sometimes look after the lamp. She would clean it and top up its oil. The two old people were very respectable and honest. They had always taken good care of the lamp and never spilt a drop of oil.

It was understandable that the lamp was rather sad and so was not shining so brightly. All kinds of other memories, happy memories, came flooding back. It had seen so much! Even things that no one else knew anything about ... But it kept quiet and did not talk about everything it knew, because it did not want to offend anyone, and it was full of respect for anyone who was more important than it was. The street lamp thought more and more about the past and softly began to mutter its memories under its breath.

"That nice boy – now wasn't that a long time ago – who had a letter on pink paper in his hand with a ribbon round it. The letter had been written so neatly you could see at once that it came from a girl. The boy read the letter twice over, kissed the paper and looked up at me with such a smile that you could see he thought he was the luckiest person in the whole world. Only he and I know what was in that very first letter."

It was this sort of thing the old street lamp remembered on its last evening.

If someone on guard duty is relieved, at least he knows who the new guard is. Then the two of them can have a bit of a chat. But the street lamp had no idea who would come after it, and this, it thought, was a pity, because it had so much experience that it could have explained so many things to the new lamp and could have given it advice. It knew everything about the rain and the fog, for example, and it could say exactly how far the moon shone into the street and from which direction the wind blew.

On the sewer grate by the street lamp were three objects that were keen to follow in the street lamp's footsteps and, since they thought that the street lamp could choose the new lamp itself, they began to blow their own trumpets. The first object was a herring's head, which itself gave out light when it was dark. It did not need any oil, so thought it would be much cheaper and easier to use than the lamp.

Object number two was an old piece of wood that also gave out light in the dark. It said proudly that it was a grandson of an old tree that had once been the most beautiful tree in the whole forest.

The third object was a glowworm. The street lamp had no idea where it came from, but the herring's head and the wood kept saying that the glowworm only gave out light now and again and so was by no means as useful as they were. The old street lamp explained that none of them gave out enough light to follow in its footsteps as a street lamp, but they would not listen.

When they heard that the street lamp was not allowed to choose the new lamp itself, they were glad and made out that it was too old to make a good choice anyway. Just at that moment the wind came round the corner of the street and blew through the street lamp's vents.

"What's this I hear?" asked the wind. "You're leaving tomorrow and this evening's the last I'll see of you? Then I must give you a going-away present. I shall blow so hard through your vents that in future you'll be able to remember everything you have seen and heard. You'll also have a light in you that is so bright that you can see everything that is said or written, wherever you may be."

"That's far too much, you really shouldn't," said the old street lamp, which

466

was very modest. All the same, it beamed with pleasure to be receiving such a wonderful present from the wind. "Thank you very, very much. I only hope that I'm not melted down."

"That won't happen straightaway," said the wind. "Let me freshen your memory in any case. With presents such as these you'll have a lovely old age."

Then the moon came out from behind the clouds.

"What are you giving the street lamp as a going-away present?" the wind asked the moon.

"Nothing," replied the moon. "I'm getting smaller at the moment and the lamp has never shone on me, while I have given it light often enough." And with these words the moon slipped back behind the clouds, because it did not want to talk about it any more.

Then a drop of water, which seemed to come from the roof, landed on the lamp. The drop explained that it came from the clouds and was also a present, perhaps the loveliest present of all.

"I shall work my way so far into you that you can rust right through in just one night and fall apart if you want," it said.

But the street lamp and the wind did not think this was a nice present. The wind asked, while it was blowing as hard as it could, whether anyone else wanted to give the street lamp a present.

Just then a star fell from the sky, leaving a long streak of light behind it. "What was that?" cried the herring's head. "I think that star has fallen into the street lamp! If even the stars are coming to help, then we might as well go home!" And this they did, all three of them. The old street lamp cast a dazzling bright light all around.

"That was a wonderful present," it said. "I have always looked up to the stars because they can shine far more prettily than I can, however hard I try. And now the stars have seen me, an ordinary old street lamp, and they've made sure that I can show others everything I know and everything I see before me. That's splendid, because if you can share lovely things with others, they become even lovelier."

"That's very nice of you," said the wind. "But remember you need candles to do that. If you don't have a candle burning in you, no one else will be able to see what you can see. The stars probably think that you and all the other street lamps are wax candles. Goodbye, I'm going to die down now!" And that is exactly what it did.

The next evening the street lamp was sitting very comfortably in an easy chair at the lamplighter's house! The old lamplighter had gone to his boss at the depot and asked if he could have the street lamp, because he had been lighting it every evening these past twenty-four years and he looked upon it like his child, since he and his wife did not have any children of their own. The lamplighter had been allowed to take the street lamp home with him.

Now the street lamp was sitting in the armchair by the hot stove. In their little house the lamplighter and his wife seemed much bigger than outside on the street and the chair had been almost too small to see. The two old people sat there eating, and every now and again they would give the street lamp a friendly smile, because they were glad that it had not been melted down.

The lamplighter lived in a cellar two metres under the ground, at the bottom of some stone steps. It did not seem very big from the outside, but inside it was nice and warm, and everything was clean and well looked after. There were curtains round the bed and in front of the window. On the windowsill stood two strange flowerpots that the

lamplighter had brought home with him from a far-off land long ago, when he had been a sailor. They were made of clay and looked like elephants. They both had a hole in their backs filled with earth. Chives were growing in the back of one elephant. This was the vegetable garden. A geranium had been planted in the other elephant and this was the flower garden. There were brightly coloured pictures hanging on the wall. A big clock kept on saying: "Tick, tock, tick, tock."

The old lamplighter and his wife ate their meal and the street lamp sat in its chair. It felt as if it had ended up in an upside-down world, because now it was the old lamplighter who gazed over at it and told his wife of all the memories going through his head.

He thought of all those evenings and nights when he and his wife had set out, short nights in the summer and long ones in the winter. Sometimes the weather had been so bad – it had even snowed sometimes – that they had just wished they could be back home indoors again. They also had gentle, muggy evenings. They were wonderful – those evenings never lasted long enough.

The street lamp listened and remembered it all. Yes, the wind and the stars had lit up a lovely light in it, because it could see everything as if it were yesterday.

The lamplighter and his wife were always busy. There was never a moment when they were not doing something. On Sunday afternoons they would take out a book for the day, usually one full of stories about journeys to far-off places. The old man would read out loud about Africa, about the big forests where elephants and lions lived. The old woman would listen carefully and glance at their clay elephants on the windowsill. "I can see it all in front of me," the street lamp would say. It just hoped that someone would light a candle in it, because then the woman would be able to see everything, just like the street lamp could, even the tiniest things.

"What good is it to me that I can see everything while there is no candle burning in me," sighed the lamp. "All they have here are oil lamps and they are not enough."

One day the lamplighter came home with a big bag full of broken candles he had been given by his boss at the depot. The big pieces were simply used as candles and put in a pot. Now there were plenty of candles, but the lamplighter and his wife did not think to put one in the street lamp.

But the street lamp was cleaned and polished nicely, and when it shone all over it was put in a corner of the room where everyone could see it. Visitors often thought it strange that the lamplighter and his wife had a street lamp in their room, but this did not worry the old people.

One day it was the lamplighter's birthday. His wife wanted to decorate the house, but she did not have many streamers or anything else she could use. With a smile on her face she went up to the street lamp and said: "Today I'm going to put a candle in you and light it as a party light for my husband on his birthday."

The street lamp began to tremble so much that its glass began to rattle. At last it was going to be able to share the present the stars and the wind had given it with someone! But the old woman only put oil in the lamp and no candle. She had forgotten again. The street light shone throughout the evening and slowly it began to realize that the present it had been given would always remain hidden.

That night the street lamp had a dream. In its dream both the lamplighter and his wife had died and the street lamp itself had been taken back to the depot to be melted down.

The street lamp was just as frightened as the first time. But it did not want to use the present that the drop of water from the cloud had given it, that is, that it could turn to dust in just one day if it wanted. In its dream it was melted down, and when it came out of the melting pot it had become an iron candlestick. It was so beautiful! The candlestick was in the shape of an angel holding a bunch of flowers. In the middle of the flowers there was space for a wax candle.

The candlestick ended up on a green writing table in a very cosy room. There were shelves of books on nearly every side and in the gaps there were lovely pictures. It was a poet's study. And because a candle burned in the candlestick, the poet could see everything that the lamp saw. Sometimes he saw thick, dark forests, or meadows and ditches with frogs in them, or a ship on a stormy sea, or the night sky with many, many stars. And the poet saw so many things around him that he kept on writing poetry and as he wrote so many lovely poems he became very famous. Suddenly the street lamp woke up and knew that it had been a dream. It sighed: "How wonderful it would have been if I could have used my present like that. I could almost wish that I had been melted down. But no. As long as these old people are alive, that will not happen. They really love me. They have cleaned me, polished me and given me oil. I'm better off than I ever dared imagine."
And from that time on the old street lamp felt at ease and content. Just as it deserved to do!

The beetle and the world

ne day the emperor of a very big empire had his horse shod in gold. For each foot the animal was given a golden horseshoe made specially by the smith who worked for the emperor in the imperial stables. Gold is very expensive, of course, so some people wondered why the emperor was spending so much money on his horse.

But the emperor was not doing this for nothing; his horse was one of the loveliest horses in the whole empire, with long, slender legs, big, bright eyes, and a lovely, long mane that covered his whole neck. The horse had always carried the emperor into battle, which had been very dangerous. It had even helped its master by biting and kicking. And because it could gallop so fast, the emperor had escaped from the enemy a number of times. So the horse had saved the emperor's life.

The horse already wore a golden crown that was only a little smaller than the emperor's. The emperor thought that everything the horse had done for him was worth far more than the money for four horseshoes.

A few days later a beetle came crawling along, on his way to the smith who had shod the emperor's horse.

"First the big animals," he said, "and only then the small ones. But size is not the only thing that is important." And as he said this, he stretched out his thin legs.

"What can I do for you?" asked the smith.

"It seems clear enough to me," replied the beetle. "I want some golden shoes too."

"I think you're rather silly," said the smith, in surprise. "Are you sure you want golden horseshoes?"

"Yes, of course, and nothing else," said the beetle firmly. "Am I any less important than that great beast there, which is looked after, and brushed, and does not even have to find its own food? Do I not also have the right to live in the emperor's stables?"

"But don't you understand why the horse has golden horseshoes?" asked the smith.

"Understand? All I understand is that it's not fair to me," said the beetle angrily. "That horse only has these things to make me jealous, so I am going out into the world to seek my fortune. Then I can make him jealous of me."

"Have a safe journey, then," said the smith.

The beetle muttered something and left the stables. He flew for a while and suddenly realized that he had come to a lovely garden, full of flowers and with a lovely smell of roses and herbs.

"Don't you think it's wonderful here?" asked one of the ladybirds that were flying around there with their thin wings and their red wing cases with black spots. "It's lovely and peaceful, and so beautiful!"

"I'm used to something better," said the beetle. "You call this beautiful? There isn't even a dungheap!"

He flew on a little further and soon met a caterpillar.

"Isn't the world lovely!" sighed the caterpillar contentedly. "The sun is nice and warm and the leaves of the plants are really tasty. Everything is perfect. Soon I'll be going to sleep for a long time, and when I wake up again I'll have turned into a lovely butterfly, and then I'll finally be able to fly wherever I want."

"Aren't you conceited!" exclaimed the beetle. "How are you going to fly? All you can do is crawl! I've just come from the emperor's stables. No one thinks that much of themselves, not even the emperor's horse, who is wearing my old gold shoes, by the way. Sprouting wings and flying! Now why am I still here? At least I can fly!" And the beetle spread his wings and flew away.

Not long after he landed in a big field. It was late and the beetle was tired from all that flying, so he lay down for a while and at once fell asleep.

While the beetle lay asleep, it suddenly began to rain very hard and all the noise woke him up. He tried to crawl into the ground, but he could not, of course. It rained so much that the beetle was washed off his feet and fell over. He had to start swimming, first on his front and when he could no longer continue, on his back. Flying was completely out of the question and the beetle began to wonder whether he would survive it all. He had never experienced such terrible weather! After a quarter of an hour he was so tired that he just lay there and allowed himself to be carried along by the current.

Finally, the rain began to ease off and it started to brighten up again. The beetle dared to open his eyes again and when he had wiped the water from them he saw something white: it was washing that someone had laid

out to bleach in the sun. He crept towards it and took refuge in a fold of a soaking wet sheet. It was not such a nice spot as in the emperor's warm stables, but it was the best he could do at the moment. He lay there for a day and a night and all this time it just kept on raining. After two days the beetle crawled out again, but he was in a very bad mood because of the rain and he was feeling very cold. On the other side of the sheet sat two frogs and to the beetle's amazement both their faces were beaming with pleasure.

"Lovely weather, isn't it?" called one of the frogs. "So nice and fresh. And this sheet stays nice and wet. My back legs are nearly awash!"

"Have you ever been in the emperor's stables?" asked the beetle. "It's damp and fresh there too, but at the same time it's nice and warm. That's the climate I like, but I couldn't bring it with me when I set out on my travels, more's the pity. Isn't there a dungheap anywhere in this garden where a noble beetle like myself can feel at home and live?"

The frogs did not understand, but that was hardly surprising because they had never seen a beetle before and they were not very fond of dungheaps. They found them far too dry.

"I never ask anything twice," said the beetle angrily, and off he flew..

A little further on he almost ran into a shard, which was sticking out rather dangerously, but which did provide shelter from the bad weather. There were some earwig families living there, so the beetle had to look a little more friendly than he did just then. The earwig mothers all had little children and, of course, each mother thought her child was the prettiest and the sweetest. They all began jabbering at the poor beetle together about their sons, who were betrothed, and their daughters, who were so beautiful.

The beetle was allowed under the shard, but grew cross because no one would leave him in peace, so he asked the earwigs how far it was to the nearest dungheap.

"It's a terribly long way off, right on the other side of the water," said an earwig. "I hope that none of my children ever wanders so far from home. They would be sure to lose their way!"

"I'm going to try it anyway," said the beetle, and off he set without saying goodbye, which was very unfriendly of him. By the water he met some other beetles. They were beetles he knew.

"We really like living here," they said. "Why don't you join us? The ground is full of food and you must be tired from your journey."

"I certainly am," admitted the beetle. "I have lain in the rain and taken shelter in a soaking wet sheet. And my wings are hurting because I stood under a shard in the cold. It's lovely to see other beetles again."

"Have you come from a dungheap?" asked one of his hosts.

"You could call it that, but really it was something far grander," replied the beetle. "I have come from the emperor's stables, where I was born with golden shoes on my feet. Now I have a secret message to deliver and you are not allowed to ask me anything at all about it; it is something I cannot give away."

With these words the beetle stepped into the soil, where three young girl beetles were sitting, giggling softly because they did not know what to say to such a noble beetle.

"None of these three has a husband yet," said their mother, and the girls started giggling again, this time because they were embarrassed by what their mother had said.

"Even in the emperor's stables I have never seen such beautiful girls," said the beetle, flatteringly, to make a good impression.

"You mustn't make them conceited," the mother warned. "If you don't mean it, you must stay away from them. But of course you mean it, so I'm delighted that you're coming to live here."

"Hooray!" cheered all three girls, and the family decided at once that the beetle should marry the eldest of the girls. The wedding was set for the next day, because there was no reason at all to put it off.

The next two days were very enjoyable and the beetle really had nothing to complain about. But on the third day it was time to start thinking about food for his wife and even about children. By now the beetle had had enough; he did not think that anyone could tell him what to do and he left the house. He did not come home all day, nor that night, and his wife stayed behind on her own.

The beetle continued on his travels. He had sailed across the water on a cabbage leaf. The next morning two people were walking by. They saw the leaf with the beetle on it, picked him up, examined him from every side, and began talking about him very knowledgeably, especially one of them, a boy. He translated the name of the beetle into Latin and explained to the other boy what kind of a beetle it was.

The second boy suggested that they take the beetle home with them. He said that it was just what he wanted for his studies. The beetle thought this sounded scary and, as his wings were now dry again, he quickly flew off out of the boy's hand. He came to a row of greenhouses, flew through an open window and crept into the warm earth. "This is nice," he said contentedly.

He quickly fell asleep and dreamt that the emperor's horse had fallen and could no longer walk and that the beetle was allowed to have its golden shoes. It was a lovely dream and when the beetle woke up, he decided that the greenhouse was a very nice place to live. There were lovely tall palm trees at the back, there was a great pile of leaves on the ground, and there were all kinds of brightly coloured flowers growing there.

"What an enormous pile of plants!" exclaimed the beetle. "Won't they taste wonderful when they start to rot! This is an enormous store room! I must have family living here somewhere that I can team up with. But they must be just as noble as I am."

He rummaged around a little, looking for something nice to eat. All of a sudden a hand took firm hold of the beetle and lifted him up. The beetle was turned round and round. The gardener's son was playing in the greenhouses with his friend. They had seen the beetle and now they wanted to play with it. They wrapped him up in the leaf of a big plant and he ended up in a warm trouser pocket.

The beetle thrashed about and struggled to free himself, but the boy pressed his hand more firmly into his pocket so that in the end he had to

give up. The boys ran to the lake, which was right next to the garden, and there they put the beetle in an old, worn out wooden shoe. The boys put a stick on it for a mast and tied the beetle to the mast with some thread, because they wanted to see what would happen when they put him on the water.

It was by no means a big lake, but it seemed like an ocean to the beetle and he was so frightened that he lost his footing. Thrashing about wildly, he lay there as the wooden shoe set sail. The little boat was dragged along by the current, but if it drifted out too far, one of the boys would roll up his trouser legs, step out into the water, and bring it back. After a while an angry voice called to the boys that they must come in at once.

They obeyed at once and left the little boat and the beetle behind on the water. Of course, the boat drifted a long way from the shore, further and further, until it finally reached the middle of the lake. It was terrifying for the beetle, because he was tied to the mast and could not free himself.

Just as he was beginning to despair, he had a visit from a fly.

"Lovely day," said the fly. "I've just come to rest awhile and have a sit in the sun. You're all right here, aren't you?"

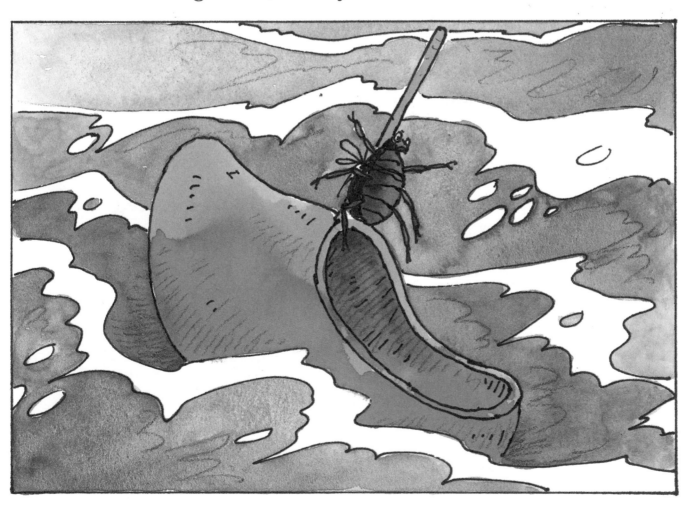

"You really don't understand," replied the beetle. "I'm stuck and I cannot fly away!"

"I can," said the fly, and just to prove it, off it flew.

"Now I know what the world is like," said the beetle. "Nothing but misfortune! I'm the only one who is completely honest. First, no one wants to give me golden shoes, then I have to sleep under a soaking wet sheet, then I stand in the cold and let them marry me off. And when I'd finally found a nice place to live, those two tiresome boys came along, tied me up and pushed me out onto this ocean. And in the meantime the emperor's horse is going around, showing off his golden shoes. That's what I really think is the worst of all. Now I'm never going to get back to the stables and I'm never going to get out of here."

But all hope was not yet lost. A small boat came sailing by with some girls in it.

"Look, there's an old wooden shoe floating in the water," said one.

"And there's a small creature tied up in it," said another.

The girls steered their boat close to the wooden shoe and one of them fished it carefully out of the water. Another girl took out some scissors and carefully cut the thread so that she did not hurt the beetle. They rowed to the side and put the beetle on the grass.

"Crawl away quickly," they said. "Or fly, if you can. It's wonderful to be free, so enjoy it."

The beetle spread his wings and off he flew. It was wonderful! He was free again! He would have cheered, if he had known how.

Suddenly the beetle spied a house in the distance. He flew towards it and went inside. He landed exhausted on something soft and warm. When he looked more closely he saw that he had landed on the mane of the emperor's horse. He was back in the stables! It took the beetle a while to recover from the shock and he said to himself: "Here I am, sitting on the emperor's horse. I'm just like the emperor himself!"

And suddenly the beetle remembered something. The smith had asked him why the golden horse had been given golden horseshoes. Now the beetle knew why it was. "They gave the horse those shoes to do me a favour!" he exclaimed with glee. "Because now I have travelled the world, and seen and learnt so much." Finally, the beetle was in a good mood again. The sun shone into the stable and everything looked so very nice and cosy.

"The world is not such a bad place," said the beetle, "if you take things as they are."